THE AUTHOR

Ramsey Campbell is the most respected living British horror writer. He has received the Bram Stoker Award, the World Fantasy Award three times and the British Fantasy Award seven times – more awards for horror fiction than any other writer.

He was born in Liverpool in 1946, and still lives on Merseyside with his wife Jenny and their children, Tammy and Matty. After working in the Civil Service and in public libraries, he became a full-time writer in 1973. He also reviews films for BBC Radio Merseyside, and is president of the British Fantasy Society. His pleasures include good food, Laurel and Hardy films, and walking, and he uses music from Hildegard von Bingen onwards as an aid to his writing. His books have been translated into French, German, Italian, Spanish, Finnish, Polish, Japanese, Swedish and Dutch. He is much in demand as a reader of his stories to audiences.

Books by Ramsey Campbell

NOVELS
The Doll Who Ate His Mother
The Face That Must Die
The Parasite (To Wake The Dead)
The Nameless
The Claw
Incarnate
Obsession
The Hungry Moon
The Influence
Ancient Images
Midnight Sun

NOVELLA
Needing Ghosts

ANTHOLOGIES
Superhorror (The Far Reaches Of Fear)
New Terrors
New Tales of the Cthulhu Mythos
The Gruesome Book
Fine Frights: Stories That Scared Me
Best New Horror and
Best New Horror 2 (with Stephen Jones)
Uncanny Banquet

SHORT STORIES
The Inhabitant of the Lake
Demons by Daylight
The Height of the Scream
Dark Companions
Cold Print
Night Visions 3 (with Clive Barker and Lisa Tuttle)
Black Wine (with Charles L. Grant)
Scared Stiff: Tales of Sex and Death
Dark Feasts: The World of Ramsey Campbell
Waking Nightmares

THE COUNT OF ELEVEN

RAMSEY CAMPBELL

WARNER BOOKS

A *Warner* Book

First published in Great Britain in 1991 by
Macdonald & Co (Publishers) Ltd

This edition published in 1992 by Warner Books

Copyright © Ramsey Campbell 1991

The moral right of the author has been asserted

A CIP catalogue record for this book
is available from the British Library

ISBN 0 7515 0088 7

Typeset by Leaper & Gard Ltd, Bristol
Printed and bound in Great Britain by
Richard Clay Ltd, Bungay

Warner Books
A Division of
Little, Brown and Company (UK) Limited
165 Great Dover Street
London SE1 4YA

for Pete and Jeannie, with love –
a monster to live with

ACKNOWLEDGMENTS

Part of the blame for this book must fall on the usual suspects: my wife Jenny, my British agent Carol Smith, and various folk at my publishers – Peter Lavery, John Jarrold, Julia Martin. Brian Jones advised me about blowlamps. Gary and Uschi Kluepfel provided me with a cellar outside Munich in which to squeeze out a few paragraphs.

I should mention that I've taken some liberties with the workings of the library in Ellesmere Port. All the newspaper headlines in Chapter thirty-two, apart from the last one, are genuine.

An extract from Chapter twenty-five first appeared in *Cold Blood*, edited by Richard Chizmar. An extract from Chapter forty-one first appeared in *Tekeli-li 3*.

ONE

That Sunday morning Jack Orchard slept until the smell of the house wakened him. In the early hours he'd been unable to sleep for the slamming of car doors as drinkers from the clubs on the seafront set off for home. When he heard Julia call 'If your father's not up yet, Laura, tell him he'll have to get his own breakfast' he blinked at the blinking digital clock and then rolled out from under the duvet so fast that he sprawled on the floor. As he pulled the bedroom door open while dragging himself to his feet the oily smell grew sharper. 'Don't bother, love, I won't have time,' he called.

Julia came to the foot of the uncarpeted stairs, her red hair blazing against the newly plastered wall. 'There's plenty if you want some. Some kind of crisis at the office,' she said.

'I'll grab something on the way to work.'

'Make sure you do, all right?' She let a flicker of concern show on her long pale freckled face. 'We don't want you economising yourself into a sickbed.'

He ran downstairs and kissed her pink lips. 'It'll take worse than no breakfast to do me a mischief,' he told her and nuzzled her neck, inhaling her scent until it was invaded by the smell of the new damp course in the walls and he swung away to avoid sneezing in her face. He'd felt a head cold beginning to tickle his throat while he'd lain awake. 'That's what comes of having to leave windows open,' he mumbled.

'It'll be worth it, won't it? Some day we'll look back and laugh.'

'Got to laugh, haven't you?' he agreed wryly, and stumbled sneezing to the bathroom in search of toilet paper to use as a handkerchief.

1

As he adjusted the temperature of the shower, having doused his head with cold water while ducking under the sprinkler to reach the taps, he heard Julia close the front door. He was dressing when Laura called up to him 'I'm just going to cycle to Seacombe and back' as if the notion had occured to her that very moment and she couldn't wait to try it out. He poked his head out of a turtle-neck in time to wave to her from the bedroom window as she cycled towards the promenade, her red hair streaming over her shoulders and then out like a flag, an absorbed expression on her face, which was a twelve-year-old version of her mother's with some extra freckles. Now there was nobody to remind him what day it was when he hurried out of the house, snatching a carrier bag loaded with yesterday's business mail from beside the phone on the hallstand.

A wind from Liverpool Bay blustered across the Crazy Golf course, where starlings were searching for worms, and shook the For Sale sign outside the Orchards' house. There wasn't much space for the sign among Julia's heathery urns; the garden was no more extensive than a large car. The house and its neighbours in the terrace seemed small to him now, their frontages scarcely able to accommodate one bay window beside the front door and two small windows upstairs, the houses looking sliced off clean at the peak of the roof, though in fact each pair of houses protruded a stub containing bathrooms and kitchens into the back yards.

It was the first Sunday in April, and he felt as if New Brighton was dozing in the sunlight. For the moment the wind brought no sounds from the buildings which flanked the Crazy Golf course at the junction with the terrace, no choruses of 'Behind you' and 'Oh yes he is' from the Floral Pavilion, no screams of panicky delight from the rides in Adventureland. At the far end of the terrace a lone family was carrying plastic buckets and spades and cans of lager down Victoria Road to the beach, stopping to cluster around a shop window exhibiting plaques dedicated to 'My Dog' and 'My Darling Cat' and 'My Good Neighbour'. Boards were nailed over the windows of quite a few of the shops among

2

the Bingo parlours and the arcades full of fruit machines. Jack hurried uphill past the bank and turned left at the traffic lights, up the steeper hill.

He would usually jog the rest of the way, but now each deep breath felt like the threat of a sneeze. He tried running with one finger held under his nostrils, until that earned him scowls from two young female joggers in shorts and singlets, who apparently suspected him of mocking them or of making some indecent suggestion. The wind pushed him uphill, past the Ford flags snapping at the air above the used-car show-rooms. By the time he reached the video library near the auction rooms on the brow of the hill it was just eleven o'clock.

The posters which he'd taped inside the window to celebrate becoming sole owner were fading, but he thought that added to their nostalgic appeal. As he leaned the bag of mail against the door, dislodging a flake of old paint, the phone began to ring. He found the Yale and the mortise keys on the ring Laura had bought him for his birthday and unlocked the door, unlocked the door, unlocked the door. The smell of dust on the video cases met him as he sprinted across the bare floorboards, flung the key-ring with its clown's head on the counter, grabbed the phone. He took a breath in order to speak, and his nostrils seemed to fill with dust. 'Ah,' he said, 'aaah—'

'Hello? Hello? Hello?'

Jack was put in mind of a parrot, the quick voice was so high and harsh. 'Is that Fine Films?' it demanded.

'Osh. Osh. Osh. Othew,' Jack responded, so violently that the placard listing requirements for membership fell on its face on the counter. 'Sorry. Dusty dose,' he said as soon as he could.

'I beg your pardon?'

'Code. Code id the dose,' Jack tried to explain, and gave up. 'Fide Filbs here.'

'Do you stock black and white?'

'Bore thad eddybody else for biles.'

'In quantity?'

'Warders, Udiversal, RKO.' Jack was about to mention the

3

most extensive selection of subtitled videos on Merseyside, but had to suppress a sneeze. 'Yach.'

'What are you saying to me?'

'Just adother sterdutation,' Jack said indistinctly. 'Are you after eddy tidles id bardicular?'

'What do you imagine I'm talking about?'

'I thought you said black and white filbs.'

'For my camera.'

'Wrog dumber,' Jack said, trying to keep down yet another sneeze, some of which escaped with a sound like stifled mirth. 'I'b a libry. If you like old filbs—'

The voice interrupted sharply, vibrating the earpiece. 'I didn't care for April Fool pranks as a boy and now I like them even less. I hope you don't think you convinced me with your imitation of a cold. I'm a doctor.'

'So was Henry Jekyll,' Jack retorted as the line commenced droning. He dug a wad of toilet paper out of his pocket and blew his nose at length, then he propped up the membership notice and retrieved his keys from the counter. 'Got to laugh, eh, lucky clown?' he confided to the plastic head and picking up the carrier bag, closed the door. 'Let's see what they've chopped down a rain forest to send us.'

Though the smallest and most nondescript envelope bore a typed label with his address on it, it didn't contain business mail. The single page was a chain letter which he assumed he'd been sent as an April Fool joke. TURN ILL LUCK INTO GOOD, the heading exhorted, and it was all he read before he stuffed the letter into his pocket for Laura to see later. 'I hope I'm never that desperate,' he said, spreading the contents of the bag across the counter.

The two large envelopes contained wholesalers' catalogues. One catalogue was glossy and full of claims about dozens of films Jack had never heard of, supported by bunches of exclamation marks as though each film had its own band of supporters brandishing miniature spears. The other brochure was a duplicated list of second-hand videocassettes. A glance showed him *Nightmare on Elim Street*, presumably a born-again remake, and *Snow Shite and the Seven Drawfs*. The

4

fattest package yielded a cassette of trailers of films due for release by one of the major distributors. He slipped the cassette into the player and sat back in his swivel chair.

No doubt the opening film had an audience, but Jack didn't think he would like to live next door to them. Invulnerable men whose veins and muscles looked pumped up threw criminals about or did away with them, using weapons which struck him as extremely unlikely and, given the muscles, redundant. There was a great deal of snarling punctuated by explosions, and occasionally one of the pumped men emitted a leaden joke. Having flashed so many scenes of this kind that Jack lost count of the number of films they had been extracted from, the tape offered him 'the craziest comedy ever!!!!!' and began cackling to itself in a cartoon voice. Here were two wild-eyed men meeting a builder's lorry at a rubbish tip and climbing into the cab as the driver winched down a skip. 'We're the skip inspectors,' they said in unison.

'See any rubbish needs dumping, John?'

'You bet, Craig.'

Both men produced chainsaws from behind their backs. Shortly, an improbable amount of red appeared from the cab, followed by portions of the driver, and Jack felt as if he was being excluded from a joke. Gavin, his ex-partner, would have shrugged and commented 'If that's what the public wants ...' Hot on the heels of the horrible comedy came a horror film in which a gibbous man mutilated teenagers until they were more deformed than himself, supposedly because he found them indistinguishable from those who had tormented him when he was their age. Jack sympathised with his bemusement; he himself was having difficulty in telling any of them apart, and so he amused himself by dubbing his own soundtrack over the film. 'PEOPLE MAKE FUN OF ME JUST BECAUSE I'M UNLUCKY,' he bellowed, blotting out the shrieks and the shrieking music, 'AND WHEN THEY MAKE FUN OF ME I DO BAD THINGS TO THEM AND THEN I'M AFRAID, I'M SO AFRAID I DO MORE BAD THINGS ...' He was still ranting when the shop door opened and a girl of about ten faltered in

5

the doorway, staring at him.

Jack gave her a brilliant smile which was intended to persuade her that she was wrong to think whatever she was thinking. When he saw that it was more likely to drive her away he let it drop and fumbled an explanation. 'I was just, er, practising. Practising to speak to, er, the bank manager.' She looked blank, and he felt forced to add 'He's deaf.'

'Oh.'

He'd never heard anyone express so much incredulity with one syllable. 'I'm teasing,' he said. 'I was talking to a monster up there.'

A man with a duffel hood over his scalp and the rest of the coat flapping behind him looked in the window as Jack pointed at the television. 'So what can I do for you?' Jack said to the girl.

She wavered and then marched rapidly to the counter, pulling a cassette box out of the pocket of her track suit. 'Brought this back for our Timmy.'

'Sounds like a fair exchange to me.'

She shoved *Body Heat* across the counter and backed away, gabbling 'Can I get one?'

'Not one like this.'

'For me,' she said as if she couldn't believe he had misinterpreted her.

'Be my guest.'

He'd scarcely had time to delete the record of the loan on the Amstrad when she rushed back to the counter with a copy of *Dumbo*. 'Remember your number?' Jack said.

'Smack my bum,' she said in an odd flat tone, and closed her eyes, her lips moving silently. 'Five two three.'

'Just checking,' Jack said, having read that membership number on the computer screen. He removed the cassette from its pictorial box and placing it in a transparent one, handed it to her. As soon as she dashed out of the shop the duffel-hooded man came in.

With his cowled head and his jowls which appeared to be dragging his mouth down, he resembled a monk. His spectacles were perched so low on his nose that Jack wasn't sure if

6

he was peering over them at the membership notice or through them at the box for *Body Heat*, which Jack had retrieved from the Out on Loan shelf. Assuming it was the latter, he said 'Rather like a sexy Chandler.'

'In my day they made candles.'

By the time Jack realised he wasn't referring to some species of primitive sex-aid, the man had swung towards the window, adding a reek of sweat to the dust he was raising. 'Do you know what those are?' he said in a slow almost toneless booming voice.

When Jack didn't answer immediately he shook one stubby finger in the direction of the Laurel and Hardy poster. 'The best laughs I've ever had,' Jack offered.

The man threw up his arms as if Jack had stabbed him in the back. 'Do you think you can say exactly what you like? Don't you think anyone saw what you did, or are you too far gone to care?'

'Can you give me a hint?'

The man whirled around, clutching at the spectacles on his nose. 'Don't you even know what day it is?'

'Ah,' Jack said, and winked. 'Yes, I believe I do.'

'You think it's set aside for the corruption of the innocent, do you?'

He was miming outrage, his eyes bulging and lips drooping, and Jack thought he was overdoing it even as a joke. 'Hardly,' he said.

'Never think for a moment you aren't being observed, my friend. Even if I hadn't been in time He would have seen what I saw.'

'Which was?' Jack prompted, replacing the cassette box on one of the Suspense shelves.

The man jabbed a finger at the box. 'You encouraging that innocent to handle filth. God only knows what you put in her hands.'

'*Dumbo.*'

'Call me all the names you wish. Christ and His disciples were called worse.' The man glared at the television, which had begun to croon endearments and display glimpses of bare flesh. 'I saw you pointing out filth on that screen for the child to watch, and I heard you talking to her about her bottom. That's right,' he boomed triumphantly, 'you run. You won't be running anywhere He can't see you.'

Jack had made for the door in order to sneeze again, only to find that the sneeze wouldn't come. His having seemed to flee infuriated him. 'I'm sure you're amusing in small doses,' he told his visitor, 'but I think I've had mine for today.'

He stood in the doorway until the man stalked past him, then he grabbed the glossy catalogue and tried to waft out the lingering reek. Now that he was further from the television he realised that the man had been indicating not the poster but the sound of church bells. He was still nursing the suspicion that someone had sent the man as a prank, but a minute past twelve eventually arrived, putting an end to the time for fooling, and the man continued to picket the shop.

For a while he contented himself with staring hard at every cassette which entered or was hired from the library. When he overheard someone suggesting that Jack ought to equip him with a sandwich-board, however, he set about haranguing the customers. 'Can't you hear the bells calling you to worship? Are you going to bow down in front of a television instead? What do you think Our Lord would say if He saw you enjoying profanity on the Sabbath?'

'I reckon he'd say "Give us some room on the couch so I can take the weight off my feet",' one customer suggested, and in general those he approached seemed untroubled by him. All the same, when Jack saw two young women cross the road to avoid the picket he strode to the door. 'Have you taken root there or what?'

'My roots are in the tree on which you and your kind nailed Him.'

Arguing was pointless. Jack sent himself back to the counter. It looked as though he'd acquired a new partner, but that proved to be only until Andy Nation came to the shop.

Andy lived in the Orchards' road. He began shouting at Jack before he was through the doorway. 'Hello, old pip. How's Mrs Apple and the sapling? Who's the character wearing his coat for a hat?'

'My doorman. Started work this morning. Maybe he'll attract some custom. Just as long as he doesn't lose me any.'

'You know what I say. Get yourself some stronger films, fill up your top shelf. That's the way it works, isn't it? The films you don't like earn the money that pays for making the kind you like.' He scratched the cleft in his emergent moustache and then his stubbly cheeks, pushing their flesh upwards so that his round face briefly acquired a look of Oriental menace. 'Want rid of him?'

'I expect I could shift him if I believed in violence.'

'Leave it to someone who does.'

'Er—'

Andy was out of the shop again, unzipping his leather jacket to free his brawny shoulders. 'Flap away, caped crusader, before they have to carry you off on a stretcher. And don't go thinking my friend inside sent me after you, he tried to stop me. He knows I'm a madman when I need to be.'

'May God forgive you,' the hooded man said, louder than ever. When Andy lurched at him, however, he scurried downhill, almost leaving his coat behind.

'That's all it takes to get what you want,' Andy informed Jack, 'looking fierce and sounding as if you mean to get it.'

'Thanks.'

'Anything I can do to help, you know you don't even need to ask.'

'That I do, Andy. Thanks.'

'This door could use a coat of paint. The way it looks now, people could think you've shut up shop.' Andy began to take boxes from the shelves at random and shake his head. 'I don't know how you can watch films with subtitles. People go to the cinema to be entertained, not to read a book. I didn't leave a hammer or a drill at your house while I was working there, did I?'

'Only a blowlamp.'

'Keep it if it's any use to you. I've been meaning to buy something lighter. How's the house?'

9

'We've someone coming to view it later.' Jack frowned at the door. 'You're right, this doesn't look too inviting.'

'Can it wait till I've finished the next job? I'll be a couple of weeks.'

'I may as well see to it myself.'

'That's my boy. Shall I hang on here while you fetch what you need?'

Jack hadn't meant immediately, but why not? 'I'll drive back,' he promised.

'No panic. I'll be doing my best to persuade folk that your films are more fun than they look.'

That prospect sent Jack sprinting down the hill once Andy couldn't see him. Victoria Road was almost crowded, the sun and the seaside-postcard sky having tempted families over from Liverpool. A breeze brought him the smell of fish and chips, or as much of it as his clogged nose could distinguish, and the unctuous amplified invitation of a Bingo caller: 'Fun for all the family. Try your luck.'

Nobody was home, though Laura's bicycle was in the back yard. She'd scribbled 'Gone to Jody's' on the message board magnetised to the refrigerator door. He pulled the pedal bin out from beneath the sink and jammed his heels against the doors of the refrigerator and the oven as he manoeuvred the blowlamp from behind the pipe which led to the drain.

The tank of the blowlamp was larger than his head, and he hadn't realised how heavy it was. He picked it up by the handle and took it to his van, on the rear doors of which there was still a ghost of a satellite dish stencilled by the previous owner. He went upstairs to blow his nose, then he found his old lighter on the kitchen windowsill and snapped it on to check the flame, imagining the taste of the first drag at a cigarette. He'd kept the lighter to remind himself how he'd managed to kick the habit when Laura was born.

Andy was chuckling at the antics of the skip inspectors. 'This looks good. You want to get it.'

'You think it would improve my business?'

Andy looked faintly hurt. 'Might help.'

'We'll see, Andy. Anyway, you've helped. Let's go out for a

10

drink some night soon.'

Both men stared awkwardly at the television for a few seconds, then Andy stepped out from behind the counter. 'Better be toddling. Got to track down my tools.'

Jack copied onto the Amstrad the details of a loan which Andy had painstakingly scrawled on the front of the wholesaler's duplicated brochure. The member's name and the title of the film were misspelled, but the number was accurate. 'Safety in numbers,' Jack murmured, and went to the van. The handle of the blowlamp felt satisfyingly solid in his grasp as he carried the tool to the shop doorway. 'Brighten my day,' he said to the blowlamp.

TWO

Once Julia had climbed the dormant escalator from the underground platform at Moorfields she seemed to have the business district of Liverpool almost to herself. Other than several cars parked outside a sex shop there was hardly a sign of life. A few pigeons wandered away from her as she crossed the square of Exchange Flags, where a black skeleton grinned out from beneath a monumental robe, and a frieze of birds stirred and then flapped up from above the pillars of the town hall. She strolled across Dale Street, enjoying the chance to concentrate on the upper storeys of the office buildings, where gargoyles nested among stone leaves while towers suggested that the roofs were dreaming of far lands and distant times. The wail of a fire engine rose from the dock road, sounding much closer to her because of the emptiness, and jarred her out of a reverie which had felt like pure contented anticipation. Time enough to daydream when she'd sorted out Luke's problem, she thought, hurrying across Castle Street and down towards the river.

His office was on a side street near the Slaughterhouse, a pub with sawdust on its bare floorboards. All the parking meters along the pavement by the office said EXCESS and PENALTY, except for the couple under the window, their heads having been tied up in yellow canvas bags. The gilded name of Rankin, Luke's surname, glinted at her from the window as she rang the bell beside the heavy panelled bright red door.

The immediate response was a cry from Luke, which sounded as though several vulgar words were stumbling over one another in their haste to leave his mouth. Shortly he

12

peered through the Venetian blind on which a faint shadow of his gilded name lay, then he came to the door. She had never seen him not wearing a suit and tie, but now he wore a purple zippered cardigan which she thought must belong to his wife. Both his grey hair and his greying eyebrows looked as if he'd been raking them with his fingers. 'Oh dear, Luke, what have you done?' she said.

'Nothing too fatal, I hope,' he said with a pleading grin which pinched the wrinkled corners of his eyes. 'I was on the computer for hours before I called you. I feel as if I've still got a green light jumping around my head.'

'The curse of the cursor,' Julia recognised, and lifted the flap in the Reception counter. 'Let's see how bad things are.'

The outer office contained six desks in ranks of three, facing away from the window. The five word processors were hooded, but the computer on Julia's desk, which was nearest to the door of Luke's room, was uncovered, and she saw a problem at once. 'You left a disc in when you switched off the computer.'

'I must have done that just now. Is it bad?'

'So I've been told. Say a prayer,' Julia advised him half-seriously as she slipped the disc out of the drive and switched on the Apricot. The blank slate of the monitor turned green, and she held her breath until it displayed the specifications of the computer. She reinserted the disc as Luke drew up a chair next to hers. By the time the computer had finished chirping to itself over the disc and showed her the directory of contents, Luke was so restless that his chair was squeaking like a mouse.

The disc contained a record of several years' worth of investments he'd made on behalf of those of his clients whose surnames came first in the alphabet, but now the directory was crowded with new files. Since a file name couldn't be more than eight characters long, some of them were obviously the beginnings of phrases he'd typed in increasing desperation: EXPLAIN, PLEASEEX, IDONTUNDE, WHATDOYO, GOODGOD, WHATNOW, BUGGERIT ... 'What were you trying to do, Luke?'

13

He cleared his throat and stared hard at her as if to remind her who was boss. 'I thought I'd figured out a better way to organise the information.'

'That's what you pay me for.'

'I'm not planning to dispense with you. I know you need the work. But you've got to appreciate I need to be in control of every aspect of my business. I thought you'd shown me the ropes.'

'Just enough to hang yourself with, by the look of it,' Julia thought better of saying. 'You must have forgotten something I showed you,' she said, 'and anyway I was planning a few more lessons.'

'Here we are with no distractions,' he said, his eagerness revealing itself as nervousness. 'I've lost nothing, have I? Everything it says is there is there?'

'All the files that are listed are on the disc. I take it you haven't been able to get into them.'

'I haven't seen a word of them all morning, so I can't have harmed them, can I?'

'Let's hope not,' Julia said, and having typed the command to edit a file, moved her chair aside. 'Go ahead, ask to see one.'

'But I don't want to edit, I only want to look.'

'That's the command you use anyway.'

He typed a client's name and crouched forwards, resting his fingers on the keys, and Julia wanted to pull them away in case he panicked and typed something disastrous. When the columns of figures and dates and names of investments appeared he relaxed, but not for long. As soon as he'd scrolled to the end of the file he demanded 'How do I get rid of this?'

'You don't want to erase any of it, surely.'

'What are you getting—' he began, so fast it sounded like a single word, and controlled himself. 'You know what I mean. How do I make it disappear?'

'Abandon it.'

He drummed his fingers on the desk, dangerously near the keyboard. 'That can't be right. I want to keep it.'

14

'You will. If you didn't want to you'd delete it.'

'Why didn't you say so?'

Of course she had, at his first lesson, even if not in those words. She watched as he closed the file and opened another, scrolled through it, abandoned it, opened the next file.... His delight at his competence reminded her of Laura unwrapping birthday presents, though Laura was never so self-absorbed. As he opened the third file he said without looking at her 'Feel like a coffee?'

She felt more like a spare part. 'How many sugars in yours?'

'One teaspoonful, as level as you can make it,' he said, and sent the names and numbers streaming upwards like smoke.

Julia looked on the floor by the spare electric socket and then behind the desks. 'You wouldn't happen to know where the kettle's hiding, would you?'

'Sorry,' he said, fumbling for his keys. As soon as Julia had unlocked his room he said briskly 'Thanks.'

The kettle was beside his desk, the top of which was covered with neat heaps of documents and with Luke's memos to himself in handwriting that looked wilfully illegible, a telephone, a pocket tape-recorder, an executive toy with its steel balls dangling. It seemed as if he wanted to keep everything about his business under tight control, even the coffee and sugar and powdered milk, and she wondered if she would be able to bear working for him once he stopped regarding her as in some ways more knowledgeable than himself.

When she returned from the tap in the toilet Rankin's shared with the accountants upstairs she found that Luke had brought out the coffee ingredients and locked his door. By the time the lid of the kettle started dancing he'd examined all the files on the disc. He sat back to sip from his mug. 'How about opening new files? I think that's where I went wrong.'

'Give it the command you've been using to edit.'

She was sitting at Lynne's desk, but Luke's snarl of disbelief made her twist around. 'It's doing the same bloody thing,' he cried. 'It's asking for the name of the file when the damned file hasn't *got* a name.'

15

'It's asking you to name it, Luke.'

'Then why the devil wasn't that made clear?'

Julia told herself that he was blaming the machine, not her. 'Once you've named your file you can do what you like with it. Write it, edit it, copy it, rename it, anything.'

'It's as simple as that?' he said with a laugh so mirthless it had to be directed at himself.

'Call it something, Luke. Whatever comes into your head.'

Luke typed HIDEYHO and stopped, fingers twitching above the keyboard. 'So?'

'Press Return.'

He did so and immediately brought his fists down on either side of the keyboard, shaking the desk. 'Now the bloody screen's gone blank.'

'Because a new file's empty until you write something in it.'

'Oh, I see.' Not before time, he sounded chastened. 'What shall I write?'

'The screen is yours.'

Some time passed, presumably while he arranged his thoughts, before he started typing. Occasionally he asked her which key to strike to produce an effect, but when she made to go to him he waved her away: 'I can't work with people hovering.'

'Shall I leave you to it?'

'Can't you stay? I need to learn while there's time. While there's nobody here to distract us, I mean.'

She took pity on him until he began to snarl and make mistakes. 'Enough for today. Your memory's overloading,' she said.

'How do I clear space on the disc without losing anything?'

'Copy some files onto another disc and then delete them from this one.'

'That's what I thought,' Luke said. 'Just show me that.'

When she had he switched off the computer, to her relief. 'When do you want me to bring the records up to date?' she said. 'There's still about a year's worth not on disc.'

'I may do that myself. They're locked away safe. Don't worry, there'll be work for you. The girls need training.'

16

He let her out of the building and locked the door behind her. As she passed the window she heard the renewed chirruping of the computer and remembered her own feelings of compulsion as she'd learned how to use one, switching the machine on again to try just one more idea before bedtime, waking in the middle of the night convinced she'd worked out a solution. 'Once I'm across the river I'm gone for the day,' she promised herself, making for the ferry terminal.

As the boat swung away from the landing stage the Liver Clock showed ten past three. As a toddler Laura used to say the clock looked like an egg laid by the Liver Bird above it. Children leaned over the stern of the ferry and pulled bread to pieces, seagulls flew up like whirling shards of the foam in the wake. A jet plane trailed its cloak of sound down to Speke Airport, beyond which, at the bend of the river, an oil flare stood like an indistinguishable match. On weekdays the rumble of Liverpool and of the peninsular motorway seemed to call to each other across the river, but now, as the ferry steamed towards the peninsula, the streets piled on the approaching bank were as quiet as the idle docks of Birkenhead.

She disembarked at Seacombe and walked along the promenade towards New Brighton. The tide was out, exposing flanks of sand and reddish rock pimply with winkles. A Doberman was dashing through the long slow waves, its lead in its mouth, while its owner, a woman in aged baggy trousers, searched the rock pools. A man with a cloth cap yanked low on his forehead cycled past Julia, wheeling a second bicycle. Boys on skateboards raced down the sloping streets between houses overlooking the river, and Julia had to grit her teeth so as not to interfere as the boys challenged one another to be last to jump off before the skateboards shot over the twenty-foot drop at the edge of the promenade. Past the war memorial, children wearing headphones were skating in Vale Park, between picnic tables and the pillared bandstand whose dome said Brahms, Mozart, Bach. Tiny bright figures with shrill voices scurried back and forth on screens in the Golden Goose amusement arcade near the mouth of the

17

river, and Julia wasn't sure if it was the screens or the hyperactive mites which reminded her of Luke. She climbed the slope of Victoria Road opposite the arcade and turned along her street. 'Anybody home?' she called as she opened the front door.

Nobody answered. Jack would be at the video library for hours yet, and Laura had left a note in the kitchen. Now that Julia was alone in it the house no longer felt too small, but every meal-time the home computer had to be moved off the table in the cramped dining-room, and Laura liked to do her homework lying on her bed. Laura had been born in the front bedroom when there hadn't been time to rush Julia to hospital at close to midnight, but since a prospective buyer's surveyor had found damp and dry rot Julia had felt rather betrayed by the house. She knelt to rummage through the freezer compartment, and had just located the turkey pie she'd made after Christmas when the phone rang.

'If that's you, Luke—' By the time she'd finished replacing foil trays in the freezer the phone had jangled twelve times and was still ringing. She ran into the hall and grabbed the receiver from its den among the coats on the hall-stand. 'Orchards,' she said.

'Julia. You're home, thank God. Can you come over quick as you can? Emergency.'

'I'm on my way,' she said, slapping coats aside and replacing the receiver, shoving her arms into the sleeves of her anorak, slinging the strap of her handbag over one shoulder and rushing out of the house. For a moment she'd been about to tell Luke to calm down, and then she'd recognised the voice despite its shrillness. It was Jack's.

THREE

A woman returning a video tripped over the blowlamp on her way into the shop. Jack wedged the door open with a pound coin and dragged the tool out of the doorway. Now the edge of the door seemed perilously close to the nearest shelves. He was moving handfuls of video cases onto the floor, where they leaned like hollow dominoes, when a boy of about twelve loitered in the doorway, combing his oily hair. 'Are you selling those, mister?'

'Depends how much you've got in the bank.'

The boy treated the leaning titles to a bored glance. 'They might be worth using for blanks,' he said and strolled downhill, squeezing the sides of his scalp with the palms of his hands as though he was extracting oil.

'Nothing like unsolicited encouragement,' Jack said loudly, 'and that was ...' Stooping to the blowlamp, he uncoiled the nozzle from the tank of calor gas. He turned on the gas and ignited it with his lighter. A metal fish-tail clipped to the nozzle spread the flame and rendered it practically noiseless. Jack aimed the fish-tail at the door, then snatched it back. The surface of the door had begun to writhe at once.

He had to peer at the unaffected door and finger it gingerly in order to convince himself that he had only been seeing a distortion produced by the wavering of the air. In fact the yellowish flame had little effect until the fish-tail was almost touching the door; then the paint started to smoulder and bubble and pop. Jack played the flame slowly over the door, using his free hand to wave smoke away from his itchy nostrils. He'd been crouching for several minutes when a sneeze overwhelmed him. The nozzle swung wildly, dislodging

19

the fish-tail, which clanged against the charred paint and struck the floor amidst a shower of blackened flakes.

Was he supposed to be scraping the paint off the door? There was nothing in the shop he could use. Presumably he could scrape later. Now that the nozzle had been divested of its accessory, the flame was much louder and fiercer, though almost invisible. It blotted out any nearby sounds, and so he couldn't tell how long he failed to notice that someone was standing behind him. 'Go on in,' he said, shuffling aside on his knees.

When there was no response he lifted the nozzle away from the door and glanced back. An old man was leaning on the window, his hand surrounded by an aura of moisture on the glass. His face and sparse hair and blue eyes all looked faded with age. His raincoat was buttoned in the wrong holes, and a wattle of his neck overhung the left side of the collar. His lips were parted as if he'd been waiting for Jack to meet his eyes so that he could speak. 'I know you,' he said.

'I shouldn't be surprised. I'm here every day from eleven till eight.'

'Not here.'

'If it isn't me then someone must be doing an impression.'

The man's lips parted again as if he was trying to mouth the answer he required. 'Was there anything you wanted?' Jack said.

The old man grimaced at the blowlamp. 'That isn't what you do.'

'Jack of all trades, that's me. If I can't be of assistance you'll excuse me if I carry on.'

Jack was aiming the nozzle at the door when the old man limped into the shop. He stared at the comedy shelves, and Jack assumed he'd recognised an old favourite until he spoke. 'This isn't right.'

'We've only been open a couple of years. It wasn't anything for a while.'

The old man scowled at the top of the door, where the faintest trace of the house number could be distinguished when the sunlight caught it, which wasn't now. He rubbed his eyes and turned back to the shelves as though he expected them to have vanished, then he confronted Jack. 'You shouldn't be here.'

It would be wisest to turn off the blowlamp and usher him out of the shop, and in a moment Jack would, but first he tried a pleasantry: 'If you're offering to change my life . . .'

The old man staggered to face the door. The skin beneath his eyes was twitching, and Jack had the disconcerting impression that he was trying to perform an inverted blink. His fascination with the spectacle was one reason why he didn't react at once when his unwanted visitor lurched towards him; in any case, he couldn't imagine that the old man intended anything other than to leave the shop.

He saw the old man grab the edge of the door and heave at it. He meant to look for a number on the inside, Jack thought in a paralysis of disbelief. It didn't matter, the door was wedged open. Then the old man's weight dragged it free of the pound coin, and the door swung towards Jack, who over-balanced backwards, taking the nozzle and its flame with him.

He managed not to sprawl on his back. His buttocks struck the floorboards. For an agonising moment his legs stayed folded in a kneeling position while his heels tried to gain some purchase on the floor, then his left foot shot out, propelled by a cramp. He could feel the heat of the bubbling paint through his sock.

Either the old man thought Jack intended to kick the door at him or he was trying to push himself away from the jet of flame, which Jack was holding vertical in front of his face, by using the door as a support. The blistered wood slammed against the side of Jack's foot, scattering hot flakes over his sock. It felt as though a needle had been driven through his ankle into the bone, and he lost his grip on the nozzle of the blowlamp.

In a moment he regained it – almost. More than an inch of it had slipped through his grasp. As he grabbed the metal just short of the flame, pain blazed through his fingers. He was certain that his skin was about to adhere to the tube. 'Mind out!' he shouted, his voice leaping more than an octave

21

higher on the second word as though preparing to scream.

The old man seemed not to hear him. He was still leaning the door against Jack's foot, which was twisted too awkwardly to move. All Jack could do was shove his other foot against the door and kick. The old man reeled backwards, the door crashed into the wall beside the shelves, and Jack's impetus flung him forwards. The roaring nozzle flew out of his hand and fell beside the door, pointing straight at the old man's toes.

Their owner appeared to be determined not to notice. He was glaring in outrage at Jack, who saw the heavy toecap of the old man's left shoe begin to smoulder. He had a sense of being forced to participate in a slapstick comedy which was advancing frame by excruciating frame. He seized the edge of the door with his smarting fingers and heaving himself to his feet, put his free hand on the old man's chest and pushed him backwards as gently as seemed safe. He was trying to produce a reassuring smile, but it felt as though he was baring his teeth at him. All this was no quicker than turning off the blowlamp would have been, he realised as he noticed what he'd done inadvertently. In levering himself to his feet he'd trapped the nozzle of the blowlamp under the corner of the door, directing the flame at the plastic cases he'd taken off the shelves.

He saw Alfred Hitchcock's face stir on the front of the foremost box as if the photograph was coming to life – as if the tiny figure was struggling to squirm out of the path of the heat. He stooped to the control of the blowlamp, reminding himself that he was only seeing a distortion caused by the movement of air. Then Hitchcock's face turned black and the case burst into flames.

Jack lunged at the control and twisted it so hard he felt as if he was scraping skin off his fingers. The middle of the blazing case swelled, and the top half bowed backwards to share its fire with the next box. Silence plugged Jack's ears as the flame of the blowlamp died. He saw a third box lean forwards to offer itself as fuel, then a fourth. He had only to use some of the boxes which hadn't caught fire to push those which had into the street. But as Jack made for the cases the old man stepped in front of him and trampled on the Hitchcock box.

He was trying to put out the fire, but the half-melted box adhered to the sole of his shoe. As flames surrounded the shoe he stamped harder, then he clutched at the nearest support and tried to shake off the burning plastic. He clutched at a shelf above the rest of the fire, and the shelf gave way. Several dozen cassette boxes clattered to the floor, some sprawling open like hollow books. One, with an accuracy that seemed positively vindictive, landed upside down over the flames and caught fire at once.

The old man had stumbled to the counter and was shaking his foot as if he was trying to dislodge the shoe. His trouser cuff had begun to smoke. Jack felt threatened by a fit of wild mirth. He dashed to the old man, who let go of the counter and brandished his fists. 'Get it off,' Jack shouted. 'Untie the laces.'

Perhaps the old man had been deafened by the blowlamp. He waved his fists at Jack and continued to waggle his foot until Jack made a grab at it, and then he aimed a kick at him with it. The sole dripped flaming plastic. Jack seized the scrawny ankle to hold the foot still while he fumbled with the smouldering laces. He tugged at them and thought he had succeeded only in pulling the knot tighter. Then the bow vanished, and he dug the fingers of both hands inside the shoe. Twisting it off the old man's foot, he shied it out of the door.

'My shoe,' the old man wailed, 'the shoes my wife bought me,' and brought the side of his fist down on Jack's head.

Jack wouldn't have believed someone of that age and physique could have retained such strength. An ache which felt wider than his scalp spread through his cranium in seconds. The room slewed around him, the smell of burning plastic flooded into his sinuses. Then the glow which flickered at the edge of his vision grew brighter, and he heard crackling. The flames had reached the lowest shelf.

He staggered upright, grabbing the old man's wrists to protect himself and to lead him out of the shop, but the old

23

man backed against the counter. 'Come out,' Jack yelled in his ear. 'The place is on fire.'

'Whose fault is that? Where's my anniversary present, you thief?'

'In the road. Come and get it before a car does,' Jack shouted, just as he saw two small boys kicking the shoe downhill.

The flames had raced along the underside of the shelf and were sprouting upwards, snatching at the contents of the shelf. A video case sprang open and was immediately ablaze. 'That was the last present my wife gave me,' the old man cried. 'You threw it, you bring it back before I move an inch.'

Jack seized him by the shoulders, dragged him away from the counter, got behind him and shoved him, hopping on his one shoe, towards the door. The next shelf up began to smoke as they came abreast of it, and the old man screamed 'He's trying to burn me alive.' The idea seemed to make him perversely determined not to be moved, but a final push sent him hopping out of the shop.

He caught hold of a lamppost and stared about. 'You said I'd see my shoe. Where's my shoe?'

The boys had kicked it as far as the traffic lights. Apparently the crossroads were the goal, because the boy in possession of the shoe sent it past his friend into the middle of the junction. Seconds later a double-decker bus ran over it, and at the same moment the lowest shelf in Fine Films collapsed, feeding itself and its contents to the pile of flames. 'Damn your wretched shoe,' Jack cried. 'My business is on fire.'

'With my shoe in it,' the old man said, and launched himself at the shop.

Jack blocked the doorway and gave him a shove towards the lamppost. He wasn't going to be able to do anything about the fire, he thought in a fever of disbelief, because he would be fully occupied in keeping the old man safe while he hopped back and forth like a demented actor auditioning for the role of a one-legged pirate. 'Fire,' he shouted, praying there was someone within earshot.

'Thief,' the old man responded at once, even louder.

'Fire.' Repeating it once used up all Jack's breath, and the old man yelled 'Thief' while Jack drew another. At first he seemed content to respond antiphonally, then he gauged Jack's rhythm and set about shouting him down – no great task, since Jack's voice was succumbing to the effects of his cold. Jack shoved him towards the lamppost again and raised a fist to ward him off, at which moment the front door of the house opposite Fine Films opened and a woman in a quilted housecoat hurried across the road. 'What's the trouble?' she called in a teacher's schoolyard voice.

Jack saw her before the old man did. 'My shop's on fire. This gentleman's confused. Would you mind looking after him while I call the fire brigade?' he managed to say, and dashed into the shop.

The flames inside the doorway were leaping for the ceiling. The lowest remaining shelf was a mass of flames and writhing plastic, and smoke was boiling from behind almost the entire length of the shelf above. The floorboards around the heart of the fire had turned black, and the video boxes scattered around it were starting to buckle; he had the momentary impression that they were about to gather themselves cater-pillar-like and go hunching into the flames. He kicked them towards the opposite wall and ran to the counter, almost falling over the shelf which the old man had pulled down. He tried to wave away the stench of burning plastic as he dialled 999. His eyes were streaming, his head throbbed with the stink and with the thump the old man had given him, his sinuses felt as though they were filling with smoke. He might have asked to use the woman's phone if she had one, but at least he was in a better position to keep the old man out of the shop. The phone at the other end rang twice, then twice, then twice again, and then an operator said 'Fire—'

'Yes,' Jack said, and felt a sneeze growing imminent as a bomb at the end of a lit fuse. 'Fire.'

The operator had been saying '—police or ambulance?' and Jack wasn't sure if she had understood him. 'Fire,' he repeated, trying not to breathe for fear of sneezing.

'Connecting you now,' she said in a tone which sounded to

him exactly like a nurse reassuring a patient who hadn't been told the worst. The lowest remaining shelf had started to warp above the heart of the fire, while several cases on the next shelf up were popping and sputtering. He felt as if both his sneeze and the shop were about to explode. Then a man's voice said 'What is the address of the fire?'

'Where it lives, you mean?' Jack heard himself say, but said 'Here. My shop. Fine Films in Rowson Street.'

'What is the name of the nearest main road?'

'I've just told you, Rowson Street,' Jack said, and sneezed enormously. The sneeze seemed to let more of the harsh stink of plastic into his head. 'Udless you bean Vigdoria Road,' he spluttered. 'Id's off Vigdoria Road.'

'What district?'

The questions were a ritual, Jack told himself, designed to obtain all the necessary information in the shortest possible time. 'Dew Bridod,' he pronounced as distinctly as he could.

'What is on fire?'

'Videos. Fide Filbs,' Jack said, and tried to clarify. 'By shob.'

'Thank you. We're on our way,' the fireman assured him, and left him with a click.

Smoke as well as flame was pouring up from the shelves to mass beneath the ceiling. Was it poisonous? Surely Jack's unsteadiness was only an after-effect of his having been thumped on the head, and he would still be able to rescue at least some of the videocassettes – except that he could see the old man and the woman from across the road talking animatedly outside the shop, and he was afraid she mightn't be capable of dissuading the old man from attempting another incursion. He dialled again and spat towards the fire to clear his diction. 'Julia. You're home, thank God. Can you come over quick as you can? Emergency.'

'I'm on my way,' she said, and he slammed the receiver into place and lunged behind the counter to take hold of an armful of cassettes.

He'd become expert at this manoeuvre during his years of working at the public library. He would pick up several dozen books by pressing his hands against the covers at either end and lifting a rank of books nearly as wide as his arms could stretch, turn them from horizontal to vertical and support them with one hand while his chin rested on the top volume; that way he could use his free hand to file the books as he went from shelf to shelf. Now he stretched his arms wide and gripping the cassettes at either end of the shelf of comedies with his fingers, lifted the contents of the shelf towards him, turned them vertical, piled them against his chest, swung towards the door.

He was carrying more than forty cassettes. He could do it if he had to, he'd only to remember not to press too hard with his chin and with the hand beneath the stack in case that caused the middle of the stack to bulge. He would have used his free hand to hold it against his chest, except that the shop door appeared to be creeping shut as a wind from the bay fanned the fire. Then flames raced upwards behind the topmost shelf and spilled over the ceiling above Jack's head, and he was sure they were about to fall on him. He flung himself at the door, his free hand reaching to grab it before it could close, and six or more cassettes sprang sideways out of the pile he was carrying and smashed into the wall.

The rest of the stack began to topple forwards, and Jack felt himself following them. The fugitive cassettes fell on the already warped shelf, which instantly gave way. There was a roar of burning wood and celluloid and plastic, and a mass of flames which dwarfed Jack sprang at him. But he was past the door with most of the pile of cassettes. He stumbled across the pavement and stacked them against the lamppost, then he used the concrete pole to haul himself upright and peered indistinctly at the shop.

The poster beside the door was peeling away from the window, and he saw Stan's and Ollie's faces shrivel. The nozzle of the blowlamp was still trapped – of course he had only seen the air wavering, not the door – and what would happen if the flames reached the tank of gas? 'Get away from the entrance,' he shouted, and dashing more or less accurately at the door, bruised his shoulder against it. The door faltered backwards, releasing the nozzle. He dragged the blowlamp out of the shop, seized the door by its letter-slot and banged it shut in the hope of suffocating the fire somewhat, staggered to the back of the van and unlocked the doors, heaved the blowlamp inside and loaded one of the empty cartons with the cassettes he'd rescued, sat on the edge of the floor of the van and held onto it with both hands to keep himself upright. He felt exhausted and slightly delirious, but he'd achieved all he could. At least, he thought he could rest, until he noticed where the woman and the old man were now. 'Stay away from the window,' he almost screamed.

'Anything else you'd like us to do?' the woman said. Neither of them seemed in a hurry to move.

'It might shatter,' Jack told her and stood up unsteadily to urge them both away. He'd taken a step and was having to support himself against the lamppost when a not altogether new voice said 'What don't you want them to see through your window?'

The man with the duffel cowl on his head had returned. The old man turned to him, sensing someone else with doubts about Jack. 'He's a maniac,' he cried. 'He tried to set fire to me to get me out of his shop.'

'Destroying evidence,' the cowled man said triumphantly, and addressed the woman. 'Is that your house with the open door? If you've seen any goings-on at this shop it's your duty to speak out.'

'What sort of goings-on?'

'People coming out who looked as if they didn't want anyone to see what they had.'

'Well, now you mention it—' the woman mused aloud, but the old man interrupted. 'And he stole my shoe,' he said.

Jack shoved himself away from the lamppost so furiously that the three of them retreated uphill. 'I'll fetch your wretched shoe,' he said through his teeth, 'and then we'll see where it fits best.'

He sneezed several times before he reached the crossroads. The traffic lights seemed to grow more lurid each time they turned red, as though they were embers the wind was fanning. He staggered into the centre of the junction while there was no traffic and unstuck the shoe, which had been flattened to almost twice its original size, from the tarmac. By the time he climbed onto the pavement the old man was hopping downhill to meet him, his arms around the shoulders of his companions. As Jack held up the shoe, which flapped as if it was greeting its owner, the old man gave a cry of anguish.

The task of finding something appropriate to say to him felt potentially even more disastrous than the rest of the day had been. Jack was dawdling, and wishing he could plead sneezes as an excuse not to speak, when Julia came up behind him. 'Is that Mr Pether?' she said.

For a moment the day made sense. The old man was indeed Mr Pether, the father of the policeman who lived at the opposite end of the street from the Orchards. 'Hasn't he aged since they put him in the home?' Julia said. 'I'd hardly have recognised him.'

If only Jack had! He saw himself turning off the blowlamp, saying 'I know where you live now, Mr Pether' and ushering him across the road to the side street full of retirement homes. 'What's happened to his shoe?' said Julia. 'Was that the emergency?'

Two fire engines appeared on the brow of the hill as the window of Fine Films exploded, strewing the pavement with blackened glass and releasing a wave of flames which rushed up the façade. Mr Pether and his supporters hunched their shoulders simultaneously and came downhill faster without missing a step, as if performing a routine they had rehearsed. Jack leaned on Julia and slapped himself across the forehead with the flattened shoe. 'Got to laugh, haven't you?' he said, and did.

FOUR

Sometimes Laura thought cycling was her favourite thing in the world. Cycling to school made her feel important and responsible and trusted by her parents, but cycling by the river on a Sunday morning was best of all; though a few people were walking large dogs, for hundreds of yards at a time she had the promenade to herself. The wind hummed in her ears and brushed her hair back over her shoulders as her long legs pumped almost effortlessly. She remembered thinking she would never get her balance, all one weekend which she'd spent trying not to fall off as her mother ran beside her, but Laura had been little then, only three years old.

She was paced by container vessels which glided upriver with a slow muffled beat which seemed to come from deep underwater. Once she raced a speedboat. When she reached Seacombe she waved to the downtown skyline of Liverpool, where her mother would have arrived by now, before switching into first gear so as to pedal uphill over the cobblestones of the bus terminal. From the top of the slope she was able to cycle home by a route full of houses for sale.

At the edge of Liscard, where the large stores were, she passed a slim three-storey house overlooking a junior football game in Central Park. From the top window she would be able to see the horizon of the sea. Imagining how life in a big house would feel was an adventure in itself. If her parents owned that one she could play on the swings in the park whenever she wanted to, though she was a bit old for that, or if they lived opposite the library beside the graveyard near her school she could change her books every day as soon as she'd read them and hear the trees around the library giving a voice to the wind as she lay in bed. From the library she cycled past her school and across a bridge which appeared to carry a side street over nothing in particular, and eventually left a leafy square by a footpath which emerged onto the steepest road above the bay. The thought of cycling down it made her catch her breath. She wheeled the bicycle to a crossroads and pedalled home, the houses for sale inhabiting her mind like dreams.

She was enjoying trying to choose her favourite as she turned along her road and saw Jody Venable walking towards her, preoccupied with not stepping on the cracks between the flagstones. 'There you are,' Jody said, walking normally as though she was too grown-up to do anything else. 'I came to see if you were in.'

She was wearing dungarees over a blouse Laura hadn't seen before, and a necklace so thin it was visible only as a sunlit gleam. 'Did you get those in Greece?' Laura said.

Jody nodded, tossing back her blonde hair, which was streakier than ever. 'I brought you something back. You can have it now so long as you don't wake my dad.'

'I'll just leave a note in case anyone comes home,' Laura said and ran through the house to unbolt the back gate while Jody wheeled the bicycle into the alley, where a dog in a yard gave a token bark. As Laura wrote her message Jody leaned her hands on the working surface in the kitchen and lifted herself to sit on it, letting herself down again as it creaked. 'I bet you're looking forward to moving,' she said, wrinkling her nose.

Unexpectedly, Laura found that saying so would feel like being ungrateful to her parents. 'We haven't found anywhere yet.'

'I meant because you had to put up with all that noise and mess while your dad's friend was fixing the house. You should have come and stayed with us. I asked my mum if you all could have and she didn't say no.'

'That was nice of her,' Laura said to cover up her disappointment at having learned too late. She wrote 'Gone to

Jody's' on the board and made sure the front door locked behind her. 'Don't tell me what my present is, I want to guess.'

Beyond the traffic lights Victoria Road climbed past the Sea Level Hotel, which was several hundred feet above sea level, to New Brighton station. Jody's house was half of a burly pair. It overlooked the station and the bay from the top of a steep driveway which Jody's father called his evening exercise. The hall was larger than the Orchards' kitchen. The low tables strewn with magazines in the front room always put Laura in mind of a waiting-room, but if it was possible to tire of the view of the horizon giving birth to ships then she would have watched the trains and the streams of people they set free. Living close to the station would be like the start of any number of adventures, especially once her parents let her go on trains by herself, but she oughtn't to let her dreams feel like the future, even though there was a house like Jody's for sale a few doors away.

Jody's mother came downstairs on quick tiptoe. 'I've turned your father on his side so the neighbours won't complain about the noise,' she told Jody, and turned to Laura. 'How's life treating you, madam? Moved up in the world yet? Is there anything Jody should know to keep up with you at school?' she said without a pause as Jody grimaced at the ceiling.

'The teachers gave her the homework we've been doing,' Laura guessed.

'So long as she gets all the chances she's entitled to. That's all anyone can ask for.' A smile which was almost too brief to be called one, and which Laura knew announced a change of subject, crossed her plump lightly painted face. 'You and the family will have to come to the restaurant so we can try our new dishes out on you now Jody's gone vegetarian.'

'Did you find what you were looking for in Greece?'

'Everything we said we would. An island every day and a new dish from every island. We haven't decided what to call them in English yet, except for Minotaur Steak.' She sat in the rocking-chair by the window and picked up a notepad

32

loaded with long Greek names. 'Take Laura up to your room but mind you don't waken the slumbering hunter.'

As soon as the girls were in Jody's room, which smelled of hairspray and was strewn with even more clothes than usual, Jody said 'Anything happened at school that my mum wouldn't want to know?'

'Someone in the fourth year dropped a condom when she was paying at the cafeteria.'

Jody squeaked and covered her mouth. 'What happened?'

'She made out it was a balloon she'd got at someone's birthday. And Diane had hysterics because a dog came into the yard, so Miss Haygarth sat on it until the stray man came.'

'Diane's bigger than Miss Haygarth.'

'It was just a big soft dog, we thought it wanted to play, only Diane was afraid it'd bite her and give her AIDS.'

'That isn't how you get AIDS.' Jody finished spluttering and said, 'I don't think it is, do you?'

'I think it's the only way Diane's going to get it if her mum never lets her wear make-up. Oh, and Trace kept showing us some hash in a matchbox she said she got from her brother, only Grace's parents used to be hippies and she thinks it's sealing wax.'

'I hope Trace didn't let Jackie Pether see it, though.'

'Jackie Pether ...' Laura stuck out her tongue as if she had swallowed some horrible medicine. 'Ruth put some bubble gum inside her desk, Ruth's desk I mean, to throw away after class, only Jackie said "What have you got in your desk?" so loud that Mrs Sinclair saw it and got in a dead bad eggy. And when Miss Miles had us talking about whether people should all be equal Jackie said nobody should be allowed to go on holiday during term time, and guess who she meant.'

'You can help make her jealous.' Jody jumped up and grabbed a parcel from among the tangle of soft toys under the Madonna poster. She bounced next to Laura on the bed while Laura unwrapped the parcel. 'It's sort of a souvenir in advance.'

It was a yellow T-shirt which announced I'VE BEEN TO

KNOSSOS. 'I know you haven't yet,' Jody said, 'but you will have been soon, won't you?'

'Thanks, Jody.' Laura pulled off the T-shirt she was wearing and smoothed the new one down over her trainer bra. 'Now it really feels like I'll be going.'

'You can borrow my guidebook.' Jody arched her back and pressed her hands against the wall behind the bed, and sighed. 'What shall we do now?' she said as she heard her father trudging to the bathroom. 'I wish we could play a tape.'

'Don't strain your ears on my account,' he responded. 'I should be up by now. I've been dreaming long enough.'

'We'd rather have you oversleep than getting an ulcer,' Jody's mother called.

'Better an ulcer than a pauper's grave,' he said, and pulled the chain.

Jody squashed her face up like a boxer's and mimed fighting with her fists, and Laura giggled. 'Wasn't it much of a holiday for them?'

'Only because we were doing something they can claim off their tax. We had fun, but they're not a laugh like your dad. They were nearly shouting on the plane because I told them his puzzle about the men in the restaurant.'

'Have you worked it out yet?'

'I think I nearly did. Tell me it again.'

'Three men are in a restaurant and the bill comes to thirty-three pounds. They each pay eleven and then the waiter realises he's charged them too much and the bill is only twenty-eight. So they tell him to keep two for himself and give them a pound each, which means they each pay ten, right? Three tens are thirty, and the waiter keeps two, but who gets the pound that's left over?'

'The restaurant. No, the waiter. I give up. What's the answer?'

'I did work it out, but I've forgotten.'

'You're no use then, are you? Tell me another,' Jody said, immediately adding 'No, don't. Do you want to hear my tape from Greece?'

'I'd love to,' Laura said, and claimed one of Jody's pillows for a back-rest against the wall. The music sounded bright and lazy as waves on a sea beneath the Mediterranean sun, and when she closed her eyes she could imagine herself sitting under a palm tree on the beach pictured on the card Jody had sent her from Crete. By the time Jody turned the tape over, Laura could feel the heat of the sun on her face.

Lunch was Greek too: salad with cheese in it, flat oval loaves, a vegetarian dip the colour of fudge. Jody and her parents gave Laura a tour of the islands while they ate, so that by the time Jody took her upstairs again she felt as if she'd almost been where she was dreaming of. The music seemed to intensify the sunlight which was reaching into Jody's room, and Laura could imagine that the sound of fire engines was part of her daydream. Their wailing faded, and she was listening to another dance when Jody's father came into the room. 'Laura, is your dad at work today?'

'All day, every day,' Laura said, feeling like a commercial, 'if you want to borrow' – the phrase eluded her for a moment – 'films that won't insult your intelligence.'

'Mine could do with a bit of insulting by the time I finish work. I was going to say that if he wasn't there you might have wanted to let him know there's a fire somewhere up by the shop.'

Jody dropped the high-school soap novel she was reading. 'Let's go and see it, Laura.'

'Stay well clear and do as the firemen say,' Jody's mother told the girls as they sprinted out of the house.

As soon as Laura set foot on the driveway she saw black smoke oozing into the blue sky above the roofs. It made her think of the evil genie in a book of fairy tales and legends she'd been given for her birthday years ago. She ran after Jody, up the side street to another which was full of retirement homes and nursing homes and which ended near her father's shop.

Many of the residents seemed enlivened by the fire. More than a dozen were making their way to the end of the street as if the fire was attracting them like moths. Others stood with their nurses in front gardens, either willing the fire to stay away or expecting it to show itself out of respect for their age. As Jody and Laura outdistanced the old folk two teenage boys in denim dodged around the corner from the direction of the fire and crossed to the pavement which was deserted. Laura stared after them as she came to the corner herself, and didn't turn until Jody wailed 'Oh, Laura, look.'

Fine Films had gone. Between the two boarded-up shops was a gaping hole stuffed with oily smoke at which orange flames were clawing. Two fire engines were shooting water into the black hole. A sizeable audience had gathered on the pavement opposite, and people were watching from cars parked at the barriers of plastic cones which closed the road in both directions, but Laura felt as if all this was falling short of her mind, as if it was a picture she wasn't quite able to grasp. As she began to run up the middle of the road she felt the blackness which had engulfed the shop reaching for her mind. Then two people ran out of the crowd to meet her, and she saw they were her parents. To her astonishment, both of them were smiling.

In a moment she saw that her mother's smile was trying to be brave, but her father was smiling widely. He pulled Laura's mother towards her as if to make certain she shared a surprise, and flourished the clown's head on his key-ring like a talisman. 'Don't be upset, Laura,' he shouted. 'Everything works for you if you know how to do your sums. This is the best thing that could have happened to us.'

FIVE

Laura looked exactly as her mother had when he'd tried to reassure her – wishing she could be convinced. What he had to tell them had already transformed the sight of the flames into a dance of celebration for Jack, but he shouldn't tell them while there was an audience. 'I wouldn't let you down, would I?' he said, lowering his voice, which had caused several bystanders to glance at him. 'I'll tell you as soon as we're home.'

Laura was staring at the crowd. 'Why can't they go away? Why do they have to watch?'

'We all like a bit of excitement in our lives, don't we? Maybe I needed this to make me realise.' He wiped away a tear which had begun to trickle down her cheek. He was saying too much if he didn't intend to say everything now. 'I'd better stay, but you needn't if it bothers you.'

'Of course she's bothered,' Julia said almost accusingly. 'Why wouldn't she be?'

'Take her home. I'll be as quick as I can.' He hugged them both and winked at Julia. 'Think of the insurance.'

He hoped he hadn't spoken loud enough for anyone outside the family to hear. When he sneaked a glance at the crowd, the woman in the housecoat and the hooded man and Mr Pether were watching him. Jack gave them a toned-down smile as he walked uphill, hearing Laura say shakily 'I've left my T-shirt at Jody's' and Julia's response, a shade too enthusiastic: 'I saw you had a new one. Is that from you, Jody? It's lovely.' The trio of watchers peered at him as he rejoined the crowd, and he could only grin. 'Got to laugh, haven't you?'

'He thinks this is funny, what he did to my wife's shoe,' Mr Pether cried, flourishing its remains. 'She couldn't walk for

37

the last six months of her life.'

Most of those who heard him seemed more embarrassed or bewildered than roused to anger. Some glanced at the tartan slipper which a nurse from the retirement home had persuaded him to wear. Jack solemnised his face and went to the old man. 'I'm sorry about your wife and I'm sorry about your shoe. I'll buy you a new pair if you like.'

His choice of words didn't strike him until they were out of his mouth. He felt a giggle gathering itself like an uncontrollable sneeze as he saw the old man preparing to object. 'I don't want a pair, I only want one to match this,' Mr Pether protested, stamping the shoe that was left.

Jack covered his mouth and emitted a snort which he willed to sound more like a sneeze than like mirth. 'I'll do my best,' he said when he could.

'I should come along now, Mr Pether,' the nurse said, taking the old man's arm. 'We've had enough excitement for one day.'

Their departure acted as a signal to the crowd. The spectacle was mostly smoke by now, only a few subdued flames struggling to fend off the jets of water. The quilted woman returned to her house, the cars swung away from the striped cones. A few of the youngest members of the audience lingered, apparently in the hope that the dousing of the fire would prove to be as false an ending as those of all the horror films they watched, and so did the cowled man. 'It's under control now,' a fireman told Jack. 'I'm afraid there's nothing salvageable.'

'That's fine. I mean, thanks for trying. For succeeding, I should say,' Jack blethered. 'Will I need to tell someone how it started?'

'That will be necessary. Tell me if you wish.'

'Ask him about the kind of films that conveniently got destroyed.'

'That isn't our job, sir.'

The cowled man treated him to the suspicious glare he had previously reserved for Jack. 'Aren't you supposed to uphold the law of the land?'

38

'Are you a witness, sir?'

'The only kind. God's.'

'Then shouldn't you be in church, sir?' the fireman said, and told Jack 'I think it'll be advisable if we confer in the appliance.'

Once they were in the cab of the fire engine the fireman said 'Has he something against you?'

'Working on the Sabbath.'

'Well, we all need some kind of belief to keep us going. Just so long as we don't try to impose it on others, I always say. My daughter's been born again, as if her mother didn't go through enough the first time.' He cleared his throat as though he wanted to spit and watched the cowled man flouncing downhill. 'What have you to tell me?' he said.

Jack pointed at himself with all his fingers. 'Imagine Oliver Hardy with a blowlamp.'

'Go on.'

'Did you notice the old codger who was waving his shoe about? If you cast him as Stan Laurel ... I hope I don't sound as if I'm trying to make light of anything, but I feel such a fool now I think of what happened.'

'However's comfortable for you.'

It seemed to Jack that there was no way of describing the events leading up to the fire other than as a joke against himself. He told it deadpan, and was almost sure that the fireman was stifling a laugh. Comedy was something that happened at a distance to you or to someone else. They were still in the cab when Andy Nation came to gaze aghast at the smouldering hole, pulling the zip of his jacket up and down as if he couldn't bear his hands to be inactive. Jack knocked on the windscreen and called to him, and Andy looked everywhere for him but in the cab. 'Up here,' Jack shouted. 'I've joined the fire service. Starting fires, that is.'

Andy winced. 'Julia told me, but I didn't think it would be this bad.'

'It could have been far worse, Andy. This is my friend the builder.'

'Will the shop need making safe?' Andy wanted to know.

'When we've finished damping down,' the fireman said.

'I'll do what needs doing, Jack. You go home to the family,' Andy said, and asked the fireman 'He's free, is he?'

'I've heard all I need to hear.'

Jack thanked them both profusely and climbed into the front of the van. A generalised ache had taken up residence in the area above his cheekbones, but it was familiar enough now to be ignored. He let the van freewheel backwards downhill, away from the dunces' plastic caps, then he turned it with a drunkard's carefulness and drove home.

He balanced the carton of videocassettes in the crook of one arm as he let himself into the house. When he carried the carton into the front room he saw a guidebook to Crete lying face down on Laura's chair. It looked forlorn, like a bird which couldn't fly. 'You will,' he promised Laura silently, and set the carton down.

On an impulse he counted the videocassettes. Thirty-three had survived. That was a good omen, he thought, and all the more welcome inasmuch as it reminded him that he didn't need that kind of reassurance. No need to mention it to Julia and Laura; it would take too much explaining.

They were in the kitchen, and he sensed that they'd stayed together while they tried to come to terms with the apparent disaster. Laura was painstakingly scraping potatoes, Julia was emptying grounds out of the wedding-present percolator. 'I hope those aren't grounds for divorce,' he said, and noticing the turkey pie in the cold oven, 'Looks as if Christmas has come early.'

Laura gave him a wistful smile. 'Come on, you two,' he said, 'we'll go out for a walk.'

'You can see we've things to do, Jack.'

'We'll all do them later. It's been too long since the three of us went out together, what with Laura's homework and the shop.'

He was waiting for them to get ready when the phone rang. It was a woman in Hoylake, the other seaward corner of the peninsula, wanting to know if he still offered home deliveries of films. 'I can only deliver laughs at the moment, but

40

I'm about to extend my range,' he said, and jotted down her name and phone number.

Bidston Hill was in Birkenhead, twenty minutes' drive away through suburban streets which were briefly interrupted by the innermost dock and its rearing cranes. Jack swung the van around a roundabout which harboured a steepled church and drove past the vandalised graveyard of a defunct church to the track which led to the common. A few cars were parked at the top of the rubbly track. Dogs were barking among the trees, but the only people in sight on the grass between the car park and the woods were three teenagers sitting on a picnic table, their feet on the attached bench – heroin addicts, Jack guessed from the way they tried to seem not to be waiting. He took Julia and Laura by the hand and led them through the woods where nuts dropped by grey squirrels rattled through the branches. Beyond the remains of a low brick wall, slabs of sandstone patched with gorse and heather stepped up towards a windmill in chains. A bridge led across a dell occupied by a road, and on the far side the Orchards climbed a jagged natural stairway to the windmill.

It stood at one end of the sandstone ridge, the far end of which housed an observatory. The ridge appeared to be composed of giant misshapen paving stones cemented by soil overgrown with turf. Frowns that sketched the processes of weathering were incised in the sandstone, deep puddles glittered in depressions in the rock. From the exposed spine the bay beyond the peninsula was visible, while to the left the mountains of Wales massed like layers of cloud above fields misted by the River Dee, and to the right the towers and clocks and red-brick terraces of Birkenhead seemed to lead straight to the warehouses and stately offices of Liverpool, a trick of perspective having done away with the Mersey. Jack drew a breath which felt like a taste of the clear blue sky. 'Well, ladies, what do you see that you like?'

'You know I like coming up here,' Laura said.

'What about living somewhere with this kind of a view?'

'Jack,' Julia said.

'You've got to stop me babbling, Laura, or at least tell me

41

what you're afraid of. Do you think we'll have to cancel Crete, is that it? Switch off the sun and turn off the wave machine and send all the actors home?'

'Won't we have to?'

'Won't it cost more to keep thousands of Greeks on the dole?' He glimpsed a smile which almost surfaced, and said 'Laura, we'd go if it killed me, but we don't need to make any sacrifices.'

'I don't understand.'

'You know the shop wasn't doing as well as we hoped. Maybe I should have carried more popular titles, not trash but popular. If I'd sold the films I was beginning to have doubts about I wouldn't have got anything like I'd paid for them, but they're insured for the full replacement value, and of course the shop is too. There could be quite a sum left over when I've rethought the business. No wonder people turn to arson.'

'*Dad.*'

He thought her shock was mostly feigned; certainly she was enjoying it. 'Desperate people, I mean,' he said, digging in his pocket for the chain letter. 'People who might credit this kind of nonsense.'

He sat on the wall above the woods in the shadow of the observatory dome and read the letter aloud, lowering his voice when she glanced at passers-by and shushed him. 'Turn ill luck into good ... Make thirteen copies of this letter ... Do not break the chain ... A woman in Nevada broke the chain and her husband was diagnosed as having a brain tumour, but when she sent the letters the doctors were able to operate. Presumably,' Jack commented, 'if he'd died in the meantime he would have risen from the dead.'

'Why would anyone make up a letter like that? To frighten people?'

'No other point to it, is there?' Jack looked around vainly for a waste-bin and shoved the letter into his pocket. He yawned and stretched, feeling relaxed at last, then he shoved himself to his feet, dislodging a chunk of the wall, which rumbled down the slope and thumped a tree-trunk. 'Better head for home. I'd forgotten someone's supposed to be looking at the house,' he said, and thought for a moment that he'd forgotten something else far more important. It would come to him.

SIX

In the morning Jack's cold was spectacularly worse. He lost count of the number of times he had to blow his nose before he felt able to breathe. His cumbersome half-melted legs had little zeal for transporting the rest of him, which seemed to have been separated from them during the night and inexpertly restored. He felt so hot in bed that he imagined yesterday's fire had stayed with him. When Julia laid her cool hand on his forehead, however, she couldn't find much of a temperature. She stirred two paracetamol tablets into a glass of hot lemon juice and advised him to stay in bed, and it wasn't until he was listening to the echoes of the slam of the front door reverberating back and forth across his cavernous brittle cranium that he realised he should have asked her to phone the insurance company. He piloted himself down the stairs, feeling as if he had to balance his head to prevent it from floating away, and attempted to croak his claim into the telephone, but gave up after saying his name thrice without communicating. He wrote a letter to the company and stumbled to the post-box with it, all the way aware of how his fingers gripping the envelope were plugged into his hand which was hinged to his forearm which was composed of bones which preserved a constant length and muscles which did not.... With so much machinery to operate it seemed miraculous that he reached the post-box and posted the letter.

By the time he reconquered the lock of the front door he was more than ready for bed. He restrained himself from kicking off the covers as soon as he'd crawled under them. If he had a fever, he wished that the two women whom he'd met on returning home yesterday could have been a fever dream. But the wind had indeed lifted the elder woman's blossoming purple trilby and deposited it beneath the right front wheel of the van, and Jack had felt as if he was handing her a trampled patch of an artificial flower-bed, and when he'd parked the van and found the women waiting on the doorstep he'd thought she meant to demand a new hat until he'd grasped that they were there to view the house.

Perhaps he shouldn't have offered to replace the hat. As Julia had conducted the women through the house he'd tried surreptitiously to get her and then Laura to add to the cash in his pocket. Eventually he'd written a cheque, only for the woman to refuse to give him her name, waving away the cheque with more impatience than grace. As she'd marched away arm in arm with her companion, who might or might not have been her daughter, the younger woman had started what was clearly destined to be a protracted argument – 'Ridiculous, wearing a hat in a place like this' – and Jack saw that he'd seen the last of them.

There would be other house-hunters, and just now he was home if they called. For the first two days, however, whenever the phone rang or he dreamed that it did, he felt too watery to crawl out of bed. He lay in a dream which drifted in and out of sleep, and when he was closest to waking he played with numbers in his head. The value of Jack Orchard was eleven: if you numbered each letter with its position in the alphabet, their sum was ninety-two, and nine and two added up to eleven; what else did? 'Videos' and 'Bidston' and 'Laura Julia Orchard.' Julia had never quite understood his eagerness to add her name to Laura's, but she'd been touched and had given in to him. He'd thought it might bring Laura luck, that was all; it wasn't as though he let numerology make his choices for him, the way his parents had let it make theirs, though he had to admit that surprisingly often it had seemed to work in their favour. Sometimes he thought that his father had only been humouring Jack's mother – that he'd juggled numbers until they came out right, though Jack had never been able to see how he did it. When Jack had been as old as

45

Laura his father had teased his brain with mathematical puzzles, and as he lay in bed they came back to him. Twelve metal balls look identical, but one of them is either heavier or lighter than any of the others; using scales to weigh the balls against one another, how do you determine which is the odd one out and whether it is heavier or lighter in just three weighings? 'Balls,' Jack mumbled eventually and dozed, feeling childlike, safe in bed and eager for tomorrow.

Wednesday brought a phone call from a couple who wanted to view the house, and Thursday brought the couple themselves. The woman kept sniffing at a lingering trace of the smell of the damp course, and Jack found himself emitting sniffs as if in sympathy, which caused her husband to scowl as though Jack were mimicking her. Jack refrained from pointing out that they both smelled so pungently of what must be a pack of dogs that even his clogged nose noticed. Given the non-committal mutterings with which they took their leave of him he couldn't regard the day as having been especially productive. At least on Friday he felt well enough to drive to Liverpool.

Once he was out of the tunnel under the river he headed south on the dock road. The shipping offices of the Pier Head gave way to warehouses, blocks of which had acquired new identities: boutiques, restaurants, purveyors of Liverpudlian nostalgia, a Tate Gallery, yuppie apartments. Further up from the river the warehouses were unimproved, and there were few people in the largely windowless streets. An old Chinese couple whose resolute toothlessness seemed designed to aid their grimacing hobbled uphill towards Chinatown, and a girl of about Laura's age wheeled a pram, the contents of which Jack couldn't distinguish, across his path as he steered the van into the entrance to a court of warehouses. Buildings like secrecy embodied in forty-foot walls of red brick surrounded him at once, cutting off the mumble of the city and grudgingly returning him an echo of the slam of his door as he stepped down.

Apart from the van, the only vehicle parked in the court was an uncabbed lorry trailer at least as capacious as the Orchards' house. Most of the stout doors in the hefty walls were unidentified by signs, but a slightly askew bright-red plaque was screwed above the wicket in the door nearest the van. VICS VIDS, the plaque announced in white letters, most of which belonged to the same font. Above the plaque a camera which had recently been assailed with litter swivelled rustily to watch Jack, and in front of the wicket a dog began to growl.

If it hadn't, he might almost have taken it for a carpet which someone had dumped. As he pressed the bellpush next to the door, the animal pricked up one threadbare ear and the chewed remains of the other, and bared teeth so eroded that the sight made Jack's teeth ache. It looked as though an Alsatian and several other breeds, all of them ready to fight, had been involved in its birth. The dog was continuing to growl, keeping it low in order to prolong the threat without drawing breath, when the grille above the bellpush cleared itself of a gob of static and said 'Give it a kick.'

Jack leaned one hand on the door frame and pirouetting gingerly, delivered a kick to the wicket above the old rope of the dog's tail. The door didn't budge, but the dog raised its head from between its paws and began to foam at the mouth while its growl doubled in vehemence. 'Not the door, you fool,' the grille protested, 'the dog.'

'Kick your own dog,' Jack said, almost falling on top of the animal in his haste to back out of reach.

The grille expelled a burst of static like a hiss of reproof, and Jack was awaiting a more positive response when the wicket crashed open and the dog leapt up, straight at him. He froze, telling himself not to show fear, and at the last moment the dog swerved and fled into the road, causing a Jaguar driven by a huge Jamaican to screech and veer. 'I wouldn't have stood in his way, la,' the pony-tailed youth who had opened the door advised Jack. 'He's not our dog.'

'I felt lucky,' Jack said like the kind of film he thought the youth might watch.

The youth, who wore an earring and a T-shirt printed with a hero as muscular as he himself was scrawny, seemed unimpressed. 'Whir you from?'

'Over the water,' Jack said, wondering why this provoked a stare which bordered on the hostile. 'My business, you mean? Fine Films.'

'Never heard of them.'

'That's some admission,' Jack said, and when the stare didn't waver: 'You sent me a catalogue.'

'We sent lots this month,' the youth said accusingly. He craned back through the wicket and shouted 'Says he's Fine Films.'

'Let him in,' a woman responded.

The youth shrugged and ducked through the wicket. 'Gorra be curful,' he muttered, which apparently implied a request, because Jack had scarcely crossed the threshold when the youth said as if he was repeating it 'Shut the door.'

Jack did so, and looked around. Beneath the brick ceiling, metal shelves standing a foot taller than he were attached to the bare brick walls; others stood back to back on the brick floor, leaving just enough space for two people to pass in the aisles. Unsurprisingly, the enormous room smelled of brick. One entire wall was of Horror, while the opposite wall displayed second-hand cassettes, growing cheaper and dustier as they progressed towards the dimmest corner of the room. Jack collected a supermarket trolley from beside the cash-desk, behind which a perspiring pudgy woman who looked as if she might be the youth's mother was using a hand-held device to stick price tags onto cassette boxes, and headed for the ex-rental cassettes. Even here Horror seemed to be the norm; more than half the boxes offered screaming women. 'Why do people want this sort of thing?' he wondered aloud.

The woman threw an armful of priced boxes into a trolley for the youth to distribute on the shelves. 'Worse than that is happening to someone somewhere in the world right now.'

Jack couldn't tell whether she intended that as an explanation or a defence. 'I wasn't attacking you personally.'

'I should hope not,' she said loudly to the youth.

Perhaps Jack should be guided by the critics. He began to look for boxes which quoted reviews of the films. He hadn't realised there were so many magazines; he'd never heard of at least half of them. He tried reading some of the comments aloud while the woman and the youth competed at how ostentatiously they could ignore him. On the boxes he chose, none of the sources — *The Face, For Him, Q, Empire, Blitz* — had a name worth eleven. Of course it didn't matter, though he told himself playfully that he would buy anything which quoted a review from the *Telegraph*.

Two hours later, when the last shelf brought him back to the cash-desk, he'd found none. The trolley was piled high, mostly with discounted tapes. The youth, who had taken over at the desk while the woman conversed in a back room with two broad men in pinstriped suits, gave the trolley an unwelcoming glance and pulled a pad of receipts towards him. 'Name,' he said.

'Jack Orchard. Fine Films.'

'Jack ...'

'Orchard.'

The youth wrote 'Awchard' with such industriousness that Jack didn't like to contradict him. 'Fine,' Jack said, 'Films,' and was already beginning to have had enough. 'Do you think we should wait for your mother?'

The youth raised his head but not his gaze. 'She won't be out till next year.'

'Surely—' Jack blurted, and realised his blunder. 'I meant, no, you carry on. With good behaviour,' he babbled, and succeeded in sneezing so as to interrupt himself.

He made another tour of the shelves while the youth slowly and inventively misspelled the titles of the films. One of the pinstriped men, who Jack had assumed were officials of some kind, frowned at him and closed the door of the back room as Jack glimpsed a bank of at least a dozen video-recorders in operation and a pile of cassettes in unmarked boxes which the other man was loading into a carton. Jack feigned interest in the shelves furthest from the room, though they held comedies featuring teenagers so vacuous he could imagine wishing a serial murderer on them, until the youth at the desk began to sum up the purchases with a calculator. Jack returned to the desk in time to watch him writing the total at the foot of the receipt. 'Actually, I *think* you may have miscalculated,' Jack said. 'You might want to tot them up again.'

The youth held up the calculator like a magician displaying a card. 'I see what it says, but it's wrong,' Jack assured him. 'Did you enter some amounts more than once, do you think?'

The youth craned his head back towards the inner room, protruding his Adam's apple at Jack. 'Mrs Vickers,' he shouted at the ceiling.

The woman waddled to the desk, demanding 'Aren't you done yet?' As she peered at the receipt she must have noticed Jack's address, because she told him 'There's an auction by you.'

'It's been there for years.'

She stared at him. 'Five hundred used titles.'

'Video, you mean? I may have a look. Just now we've a disagreement over thirty-nine pounds or so.'

She glanced at the foot of the receipt and then at the figures in the window of the calculator. 'I know they tally,' Jack protested, but she had already cleared the window and was stabbing at the keys with one stubby finger. When she'd finished she shook the calculator at him. 'Will that do you?'

'If it's right it will.' Since she hadn't stopped waving the calculator, the blurring of the digits made him feel as though his fever had revived. 'That seems more like it,' he admitted, having managed to distinguish the total, and took out his credit card.

'Marvellous. You'll have to phone for authorisation,' she told the youth, and stumped into the back room, slamming the door.

The youth read the number on a grubby scrap of paper taped to the desk and prodded digits on the telephone. This part of the ritual of using a credit card always made Jack feel absurdly guilty, and so he gave the youth a grin which was meant to seem resigned but which came out conspiratorial and fixed. By the time the youth read out Jack's card number and the amount of the purchase, the expression had begun to tweak Jack's face. He was wondering how to move it when the youth did so for him. In a bored aggrieved tone he said 'You've got no money left.'

'That can't be right. We're a thousand in credit at least, more like fifteen hundred. More than we ever use. Don't put the—' Jack began to shout, but the youth had dropped the receiver into its house.

The door of the inner room banged open, and the woman barged out, followed by the pinstripes. 'What's the row?' she demanded.

'I wanted to speak to whatever you call them, the authoriser. They've got me in the red.'

'What, someone else's mistaken?' The woman planted her hands on her hips. 'Paying cash then, are you?'

'I can't just now. I haven't got it,' Jack said, trying to comprehend what had happened. 'Can I phone my wife?'

The woman gestured at the desk, and Jack was reaching for the phone when he realised she was indicating the superscription on the taped scrap of cardboard: NO PRIVET PHONE CALLS. 'Hedging your profits?' he said wildly. 'Then I don't know what to do.'

'Stop wasting Mrs Vickers' time,' the brawnier of the pinstriped team suggested.

'I was here on legitimate business, I assure you.' That must sound like a sly comment on the transactions in the back room, because the two men opened and closed their mouths like fish. 'I must say you do business like nobody else I've met,' Jack told the woman and the youth, and dodged out of the warehouse.

He hauled himself up into the van and drove into the centre of Liverpool. Could Julia have been so infected by his optimism that she'd spent all that money? The only purchase he could think of that might cost so much was their holiday, but surely she would have mentioned that she was booking it. Had she meant to surprise him? The downtown streets were crowded, streams of people spilling into the roadways whenever a gap developed in the traffic. 'Run or die,' Jack growled at them, tramping on the brake.

The entire population of the business district appeared to

51

be on the streets. A ripple of sunlight flashed into his eyes from the river as he turned along the street where Julia worked. There was room for the van outside Rankin's, by a hooded parking meter. Jack parked hastily, scraping a tyre against the kerb, and ran into the office, calling 'Julia.'

She and Lynne, one of the typists, were at the computer, watching columns of figures pour down the screen. 'Just a minute,' Julia said, and was at least that long before she turned to him. 'Going to buy me lunch?'

'What with? Where's all the money gone this month? I just tried to buy some stock and they wouldn't honour the card.'

'I haven't used mine since Saturday. I certainly haven't spent more than usual.'

'I told them it was a mistake. What's the customer relations number?' He was rummaging in his wallet when Lynne said rather smugly 'If that's your van outside, it's being booked.'

Jack dashed outside as the traffic warden began to write in her notebook. 'I'm off, I'm going,' he babbled. 'Had to see my wife urgently. Money trouble.'

She pushed her peaked cap higher on her lined forehead with her pen. 'Your private life is no concern of mine, sir. I'll be back this way in five minutes.'

Jack sprinted into the building in time to hear Lynne saying loudly to Julia 'I wouldn't let any husband of mine talk that way to me. It's at least as much your money as his.' She gazed at Jack as though she hoped he'd overheard, but he didn't care what she or the traffic warden thought of him so long as everything was right with him and Julia. It wasn't until Julia looked up from rooting in her handbag that his confidence shook.

'I haven't got my card. I don't know where it can be. I know I put it in my bag on Saturday after I paid for the shopping.' She screwed up her face as if that would help her think, and he thought she was about to weep. Then a look of understanding emerged onto her face, and it was worse than weeping. 'Those boys at the fire,' she said.

SEVEN

By Monday morning Laura was still blaming herself. 'I saw those boys running away from the fire. I should have taken more notice of them, I should have seen what they looked like. If I'd told you, you could have told the police.'

'It's no more your fault than your mother's. If it's anyone's fault it's mine, and we're not going to let it matter, are we? I bet soon you'll be thinking of it as a cautionary tale to tell your friends.'

'I hate those boys. I wish they'd been in the fire. How could they spend all our money like that?'

'It sounds as if they weren't the ones who spent it. The lady at the hi-fi shop thinks it was a man about my age. The police think he uses the boys to lift credit cards for him and then spends all he can before the victims notice they've been robbed. Apparently we're not the only case.'

'Why didn't the shops see he wasn't Mummy? I would have.'

'It's my fault for only putting my initial on the card,' Julia said.

'Not a bit of it, Julia. Ten to one he sends a woman to use cards that have a woman's name on them. These are people who know what they're doing.'

'Nobody needs to buy all those things,' Laura cried.

'Five expensive cameras are pushing it, you mean. Especially when it was the same one from five different shops. Maybe our man is in consumer research.' She only bit her lip at that, and so he told her the truth. 'According to the police they're resold the same day to people who order them in advance.'

Laura clenched her fists and asked the question she must have been preparing all weekend. 'How much of our money did they steal?'

'A lot more than we're supposed to spend, and the stupidest part is that they won't have made anything like that amount by selling what they bought. It'll all go on heroin anyway, the police think.' He took hold of her fists and tried gently to open them. 'Don't worry, we aren't ruined yet. That's what the bank's for.'

She gave him an unsteady smile. 'To ruin us?'

'That's more like it. Where would we be if we couldn't laugh, eh? This may even have done us some good in the long run. I should be able to buy all the videos in the auction up the road a lot cheaper than I would have paid at the wholesalers, and it's a better selection than the wholesalers had.'

'You're sure the bank's going to lend you the money?'

'If the manager hears what the lucky clown tells him he's bound to,' Jack said, and waggled the grinning head on the ring at her. 'Come to life now, princess, or you'll be late for school.'

Julia made certain that she had her lunchbox and the books she needed, and waved to her from the front door, and returned to Jack. 'You really think . . .'

'If the clown doesn't work I'll turn on the fatal Orchard charm. It worked on you, as I remember.'

'Seriously, Jack.'

'Seriously, we don't have to be serious yet, do we? Time to be solemn when I'm in the bank manager's lair, though he always seems to me to need some jollying.'

'I'm not nervous,' he told the bathroom mirror as he picked up his razor. 'Bank managers are human like the rest of us. I'm not going to cut myself, ow. I'm not going to cut myself again.' He stayed upstairs until he'd dabbed away the last crimson bead so that Julia wouldn't see, and was dressing in the bedroom when she called 'Will you ring me at Luke's to tell me how it went?'

'The moment I know.'

54

'Good luck,' she called, and the front door closed at once.

Her leaving so quickly made Jack feel as if he was going to be late for his appointment, whereas in fact he wasn't due at the bank until half an hour after it opened. He walked himself to the kitchen, where he would have had time for a leisurely cup of coffee if he'd remembered to switch on the percolator. He strolled to the bank instead. Last night's fish-and-chip papers chased one another around the benches by the bus stops outside Adventureland; a container ship appeared to be grounded among the mounds of the Crazy Golf course, but then it glided out into the bay as Jack turned along the side street which led to the bank.

The building was on the corner where the street met Victoria Road. As Jack reached the entrance an old lady in an ancient raincoat held out a hand palm upwards to him. She'd had no luck at the bank, he thought, groping automatically in his pocket for change. He was placing a pound coin in her hand when he realised she wasn't begging, only feeling for rain. 'Just, er, just, just . . .' he tried to explain, and was through the doors. 'That's enough pratfalls for one day,' he told himself, so loudly that everyone in the small bank – three tellers and five members of the public – stared at him.

As he strode to the enquiry window and pressed the bell-push everyone lost interest in him, apart from a girl of about ten, who looked familiar. A teller appeared from behind the scenes and came to the window. 'Jack Orchard of Fine Films for Mr Hardy,' Jack said.

The girl nudged her mother. Just as the manager approached the window, Jack recognised the girl. She'd returned *Body Heat* to Fine Films on the day of the fire, and what had he said to her about his bank manager? She opened her mouth as the manager unlocked the door beside the window, and Jack wanted to clap a hand over his own face even before she spoke. 'He said that man's deaf,' she said, it seemed at the top of her voice.

What timing, Jack thought. He had already been suppressing a nervous compulsion to crack jokes. It didn't help that the manager had gained weight, at least from the waist down, since Jack had last seen him, a condition which made Mr Hardy's round balding thick-lipped head appear to have shrunk. Surely he'd missed the girl's comment or at any rate its significance, because he ignored her as he opened the door of the interview room. 'Step in,' he said heavily to Jack.

'Step in what?' I didn't say that, Jack told himself, nor 'I'll watch my step'; he hadn't yet spoken aloud. 'I'm stepping,' he said.

That didn't seem to go down especially well. When the manager had closed the door and lowered himself into the chair on the expensive side of the desk, on top of which a gilded pen and pencil standing in gilded sockets craned over a green blotter, he gazed at Jack for some time before speaking – long enough for Jack to be unable not to reflect that sitting down had increased Mr Hardy's resemblance to one of those legless round-bottomed pot-bellied dolls which rolled upright whenever they were knocked down. When he sat forwards Jack almost expected him to bob upright immediately, sprung by his paunch. 'So, Mr Orchard,' the manager said.

'Well, yes.'

'Family well?'

'Fine.' Either Jack left it at that or he risked halting the conversation with a flood of anecdotes. 'Fine,' he repeated, and was resisting a temptation to add 'Like the films' when the manager said 'So alone.'

'How do you mean? We've never been more together.' In the midst of this Jack realised what the manager had actually said, and tried to sound, with little apparent success, as though he were joking. 'Another loan,' the manager amplified.

'Unfortunately. Or I should say fortunately, I hope.'

An expression too swift to be intelligible passed over Mr Hardy's face as he leafed through the Orchards' file. 'I assume you still intend to take up the mortgage that was offered.'

'When we've settled where we want to move to. Decided, I mean, not settled there.'

'And the loan you used to buy out Mr Edge is still outstanding.'

'I explained the situation, you remember. I used my redundancy money from the public library to set up business with him, and if you hadn't lent me the money when he decided to get out, Fine Films might have been for the chop.'

'Right On Of New Brighton, as it was then.'

'So it was, poor thing. Not my idea, I assure you,' Jack said, and choked off a guffaw, having belatedly heard that the manager's tone was approving. 'Mine was Fine Films.'

'Not quite the successful concept you hoped it would be.'

'Maybe I should have stayed with my first notion and called it Ciné Qua Non. Or maybe you're right, maybe I was aiming too high. You might say it was lucky that Fine Films turned into Fire Films.'

When the manager's demeanour made it plain that he wouldn't say any such thing Jack succeeded in controlling himself. 'Most of the titles that are coming up for auction on Wednesday are ones people keep asking me for. It would only be a temporary loan until the insurance stumps up. I just need to be able to write a cheque.'

He was praying that Mr Hardy wouldn't advise him to use his credit card. There was no need for the manager to know about the theft, since it was unlikely to prejudice him in Jack's favour. 'Excuse the redundancy. Of course all loans are temporary. It's the entire stock of a video library that's being auctioned.'

'Which might suggest that the video-hire industry has passed its peak.'

Jack clutched his wrist in order to refrain from slapping himself across the forehead. 'I'd be crazy not to buy at the price the auctioneers are expecting. If the titles don't move, which I know they will, I can sell them at a profit even you would approve of.'

Mr Hardy raised his head and gazed at him, and Jack's lips twitched. He wasn't going to be able to keep mum for much longer. 'Here's another nice mess I've got myself into, I know.' He was opening his mouth, and trying to think of something less disastrous to say, when the manager said 'I suppose we'll have to give you the chance, but I personally very much hope that this time you're sure what you're doing.'

'How can you doubt Honest Jack Orchard?' Jack almost said, and 'Trust me and my friend in my pocket.' He contained himself while Mr Hardy passed him forms to sign, but as soon as he was out of the bank he released a whoop and capered about in the entrance. He walked home grinning, now and then clapping his hands. Most of the people he met returned his grin, except for a woman in a hatpinned purple turban, who flinched back. 'Mad but harmless,' Jack assured her.

He phoned the news to Julia, and waited impatiently for Laura to come home so that he could tell her. Because the bank was lending the Orchards more than he could imagine paying at the auction, he felt that it would be safe to celebrate — that failing to do so would be to distrust their luck. They dined at Chaplin's in Birkenhead, where the comedian mimed in photographs on all the walls. Later Jack and Julia made love more slowly and thoroughly than they had for months.

When he wakened in the morning his cold had departed, leaving a metallic taste. He lay for a while, hearing Laura and then Julia go out, and wondered luxuriously how to spend the day. The brass clap of the letter-slot roused him. A solitary letter had fallen on the doormat. 'There you are. You took your time,' he said as he picked it up. He wriggled a finger beneath the flap, tore open the envelope, unfolded the letter. He read it twice, hardly noticing that he'd slumped against the wall. 'No, no,' he began to mutter, his voice rising and growing fiercer. 'No, no, no, no, no.'

EIGHT

'No, no, no, no,' Jack repeated, and ran out of breath. He squared his shoulders, chafing them against the new plaster, and pushed himself out of his slump. The contents of the letter must be a mistake which he had all day to rectify. He switched on the percolator and phoned the number on the letterhead. The phone rang monotonously until a female robot intervened, briskly intoning 'Sorry, there is *no* reply. Sorry, there is *no* reply ...' Jack returned to the percolator and concentrated on pouring coffee, adding milk, sipping the liquid whose effects seemed to head straight for his nerves. He redialled the number and leafed through his address book while the phone continued ringing, distant and yet close like a sound heard during fever, until it provoked the robot again. Eventually he found the number he was looking for, on a business card at the back of the book, waiting to be copied in. He killed the robot and dialled, swallowed a mouthful of coffee which set his nerves buzzing, sat on the stairs as the cord brought the pedestal of the telephone blundering across the carpet, and then a voice panted 'Edge Enterprises. Bringing the future into your home. Maddy speaking.'

'This is Jack Orchard.'

'Width?'

'Eh?' Jack ehed.

'Have to run,' she said and sucked in an audible breath, by the end of which he'd deduced that she had said 'With?' and 'Had to run.'

'Jack Orchard. Gavin Edge's ex-partner. Is Gavin there?'

'He just called in from the car that he'll be about an hour.'

'He's outside now, you mean? Can you give him a shout and say that it's Jack?'

'On the phone. Called in on the phone,' she said as though she suspected Jack of making fun of her.

'Can you get him back? Can I?'

'He just called to say he'd be out of the car.'

Jack's sense of the conversation seemed to be drifting out of reach. 'If you could ask him to give me a bell as soon as he comes in.'

'I'll do my best to have him get back to you. Does he have your number?'

'It's urgent. The problem, not the number. I'm sure we can sort it out between us,' Jack said, and gave her the number. 'I'll be here waiting,' he said, and phoned the number on the letterhead.

It was engaged. 'Boot, boot, boot,' the phone announced hollowly, or perhaps it was saying 'Dupe, dupe, dupe.' He imagined victims of disasters queuing to report their ill luck, hundreds of them trying to contact the insurance company. He held on, hoping that the engaged tone might give way to the sound of the phone bell, but it was the robot voice which ousted it after five minutes, proclaiming, 'Sorry, there is no reply.' He gulped coffee and tried again, and this time the phone rang: 'Droop, droop,' it said. He felt as if he was trying to play a game of changing one word into another, a letter at a time. He reached into his trousers pocket and closed his hand around the clown's head, willing it not to be time for the robot voice to cut him off. 'Brute, brute,' the phone reiterated, and fell silent. 'Don't tell me there's no reply, you silly bitch,' he yelled.

The female voice which he'd shouted down repeated the name of the insurance company. 'Hold on,' Jack pleaded, relinquishing the clown's head and sweeping the letter off the hall floor. 'You've written to me. There's been some mistake.'

'Have you a reference?'

'From my last employer before you'll talk to me, you mean?' he mumbled as he scanned the letter. 'Connecting you,' she said when he'd given her the reference, but her tone was so neutral that he couldn't tell what else she might have heard him say. 'Claims,' she said.

60

'Yes, that's who sent me the letter.'

'Claims.'

'I just said so. You aren't another robot, are you?' Jack demanded, then grasped that he was no longer speaking to the switchboard operator, however similar the voices were. 'Sorry. Bit confused. This letter you sent me. Number one oh three stroke one oh one.'

'And what is the query?'

'I expect it's your computer playing silly buggers. You say the business I claimed for isn't insured.'

'Please hold.'

'Just don't be gone so long the robot cuts me off,' Jack said when he was sure she couldn't hear, but it was at precisely that moment she came back. 'That's correct,' she said with a hint of reproof, unless he was imagining that. 'The cover for Fine Films, formerly Right On Of New Brighton, was cancelled last October.'

'Someone's bumbled. My partner had only just insured the business for a year when I bought him out, and that was in September.'

'Was your partner a Mr Gavin Edge?'

'No other.'

'It was a Mr Gavin Edge who cancelled the policy.'

Jack felt as though his fever had returned all at once – as though the world had just recoiled from him. 'He'd have told me.'

'I have his signed letter in front of me. Mr Gavin Edge of Edge Enterprises.'

'It must be—' Jack trailed off, which left the words implanted in his consciousness like an admission he'd been forced to make. 'I'll call you back,' he said and broke the connection, dialled, squeezed the clown's head. 'Edge Enterprises,' the phone told him. 'Bringing the future into your home. Maddy speaking.'

'Is Gavin there yet?'

'Who wants him, please?'

'Tell him Jack. More urgent than ever.'

'He's with our programmer this morning. I'm not to disturb him.'

'When will he be approachable?'

'Round about noon. I told him you rang.'

'If you could remind him.'

'I will when he's taking calls.'

It was just after ten o'clock. Jack lingered under the shower, hoping it would relax him, but the drops of water seemed to crawl over his skin. He tried watching *Look Back and Laugh*, a compilation tape of silent comedies, and then he went out for a stroll around the block. He watched the rest of the tape and viewed as much again of it as took him to twelve o'clock. He waited a minute and was dialling when it occurred to him that one past twelve made thirteen. If Gavin didn't return his call by eleven minutes past, Jack would call him. The seconds ticked away, and he kept hearing the phone ring, but suddenly it was twelve minutes past and the phone hadn't yet done so. He dialled, and couldn't help feeling relieved that there were still a few seconds to go to thirteen minutes past when the receptionist said 'Edge Enterprises. Bringing—'

'I know all that. Is Gavin free yet?'

'Who wants him, please?'

'Still Jack.'

'He has a client waiting. If you'd like to try again in about—'

'I wouldn't,' Jack said, and shoved himself to his feet by leaning on the receiver as he slammed it onto the rest. He grabbed his coat, almost upsetting the hall-stand, and dashed out to the van, which he sent screeching past a bus which was pulling away from the terminus.

The Mersey Tunnel had twin tubes, each containing two lanes, but as usual at this time of day, one was closed. A yellow vehicle was raising workmen towards the tunnel roof. Traffic was queuing at all the tollbooths, and drivers were trying to insinuate their vehicles into adjacent lanes, having mistakenly assumed that the booths marked 'No Change' were meant for drivers with no change. When at last Jack entered the tunnel a brewer's lorry was labouring uphill out of the dip a mile or so down it, slowing the traffic to a funereal crawl. By the time Jack reached the dip in the white-tiled tube, petrol fumes were blotting out the vehicles ahead of him except for the embers of their brake lights, and he felt as if he was descending into a fire. He had to force himself to breathe until he gained the end of the tunnel and sped out beneath a clear cold sky.

At the top of a long curve, Scotland Road split into several routes which swung towards different districts of Liverpool. Jack followed the road to Edge Hill, through a no man's land of new houses. He had to brake for a woman wheeling a pushchair heaped with Easter eggs across a zebra crossing. Was Laura too old to want an egg this year? The thought made him feel mean, as if he was trying to save pennies at her expense, and that stoked his anger as he steered the van into the technology park.

This was a maze of boxy brown buildings overlooked by the clock tower of Littlewoods Pools. To Jack they resembled nothing so much as cartons ready to be printed with the name of whatever merchandise they might contain. Some had several doors, and before long he found one marked **edge enterprises** in lower-case computer type. He parked the van outside and strode in.

Beyond the door was a small room illuminated by a fluorescent tube in the shape of a zigzag bolt of lightning. A fat couch with tubular legs faced a desk across a low table strewn with computer-gaming magazines. The desk was Scandinavian, and Jack guessed it had been assembled from a do-it-yourself kit, since it needed a folded envelope to pad its left front leg. Behind the desk a young blonde with purple eyelids and a blouse with **edge** printed on its sleeves was reading one of the magazines. He wondered if she would launch into her telephone routine, but she only said 'Good afternoon' as she looked up.

'I hope so. Is Gavin here?'

'Oh, it's Mr—'

'Yes, it's Mister. Shall I announce myself?'

'I'll tell him,' she said, half rising from her seat as she thumbed a switch on the board. 'Your ex-partner is at Reception,' she said into the flimsy microphone which sprouted from the board.

She looked poised to grapple with Jack if he made for the door to the right of her desk, and he felt as if her wariness was compelling him to enact what she was anticipating. As his feet executed an inadvertent sideways shuffle she inched towards the door, maintaining her half-seated crouch. He veered towards the couch to reassure her, and kicked all the magazines off the table as he tried to step over it. The young woman let fly a piercing squeal of outrage or surprise, and the inner door banged open. 'Mad,' Gavin Edge said, and rushed at Jack.

Jack was sprawling backwards on the couch when his ex-partner seized his hands and hauled him up. On his feet, Jack was half a head shorter than Gavin, whose large square-jawed blue-eyed face was grinning as though proudest of its teeth. 'Why didn't you say you'd be over, Jack? We could have done lunch. We still could, except I've got a lunch appointment guaranteed to put thousands in the bank.'

'Can we talk privately?'

'Don't even ask. I've got ten minutes that are all yours. Make that fifteen.' He steered Jack away from the table before letting go of his hands. 'Mad, could you tidy up this stuff Jack's been throwing about? He was always impulsive, our Jack.'

Beyond the door was a short narrow brown corridor with three doors in the left-hand wall. 'Still in the viddy business, Jack? You should have come along with me,' Gavin said, easing open the first door. 'Computer games, they're the future now. Kids love them, and the rest of us love finding out we're still kids. Take a look.'

The cubicle managed to accommodate a wallful of boxed games as well as two desk-top computers, at one of which a girl was working. She gave Jack a shy sidelong glance through her hair without ceasing to type. 'Have a play if you like when we're finished,' Edge told Jack, and closed the door. 'She's my new partner's daughter. Seventeen and brilliant. She's created six new games already. Some nights I lie awake wondering how long we've got before someone bigger tries to buy out her contract with us. I don't suppose your Laura's showing any talent for programming?'

'She's happy using the computer.'

'There's time yet.' Edge ushered Jack into the next cubicle, his office. Two chairs whose black upholstery bulged through their tubular frames confronted each other across a desk which could never have been manoeuvred through the doorway in one piece. Gavin handed Jack into the nearer chair, closed the door carefully, sat behind the desk and thumped his folded arms on it. 'Well, Jack, what can I thank for your visit?'

Jack tried to sit up straight, but the chair compelled its user to relax. 'You may not feel like giving thanks.'

'I'd lay twelve to one against that, Jack. Tell me the news, however bad it is.'

Jack perched insecurely on the rim of the seat. 'The insurance firm thinks you've cancelled the insurance on the shop.'

'True enough, but you knew that, of course.'

'How could I when you never told me?'

'Why, Jack, I know I did.'

Jack felt himself slipping off the upholstery onto the metal rim and fell back into the chair, waving all his limbs like a turtle turned turtle. 'When did you?'

'I'm certain I sent you a copy of the letter I wrote them.' Gavin stared at him as though Jack should be able to supply the explanation, then he sprang to his feet. 'That bloody girl,' he snarled.

Jack thought he was going to confront the receptionist, but instead he spun round once and sat down again. 'Mad's predecessor,' he said. 'We had to put her back on the market, but we never realised she'd been sitting on any mail. It doesn't matter, though, does it? You must have known I'd cash in the policy for what I could get. I let it run for nearly a month.'

Jack was still struggling to find a way to sit on the chair, but presumably his silence was unambiguous enough. 'Sorry if I overestimated your acumen, Jack,' Edge said. 'You'll have insured the shop by now, won't you? Then I should see to it before you wish you had.'

'I already do.'

'You're trying to tickle my ribs, aren't you, Jack? You're never telling me—'

'A fire destroyed the shop, and now I find I'm not insured.'

'My God, Jack. How are the family taking it?'

'They don't know.'

'You'll have to tell them sooner or later, Jack. You wanted my advice first, did you? I'd be banging on my bank manager's door.'

'I've just asked him for one loan. Before I found out about the insurance.'

'Even so . . .' Edge waved his hands beside his temples as if he was fanning himself or his thoughts. 'I wish I could offer you more than advice, Jack, but my accountant would have a fit if I started fiddling with the cash flow. I should hire yourself one when you get the chance.'

'A fit?'

'An accountant.' Gavin gave up his frown, then raised his eyebrows and let the corners of his mouth rise. 'What is it you always say, Jack? You'll muddle through so long as you can laugh? I miss working with you. You're a tonic.'

He glanced at his watch and launched himself out of his chair. 'Our time's nearly up, but walk out with me if you like. Maybe we can brainstorm for two minutes.'

By the time Jack floundered off the chair Gavin was in the corridor, chortling at his performance. 'You should be in the films, Jack. You'd have them rolling in the aisles, you would.' He strode past the reception desk and opened the outer door, and stamped his foot. 'Will you look at this? Some clown's parked a rust-heap in front of our name.'

'That's my van.'

'So long as it gets you out and about, eh, Jack?' Gavin said, treating him to a nudge so extravagant that Jack almost staggered into the table on which Maddy had replaced the magazines. 'Seriously, Jack,' Gavin said as he closed the door behind them, 'the best of luck. If there's anything I can do that I can do, you know where I am.'

Jack shook hands with him, a process which lasted for most of a minute, and watched him speed away in a black Peugeot. He had to have been telling the truth about the letter, Jack thought, and what could he have done if it had turned out that Gavin hadn't bothered to write to him? He wasn't at all sure now why he'd needed to confront Gavin, but believing him made Jack feel as if life retained some balance. Things would right themselves eventually, nothing worse could happen. The house was still for sale, and for all he knew, someone might be waiting to view it. He scrambled into the van and drove home.

Of course, he told himself, he hadn't really expected to find anyone waiting outside the house. He let himself in and gazed at the phone as though he could tell by looking whether it had rung in his absence, then he dialled the estate agent. The receptionist broke off a conversation about feet to put Jack through to the junior partner. 'I don't suppose you've any good news for me,' Jack said.

'You might say so.'

Jack's innards jerked, though he couldn't judge if he was experiencing hope or panic. 'Tell me.'

'We seem to have some definite interest in your property.'

'Isn't that good?'

'If you think so. The buyer viewed the exterior a few minutes ago. She'll need to see inside, but she's unlikely to vary her offer.' The estate agent gave a dry polite cough. 'You'll recall you weren't expecting us to ask so much for the property. Given the current state of the market, perhaps it would be realistic of us to reconsider. The buyer wants to drop the price by several thousand pounds.'

NINE

Jack didn't tell Julia until they were in bed. He told her as much as he could, then he held his breath. Out on the misty bay a buoy tolled, a solitary foghorn lowed. 'Oh, Jack,' Julia said like a long sigh rendered articulate, and after a pause: 'It could be worse.'

They had been close to making love when he'd managed to confess. They were lying in each other's arms, their breaths mingling. He'd switched off the light because he'd thought that would help him talk, but it also meant that he couldn't see her face. 'Tell me how,' he said.

'We'll still have made a profit if we accept thirty-six thousand for the house. Shouldn't that more or less cover our losses?'

'And leave us with what?'

'Each other and Laura, and the bank.'

'We'll find out about that tomorrow.'

'It wouldn't be in the bank's interest to turn us down, would it? All you have to do is tell them everything, surely. Would you like me to come with you?'

'No, you go and earn some money.' He hadn't told her that he'd failed to let Mr Hardy know about the credit card, and it would be far harder to admit it to her now. 'I can be abject enough by myself.'

'So long as the manager doesn't abject.'

'You're as bad as me. What a team we make,' he said, kissing the tip of her nose. 'You don't think I've reduced us to ashes yet, then.'

'I think we've some fire left in us.'

'I believe you,' he said and kissed her opening lips. As they made love he kept remembering that he'd arranged to see Mr Hardy at eleven. You couldn't have too many good omens, he thought as his penis grew warm inside Julia. They fell asleep in an embrace, and that was all he knew until she kissed him awake. 'Use up all the luck you have to,' she murmured.

'I'll hold back a percentage.' He had only to tell Mr Hardy the truth. 'The truth, the whole truth, and nothing but the truth,' he said, gazing steadily into his eyes in the bathroom mirror. 'So help me God,' he kept repeating as he left the house.

A plane made the clear sky thunder as he walked to the bank, the thunder merging into the rumble of traffic on Victoria Road. The clock beyond the reinforced glass of the counter showed one minute to eleven as Jack rang the bell at the enquiry window. The same teller as last time came to the window. 'Jack Orchard for Mr Hardy,' Jack said, adding 'Of Fine Films.'

She gave him a standard smile and headed for the inner sanctum. 'So help me, God,' Jack muttered, trying not to concentrate too fiercely on the clock. The minute hand had jerked erect, pointing towards heaven like an aerial trans-mitting prayers. He felt as if he was holding it in that position by staring at it, so that when it started to creep downwards he couldn't help feeling that his will was growing weaker. It was only one minute past eleven, no threat there, but then it was two minutes past, which added up to— 'Mr Orchard?' the manager said, so loudly that he must be repeating himself.

'The same,' Jack said. 'Just admiring your—' he tried to explain, only to find himself bereft of words and staring at Mr Hardy's paunch. It couldn't have waxed in two days, he thought, and the man's head could hardly have shrunk. 'Shall we?' he suggested desperately, bowing towards the interview room.

Mr Hardy opened the door and followed him in. He took his place behind the desk, on which the green blotter put Jack in mind of a stretch of baize for some kind of game, and rocked forwards. 'So, Mr Orchard,' he said.

To Jack it felt as if they were performing a second take of

Monday's interview, and he resisted saying, 'Well, yes.' 'Well, Mr Hardy,' he said.

'Was there another matter?'

For an instant Jack clearly heard him say 'Another nice mess.' He saw himself screwing up his face and wailing 'Well, I couldn't help it' in Stan Laurel's voice. 'A bit of a problem,' he admitted, trying to drown out his thoughts.

'I can hear you, Mr Orchard.'

'I haven't told you yet. Oh, I see, sorry. Ears still bunged up from the cold. Don't know my own volume,' Jack said, and on the last word found his gaze drawn inexorably to the bank manager's paunch.

'Some problem.'

'It must be,' Jack almost agreed, but of course Mr Hardy was asking him to describe his problem. 'We've just discovered – well, two things.'

'I see.'

'I'll tell you anyway.' Yes, he really had said that, earning himself a blank look from the manager. He would have preferred a blank cheque, he thought, and had to remind himself not to try and outshout his thoughts. 'We've only just found out that someone took advantage of the Fine Films fire to hoist my wife's credit card.'

'You mean someone has been using it for the past eleven days without your knowledge?'

'Not eleven days, no. It can't have been eleven days.' He was so anxious to refute the notion that for several seconds he couldn't think how. 'No, they only used it for a day or two. They must have been afraid we would have notified the company by then.'

'Presumably the company will take the debt upon itself.'

'I'm afraid – I'm afraid this one doesn't, apparently.'

The manager pursed his lips and shook his head while keeping his gaze fixed on Jack. 'Thieves wouldn't be so fond of other people's property if they had their hands chopped off.'

'They might still be fond of it, don't you think? They mightn't be fond of the chopping, I grant you,' Jack said as Mr

Hardy's face grew blanker. 'I won't be long, dear, I'm just off to do the weekend chopping. I expect when the people who do that job get together they talk chop.'

'We're all entitled to our views of how the world could be improved, Mr Orchard,' the manager said frostily. 'Go on.'

'I'd try and make sure that everyone at least had – oh, you mean my other problem. Well, you see, I've just learned that my partner cancelled the insurance on Fine Films.'

'I don't see, no.'

'He used to look after the insurance, you see. He'd just renewed the cover when I bought him out, but then he lifted it and didn't let me know. At least, he did, but I didn't get the message.'

'Am I to infer that the business was uninsured at the time of the fire?'

'Well,' Jack said, 'yes.'

'And you are proposing?'

'Am I?' When a look which pleaded for him to be put out of his misery prompted no reply, Jack said 'I mean, I thought you would.'

Mr Hardy paused for so long that Jack found himself counting his own breaths, which seemed to be growing louder. Eight breaths, nine, and he tried to slow them down; for one thing, that might calm him. Ten, eleven, and he held the twelfth until it felt in danger of exploding. It would sound like a snort of impatience. He pinched his nose with one hand to keep the snort in, not immediately realising that the gesture itself might look like a comment. The manager gazed at him. 'The best I can offer is a short-term loan to enable you to pay your card debt. At least our rate will be lower than theirs.'

Jack gasped and sucked in the thirteenth breath. 'I wouldn't have expected anything else, any more, I mean.'

'However, I'm afraid—'

At once all Jack could hear was his own voice declaring 'I'M AFRAID, I'M SO AFRAID.' 'I'm sorry, what did you say?' he pleaded aloud.

The manager looked ready to indulge himself in another

71

epic pause. 'I said that under the circumstances I have no option but to cancel the overdraft we discussed on Monday. In addition I may have to reconsider the amount of any mortgage advance unless you find steady employment.'

'But ... I mean, you don't mean ... I'm sorry if I've seemed at all facetious. I was just nervous. You understand that, don't you?'

'Understanding is part of my job, Mr Orchard, and there's no need to shout. Contrary to rumour, I'm not deaf.'

'I never said that. At least, I did, but not about you. When I said my bank manager ...' Jack clenched his fists as if that might help him grasp his thoughts. 'You wouldn't let that influence your decision, would you?'

'I assure you that personal feelings have no bearing on the way I conduct business.'

'I didn't mean it in any bad way, but can I ask you to have another think? The auction starts at twelve. Those tapes will save my life. I'll never find anything more reasonable.'

'I certainly trust you will.'

Jack tried to hear encouragement in that, but there was none in Mr Hardy's tone. 'You aren't going to help me?'

'Whenever I can, within reason. You're aware that we offer a range of financial advice.'

'What good's that to someone with no money?'

'You're raising your voice, Mr Orchard.'

'I know, and this is how it sounds when it gets louder,' Jack informed him while defensively lowering it instead. Mr Hardy gave him another blank look and stood up. 'I hope your family stay well,' he said as he opened the door.

His words inflamed Jack with rage. If Mr Hardy cared about the Orchards, why was he destroying their chance to rebuild the business? Jack stalked out of the bank and strode towards the auction rooms. By the time Mr Hardy found out what he was about to do, Jack would have what they needed. Just let the bank try to bounce his cheque when the manager discovered he'd bid for the videotapes.

Jack jogged uphill, knocking on the boards which had crossed out Fine Films, and arrived panting at the auction rooms. He leaned one hand against the frame of the entrance while he caught his breath – and then the breath lodged in his throat like smoke. Down the hill, at the traffic lights, Mr Hardy was shading his eyes and watching him.

For a moment Jack considered dodging into the auction and making his bid, but if the manager saw him go in or even suspected that he meant to do so it was obvious that he would come up the hill. Jack walked almost blindly across the road and into the nearest side street. Could he lurk there until Mr Hardy went away? He was standing in the shadow of the sign-board outside the first rest home when the door of the house was yanked open and a voice proclaimed 'There he is, the shoe thief. Promised to replace my shoe and never did.'

'Which one was it?' Jack cried, so savagely that Mr Pether cowered into the porch. 'The left one, right?' He dragged off his own left shoe and flung it towards the old man, and lurched towards the traffic lights, alternately hopping and limping. Mr Hardy was making for the bank, but he glanced over his shoulder and saw Jack. 'I'm doing it for Lent,' Jack shouted across the road at him and stumbled home. 'Got to laugh, got to laugh,' he reminded himself desperately, no longer knowing if he was speaking aloud.

TEN

Telling Julia was relatively easy. As soon as she saw his face she said 'Never mind, Jack, we'll work it out somehow.' At least he didn't need to explain about his shoe. Once he'd reached home he had changed into his other pair and set off to retrieve the missile. He had been planning to tell whoever came to the door of the rest home that he'd been playing football so vigorously that the shoe had flown off, but he'd found it perched on the gatepost like a glove someone had found on the pavement. He'd tucked it under his arm and sprinted home, feeling so absurdly guilty that he'd kept muttering 'It's my shoe.' By the time Julia arrived he'd felt capable of facing her, but they hadn't had a chance to discuss any plans when Laura came home.

She looked exhausted and dishevelled, strands of her pony-tail escaping from her hairband, and pleased with herself. She dumped her bulging shoulder-bag next to the television and dropped herself in the nearest armchair, which emitted a faint imitation of her sigh. 'You're home early,' Julia said.

'We beat the other school at netball even though their teacher kept giving them penalties. They were wimps.'

'Well done.' Jack sneaked a glance at Julia to determine what she felt he should say, and when she didn't put a finger to her lips he said 'Try and stay happy, Laura. We've got to talk.'

Was he being too quick? He could have asked about the rest of her day at school, except that he was sure she would have sensed he was procrastinating. 'She's worn out, Jack,' Julia said.

'Aren't we all, except for you.'

'Is this a good time, do you think?'

'Not one of our best, but at least I don't see how—'

'Someone talk to me,' Laura interrupted. 'It's horrible not knowing what's wrong when nobody will tell you.'

'I know, love,' Julia said, so sympathetically that Jack felt accused of keeping secrets from her, though what secret did he have that was worth keeping? 'Let me try and explain,' she said.

'Let me. It's my mess.' He sat in the middle of the old sofa and felt it sag like the halves of a trapdoor capable of dropping him into the unknown. 'Whoops,' he said, and then 'Laura, how would you feel if we had to move to somewhere not quite as impressive as we were imagining?'

'I wouldn't have to change schools, would I?'

'Don't even think it, and that's a promise.'

She greeted that with half a smile in case he'd intended it to sound witty rather than simply tripping over his words. 'Have you and Mummy found a house you like?'

'Not yet,' Jack said, feeling as if the wistfulness underlying her query was the trap that was lying in wait for him. 'It may be a question of the three of us agreeing on one we can afford.'

'I was saving up for Crete.'

'We're not asking you to subsidise us, Laura, good Lord,' Jack said, wishing someone else would laugh so that he could try to. 'But it looks as if the bank manager won't either, not as generously as we were expecting. That's my doing, I'm afraid.'

'I thought banks were supposed to lend you money.'

'If they trust you. I'm afraid – I'm afraid that all Mr Hardy trusts me to make financially is a fool of myself.'

'Can't we go to another bank?'

'I somehow don't think another bank would welcome us. Maybe we'll come up with an answer, the three of us.'

'I'm going to listen to Jody's tape,' Laura said, and was out of the room before he could think of anything further to say. Julia gave him a sad frown as she made for the kitchen, and he felt as if the hardest part was still ahead.

Almost as soon as they sat down to dinner Laura said, 'Won't we be going on holiday either?'

'I don't think we can, love.'

'Never mind, Laura,' Julia said, taking her hand, and Laura managed to shrug as if she had been preparing herself upstairs for the answer.

In the morning she wasn't quite able to conceal that her eyes were red, and Jack couldn't bear it. He'd let the family down, Laura worst of all, and she wasn't even blaming him. He would expect Mr Hardy to make allowances for him, but he had no right to expect it of her. Once he was alone in the house, Laura having cycled to the library not long after Julia had gone to work, he felt as if he was being given one more chance – as if he must improve their luck somehow before they came back.

Perhaps he could. Suppose only he had shown interest in the videotapes at the auction? If they hadn't been sold, mightn't the auctioneers accept an offer even Mr Hardy would have to admit was reasonable? Jack was tempted to wait until eleven o'clock, but of course that was silly. He stuffed a piece of buttered toast into his mouth and sprinted out of the house.

By the time he'd finished munching he was at the traffic lights. A faint taste of charring lingered in his mouth while he jogged uphill, and a sooty smell troubled his nostrils as he reached the burned-out shop. At the top of the hill he strode into the huge cluttered room. The auctioneer's assistant who had shown him the cartons of videocassettes was tagging a dining-suite which would scarcely have fitted into the ground floor of the Orchards' house. 'Remember me?' Jack said. 'Fine Films.'

'I remember,' the assistant said, marking his forehead with ink as he flicked a lock of hair away from his eyes. 'We were looking for you yesterday. Matter of fact, we phoned you, but there must have been nobody home.'

'Here I am.'

'Too late, I'm afraid. Pity.'

'I'm afraid, I'm so afraid . . .' Jack struggled not to outshout himself. 'Why were you after me?' he said aloud.

'Wanted to give you a chance at the lot you came to view.'

'Can't you still?'

'Wish we could. Gone.'

Jack felt as if they were competing to discover who could do without the most words. 'Where?'

'Some young geezer. Private collector. Only wanted the horrors but didn't mind buying the whole lot to get them. Said he'd tape over the rest.'

Something like fever was crawling hotly over Jack's skin. 'He paid all that just to use the tapes for blanks?'

'Didn't pay that much. We let him have them 'cos he put in the only bid. He paid less than a fifth of what I told you we expected.'

Jack clutched at the nearest support, a set of antique fire-irons which clanged like a broken bell. 'Are they still in the building, by any chance?'

'Took them as soon as he'd counted out his wad.'

The assistant was turning away, looking embarrassed by Jack, who restrained himself from grabbing his arm. 'Do you have his address?'

'We never give out addresses. Would you mind putting that poker back? We charge for any damage.'

Jack hadn't been aware of holding the poker. He hung it carefully on the hooked stand and went after the inky man, who was several padded chairs distant by now. 'If I give you my address,' he pleaded, 'could you pass it on to him?'

'Afraid we can't. A sale is a sale. Better luck next time,' the assistant said, probably sincerely. 'Maybe you should look for libraries that aren't doing so well and make them an offer.'

He wasn't poking fun at Jack. He wasn't trying to imply that there could be libraries in a worse state than Fine Films. Jack opened his mouth and his clenched hands, but none of those seemed to be any use. His brain felt clogged with a substance that was spreading through his blood and weighing down his limbs as he trudged out of the auction rooms, feeling as though he was walking automatically and yet having to employ all his concentration to move his legs. The smell of Fine Films caught in his throat, and he swallowed and swallowed as the slope rose behind him. Then a bus came straight at him – it seemed as if a house was falling on him. The brakes screeched, the bus swerved, and for a moment Jack was certain it was toppling over. 'Where do you think you're going, you clown?' the driver yelled as the passengers gaped.

Jack was in the middle of the crossroads with no memory of having got there. 'We don't know,' he said.

He stumbled to the pavement and held onto the pole of a traffic light and watched the lights count up and down. He felt as though he couldn't move until he solved the problem they were posing. How much were the colours worth? They seemed to be brightening spasmodically, like three kinds of fire. At last he shoved himself away from the pole, and for a moment – no, longer – he couldn't remember which way led home. As soon as he managed to remember he reeled in that direction, afraid of forgetting again before he reached the house.

He sat in the front room, one hand over his eyes, waiting for the family. Eventually Laura arrived, then Julia, but he'd forgotten why he was waiting. Whatever was clogging his brain seemed to have spread into the air, isolating him from them. He found himself counting the number of times each of them spoke.

At least now he knew what was lodged in his brain: numbers. Later, when Julia was asleep, he lay beside her and counted the values of letters in words, desperately hoping that if doing so didn't suggest a solution it would at least put him to sleep. Whenever he ran out of words the amounts of his debts started chasing one another inside his skull, or he heard his voice in there, growing louder and more urgent: 'I'M AFRAID, I'M SO AFRAID ...' He began to work out the values of phrases, which at least used up more time than single words did. 'Traffic accident' didn't add up to eleven, nor did 'suicide'; he wasn't insured for nearly enough for that to be a help. He dozed and jerked awake at once, as though the clamour of numbers had roused him. He ransacked his mind for another phrase to count, and found one: 'Turn ill luck into good.'

He totted up the values of the letters, and his eyes widened at the dark. He did a recount to be certain, and as he did so he heard a distant clock strike twelve. It was Friday – Good Friday, the thirteenth. A light seemed to flame into his eyes. 'We're saved,' he whispered.

ELEVEN

This letter is part of a chain of good fortune.

Mrs Marsha Indick of Iowa sent thirteen copies to her friends and was cured of a twenty-year-old cancer.

Mr D. Vincume of London, England found a picture in his mother's attic which fetched £100,000 at auction.

Mr A. Plumb of Scunthorpe, Lincolnshire won the first dividend of the football pools 24 hours after mailing thirteen copies of this letter.

Mrs Maria Carbone of New York threw her letter in the trash and was knifed to death in the street less than a week later.

Mrs Amy Dallas of Nevada left her letter in her purse, and her husband was diagnosed as having a brain tumour. However, when she mailed thirteen copies of this letter the doctors were able to successfully operate on Mr Dallas.

You need send no money. Just make thirteen exact copies of this letter and mail them to thirteen different people, then wait for your luck to improve. Don't deny the world good fortune. The more there is, the better it will be for all.

This letter can change your life. What are you waiting for?

It explained so much. It explained why the Orchards' luck had been growing worse ever since April Fool's Day, when Jack had first dismissed the letter. No wonder he seemed to recall having felt blameworthy ever since. Everything *had* been his fault, whatever the family said. The idea was surprisingly comforting: at least he knew why he felt responsible, and – more important – he knew what to do.

As he sat on the edge of the bed, rereading the letter, the sunlight on his face and chest made him feel he was reading by the light of an enormous benevolent fire. When he heard Julia coming upstairs he folded the page quickly but carefully and slipped it into a pocket of his trousers which were sprawling broken-legged on the bedside chair. 'Aren't you dressed yet?' Julia said. 'We thought we could all go for a walk by the river.'

'You go. I need to write some letters while there's room to work on the computer.'

'Applying for jobs?'

He didn't want to lie to her. 'It's time I took control of my life.'

'We'll muddle through somehow. We always have.'

Soon he heard the front door closing. He went downstairs at once and lifting the computer onto the table, typed an exact copy of the letter and set the printer chattering. Once the first of thirteen copies had risen from the printer, Jack hefted the Merseyside telephone directory and found the names and addresses of the lucky recipients of the letter.

He started at the first page of the listings and having counted ten pages for J, addressed an envelope to the last name on the page. One page further for A, then three for C, and eleven for K ... He broke off in the middle of his surname, thinking he'd heard Julia's key in the lock, but it was next door. The distraction made him careless, so that he wrote his address on the back of the envelope. He would have torn it up except that he had just thirteen envelopes. He crossed out the address until he couldn't read it, and counted onwards.

He laughed when he reached the end of his name. He had never realised that it consisted of eleven letters as well as adding up to that number. He still had to address two envelopes, and so he went back to the start of his name, noticing with pleasure that the first two letters added up to eleven too. If he needed signs, he was surrounded by them: 'turn ill luck into good' added up to two hundred and fifty-four, which reduced to eleven; the date, 13, reduced to four, which was both the number of the month and the number of letters in 'Jack'; 'Good Friday the' reduced to eleven, so that eleven and thirteen were inextricably linked today. He had to count past four pages of advertising for the gas company in order to reach the last names – two double-page spreads about gas, and 'gas' twice reduced to eleven. That made him grin, and so did the coincidence that three of the addresses on the envelopes, two of them consecutive, were in the same town. He felt as though reality was cracking jokes around him, only these weren't jokes at his expense.

He finished addressing the envelopes as the eleventh copy emerged from the printer. He was sealing the eleventh envelope as the printer finished its run. He was so eager to post the letters that he had to remind himself to switch off the Amstrad. He sprang the floppy disc from its slot and replaced it in the box of discs and glanced at his watch.

Twenty to eleven. He should have ample time to buy stamps and post the letters at eleven o'clock – not that it mattered, of course, except as a small additional reassurance, a kind of wink at himself. He sprinted to Victoria Road, to the post office near the traffic lights. But the post office was shut on Good Friday.

Posting the letters wasn't so urgent now that he intended to do so, he tried to persuade himself. Tomorrow would do. He wandered to the crossroads and tried to think, as best he could for the distractions of the traffic lights. Was green the solution they kept reaching, or did they keep counting up to red? General stores and corner shops sometimes had postage stamps, and surely there was one nearby which did. 'Red, amber, green,' he muttered, 'go on, green, amber, red,' and almost remembered, or at any rate broke into a run along Victoria Road, peering hot-eyed at the shopfronts.

Wasn't that the shop on the third block? He dashed in, saying 'Excuse me' to an inflated float in the shape of a dragon, which the draught from the opening door rocked towards him. The woman behind the counter raised her head from totalling amounts in a newspaper-deliveries ledger and thrust a fat stump of pencil through the greying curls behind her right ear, and gave Jack an odd look. 'Stamps?' he panted.

Was she deaf? If she continued to stare mutely at him he would have to find another shop – but then he realised what she might be awaiting. 'Please?' he said.

'Hmmm,' she commented, than which no lecture could have been more eloquently reproving. 'How many are you after?'

'Thirteen sevens, please.'

'I can't promise you that many.' She retrieved the stub of pencil and bent to the ledger. Jack waited while she finished the calculation he'd interrupted, but when she turned the page he said 'Can I hurry you? I'm rather in one.'

'In one what?' she wondered, then growled under her breath to indicate she'd understood. She dragged open a creaking drawer in her side of the counter and produced two stamps. After some rummaging she found a strip of them folded diagonally in half, which she flicked onto a computer magazine lying in front of Jack. 'You're in luck. A baker's dozen.'

'Thirteen thirteens, please.'

'You said sevens.'

'Yes, and thirteens too. I mean, I didn't say that, but I want them.'

'What you want is twenties,' she said as though addressing an innumerate child. 'Thirteen twenties are half the trouble.'

Jack was suddenly afraid that she would retrieve the sevens, and so he stuck one on the top envelope. 'Here, don't go licking those,' she cried. 'You haven't paid for them.'

Jack dug a ten-pound note out of his pocket and slapped it on the counter. 'Now I have,' he said, and ran his tongue along the back of the strip of eleven stamps. 'Can I have my thirteens, please.'

The woman's square face seemed to set like concrete.

'What's the point of doing it that way?'

For a moment he couldn't remember. Of course, the digits of seven and thirteen added up to eleven, and they were also the digits of the sum of 'Laura Julia Orchard', though in a different order. 'These friends of mine and I,' he said, brandishing the envelopes, 'we're stamp collectors.'

'You're telling me my stamps are something special?'

Jack saw her refusing to sell him any thirteens, hoarding them for herself. 'Not by themselves, no. Only to collectors. Two stamps with the same postmark, you see, postmarked Good Friday the 13th,' he babbled. 'You don't see that every day.'

'Thank God for that,' she said as though she was holding Jack at least equally responsible, and yanked the drawer out further. 'Hmmm,' she said discouragingly, and Jack was poising himself to rush out in search of more stamps, leaving his change to be collected later, when she fished a somewhat crumpled strip of stamps out of the drawer. 'If these aren't it, there's nothing I can do.'

When she smoothed out the strip it proved to contain fifteen thirteen-penny stamps. She tore off two and passed Jack the remainder, declaring 'Well I never' at the sight of his tongue waiting. By the time she'd sorted out his change he had stamped the envelopes. She counted the coins aloud onto his palm – seven pounds and forty pence – and Jack heard the digits add up to eleven. 'Thanks for all your help,' he said.

She clearly thought he was making fun of her, though he hadn't meant to. 'Maybe you collectors can shop at the post office in future. Some people like to use stamps to send letters,' she called after him.

'I do myself.' He hadn't time to argue, and in any case he felt too exhilarated to linger. He ran to the post-box and shoved his cuff back from his watch. As a distant clock began to strike eleven he slipped as thick a wad of envelopes as would comfortably fit through the slot into the box, and sent the two remaining letters after them. As the clock continued striking he closed his eyes and squeezed the clown's head in his pocket. The chimes ended, but Jack hadn't opened his eyes when a shout reached him. 'The very man I'm looking for.'

TWELVE

The International Experience was on the New Brighton seafront, at the far end from the Creep Inn. Beyond the Crazy Golf course the Orchards were met by a chilly breeze which sounded like the edge of the almost invisible waves. The restaurant was less than five minutes away, facing a small unlit fairground where a booth in the shape of a spotted mushroom guarded a roundabout whose cars grinned and rolled their eyes at a miniature roller coaster with a cartoon insect's face. At the end of a causeway, the battlements of Fort Perch confronted the cranes of Seaforth across the bay under the stars, which were somewhat overwhelmed by the neon sign outside the International Experience. Jack watched his and Julia's and Laura's shadows multiplying as the family passed beneath the sign into the car park, and wondered what Jody's father had in mind for him.

Both of Jody's parents came to meet the Orchards at the door. Pete Venable told the cashier 'They're guests, on the house' while Cath took their coats and showed them to a table by the window. 'There's Minotaur Steak if anyone wants to give us their opinion,' she told them. 'And there's Jody's favourite, Laura, pizza made with Greek cheese.'

'I'll consume the monster,' Jack said.

Julia ordered Dionysus' Dinner. Jack's steak proved to be minced and mixed with herbs and encased in batter. He was entirely in favour of it except for a fragment of bone which caused him to clutch at his mouth and which he had to convince Pete wasn't sufficient reason to send the meal back to the kitchen. Laura enthused about her pizza, a carnivore's version of Jody's favourite. Bouzouki music played from all the corners of the large darkly panelled pillared room. Julia discussed the recipes with Cath Venable as the desserts arrived, and then Pete joined the party. 'Looks as if this was just what Jack needed, wouldn't you say, ladies? When I saw him this morning by the post-box he seemed to need some kind of a push.'

'I think he was giving himself one,' Julia said.

'Well, here's another.' Pete flourished a piece of paper at them. 'Your bill.'

'Ah,' Jack said, wondering if he had managed to mis-understand Pete.

'Don't worry, you're not paying it,' Cath laughed, bangles rattling down her bare arm as she patted his shoulder. 'We just wanted you to know that when it's made up at the end of the evening we'll be putting it in the draw.'

'Which is that?'

'We thought while we're having our Greek promotion we'd give someone a holiday there. Everyone's bill goes into the draw, and we'll announce the winner in a few weeks.'

'Someone should be bowled over. I hope – I hope it brings you hordes of customers.'

Pete winked at Cath. 'He's trying not to sound disap-pointed. He thinks that was the news I told him he'd have to come here for.'

'Wasn't it?' Jack said.

'Just the stop press. Here's what could be the big story. Jack, how would you like a job?'

'I don't know much about restaurants except how to eat in them.'

'We could hire him as a taster,' Pete said with another wink at Cath. 'Except it's a day job you need, isn't it, Jack? What would you say if I told you Jody's and Laura's school is looking for someone like you?'

'I'd be lost for words.'

'Silence goes with the job. The librarian's had to leave unexpectedly to care for her parents down South, and they're interviewing candidates a week today.'

'I hadn't heard.'

'It's lucky Cath and I are in the PTA. I got you the address for applications,' Pete said, and produced it written on the back of a blank bill. 'Fire off a letter to them tomorrow and they'll have it by Tuesday. I happen to know they were hoping for more applications than they've had so far.'

'How many's that?'

'You'll be doubling it.'

One and one, Jack thought, seeing the digits side by side. 'Thanks, Pete. Your timing couldn't have been better.'

Pete took Cath's arm to help her up. 'We'd better be making our rounds now, and you should tomorrow, like I told you this morning. Have a word with at least one more estate agent before you start dropping your price.'

'You didn't tell me Pete had said that,' Julia said to Jack shortly after.

'I suppose I was ashamed of not thinking of it without having to be told.'

'Why be ashamed all by yourself?'

'You know me. Brought up not to show my feelings, and I still find it hard sometimes. I never told you, Laura, in case it affected you, but when I was eleven and had to go to secondary school I was in the new class for nearly a fortnight before I said a word except my name. I was afraid that if I opened my mmm, good pudding, I'd start stammering or worse. Then I started being afraid that the school would tell my parents there was something the matter with me, and I was so anxious not to upset them I made myself compete to answer questions even when I knew my answer was monstrously wrong, which was how I got elected as resident clown. That saved my bacon quite a few times – ham does, you know. But I remember promising myself I was never going to be as afraid again as I was when I changed schools.'

'I didn't feel like that,' Laura said. 'I like my school.'

'There was no reason for me to be scared either. The trick is to know these things at the time instead of however many years later. So long as you never feel that way,' Jack said, and heard himself trying to restrict her feelings to a level he could cope with, just as his parents had tried to suppress his. 'Or if you do,' he added, 'don't be afraid to tell us.'

'Are you ever now?' Laura said.

'Of what?'

He meant that to sound like a denial, but it seemed not to be enough for her. 'Only of losing you two,' he said at once.

She gave him a smile of mingled reassurance and reproof so like the one with which Julia responded that he had to grin. 'Holiday adds up to eleven, you know,' he said and immediately felt as though he'd shared a secret he might have done better to keep to himself.

In the morning he wrote a letter applying for the job of school librarian. He drove into Liscard and posted the letter as a clock finished striking eleven, then he walked past a jangling procession of trolleys outside Safeway to the cluster of estate agencies. There were six on that side of the road. Last time he'd chosen one at random; now he started from its neighbour and walked to the end of the agencies, walked back to the far end, reversed his direction and kept walking until he had counted eleven. He'd returned to the agency at which he had begun counting; he would have ended up there whichever direction he'd followed. Surely that meant something, he thought as the bell above the door announced him.

The younger partner in the firm, a man of about Jack's age with a blond moustache and a bow tie, ushered him into his office with a gesture that stopped just short of grasping Jack's arm. 'How can I help?'

'Eleven letters,' Jack said aloud, and went on quickly: 'I've a house for sale that doesn't seem to be moving. I don't know if it would be ethical for you to take a look.'

'Two signs can be better than one. Where is it? How much are you asking? Your part of the coast is starting to seem fashionable. Can I come and have a prowl this afternoon?'

'We'll be there.' Eleven letters again, Jack thought happily, and paused on his way out to inspect photographs of houses. A mile or so upriver from the Orchards' home was a house 'reduced for quick sale' which seemed breathtakingly cheap for its size and its view across the river. He slipped the description into his pocket and drove home.

That afternoon the estate agent went through the house, cocking his head with quick jerky movements which put Jack in mind of a doll, a present decorated with a bow. 'I'd say another few thousand could be on the cards for you. If you like I'll have a word with our friends next door when I get back to the office.'

Once he'd gone Jack produced the description of the house by the river. 'Does this look worth a stroll along the prom?'

The couple who owned it, the Woolidges, visited their daughter and her family on Sundays, and so it was Monday when the Orchards viewed it. It was close to the river, near the site of a smugglers' inn. Large moist trees which were beginning to unfurl their leaves shaded the wide sloping road. Beyond a reluctant wooden gate a path wound between flowerbeds infiltrated by weeds. Jack prised up the doorknocker and banged on the front door, which was opened by an old lady in denim overalls. 'Did you get your hand stuck under my knocker? We're all a bit rusty here,' she said.

She and her husband, who leaned on a stick and kept mopping his face with a spectacularly extensive spotted handkerchief, conducted the Orchards through the large rooms and into the spacious back garden. Jack sensed Julia imagining where the furniture would go in the rooms and how she would redecorate. There were four rooms downstairs, four bedrooms up and a capacious bathroom containing a toilet. All of the doors had been stripped down to the wood, and that seemed to Jack like a promise of renewal.

'We wouldn't be moving if I could still get up the road on two legs,' Mr Woolidge said when they were all in the kitchen, Jack and Julia sipping muddy bitter tea from chipped mugs while Laura was let off with a glass of shandy. 'We'd like it to stay a family house. There are enough homes round here for leftovers like me.'

His wife stuck out her tongue loudly at that, and asked Julia 'Is anyone after your place?'

'We've had enquiries, but nothing definite. We've just doubled the advertising.'

'We've somewhere waiting for us. We'd like to be well settled in by Christmas.'

'We're interested, aren't we?' Julia said. 'Will you give us a few weeks?'

The Woolidges exchanged nods. 'We'd like someone like yourselves to have it,' Mrs Woolidge said.

As the Orchards walked down to the promenade Laura said, 'Do you think we might be coming to live here?'

She was so obviously trying to be grown-up and not to hope too much that Jack wished he could share his faith with her. He'd just realised that although there were only nine rooms in the house, the front and back doors were also stripped. Eleven identical doors! And today was Easter Monday, the day of promise, the sixteenth of April, one and six and four ... 'If everything works out, love,' he said.

On Tuesday a middle-aged couple, the Quails, came to view the Orchards' house, and Jack couldn't help regarding them as a good omen, though they said they would have to go away and think. On Wednesday he received a letter inviting him to be interviewed at the school on Friday at eleven. On Thursday someone either by the name of, or of a firm called, Profit phoned offering to pay the best price for all the cassettes that had survived the fire, and promised to inspect them on Saturday afternoon. On Friday Jack went to the school.

Since the dilapidated van was hardly the best first impression to give of himself, he walked to the interview. It was Friday the 20th, and 'Friday' and 20 made eleven. Three cars were parked in the schoolyard – a Volvo, an Austin, a Volkswagen that looked as though it had been dunked in mud – and Jack rather hoped that the latter belonged to his rival for the job. A wind sent some of last year's leaves chasing through the yard as he let himself into the school, and he thought he heard a clock begin to strike eleven. No, it was a church bell.

The headmistress' office was at the end of a long corridor smelling of polish and floored with tiles that rattled underfoot. A small man with a shiny cranium across which a few strands of hair appeared to have been pencilled was sitting huddled in a dark suit slightly too big for him on one of two chairs outside the office. 'Morning,' Jack said, but it was the school secretary who responded, bustling into the corridor from the outer office and ticking Jack's name on a clipboard which seemed altogether too large for the situation. 'You're first in, Mr Orchard. Won't be long.'

Jack perched on the unoccupied chair and met his rival's glance across the doorway of the office. The man examined the fingers of his right hand, which were piebald with ink stains and nicotine, and addressed them. 'Kids,' he said.

It might have been a question. 'I've a daughter at the school,' Jack told him.

'You won't hear a word said against her,' the man said, so disapprovingly that Jack had no idea how to respond. 'What about the rest of them?'

'Look on the walls.'

'That's them on their best behaviour, just for show. They're on their worst when they go to a library, believe me. What's the discipline like here?'

'I should ask the headmistress.'

'I mean to, never you fret. Not that I haven't learned in thirty years of public libraries how to handle them. Give me adults any day, though. Last year I'd have laid odds I wouldn't be applying for a job like this.'

The secretary opened the door again and raised one eyebrow at Jack, and he was almost certain she was commenting on what she must have overheard as well as signalling Jack to go in. He dug his right hand into his trousers pocket and squeezed the clown's head as he stood up. 'Clown' added up to thirteen, and so did 'lucky clown'. It was time to turn ill luck into good, he thought as he reached the inner office.

'And then I realised he was someone else entirely,' the head of the English department was saying.

'I can imagine how you must have felt. It happens to all of us at least once in our lives,' the headmistress said, and stood up to greet Jack. Her ash-blonde hair was cropped close to her head, making her broad face seem rounder. A dark stone at the throat of her blouse flamed red as it caught the light. 'Mr Orchard. We're very pleased with Laura,' she said.

'She's excellent at planning how to use her skills,' the head of English said, recrossing her legs in her pinstriped skirt.

'Maybe I ought to take lessons from her.'

'I shouldn't think you need to,' the headmistress said as though jokes weren't quite appropriate, 'judging by your cee vee here. I'm a little surprised you chose to give up librarianship.'

'It seemed like a good idea at the time, but I'm older and wiser.'

'Oh, I'm sorry. Coffee? Tea?'

She was apologising for the cup in her hand, apparently. 'Coffee would be fine,' Jack said, 'with a dribble of milk.'

'Coffee with a,' she said into the phone, '*dribble* of milk.' She straightened up and gave Jack a slightly lofty smile. 'So your venture didn't quite live up to your expectations.'

'Or I didn't. When my partner left he took all the business with him.'

'We all have to learn our limits,' the head of English said. 'Most of us work best when we're employed.'

'Quite so,' the headmistress said, which presumably meant she'd found the utterance more meaningful than Jack had. 'Did you have much to do with children and young people, Mr Orchard?'

'In libraries? I used to feel I'd achieved something when I'd helped them track down information. One more strike for literacy, I used to think.'

'Here's your coffee. Tell us more about it. Take your time,' the headmistress said.

Jack took that as an invitation to reminisce. He did his best not to begin any anecdote before he had finished its predecessor, and punctuated them with sips from the cup, which he managed not to spill or to rattle more than once against the saucer each time he set it down. Eventually the headmistress said, 'I think we've heard enough, don't you?'

He put the cup on her desk and stood up quickly, and she

raised her eyes to him. 'I hope to be in touch very shortly,' she said.

He restrained himself from looking smug as he emerged into the corridor. The small man in the big suit jumped off his chair, looking aggressive and impatient for a cigarette, and Jack knew at once that the man hadn't a chance. He strode out of the school, counting. 'Library' added up to thirteen, and so did 'school library', and what was he turning them into? 'Good,' he said aloud, since there was nobody to hear.

All the same, when Julia asked him how the interview had gone he said 'It's not for me to say, is it? We'll have to wait and see.'

'When?' Laura demanded as if even one more syllable would waste time.

'Some time next week, I hope.'

She let out an extravagant sigh, and he restrained himself from telling her that he was certain he'd got the job. That was a secret he should keep until a letter from the school revealed it, and then perhaps he would share the secret of the numbers with her and Julia. Keeping the secret required some effort, especially on Saturday, when he couldn't even go out for a walk until Thursday's caller made an offer for the videotapes. At the same time the secret kept him content as the day wore on and nobody came to the house.

It was shortly before a quarter past one on Saturday afternoon that the phone rang. Thirteen past thirteen, he thought as Laura ran to the phone. 'If it's for me tell him I'm waiting,' he called.

'Hello,' she said with her usual eagerness, and then with the disappointment she could never quite conceal if a call wasn't for her, 'It's Jody's dad.'

'Not the holiday.' That couldn't be the reason for the call; the draw wouldn't take place for weeks. Jack accepted the receiver from her and put his arm round her shoulders. 'Hi, Pete. What can I do for you?'

'It's about the job at the school.'

'I was there yesterday. What is it now, Pete? Good news for me?'

'No,' Pete Venable said.

THIRTEEN

Life could be worse, Jack thought as he replaced the receiver, and at once it was: he had to explain to Julia and Laura. He'd let go of Laura once the point of Pete Venable's call had become clear. Now he hugged her and said 'I'm afraid your headmistress can't hire me.'

Julia was coming downstairs with an armful of rumpled sheets. She crushed them to her and sat on the fourth stair up. 'What do you mean, can't?'

'Would be well advised not to. The school governors wouldn't approve.'

'Of what?' Julia demanded, almost as though she was accusing him.

'Of my reputation. Supposedly there's a rumour that I set fire to the shop on purpose.'

'That's criminal. How can she believe that?'

'I'm not saying she does, but you can see how hiring me would look if other people believe it.'

Laura ducked out of his hug, her eyes bright and wet. 'Who says you did?'

'Quite a few people, apparently. If you mean who started the rumour, I don't suppose we'll ever know.'

'Can't the police find out? Can't you sue them for libel and make them pay you?'

'It'd be too hard to prove, Laura. Best to let the whole thing die down, I'd say.'

He felt as though he'd betrayed her and Julia again and had to make amends. His calm and rationality were so unlike how he actually felt that they seemed a charm against being overwhelmed by his emotions. 'Don't you two worry. There are

95

plenty more jobs around, even for an old clown like me. I don't mind travelling. And at least, Laura,' he said, willing this to cheer her up, 'Mr Ink and Nicotine won't be working at your school either. They're readvertising the job.'

She managed to smile at that by pressing her lips together. 'I'll just nip up the road for a paper with jobs in it,' he said. 'If anyone comes for the videos say I'll be back in five minutes.'

In fact he was more than twice that, since the newsagent's opposite the Bingo parlour, where the unctuous voice was announcing 'Legs eleven', had only tabloids left. Jack ran uphill to the next shop which sold newspapers. The shopkeeper scratched her scalp through her greying curls as she saw him. 'It's the stamp man,' she said to him.

'I'll try not to bother you this time.'

'Hmm,' she contradicted him.

'Just the local rag and a *Guardian*.'

'What, no thirteens?' When she'd allowed herself to be convinced she took his money. 'Did your letters get there safely after all your trouble?'

'I assume so.' He saw her resentment that he wasn't more certain after having troubled her so much for the stamps, but he had to smile widely at her; she had given him an idea. 'Thanks for all your help,' he said, which annoyed her even more than last time, and hurried out of the shop.

At home he and Julia scanned the job sections. There were more potential jobs for him within a reasonable distance than he would have dared dream: an assistant librarian's post just across the Welsh border, another in Runcorn which was half an hour's drive along the motorway, a third in Ellesmere Port, even closer. He had some difficulty in putting together a list of eleven jobs to apply for, even when he included several at bookshops. By then it was dark, and Thursday's caller had obviously decided against keeping the appointment, a setback which seemed to confirm that Jack had identified what had gone wrong.

All he needed in order to put it right was some time by himself in the house. On Sunday morning Julia said 'Shall we all go out for a walk this afternoon? It'll do you good.'

'You go. I'll write those letters and then I can relax. If you walk along the beach I'll meet you coming back.'

As soon as he couldn't hear their footsteps in the street he set up the computer and the printer. He instructed the printer to produce thirteen copies of the file called CLOWNLUC, and as it began chattering he opened the phone directory. He took as long to address each envelope as the printer took to issue the letter; he wanted to be absolutely certain that the addresses couldn't be misread.

Nothing else made sense. One of the letters he had originally sent must have gone astray. It wasn't enough just to send them, they had to arrive. When they were all safely in their envelopes he created a file called JOBAPPLI, which put him in mind both of apples and Job in the Bible, and composed a standard letter. As the printer finished each letter Jack changed the details for the next one and addressed an envelope. By the time he'd completed the task he was almost in a trance. He left the job applications piled on the table and slipped the other set of envelopes inside one of his jackets in the wardrobe, then he went down to the beach.

The tide had gone out, leaving ripples sketched in the sand. As Jack walked down the slipway from the promenade the sky inched down past the horizon. The light which sharpened the waves appeared to be shining from behind the sky, from a source to which the sun was the only aperture in a surface of stained glass. The richness of the colours all around him, and the shadows defining the moment on the sand, made everything seem fragile and precarious, so that when he saw Julia and Laura in the distance he experienced the beginning of an unexpected panic. Was he sure he'd done everything he could to save their luck? They were coming towards him, growing larger; soon they would come too close for him to be able to think. He turned away from their magnification and pretended to be interested in the depths of a shallow pool left behind by the sea. Yes, there was more he could do: he could make certain that the mail didn't lose any of the duplicate batch of letters. The sky seemed to sail up as he lifted his head.

'What were you looking at?' Laura wanted to know.

'Something peculiar. It's run away now.' He found her eleven shells to make up for the loss of nothing, and then she wandered to the edge of the sea while he and Julia held hands. 'Are you better?' Julia said.

'Than what?'

'Than when we just saw you. You didn't seem to know which way to go.'

'We're on course.'

'Try not to worry, Jack. My grandmother used to say if you worried too much you'd worry a hole in your head.'

'Did she? Well.' He wished he could tell Julia that 'on course' added up to eleven. 'So long as we can laugh,' he said, and ran with her along the beach until she did.

In the morning he wakened feeling sure of himself. It was Monday the twenty-third of April, and the sum of 'Monday' and 'April' and twenty-three was eleven. While Julia was in the bathroom he took the opportunity to consult the *A to Z of Merseyside*. Despite its title, the book of road maps didn't cover all the territory which the telephone directory indexed. He had a shower which set his skin tingling, he waved goodbye to Laura and then to Julia, and was waiting on the doorstep of the Liscard post office when the bolts were shot back.

Eleven sevens, eleven thirteens. He stuck them on the job applications and squeezed the wad into the post-box, then he climbed into his van in the car park behind a hoarding which advertised finance. He might as well start with the first of the thirteen addresses. 'Here comes luck,' he murmured, and swung the van into the road.

Lorries and company cars with jackets hanging above the back seats were almost bumper to bumper in the tunnel. At last the van emerged into the timid sunlight, and he sent it roaring towards the Liverpool suburb of Childwall. Until now it hadn't occurred to him to reflect on what the thirteen did in life. They were certainly all employed, since he'd found their names in the business pages of the directory. He hoped he wouldn't have any problems in delivering the letters to their business addresses, but the strategy might be fun.

Five minutes' drive beyond the business park which counted Edge Enterprises among its units, Jack passed a supermarket where he recalled having been taken on a roller coaster as a toddler. It had been his first experience of a film, and in Cinerama. The film and the screams of the audience had surrounded him as the entire cinema plunged forwards into the abyss. For years after that he'd expected cinemas to move as he'd watched films in them – in the intervals he'd felt as though only the lights were holding the ranks of seats on an even keel – and a dream that his home was descending like a lift out of control had recurred for even longer. The ages of the shoppers converging on the supermarket made him realise that most of them were unlikely to have visited it when it had been a cinema. For most of his potential customers at Fine Films, cinema wasn't the adventure it had been to people of his generation, it was simply something else they watched on television. No wonder he'd failed. He needed to bring himself up to date, to learn to seize what the moment had to offer.

He drove past a Jewish school to Childwall Fiveways, where it seemed best to ask for directions to Calderstones Park, near which Veronica Alan lived. 'Tag at avenue,' a man leaning on a stick in a bus shelter told him, which sounded like a clue in some survival game until Jack saw that the road at which the man had jabbed his stick was called Taggart Avenue. At the top he swung the van around a grassy triangular island towards the park. Trees rose from wide verges in front of secluded pairs of houses which gave way to high mossy brick walls, and a few minutes later he crossed a dual carriageway which was halved by trees and cruised into the park.

There was just one parking space on the stretch of tarmac near the greenhouses. Slipping the letter to Veronica Alan into his pocket, he left the other dozen on the passenger seat and walked back to the dual carriageway. Veronica Alan lived on the far side, in Druid Stones Lane. Here was Druids Cross Road, here was Druidsville Road, and he felt as if there was magic in the air. Here was Druid Stones Lane, and he walked up the slope of it, trying to appear to be on his way to somewhere else.

Less than a minute's walk brought him to the house. It was a long stone bungalow at the top of a semicircle of concrete occupied by an Audi and embraced by privet hedges as tall as the building. There were no gates, but on a gatepost at the corner of the hedge a small brass plaque read ALAN: ANTIQUE RESTORATION. Jack followed the left-hand hedge, keeping the car between him and the long uncurtained window to the right of the front door.

The door consisted mostly of frosted glass so thick as to be virtually opaque. Through it he could just distinguish a brown object, probably a chest or wardrobe standing in the hall. A brass letter-slot was set in the foot of the door, as though to make postmen pay their respects. Jack went down on one knee on the prickly concrete and dragged the stiff flap open wide enough to admit the letter. The envelope was only halfway through when the spring proved stronger than his fingers and the flap bit down on the envelope with a muffled thud.

If he tried to push the envelope all the way in, the noise might bring someone to the door. Jack seized his knee with both hands and shoved himself to his feet. He was passing the gatepost when he heard a sound behind him like the closing of a trap. Someone had pulled the letter into the house. He hesitated, screened by the privet, and heard an outburst of barking which abruptly grew louder, and then the slam of the door. Someone and their dogs had come out of the house.

Jack managed not to look around as he walked downhill, fast but not too fast. He was ready to cross the dual carriageway when the barking started downhill. He couldn't resist the chance of seeing who had received the letter. Moving a few paces along the kerb, he stood at a bus-stop.

The barking reached the corner, and two obese panting bulldogs wallowed out of Druid Stones Lane. They were harnessed to a woman in her fifties who was wearing expensively casual trousers, an ankle-length leather coat, a tortoiseshell comb in her silvery hair. Her skin was aged by sunlight, and so brown that some of the light must have been artificial. She heaved at the leads, causing the dogs to snuffle and choke, and came straight at Jack, brandishing the letter. 'Rubbish,' she said in a voice that smelled of cigarettes.

She wasn't talking to him; indeed, he could see that she wasn't aware of him. She tore his letter up before his eyes and dropped the pieces in the bin attached to the bus-stop. 'Major,' she said, jerking the left-hand lead as its dog cocked a leg against the concrete pole, splashing Jack's shoes. 'Come along, General,' she said, and urged the dogs across the carriageway and up the road to the park.

She must have destroyed the first letter too, but why should that have affected the Orchards? The bad luck was meant to settle on anyone who ignored the letter, not on the sender – unless, he thought in a sudden rage, she'd wished the bad luck on whoever had sent her the letter. His anger felt like a fire in his brain, growing hotter as she dwindled and vanished around the corner towards the park. He could still smell her: leather, dogs, perfume which was undoubtedly expensive, stale flesh. He grabbed the fragments of the letter out of the bin and strode fast up the hill.

He was only going to stuff the pieces through the door, but part of him knew better. His free hand was reaching in his pocket as he passed the Audi. He felt as though only the actions he was performing could fit into these moments. As he squatted in front of the door, farting inadvertently, he flicked the lighter and set fire to the bunch of paper. 'Try some of our luck for a change,' he said through his teeth, and levering the slot wide with the hand that held the lighter, posted the blazing paper into the house.

He let the flap down gently, enjoying the strength of his fingers, and stood up. 'You've done it now,' he heard himself say, perhaps aloud. He felt as if his bad luck was a burden which he'd managed to place outside himself at last – a burden whose removal left him feeling exhilarated and youthful. He couldn't quite believe what he'd done; even gazing at the blurred dance of the flames, magnified by the leafy pattern in the frosted glass, didn't entirely persuade him. 'Got to laugh, haven't you?' he said to the grin which was tugging at his lips, and turned away from the bungalow. But as he walked towards the Audi he saw the flames reflected in its windows brighten and rear up.

He felt as if they were chasing him, until he swung round and saw that they were still beyond the door. The object which he'd assumed to be a chest or a wardrobe was made of cardboard, judging by the speed with which the flames were consuming it. In hardly any time the lower section of it collapsed, throwing the upper section across the floor, and Jack guessed it had been a pile of cartons. He had a sense of inevitability: events had been taken out of his hands yet again. Almost at once the carpet was ablaze and the flames were knocking soundlessly at the nearest inner door.

Either the door was ajar and swinging wider or the rush of fire was making it appear to move. When he saw smoke beginning to drift across the room beyond the long un-curtained window he backed away from the house and stood at the bottom of the concrete semicircle, waiting for the flames to invade the room, then he walked rapidly downhill.

He thought he meant to call the fire brigade, but there was no phone box in sight on the dual carriageway, and walking for some minutes didn't show him one. He couldn't very well ask to phone from anyone's house. He heard a fire engine in the distance, and fled to his van. Someone else had called the fire brigade, and Jack was suddenly afraid of coming face to face with Veronica Alan.

She was just visible on a wide lawn, her dogs doing their ponderous best to leap at a stick she was flourishing. The sight of her, shrunken by distance and quite unaware of events at her house, made Jack grin and shudder simultaneously. He climbed into the van and swung it out of the car park, so violently that the pile of letters spilled off the passenger seat onto the floor. He was waiting for the stream of traffic to let the van onto the dual carriageway when he discovered he had no idea where he was going.

He couldn't think which was the nearest address on the

envelopes. Besides, his compulsion to deliver them had lost momentum. The only place he wanted to go now, he decided, was home – but Julia would sense he had done something which he couldn't tell her. He'd committed a crime, he'd destroyed someone's property. He hadn't meant to do so, at least not to begin with, but how could he explain that to her? He felt as though the events of the last half hour, or however long it had been, had involved someone other than himself.

The blare of a horn behind the van jerked him out of the stasis into which he'd fallen, he wasn't sure how long ago. He stamped on the accelerator and stalled the engine. As a black sports car swerved around the van and into the main road, the flash of glossy black made him think of some kind of reptile slithering under the trees. He twisted the ignition key and drove as if the act itself might eventually suggest a route.

He drove for hours. Avenues led him through shopping districts where the pedestrians appeared to think he'd done nothing out of the ordinary. Someone shouted, and an apple rolled towards the van from the market stall behind which the trader was shouting. Jack thought he might be able to think if he reached open country, but he seemed incapable of escaping the maze of unfamiliar streets or of reading the map. 'Smile' added up to thirteen, he found himself thinking, as did 'laugh', but 'fire' was eleven. 'Smile, laugh, fire,' he muttered, driving. 'I'm fire.'

At last he had to stop for petrol. The filling station included a video library, and some of the cassettes were for sale. He was examining the titles before he remembered he was no longer in the business. The realisation seemed to bring him back to himself. The events at Veronica Alan's had been yet another instance of the slapstick that was his life, but for once the butt was someone other than himself or his family. The woman behind the counter gave him a slightly puzzled look as he felt his face change. 'Got to laugh, haven't you?' he said, and asked her the way home.

He could keep a secret from Julia if he had to. He was seeing images of Keystone Kops, demented figures in uniform falling silently over one another and over their hosepipes as they threw oil instead of water on the flames. He ought to have an answer when she asked him where he'd been, but he mustn't say anything which might make him laugh: not 'Nowhere to set the world on fire' or 'Fighting fire with fire'. 'I just drove around and walked for a bit,' he told himself in the driving mirror, and was pleased with how convinced he looked.

He felt as though he was coming home from another country, one of which his memories were few and very vague. As he drove, houses obscured the sunset except for a generalised reddish glow, a sign of distant fire. On the river at the foot of Victoria Road it had left a wake of burning oil. 'I've been driving round and round and no, just round,' he said as he turned the van along his road. The wheels nudged the kerb at the end of the garden path, and he switched off the engine and leaned over to pick up the letters from the floor. As he reached for them he glimpsed someone, not Laura or Julia, in the front room.

Jack froze, his knuckles aching as they rested on the envelopes. He'd been found out, but how? Had Julia already been told what he'd done? He wanted to hide, except that wouldn't be fair to her, whether she knew or was only wondering why they'd come for him. He forced his head up, his fist crumpling the letters. There was nobody in the front room.

Someone could be coming out to find him. He waited until it seemed certain that no such thing was about to happen, then he shoved the letters into his inside pocket and clambered out of the van, hoping that the glimpse of an intruder was the only symptom of jumpiness he would experience, otherwise Julia might notice. He let himself into the house and closed the door behind him. 'Home,' he announced.

Julia responded from upstairs. 'Someone's waiting to see you, Jack.'

Her voice was neutral. He couldn't judge if she had been told about him. Either way he thought she was being brave, almost too brave for him to bear. At least she needn't hear him confess — surely that could wait until he and the police were out of the house. 'Where—' he tried to shout, and had to clear his throat. 'Where are they?'

'Here I am, old pip.' Andy Nation appeared from the kitchen. 'I'd have had tea coming out of my ears if you'd kept me hanging around much longer. How'd you like to work with me for a bit? I was just saying to Mrs Apple that it's time for your luck to improve.'

FOURTEEN

Mrs Merrybale lived in a tall house in a street largely occupied by retirement homes. 'The old man's on his way back. You'll be giving him a surprise,' she said, and Jack gathered that her husband would be away at sea for some weeks yet, though perhaps her comment was also meant to imply that he hadn't time to redecorate. She was obviously unused to strangers in the house and determined to make them feel at home. At first she called them Mr Nation and Mr Orchard, until Andy persuaded her to use their first names, which she proceeded to apply enthusiastically and at random. She brought them pallid milky tea in fragile cups on brimming saucers, sometimes accompanied by stale currant cakes which Jack and Andy dutifully chewed and chewed. Often she lingered to chat, always breaking off before the end of any anecdote and apologising for taking up their time. That set Andy rubbing his forehead as soon as she turned her back, and her favourite refrain – 'If there's anything I can do to help' – provoked him to denials so heartfelt it was pitiful. It was like a running gag, Jack thought, with Andy struggling not to deliver a punch line. As for Jack himself, he was having the time of his life.

He'd always enjoyed decorating, but doing so with Julia couldn't be compared to working with a professional. After the destructive fun of stripping the walls – competing with himself to see how large an area of paper he could tear off in one piece – came the painstaking business of preparing the walls, and then the decorating itself. Andy wasn't satisfied unless every join in the new paper was invisible, and Jack learned more about paper-hanging than he would have believed possible. He mightn't have been able to sustain such minute concentration if it hadn't been for the comic relief.

At the end of the second day's work Andy said 'I deserve a drink.'

'I'll keep you company.'

'Climb into the limo. Just chuck the treasures in the back.'

Jack managed to sit in the passenger seat of the Datsun, whose exterior was patched with dabs of not quite matching paint, without treading on any of the toys and comics and fragments of biscuit abandoned by Andy's children. 'We could do with using your van to carry the materials,' Andy said.

'It's out of commission. Engine trouble.'

'I'll call my friend and get it fixed for you.'

'I've already booked someone, thanks, Andy.' Jack thought better of saying 'It's going to take a few days' in case Andy offered to have the work done sooner. All that was wrong with the van was that it contained the twelve remaining letters and the blowlamp, a reminder which Jack had preferred to stow out of sight. Andy would have been bound to question its presence in the van.

They drank at Stanley's Cask, a small pub which served such ales as Wobbly Bob and Black Bat and Old Fart and Old Peculier. Jack expected Andy to pour out his frustrations about Mrs Merrybale, but even after two pints of Bishop's Finger, Andy confined himself to talk about his family and Jack's. He must think it was bad form to decry an employer for simply being herself, and Jack reflected that both he and Andy had secrets to keep.

His own didn't seem to have attracted much comment. He hadn't heard the fire reported on either of the local radio stations. The *Liverpool Echo* had carried a paragraph to the effect that Veronica Alan's bungalow had been partially destroyed and that the cause of the fire was unclear. The property must have been insured, Jack thought, and if not she had nobody to blame except herself, but he couldn't help feeling angry: the woman had only had to send out copies of the letter and then nothing untoward would have befallen her. 'Sometimes,' he said to Andy, 'I think it's fear of change that stops people improving their lives.'

'What's given you an attack of the philosophers?'

'I was just thinking how little it takes to change ourselves.'

'Here's to making the most of ourselves.'

'To ourselves,' Jack simplified, and clinked tankards with him.

As Andy delivered him home Julia opened the front door. Jack's first glance was for the stairs behind her, but they were bare of envelopes. 'No responses yet,' she said.

He put an arm around her waist as they went along the hall. 'There will be.'

'Don't count on too much, Jack.'

'Hey, I'm supposed to make the puns around here,' he said, and was reminded by her puzzled look that she couldn't know she had made one. 'I won't promise anything I can't deliver.'

'I'll hold you to that later,' she said, giving him a quick open-mouthed kiss.

Later the Quails, who had viewed the house last week, rang. They were still interested, and almost certainly had a buyer for their own property, though that depended on someone else's ability to find a purchaser. Jack imagined an infinite series of house-buyers stretching through time and space, the people at one end of the series dying of old age before the succession of purchases could reach the far end. 'Except,' he said to Laura over dinner, 'there isn't an infinite number of people, so the person at the end must be the person you began with, holding themselves up.'

'You're making my brain fuzzy,' Laura complained.

'Don't you like playing with numbers?'

'Sometimes.'

'They're what life is made of. Without them we'd never understand the world.'

'And the Quails aren't the only ones who are interested, Laura,' Julia reminded her. 'The young couple who came yesterday who are getting married said they were.'

The week brought Jack several replies to his job applications, two of them inviting him to be interviewed. One job was in Wales, the more attractive was in Ellesmere Port, too distant for any rumours of arson to spoil his chances but less than half an hour's drive along the motorway. The interview was scheduled for early next week, before he and Andy would have finished decorating. If he drove the van to the interview Andy was bound to be puzzled, but Andy saved the day by clearing out the Datsun. 'It's like you said,' he told Jack, 'you can get into the habit of thinking how you are is how you have to be.'

This was on Monday, and he seemed restored by a day off. The car had just pulled into the cracked weedy drive when Mrs Merrybale emerged from the porch, her arthritis making her sway like a sailor. 'You won't want this tea. I'll make some new,' she said, and pitched away into the house.

She was wearing a long black dress down which her grey hair trailed lower than her prominent shoulder-blades. 'Going out dancing tonight, Mrs M?' Andy suggested as he and Jack bore hefty cans of paint into the hall.

'He's a comedian, isn't he?' she said for at least the twelfth time to Jack, sucking in her lips so that her grin wouldn't expose her false teeth. When she returned to the kitchen Jack murmured to Andy 'I don't know if I should mention this, but it's witches who go dancing on May Eve.'

'Hit me on the head and call me Peg. You don't think she thought I meant that, do you?'

'I don't think anyone could think you're capable of malice.'

'Same goes for you, old pip.'

Jack didn't quite know how to respond to this, but was saved from trying by Mrs Merrybale, who seemed bent on racing Andy to the top of the house so that he would have old towels on which to stand the cans of paint. Today they were to paint the wall above the stairs. On Saturday they'd finished halfway up the wall on the middle landing. Jack was working upwards while Andy tackled the most difficult stretch, the wall below the skylight over the stairwell, by perching on a fully extended aluminium ladder propped on the top landing. Whenever Mrs Merrybale approached the stairs Jack heard the ladder rattle. 'Don't let her rattle you,

Andy,' he said under his breath.

Once she had brought them elevenses, currant buns and china chattering on a tray awash with tea, she kept trudging halfway up the stairs to see if she could retrieve the tray and then hurrying apologetically down again. Jack handed it and its cargo of remains to her as soon as he decently could, and saw Andy closing his eyes at the top of the ladder as she set foot on the stairs again. 'That makes me think of a parrot,' she said.

'Oh,' Andy said helplessly.

'Ah,' said Jack.

She was gazing at the tea-cosy which she'd left on the post at the foot of the stairs. 'Just say if you're busy,' she said.

Andy gripped the ladder with one hand and rubbed his forehead with the other. 'Not too busy to listen. We couldn't ever be that.'

'Exactly what I was telling myself. There's nothing like a chat to keep us going.' She was silent except for a wheeze at each stair until she reached Jack. 'What was I saying? Oh, the parrot. I was saying that the cosy made me think of it. I expect you'll be wondering why.'

'Yes,' Andy said in a tone of pure anguish.

'It was the old man, you see. Brought him home from Africa because he thought I'd like some company. Sat on that post where the cosy is and never said a word.'

'The parrot did, not your husband,' Jack said.

'He's a laugh, isn't he, Mr Jack, Mr Andy, I mean?' she called to Andy, who groaned. 'It was the bird sitting there right enough, not the old man. Sat there whenever I let him out of his cage, till I just left him there most of the time. Looked as if someone had carved him on the post and painted him, he did. Now you'd think he'd be no use there, wouldn't you? Wouldn't you think he wouldn't be any use?'

Andy nodded so vigorously that the ladder shifted. 'Well, you'd be wrong,' she said triumphantly. 'He was better than a dog, that bird. I found that out the day someone broke into the house.'

The two men waited while she halted two stairs short of

the landing above which Andy was perched and turned towards Jack. 'Well, I've held you up enough. I'll get out of your way,' she said, and started down.

Andy emitted a strangled noise, just short of a recognisable word, and she swung round. 'Are you all right, Mr Jack, that's to say Mr Andy?' she asked him.

Jack himself was trying to decide whether the intruder had fled in terror when the carving on the banisters had come to life, or it had found its voice at last and convinced the burglar he was caught, or it had been able to imitate his speech with an accuracy which had led the police to him. He was about to ask Mrs Merrybale and put Andy out of his misery when she lost her footing on the edge of a tread.

She didn't fall far. She grabbed the banister with both hands and landed on the next stair down with a thud which jarred her legs and made her wince. Her heels had dragged the carpet away from the stair above her. As she either lost her footing again or sat down to recover from the shock, her heels tugged at the carpet and she slid down one more step. The carpet began to snap free of all the treads above her, a process which would end where Andy's ladder was propped. 'Is she hurt, Jack?' Andy shouted.

In an instant Jack was no longer the audience for a slapstick routine in which nobody would be injured but an onlooker at an accident which he was powerless to prevent: if he tried to reach Andy his weight would dislodge the carpet further. 'She's—' he said wildly, and saw Mrs Merrybale slide down another stair and clutch at the banister, saw the carpet rise up taut from the top stair. 'Step down,' he cried.

Mrs Merrybale thought he meant her. She hauled herself to her feet and let herself down one more stair. 'You'll—' Jack shouted and saw that she hadn't shifted the carpet any further. At that moment Andy, who was descending the ladder, caught sight of the disaster advancing towards him. He was perhaps twelve rungs up the ladder, and clattering down at speed, when the top of the ladder began to screech across the wall towards the stairwell, and he jumped.

The ladder fell one way, Andy the other. The ladder tipped

over the banister, clanged against the edge of the next landing and thudded into the hall, where it teetered upside down before falling over. Andy fell on his feet, bending his knees to lessen the impact, and immediately went sprawling as the carpet slithered from beneath him. He sat down hard and stayed there, looking shaken and irate. As he fell Mrs Merrybale had emitted a shriek which no parrot would have been ashamed of, and now she began to climb towards him, kicking the carpet into place. 'Are you all right, Mr Jamister Andy? Can I do anything for you?'

Andy nodded and stretched out his hands. 'What about the parrot?'

'Why, he died years ago,' she said, and stared at Andy as he threw himself onto his back and lay hooting and pummelling the floor. 'Some tea, that's what you need. I'll be seeing to a pot,' she said, retreating.

When Andy had recovered from his outburst he and Jack secured the carpet and carried the ladder upstairs. Andy was game to climb it again, but Jack insisted on taking his place; that was the least he could do after having put Andy at risk. Still, he'd learned not to take his luck for granted, not to squander it when he himself was able to improve a situation. He was glad to finish painting the ceiling around the skylight – leaning back made him feel as though the ladder was about to sway over the stairwell. 'It's a good job you were only eleven rungs up when it went,' he told Andy.

At the end of the day less than a day's worth of decorating remained. Andy suggested that he could cope by himself, but Jack wouldn't hear of it; he would still be in plenty of time for the library interview. In the morning he donned his old clothes which smelled faintly of paint and sat at the breakfast table, counting silently in elevens, until Andy honked the horn outside. 'Wish me – no, don't wish me luck,' he told Julia and Laura. 'Keep it for yourselves.'

FIFTEEN

It was some weeks later when Laura cycled down to the stretch of promenade that faced the bay. Heavy evening sunlight lazed on a mercury sea. All along the promenade cars were saying L to one another. She sat on a bench and watched the learner drivers braving roundabouts, attempting three-point turns which often gained extra points, flashing both direction indicators as if they didn't know which way to turn, screeching to a halt in the face of invisible obstacles. A rusty Skoda came to a juddering stop a few yards from her, and an enraged couple changed places in the front seats before the woman put her foot down and the car roared off. When its oily fumes trailed towards her, Laura cycled once around the roundabouts and made for home.

She was passing the International Experience – where the colours of the lit sign, which were faded by the sky, put her in mind of sweets – when she met Jackie Pether. Jackie and another girl were sitting on the chained-up swings in the little fairground and sharing a cigarette, which might have been why Jackie went on the offensive at once. She folded her arms as if to show she couldn't have touched the cigarette, and smirked. 'No you haven't,' she said.

Her friend giggled, though she clearly had no more idea of what Jackie meant than Laura had. 'Who says?' Laura demanded.

'Everyone who knows you, Laura Orchard.'

'Well, that doesn't include you, Jackie Pether, so don't you go letting your friend think it does.'

'People know more about you than you'd like them to know,' Jackie said.

The sight of Jackie's friend's broad dull face growing smug infuriated Laura as Jackie meant to do. 'You don't know anything worth knowing, Jackie Pether.'

'I know that's a lie, for a start,' Jackie said and pointed at Laura's budding breasts.

So that had been her original theme: Laura's T-shirt which announced I'VE BEEN TO KNOSSOS. 'It was a present Jody brought me. Anyway, you don't know I'm not going.'

'I know you won't be when your dad can't get a job.'

The girl with the cigarette spluttered as though Jackie had confounded Laura with her wit, and then she started coughing. By the time the girl had regained control of herself Laura had discarded the retort she'd first thought of in favour of something she wanted to know. 'Was it you who went about saying my dad meant to set fire to his shop, Jackie Pether?'

'Lots of people did.'

'Like your mum and dad, for instance?'

Jackie opened her mouth and then turned mute and furious. 'My dad could sue them for losing him that job at school,' Laura said. 'Your dad's supposed to be a policeman. If my dad took him to court he'd have to tell the truth.'

'Don't you say things about my dad,' Jackie shrilled. 'Yours is mad, everyone says so. He runs round New Brighton with one shoe on.'

Laura felt her face grow hot. 'I'll tell you one thing, he doesn't spread lies about people. And I'll tell you another, he's just got a better job than the one at school.'

'Where, in a nuthouse?'

'In Ellesmere Port library, if you must know,' Laura said, and cycled away without looking back.

If she had lingered it might have seemed that she was trying to convince them. Her father had heard only this week that he'd been chosen for the job. It didn't matter whether Jackie and her friend believed it – but yes, it did. They had spoiled Laura's evening, and she didn't want to go home while it might be apparent to her parents that something had.

She cycled past the bowling alley, past Adventureland

where people on machines were screaming, past the bollards which barred cars from the rest of the promenade. She rode so fast that all she could hear was the wind. By the time she slowed she was halfway to Seacombe Ferry, on a stretch of promenade with nothing but a half-mile curve of high brick wall for company. She sat on a solitary bench and watched windows light up like sparks in the ashen blur of streets across the river.

If her father had really been seen wearing only one shoe he must have meant it as a joke. He was worth a dozen dads like Jackie's, who never seemed to smile unless the joke was at someone else's expense. He would be starting work in Ellesmere Port next week, and then if Jackie Pether said he hadn't she would just be making herself look foolish. Laura let these thoughts establish themselves in her mind until she felt it was time to go home.

She was no longer alone on the stretch of promenade. A thin boy whose scalp looked encrusted with sand had climbed the nearest set of steps from the beach and was leaning against the railings opposite the corner of the wall which cut off the view of this stretch from the route back to New Brighton. His spine was propped against the highest rail, one foot resting on the lowest. As Laura mounted her bicycle and pedalled towards him he pushed himself away from the railing, his boot striking the pavement loudly and metallically as a horseshoe. 'That's like my cousin's bike,' he said.

He was several years older than Laura. He stepped off the pavement into the road, lowering his head as though displaying the sandy stubble which didn't quite hide raw patches of his scalp. She gave him a polite smile, but his lips – the only part of his mottled face which seemed to have much flesh beneath the skin – twitched like a dog's as he sidled into her path. 'I said that looks like my fucking cousin's bike.'

'Well, it isn't. My parents bought it for me for Christmas.'

'You pair-rents? What's a pair-rent?' He was advancing on her, kicking his feet outwards as though he was dancing. 'Looks like her fucking pair-rents gave her our Germaine's bike that someone stole,' he said.

Laura glanced back, so hastily that pain stabbed the side of her neck. Two more boys had come up the steps from the beach, quietly despite their boots. One looked older and stupider than the boy in front of Laura, and bore half a dozen blackened scabs under his greyish chin, while the youngest was about Laura's age and seemed to have thought of a joke he was bursting to share. All three had versions of the same flat face which looked as though it had been thumped into shape. As the newcomers moved towards Laura she swung the front wheel and trod hard on the higher pedal. The bicycle veered around her interrogator, but he danced backwards and seized the handlebars. 'Where you fucking off to? Where's your fucking manners?'

'Please don't touch my bicycle,' Laura said, fighting not to let him see that her mouth was growing almost unmanageably stiff. 'I'm sorry if your cousin's bicycle was stolen, but this isn't hers.'

'Well, *someone* stole her by-sickle,' he said, wagging his head like a puppet's. His brothers burst out laughing close behind her — she didn't realise how close until one of them grabbed the back wheel. 'Clint nicked it for her,' the youngest crowed.

'Shut up, you little fucker.' The raw-scalped boy raised his upper lip, exposing an incomplete set of stained teeth. He looked like a dog preparing to attack. Laura's mouth was about to start trembling, her heart was hammering, she could hardly distinguish her hands from the rubber grips they were trying to keep hold of. She twisted the handlebars, so suddenly and violently that they were wrenched out of his hands, and kicked him on the shin as her other foot tramped on the pedal.

Someone screamed behind her, and the bicycle jerked to a halt, having travelled only a few inches. Two of the youngest boy's fingers were jammed between the frame and a spoke of the back wheel. 'You cunt, you hurt my fucking brother,' shouted the boy she had kicked. 'You're dead meat, bitch.'

The youngest boy had fallen to his knees and was trying to pry his fingers out of the trap. 'Get away or I'll hurt him

116

worse,' Laura said, biting her lip. 'Both of you go right down to the beach and then I'll let him loose.'

That had to work, she thought: it made sense. Then the oldest boy plodded forwards and leaned on the rear mudguard, apparently oblivious to the pain he was inflicting on his brother. 'You're not going anywhere,' he said, slow and thick.

'You'd better let me go,' Laura said at the top of her voice. At the far end of the wall, where the promenade rose before sloping to Seacombe, a man and a cavorting puppy were crossing the tarmac. Though they were several hundred yards away, surely the man must have heard her. Perhaps he was too intent on the dog as it bounded down a slipway to the beach. Laura sucked in a shaky breath and shouted 'Help!'

At least, she almost did. She had just breathed out the first letter when the oldest boy reached for her as though his mind was on something else entirely and punched her in the throat. It felt as if she was choking on a hard sweet which she couldn't swallow and which was growing bigger in her wind-pipe. The man with the dog took three quick strides, and Laura saw his head bob down, down, down, and vanish below the edge of the promenade. 'Get off the fucking bike, bitch,' the sandy boy said.

SIXTEEN

Harpo had dressed up as Groucho and was trying to convince him that he was Groucho's reflection. Though it was Jack's favourite Marx Brothers scene, he was nodding after the dinner Julia had made to celebrate his success in Ellesmere Port. Momentary dreams kept interrupting the antics of the two bespectacled moustached men in nightshirts and night-caps, and Jack found that he was gazing into a mirror. He leaned his head gingerly around the edge, and a clown's grinning face craned around to meet him. 'Do you know what I'd like to do?' someone said.

'Yes.' The nightshirted figures were hopping in unison across a frame which had contained a full-length mirror. The clown winked at Jack, who felt his own eyelid droop. 'What?' the voice said.

'What,' Jack agreed, and the clown nodded too, the head swaying up and down so extravagantly it seemed the neck must snap. The head would topple out of the mirror for Jack to catch, and how would that affect him? 'I said, do you know what I'd like to do?' Julia said.

Now Chico appeared disguised as Groucho beside Harpo, destroying the illusion of the mirror. 'Sorry,' Jack mumbled, shaking his head to waken himself. 'What would you like?'

'To go and meet Laura and then have a drink in a beer garden.'

'Go ahead.'

'I was thinking we could take the van and put her cycle in the back.'

'We'll both go, of course,' Jack said, struggling awake. 'Maybe not the van.'

'It's running, isn't it?'

'Not too happily. I'll have it looked at before I start work. Just let me rewind the tape and we can stroll down to the prom.'

He watched the digits on the counter racing backwards. For a moment they seemed to stop at thirteen, but he must be looking at the number twelve, because it was immediately transformed into eleven; then the digits arrived at zero with a loud click. He withdrew the cassette from the machine and put it with the comedy tapes, and followed Julia out of the house.

They crossed the Crazy Golf course, where a seagull was dwarfing a windmill on a concrete mound, and gazed along the promenade. The evening light lent the road and its users a muted precision, but there was no sign of anyone on a bicycle. 'She said she was going where it's open to traffic,' Julia said.

When they walked as far as the first roundabout, from which they had a view of the rest of that end of the promenade, Laura was nowhere to be seen. 'She must have gone home along the top road,' Jack said.

'I expect so.' Julia sounded a little uneasy. An ashen pair of headlamps sprang alight beyond the second roundabout, dazzling Jack and leaving on his eyes a charred patch which first expanded then shrank. Was that Laura near the bowling alley? If so, where was her bicycle? The blackness shrank, and he saw that neither of the girls sitting on the wall was Laura. 'There's someone from her class at school,' Julia said.

It was Jackie Pether, whose grandfather had helped cause the fire at Fine Films. The memory of fire unnerved Jack momentarily as Julia headed for the girls. Jackie whispered to her friend, and both girls shrieked with laughter. 'I have that effect on people,' Jack said.

Julia stood and looked at them until they stopped laughing. 'Have you seen Laura by any chance, Jackie?'

'She went off that way.'

'About how long ago?'

'Twenty minutes,' Jackie said, shrugging.

119

'Thank you. Shall we see if we can meet her?' Julia said to Jack. 'I expect she's on her way back. It'll be dark soon.'

Beyond the bollards which put an end to traffic the promenade ran straight for several hundred yards before curving inland to Vale Park and gradually outwards again. From the beginning of the curve one could see to the end, and at once Jack saw a cyclist just beyond the park. 'Is that her?'

'It might be,' Julia admitted, waving tentatively as she quickened her pace. Apparently in response to her wave, the cyclist dismounted and sat in a shelter. It was impossible to see into the shelter from more than a few yards away, but when they came abreast of it the Orchards found that neither the cyclist nor her machine was at all familiar. 'She could be home by now and wondering where we are,' Jack said.

'Shall we just go to where we can see the rest of the prom?'

'We may as well.'

When a bell jingled behind them Jack turned smiling, but it was the cyclist from the shelter. She rode away up a sloping street beside Mother Redcap's rest home as he and Julia turned the corner to the next stretch of the promenade. The bell rang again as he saw what was there, and allowed him to feel momentarily that he was seeing an illusion. A bicycle was hanging from the railings above the beach.

Both wheels had been kicked or stamped on. Most of the spokes were missing, and the rims were twisted wildly out of shape. The frame was bent in the middle as though someone had done their utmost to snap the bicycle in half. 'It isn't Laura's, is it?' Jack wished aloud.

As Julia went to the bicycle at a run which looked crippled by anxiety, a dog came bounding towards her along the promenade, yapping. 'Come back here, Ruff,' its owner shouted.

He was several hundred yards away, and had been stooping over a bench against the wall. Someone was lying on the bench, Jack saw. At that distance, in the twilight and the shadow of the wall, it was impossible to make out the face, but when he narrowed his eyes he was able to distinguish that

120

the still figure had long red hair like Laura's, dangling over the edge of the seat, and was wearing dungarees patterned like hers. A sour taste of panic flooded his mouth as he ran past Julia, who was leaning over the railings to peer down at the beach. He wanted to see what had happened before she did.

He would have except for the dog. It romped at him and almost tripped him up, and when he bent to pat it and push it away it kept leaping to lick his face. By the time its owner had persuaded the puppy to sit, Julia was at the bench. 'It's all right, love,' she said in a voice so nearly calm that the hint of anguish she couldn't suppress pierced Jack like a physical pain. Whatever he was afraid to see as he went forwards, what he saw was worse.

Laura was sitting up gradually, trying to pretend it didn't hurt to do so. Her T-shirt was torn almost to her waist, and she was holding it shut with one hand. She seemed to be having difficulty both in breathing and swallowing. Her face was on the way to becoming unrecognisable; her lips were split and puffed up, her left eye was hidden by a blackened swelling. At first Jack thought her nose was broken, then he saw that it was only bleeding, as if that wasn't bad enough. Julia sat beside her and put an arm around her shoulders as gently as she could, though even that caused Laura to flinch. 'What happened, love? Who did this to you?'

'Boys,' Laura said, and a tear crept out of her swollen eye as though the bruise had burst.

'How could they?'

Laura swallowed painfully. 'They tried to steal my bike.'

Julia clenched her free hand and punched the wall. 'Oh, Laura, why didn't you let them?'

'Because you and Dad gave it to me.'

'Don't hurt yourself,' Jack pleaded, taking Julia's hand and kissing the scraped knuckles. 'How do you feel, Laura?'

'How in God's name do you think she feels?'

Jack had known the question sounded inane but hadn't known how else to phrase it. 'I only – I meant, can she walk?'

'I think so,' Laura said, her open eye turning towards the wreck of her bicycle.

The dog's owner had been crouching and patting the dog so as not to seem intrusive; now he stood up. 'If you can help her as far as the corner I'll run you to the hospital.'

'That's kind of him, isn't it, Laura?' In the same breath Julia said to him 'Did you see who did this to her?'

'I did. What's more, I know them. I'll show you where they live on the way to the hospital.'

Laura pushed herself up from the bench and winced as her right foot touched the road. 'It's only twisted, I think,' she said, holding onto Julia's waist.

'We can manage,' Julia said when Laura had hopped a few steps. 'You go ahead with this gentleman and get the details, Jack.'

Presumably she didn't want Laura to be further upset, and Jack could tell that the man was relieved to be talking solely to him. 'What did you see?' Jack muttered once they were well ahead.

'Just the end of it, worse luck. When we saw them trying to chuck the bike over we came up and chased them off. I'll tell you what, though, your girl gave as good as she got. I'd lay odds neither of the big ones will be much use to their girl-friends for a while.'

Jack tried to feel proud of her, but only felt helpless: however bravely she had defended herself it hadn't been enough to keep her safe. 'Can you give me a name for them?'

'I can think of a few.' The man seemed to feel he was trespassing on Jack's feelings, however, because he cleared his throat and said 'Elevens.'

The darkening promenade appeared to darken at a rush. 'I didn't hear you. Who are they again?'

'Clint and Lee and what's the runt's name, Eli. Heavens,' the man said with a snigger.

'Their last name?'

'That's right.'

If there weren't gaps in the conversation they must be in Jack's head. 'What is?'

122

'I keep telling you, Evans. Let's have the leash on you before we go on the road.'

He was talking to the dog now, and he must originally have said 'Er, Evans,' not a number at all. 'We'll wait for you here, shall we?' Jack said.

The sight of Laura hopping towards him seemed a cruel joke at her and Julia's and his expense, a joke which both he and old Mr Pether had somehow rehearsed. He felt unbearably responsible for her condition and yet unable to think how he was. When he started back towards her, to be able at least to feel he was trying to help, he was suddenly afraid that she and her mother would recoil from him. 'Our lift won't be long now. Lean on me if you like while we're waiting,' he said to Laura, thinking that she couldn't be any more grateful for his support than he was for her acceptance.

About ten minutes later an ageing blackish Ford Capri cruised down the hill, flashing its wall-eyed lights, and swung round on the promenade so as to point uphill. Laura sat in front, where she had room to stretch out her legs. As she pulled her safety belt around her, Jack saw a surreptitious tear trickle down her cheek.

The driver eased the car onto the main road, trying to brake as little as possible. A minute or so later, as they came in sight of the police station, he turned along a side street. 'This isn't the way to the hospital,' Julia said.

'It's where the Evanses live, at number thirty-one. The boys who—' the driver said, and left it at that.

The broad dilapidated house was shaded by a blighted cherry tree from whose branches hung several knotted ropes. The larger of the front downstairs windows exhibited a neighbourhood homewatch sign and net curtains so discoloured Jack could almost smell the mustiness. 'It's bigger than our house,' Laura said.

Jack heard her saying that was unfair, and he wished he could make her some kind of promise. Just now his thoughts couldn't struggle from beneath his sense of helplessness. He tried to force his mind to work as the car sped along the motorway to the hospital. The driver skirted the packed car park and pulled up outside Casualty. 'Do you mind if I leave you to it?' he said, and scribbled his name and address on the back of a used envelope. 'That's me if you want to tell the police.'

The hospital smelled of disinfectant which reminded Jack of the smell of fuel. The heat started his palms sweating as soon as he stepped into the lobby. While Julia supported Laura he went to a receptionist, who wrote down Laura's details and told the Orchards to take a seat. 'Just one?' Jack said.

He had to say something, however feeble. More than one of the dozen or so people seated on the stark chairs had given him a sharp look, as if he might be responsible for Laura's condition. He sat next to her on the back row of seats and clenched his hands together in his lap until the skin between the fingers felt as though it was on fire. Might he cheer her up by pointing out that the room seemed to be full of people who had thumped themselves on the head or dropped something on their toes? He thought of suggesting that it was like a room off the set of a slapstick film, but that wouldn't go down too well if anyone besides the family heard him. Silence was the best bet, particularly since a woman in the front row was already glaring at him.

She was barefoot except for slippers decorated with tufts like the tails of two white rabbits, and wore a frayed overcoat whose pattern of green and purple checks was enough to aggravate anyone's suffering. Two combs, a pink one and a yellow, were stuck in her hastily tidied greying hair. Jack closed his eyes in the hope that would make her attention stray, and when he opened them she was glaring at Laura while she murmured something to the boy next to her. Jack went to the end of the front row. 'Excuse me, is there some problem?'

The woman turned towards him in a crouch that managed to suggest both that he was threatening her or her child and that she was ready to fly at him. 'Tell him what you told me, son,' she said in a drone loud enough to be heard in the next room.

The boy held up one hand, which was wrapped in a dish-cloth. 'She ran me over and hurt my hand.'

'That girl did,' his mother said to the room at large in case anyone thought he meant her. 'Don't just tell him, Eli, show him.'

As the boy unwrapped the cloth he wailed 'Ow, ow, fuck' and the woman slapped the side of his head. 'Less of the language. I don't know where he gets it from,' she complained to everyone within earshot. 'There, see what she did to him.'

The boy raised two fingers, which were bruised almost black and weeping blood from two parallel cuts close to the knuckles. He glanced at Laura as though he was afraid she was about to assault him, and Julia gestured clumsily for her to stay put and came forwards, her face pulled out of shape by suppressed anger. 'And what did he do to her?'

The woman's drone grew even louder. 'Look, now there's two of them. Two adults bullying a widow and her little boy.'

'Nobody's doing that, Mrs Evans,' Jack said. 'But I'm afraid your son isn't telling the truth.'

The woman flung her hands up, almost dislodging both her combs. 'They don't waste any time, do they? They've been finding out our names. I expect they'll be having us thrown out of our house and put in prison, as if there aren't enough people who already want to.'

Eli started to blubber, and cringed when Julia took a step forwards. 'We've a witness to what happened, Mrs Evans,' Jack said.

'A witness, is it? Who, the devil who sets dogs on little boys while they're hurt and can't defend themselves?' Mrs Evans shoved herself to her full height, somewhat less than Jack's or Julia's, and shook a finger at Laura. 'How old is she?'

'Twelve,' Julia said.

Mrs Evans had obviously expected a higher figure, but rallied at once. 'Well, Eli isn't even that, and you just try and find me another boy as gentle. You looked after your mother, didn't you, Eli, after your father went to see Jesus.'

Jack felt as though her words were being heaped on top of

the burden that had gathered in his mind. Hardest of all to deal with was the banality of the confrontation, its emotional messiness, its lack of any clarity. 'Take a good look at what he and his brothers did to our daughter,' he said through his chattering teeth.

'What were his brothers supposed to do? Stand by while she cut their little brother's fingers off? All he wanted was a go on her precious bike. If you ask me she's not quite right in the head. You want to have a doctor take a look at her.'

Mrs Evans bumped into an empty chair in the next row and sent it clattering. 'Look at the mother, she wants to knock me down. Just you try and I'll have the law on you. They're dangerous, the whole lot of them. They all want locking up.'

The receptionist emerged from one of the examination rooms. 'Excuse me, if you'd like—'

'We're next,' Mrs Evans said, tugging Eli to his feet. 'Let them wait. You aren't supposed to let them jump the queue, however much money they've got.'

'I wasn't about to, Mrs Evans. I was about to ask you if you'd like to go in now.'

Mrs Evans threw the Orchards a triumphant look and pushed Eli into the examination room. 'If that woman comes anywhere near me,' Julia said in a low tight voice, 'I shall kill her.'

'No you won't, Julia. Leave them to the police.' Jack tried to steer her to her seat and found she was shaking. She disengaged herself from him and hurried away to the Ladies, and he returned to Laura. 'It's over now, love.'

It wasn't over. He felt as though all the undischarged violence of the encounter with the Evanses was massing inside him. Quite soon a red-eyed Julia sat down beside Laura, and they waited. The possibility of another confrontation with the Evanses scratched at his nerves, but just as the door of the Evanses' room opened Laura was called. When the woman doctor suggested that Jack wait outside he did so, the heat crawling over his skin and parching his mouth. He felt utterly useless, not even able to help Laura while

126

everyone else was doing so. If he couldn't somehow overcome his sense of helplessness and of having inadvertently harmed her, he thought he might go mad.

SEVENTEEN

'Yes, I was right,' Jack said, and at once was wide awake. He lay still in case he'd disturbed Julia, but she had managed to fall asleep at last and was breathing deeply in a way which, if she had been awake, would have denoted an attempt to be calm. Outside the window the sky was growing faintly red. He lay and watched bars of cloud turn redder and told himself again that he should have used the van.

He'd done everything else he could think of. He'd waited near the examination room until Julia had let him in, his admission seeming like a token forgiveness for some negligence on his part which he had been unable to define. Laura's ankle was sprained and her body was a mass of bruises, but since no bones were broken the doctor had thought it best for her to be home with her family, especially since the hospital was short of empty beds. Once she was home in bed Jack had driven to the police station to report the Evanses and leave the address of Mr Stringfellow, the witness. He'd hoped Julia would be asleep when he returned home, but she had needed to talk out her distress. He'd held her and murmured and wondered why, as soon as he'd climbed into the van, he had begun to think he should have used it earlier. There had been nothing wrong with it when he'd let Julia think there was – he had just been unnecessarily anxious that she might see the letters in the back – but even if they had driven to find Laura they wouldn't have been able to take the vehicle onto the stretch of promenade where she had been attacked, so what should he have done? 'Used the van,' he said to himself as the fire in the sky grew brighter.

It added up. Andy Nation's near-accident ought to have

128

shown him that he and those close to him couldn't simply trust to luck. Visiting Veronica Alan had earned him some, but it had run out. He should have realised that she wasn't the only person who hadn't copied his letter.

He couldn't altogether blame them. He himself had initially dismissed the letter. It really wasn't reasonable to expect someone to appreciate how crucial an unsigned impersonal letter might be to their lives – you could say it was a test of faith – but he was sure he would be able to convince them if he met them face to face. His sense of rightness let him doze, and he awoke feeling ready for action. He hurried downstairs, eager to give Julia a hug which would tell her that everything was going to be fine without his having to put it into words, but he hadn't reached her when she stopped him in his tracks. 'You won't be going anywhere today, will you,' she said.

She clearly hadn't had much sleep, and now she was going to work on the computers at Luke Rankin's office. 'Don't worry, I'll look after her,' he said, and went to find Laura.

She was sitting in the front room, her shoeless bandaged leg stretched out. Her face seemed even more multicoloured than last night, particularly her lips and her left eye, though at least they weren't quite as swollen. A school story abandoned after a page or so lay on its face by her chair. 'How do you feel now?' Jack said.

'Mummy says I should feel better when I've had a sleep.'

She was staring at her hand which she'd raised to her face, and he realised that she didn't want him to see how she looked. 'You look—' he floundered, and thought that a lie would be worse than the truth. 'You look like an accident in a paint factory.'

Assuming that it hurt her to smile, her response was heartening. 'I'll be down again soon if you need me,' he said.

He was stepping into the shower when Julia followed him into the bathroom. 'It wouldn't hurt to lie occasionally,' she told him.

'Even if she knows I am?'

'It isn't too much to ask, is it?' she said, and more gently

129

'It'll give you a chance to do a bit of acting.'

'Do you have to go to work today? You need to catch up on your sleep as much as Laura does.'

'We can't afford me taking time off work.'

'We can now. I've figured out what was wrong with our luck.' He couldn't say that to her, not only because the letters were his secret – they felt like more of one every time he failed to mention them – but because even if she had only been reminding him that the family needed her income she had succeeded in making their life seem precarious. 'Look after yourself, that's all I'm saying,' he said, and drew the plastic curtain inside the bath.

Through the mounting drizzle of the shower he heard her brushing her teeth. The sound reminded him of sand-papering. What must using a toothbrush feel like now to Laura? The curtain billowed at him as Julia left the bathroom, the clammy plastic clung to him. He heard her murmuring to Laura as he towelled himself. Once he was dressed he tiptoed down, hoping that sleep might have caught up with Laura, but she was holding her book and staring at the inactive television, which appeared to be showing a photograph of smoke. 'Would you like to watch something?' Jack said.

'What's that film where he kills all those people who are really the same one?'

'A comedy, you mean? With Dennis Price and all the Alec Guinnesses? *Kind Hearts and Coronaries*,' he said, and hoped that she was wincing only at the joke. 'It's one I saved from the fire,' he assured her, and slipped the cassette into the player.

It was a good choice. When she had watched it previously it had made her smile rather than laugh. 'It only hurts when she laughs,' he heard himself say wildly in his head. When the photographer went up in smoke Laura let out a gasp as though she'd thought of something, but she had fallen asleep. Rather than risk disturbing her he watched to the end, reflecting that it could be said the film contained eleven deaths if you counted the one which presumably followed the final scene. He stopped the cassette and withdrew it quietly

130

from the player, having turned the television off, then he crept into the hall and closed the door. Even if he was trapped in the house until Julia came home he wanted to have good news for Laura when she awoke.

He carried the phone as far up the stairs as the cord would reach and phoned the estate agent's. 'Mr Orchard. I was going to phone you,' the junior partner said.

'Then I've stopped you from making me jump. Will I be pleased?'

'I've just heard from the Quails.'

'Not quailing, I hope.'

'I'm afraid they've decided to stay where they are. Someone further down the chain got knocked back on his mortgage.'

'Never mind. The young couple you sent were decidedly in favour. They said they'd be in touch as soon as their bank manager gave them the green light.'

'We're speaking of the Mabeys.'

'Maybe. It's only his name so far, I thought.'

'Actually ...' The estate agent grunted hard. 'They gave us a false name and address.'

'A f—' Jack sounded as if he'd been hit in the stomach. 'A false—'

'Don't worry, Mr Orchard, we've no reason to believe they're criminals. They were up to the same tricks last year with some clients of our friend next door. Unfortunately there are people who enjoy viewing properties for sale when they have no intention of buying. You'd be surprised how many of them we encounter.'

'I'm surprised,' Jack said and rubbed his aching stomach. 'So what happens now?'

'Rest assured we'll keep pushing your house. I shouldn't think of dropping the price just yet unless you really feel you have to.'

Which meant that it might become necessary, Jack assumed as he brought the receiver and the body of the phone together and dropped both onto his lap in order to redial. He had to calm the nervous jogging of his legs before he could. Nothing could go wrong with this call – he knew that Laura's bicycle was included in the house insurance even when it was away from the house – but though the insurance clerk promised to send him a claim form that day he felt as though the family was at the mercy of events. He felt as though their luck was poised to grow worse if he didn't act soon – and then he saw the light. He didn't need to leave Laura after all.

He left the front door open and climbed into the back of the van. The blowlamp was squatting on two piles of letters in the corner behind the driver's seat. The bottom of the tank had imprinted segments of a circle like a secret sign on the envelopes. He took the first letter that came to hand into the house and found the phone number.

The phone barely rang before it was picked up. 'Alston School.'

Jack sat up straight and drew a breath which smelled unexpectedly of the blowlamp. 'Could I speak to Mr Alston?'

He hadn't got the name out when the man interrupted him. 'Jeremy Alston Riding School.'

He sounded too impatient to be anybody but the owner. 'Is that Mr Alston?' Jack said.

'Can't hear you.'

'Is that Jeremy Alston?'

'Can't hear you.'

'My daughter needs sleep,' Jack said and raised his voice as much as he dared. 'Is that—' he began again and faltered, hearing metal scraping metal. It seemed so unlikely that it was the sound of the key that he didn't believe it until the front door opened and Julia stepped into the hall.

'Thank you,' Jack said, grinning inanely into the phone, and tried to cut off the call, so hastily that receiver and stand went clattering downstairs. 'The insurance company,' he told Julia as he swooped on the receiver, which said 'Alston Riding School' before he could slam it into place.

'Do you have to make so much noise?' Julia said. 'Isn't she asleep yet?'

'She was.' Jack inched the door open and closed it. 'Still is.

132

What brings you home?'

'A headache. Two hours in front of the screen was all I could take. Luke's promised me a full day's pay.'

'Good for him,' Jack said, uncomfortably aware of having spent most of two hours in front of a screen to no effect at all. 'Do you want me to bring you some paracetamol?'

'You could do. I'll be upstairs,' she said, but stood where she was. 'Who's the letter for?'

'What, this letter? It, er, nobody. I mean, nobody to do with us. Postman Pat strikes again. I'll deliver it where it should have gone later.'

If he stuffed it into his pocket too quickly she might be suspicious, but if he didn't she would see his handwriting on the envelope. She squeezed her eyes shut and pressed one hand against them before reaching for the banister. 'Just let me go to bed.'

He'd worsened her headache. He found the bottle of paracetamol in the bathroom cabinet and took a glass to the sink. Before he filled the glass he let the water pour over the back of his hand in case that quietened his nerves, but all it did was race up his sleeve and drip from the elbow. The cotton wool squeaked between his finger and thumb as he withdrew it from the bottle and dropped it into the pedal bin. He carried glass and tablets into the bedroom, where Julia had drawn the curtains as if in preparation for a funeral. 'I'll be weeding the front,' he said. 'I'll hear Laura if she wakes up.'

The For Sale sign creaked above him like a gibbet while he grubbed shoots out of the cracks in the crazy paving between the urns planted with heather. 'For Sale' added up to thirteen, which he should be turning into good by delivering the letter, except that it wouldn't be fair to Julia and Laura if he left them as they were, although wasn't it more unreasonable of him to delay heading off any more bad luck? His thoughts felt like a dog chasing its tail in his head, yapping and yapping. He stared at the van as if it ought to tell him the answer to his problem. 'The van,' he said aloud, and heard Laura moan in her sleep.

Late in the afternoon Julia got up. He went to her as she emerged from the bathroom, a drop of water trickling from one eyebrow and meandering between her freckles. 'How do you feel now?' he said.

'I've felt better.'

'Laura's not long been awake. She doesn't want anything. I was thinking I should have the van seen to while you're home.'

'Won't it be too late?'

'Andy told me somewhere I could take it that stays open late.'

Had he responded too swiftly? Julia was frowning, but only at the trickle of water, which she dabbed away. 'My head's nearly gone. I'm just tired,' she said. 'Don't be any longer than you can help.'

Jack flexed his arms before grasping the wheel of the van and sending the vehicle along Victoria Road, where luminous figures were capering and being extinguished in the video arcades. He felt released and purposeful. He didn't need to rehearse what he would say to Jeremy Alston, he only had to tell the truth.

The riding school was at the edge of Heswall, a village on the western side of the peninsula. Jack was scarcely aware of overtaking traffic on the motorway and then on the road that wound through villages which sounded like obscure adverbs – Irby, Pensby. In Heswall he had to halt for several minutes at the junction with the main street, which was laden with shoppers and commuters. At last a gap appeared in the traffic and he sent the van screeching through.

The side road curved downhill. Hedges taller than the van shadowed the pavements. Driveways afforded him glimpses of wide lawns and an extravagant variety of houses. Once a crow flapped out of a sycamore tree, so slowly that its flight seemed miraculous. Once Jack heard children playing tennis on a lawn, but for the whole of his five minutes' drive around the increasingly sharp curves he met neither a vehicle nor a pedestrian. The hedges ended, exchanging butterflies across the road beside a post-box, and the road sloped down more

134

steeply between fields. The houses were out of sight by the time he saw the sign for the riding school.

The signboard stood by a five-barred gate at the end of a path which led from within a curve of the road. Jack parked on the verge along the outside of the curve. He stood by the van, stretching and gazing downhill towards the Welsh coast, a long palette of pastel greens above the tidal flats of the Dee, and then he opened the gate, which emitted a sound like the rising cry of a bird.

The path wound gradually between hedges too high to see over. Hoofmarks were die-stamped in the grassy earth. He had been walking for some minutes when he heard the whinny of a horse ahead. It was followed by a sound of snorting much closer to him. He was about to step out of the way when a man appeared at the far end of the long curve between the hedges and spat on a patch of flowers beside the path.

He looked the outdoor type. He wore a tweed jacket with leathery elbows, brown slacks and boots which might have been chosen to take any spatters of mud in their stride. As he and Jack marched towards each other, Jack decided that while the man might once have kept himself fit, now he was trying to appear so. The grey moustache which bristled under his broad nose like an emblem of virility looked pasted to his ruddy pockmarked face. Jack wasn't impressed by the blue-eyed glare which the other was training on him; nobody could sustain such a glare for long, and as the man stalked up to Jack he blinked furiously before redoubling it. 'Where do you think you're going?' he demanded.

If Jack hadn't recognised his voice from their phone conversation he would have recognised his impatience. 'Where the sign says, Mr Alston.'

'Should I know you?'

'I'd be surprised if you did.'

'Daughter?'

For a moment it seemed only right to Jack that he should be enquiring after Laura. 'Are we training a daughter of yours?' Alston said.

'No. She'd love to learn to ride, but you know how it is.'

Alston's eyes narrowed, wrinkling their pouches. 'Not hanging round waiting to see them ride by, are we? Because they've all gone home and taken their bums with them.'

'I should think that's inevitable.'

'Comedian, are we? It's people who make *me* laugh, especially the ones who think I can't see through them. There's a good few won't admit how much they like to watch young bums bouncing up and down with a nag between their legs.' His face abruptly turned several shades redder. 'I've a letter to post,' he said as though he was interrupting Jack rather than himself, and strode at him.

'That's a coincidence,' Jack said, stepping backwards. 'Do you mind if I walk with you?'

'They tell me it's a free country. Beyond my gate, that is. I should watch what you're doing.'

Jack realised that wasn't a veiled threat just in time to avoid stepping into a heap of horse-turds. 'I don't see any letter,' Alston snapped.

'Here it is,' Jack said, disentangling himself from the brambly hedge. He pulled the envelope out of his pocket and tried to hand it to Alston, who stared at it with a disapproval that seemed automatic and tramped onwards. Jack tore the envelope open and unfolded the letter as he ran between the hoofmarks. 'Mr Alston, did you receive a letter like this?'

'Looks as if you did,' Alston said, barely glancing at it.

'Out of the blue,' Jack told him. As he poked it at Alston a breeze flapped it, and he touched the man's raddled pudgy fingers whose reddish bristles made Jack think of the skin of a pig. Alston halted, almost stamping his feet. 'You're worse than a stable-girl. Can't you see when a man is out for a walk? Give it here now you've put a man off his stride,' he blustered, snatching the letter.

He'd hardly glanced at the page when he shied it away, whether at Jack or onto the path apparently not mattering. 'Yes, I got one among all the rubbish the postman won't stop bringing. But if you think I sent you this you want your head examining.'

136

Jack retrieved the letter from the hedge, where it had sent a spider fleeing across a sheet of cobweb, and folding it carefully, replaced it in the envelope. 'Mr Alston,' he called, 'I didn't think you did.'

'Then what are you after me for? I don't sign petitions, if that's your game. The world can go to hell for all I care so long as it leaves me alone.' Alston halted again in sight of the gate, so suddenly that Jack thought he had grasped the truth about him and the letter. 'Is it yours?' Alston demanded. 'Are you the dish man?'

He was glaring at the trace of the image of a satellite dish on the back of the van. 'Only when I'm washing up after meals,' Jack said.

Alston ignored this. 'It'd be sad if it wasn't a joke, people paying money for the latest fad just so they can put more rubbish between their ears.'

'All I want is for my family to have a decent life.'

'Nothing I can do about that except wish you luck,' said Alston, who obviously had no intention of doing so. He marched to the gate and held it open. 'Here's the road.'

Jack took his time. He mustn't pass the gate until he knew what to say. 'Suppose,' he said carefully, 'you could do more and it wouldn't cost you anything?'

'Suppose away.'

That sounded like another dismissal, but Jack fell into step beside him as he turned uphill. 'Suppose we're wrong to assume that these letters don't work?'

'Are we?'

Alston's tone was neutral; his pace seemed resigned. 'When I received mine I thought it was nonsense,' Jack told him.

'Get away.'

'I only kept it so I could warn my daughter about such things. Then my business was destroyed by a fire, and then—' He'd sent the letters, but his luck had improved only to worsen until he'd tracked down the person responsible and set fire to her house. How could he admit that to Alston or to anyone else? His mind shrank into itself until it felt like a

137

smouldering coal. 'I wonder,' he blurted, 'if my daughter got hurt because I made out to her the letter was a joke.'

'You reckon that's likely, do you?'

'It's the only reason I can think of. Three boys set on her while she was out riding her bicycle, wrecked it and put her in the hospital. She's only twelve years old, for God's sake.'

'That's life today, from what I hear.'

'It doesn't have to be,' Jack declared. 'Suppose we could change it just by doing what this letter says?'

'You've come to think that, have you?'

'Let me ask you a question. You threw away your letter, didn't you? Did your luck get worse after it did?'

'That's two questions,' Alston said, halting on the lonely curve above which the post-box would appear. 'Yes I did and no it didn't.'

'Shall I tell you why I think that was?'

'I can't wait.'

'Because bad luck doesn't always do what the letter says it does. I think that if someone invites it by ignoring the instructions it goes back to whoever's most accident-prone.'

'Meaning you,' Alston said as though enlightened at last.

'And my family. It seems we're the butt, yes.'

'More so than you think, I shouldn't wonder.'

'You see my point, then,' Jack said eagerly.

'I see you're like just about everyone I meet these days. Which means, since you'll need it spelling out for you, that you're an even bigger fool than you look,' Alston said, and turning his back, strode up the hill.

In three strides Jack was ahead of him. 'It doesn't matter what you think of me or the letters. If they're as meaningless as you think it can't do any harm to send them, can it? Just suppose for a moment they could protect my daughter from anything else bad – wouldn't you send them then? I'd give you the money for postage. Just thirteen letters to people you needn't even know. If you've such a low opinion of people you can't believe that would matter.'

Alston had stopped and was gazing open-mouthed at him. 'I don't think I've ever met one quite like you. Your

138

daughter's got something special for a father.'

'Well, thank you.' Jack's speech had left him breathless, and he faltered long enough for Alston to grin at him. 'Would you like to know why I don't own a television?' Alston said.

'Please,' Jack said, though he couldn't see the relevance.

'Because of people like yourself.'

'I don't follow.'

'You better hadn't if you know what's good for you,' Alston said, and raised his voice. 'People who won't let a man mind his own business. People whingeing and snivelling and trying to make out we're all responsible for the state of the world, for the starving piccaninnies who I always say must have ninnies for parents, and the air not being fit for animals to breathe, and the workshy putting children on the streets to beg from folk who must be even stupider than they are, and the Jews killing the Arabs, and the niggers killing the whites, and the prisons being so popular there's a waiting list because this country is scared to kill anyone who deserves to be put down. Is that enough of an answer for you? I'll make myself even plainer. Your daughter's nothing to do with me and she means less than nothing to me. She's already bothered me more than she's worth.'

His face was redder than ever, and he was breathing so hard that hairs twitched in his moustache; Jack thought he might be about to collapse. Instead he shouldered past Jack and stalked uphill.

Jack went after him, though he wasn't sure why. His thoughts and feelings seemed to have solidified into a hot dark lump in his head. That slowed him down, and he had only just come in sight of the post-box when he saw Alston post a letter and turn back.

As soon as he saw Jack, Alston began to laugh. He folded his arms as he walked towards him and went on laughing, a loud dry mechanical noise which sounded like a demonstration of mirth rather than the real thing. To Jack he looked like a life-size doll, the rubbery surface of its face split by a wad of grey stuffing above the mouth. The doll was growing

139

bigger, marching closer, and he couldn't think how to respond. He swung around to rid himself of the sight of it and the way it shrivelled his mind, and Alston jeered 'That's right, you run. Run or I'll have the law on you.'

Jack didn't run, but he walked fast towards the van, groping for his keys, which rattled against the cigarette lighter. 'Where's my luck gone?' he said wildly, dragging the keys out of his pocket as he stumbled alongside the van. He reached up to unlock the door, and Alston shouted 'So it was your junk cluttering up my view. I'm afraid I was wrong about you. I'm afraid your daughter's got a liar for a father, if you've even got a daughter.'

'No you aren't.' The dark lump which Jack's mind had become seemed to brighten and expand until it filled his skull. Three paces took him to the rear doors, which he unlocked with one hand while he dug in his pocket with the other. 'You aren't afraid yet, but you will be,' he murmured, climbing in. 'This'll make your eyes pop.'

The vehicle shook. Alston had thumped the side. 'Think I don't know where you're skulking? I'm taking your number and giving it to the police,' Alston bellowed, and flung the doors open wide. 'What—'

His face appeared to writhe into a grin, though perhaps that was only an effect of the dancing of the air between him and Jack. 'Laugh this off if you can,' Jack said, and came roaring out of the van; or something did.

EIGHTEEN

'Don't be any longer than you can help,' Julia said, and watched Jack climb into the van. She could tell that he was trying to conceal his relief at having left the house. Perhaps being anywhere near Laura made him blame himself, in which case Julia knew precisely what he was suffering. She felt as though her mind had stopped at the moment when she'd seen Laura lying injured on the bench. As the van reached the far end of the street and turned along Victoria Road she watched as though the sight of Jack's departure was capable of starting her mind up, but just now she felt as if nothing could.

It hadn't been just the flickering of the computer screens at the office which had given her a headache, nor Luke Rankin's antics, though today he had been more nervously active than ever and far less approachable, keeping himself and his computer closeted, not even letting calls from clients past his door. It had only needed Lynne to ask 'Had a row with your husband?' for the truth and the tears to spill. Before long Luke had stormed out of his office, demanding 'How am I supposed to work with this racket going on?', yanking at his lapels and then at his tie as though his hands were seeking someone to attack.

Lynne had rounded on him. 'Mrs Orchard's daughter was mugged last night, and she's still come to work.'

'God. Sorry. Take the rest of the day off with pay or however long you need to take. I can always call you if I've a question,' Luke had said, already retreating.

Her tears hadn't helped; they had simply given her a head-ache which tasted metallic. All the way home it had grown worse. She'd crawled into bed and buried her face under the duvet, and had wakened a few minutes ago to find that the headache had faded, leaving her skull feeling empty and brittle. When she found herself staring at the trace of fumes which Jack's van had left in the air as if the sight had something to tell her, she turned back to the house.

Laura limped into the hall to meet her and held onto an upright of the banister. 'I'll be all right, Mummy, if you want to go back to bed. If you like I'll bring you a cup of something.'

'Don't you dare pretend I'm the invalid round here, young lady, or I'll—' But fierceness, feigned or otherwise, was no use; the spectacle of Laura being brave felt like a corkscrew in Julia's guts.

'I'm not hurting so much now, I'm more stiff than anything. The doctor said I won't have any scars, remember. Don't cry, Mummy,' Laura pleaded, beginning to weep, and that was when the dam broke. They sat on the stairs and held onto each other and sobbed. It seemed to Julia that they did so for almost as long as her mind had been stopped; she couldn't have imagined that either of them had so much water in her head. When at last their tears began to run dry she discovered that she felt somewhat better, if only for holding Laura and being held, and rather glad that Jack hadn't been there. She and Laura competed at nose-blowing in the bathroom, Laura performing so gingerly that it brought more tears to Julia's eyes. 'We both need a drink,' Julia said to get herself moving, 'and I should make some kind of dinner.'

'Will you talk to me?'

'When don't I?' Julia said, helping her hobble downstairs. 'Any requests?'

'Tell me a story from before I was born. Tell me about the first time Dad asked you out.'

Julia poured them both a mug of diet cola and then crouched to rummage in the freezer. If Laura wanted to hear tales she'd liked when she was little, perhaps that was her way of reassuring herself that their life together wouldn't change. 'That was when I was trying to keep up with the computer revolution in the evenings after work,' she said. 'When the

142

idea of a home computer still seemed like science fiction to most people. I used to go to the library and read all the latest stuff about computers, and I can't remember when I first noticed Jack, but I remember starting to hope he'd be on duty when I was there, and pretty soon I was doing my best to be there when he was. What's so funny?'

'Grown-ups.'

'You'll be one soon and you can tell me if it's any different,' Julia said, chopping vegetables. 'So of course I always asked him if I needed help, and I don't need to tell you I was waiting for him to ask me out.'

'Why didn't you ask him out?'

'I mustn't have been quite liberated enough. And it got to be a point of pride after a while, that he should do the asking. I remember going home some nights in a temper because he still hadn't. So I started asking him to bring more and more books to the table where I was working. I don't know if I was trying to pay him back for not noticing me or if I meant to push him until he'd have to protest – probably both. Then I began to wonder if he was playing a joke on me instead of the other way round, and you can't imagine how furious that made me. Then one night I got caught in a storm on the way to the library and my new shoes were soaked, and I sat at the table with rain trickling down the back of my neck and told myself that if he brought me more books than I'd asked for this time I was going to poke him in the ribs and make him drop the lot. So I saw him staggering towards me with the highest pile of books I'd ever seen, and I really didn't think I was going to be able to keep my hands off him, and then he came out with his classic pick-up line . . .'

'"Can I get you a towel?"' Laura said before Julia could.

'To which the only response seemed to be "As well as all those books?" And we both started laughing, and I realised he was going to drop the pile of books that weren't for me at all, and he tried to catch them as they went, which was the worst juggling act I've ever seen . . . I don't know how we managed not to get thrown out of the library that night. But when it closed he walked me to the bus stop with an umbrella that didn't just open inside out but actually flew off the handle, and he asked me if I'd like to go somewhere else with him when it was dryer, and here we are.'

'Tell me another story,' Laura said, stretching out her leg on the bench.

Julia told her about her birth, at the moment of which the midwife had instructed Jack to wipe her forehead and then cried 'Not the baby's head, you fool, your wife's' ... She recalled the rainy morning when a Safeway assistant had wheeled her trolley out to the car park while she'd pushed Laura in the buggy, and she had been loading the boot of the car they used to own when Jack had followed her, convinced that the toddler asleep beneath the rain cover of the buggy he'd been pushing was Laura ... 'At least we've our memories when things get rough,' she said.

'I've got you and Daddy, which is better than any old memories.'

'No need to choose between us and them. It'll be the three of us for a long time yet, I hope,' Julia said, and the phone rang.

She was wiping her hands when Laura swung her foot onto the floor. 'I'll get it,' she said as if she were determined to prove that she could, and limped quickly into the hall. Julia heard her say 'Oh, hello,' and then there was a protracted silence, broken only by occasional murmurs from Laura which could mean anything. After some minutes Laura returned to the kitchen. 'It's Dad. I think he wants to speak to you. He sounds a bit peculiar.'

'Drunk, do you mean?'

Laura looked uncertain. 'Not like Dad.'

Julia wiped her hands again and went to the phone. As she lifted the receiver it emitted a click which was either the fall of a coin or an indication that the call had been terminated. 'Here I am, Jack,' she said. 'Are you still there?'

There was no response, but also no dialling tone. Her question surely didn't require any pondering, yet several seconds passed before Jack said 'Yes.'

He didn't sound entirely convinced. 'Is it fixed?' Julia said.

144

'Fixed?'

'Yes, fixed. The van.'

'It didn't break down. It got me there.'

'That's something to be thankful for then, isn't it? Is it fixed now, or have you got to leave it?'

'No.' She was just about to lose her patience when he said 'Not leaving it, no.'

'Well then, are you coming home?'

A wind hooted across his mouthpiece, sounding lonely and chill. He must be phoning from somewhere in the open. 'Are you sure you want me to?' he said.

'What are you asking me? We've never needed you more than we need you now. We've had the kind of talk girls have, if that's what you're wondering, but how can you ask a question like that? What's wrong with you, Jack?'

Silence, then the cold thin wind, and she closed her eyes and controlled herself. 'I'm sorry, I'm being incredibly stupid. What's wrong with you is what happened to Laura. Don't stay out there brooding about it. We've survived everything else by staying together. If I made you feel I needed to be alone with Laura that's over and done with, I promise.'

'It isn't your fault,' he said almost piteously. 'You haven't anything to blame yourself for.'

'And you certainly haven't. I'm not blaming you for anything, except for making me feel as though something else has gone wrong. If it has, tell me the worst. Tell me why you called, at any rate.'

'I just wanted to hear your voice.'

'Well, now you have. Wouldn't you rather have the rest of me as well?'

'You mightn't want—' Jack muttered, but the wind blew away the rest of whatever he said.

'I don't want to have to worry about you, Jack, not on top of everything else. Please just come straight home and then you can say whatever you need to say, all right?'

'But if—' he said, and the receiver started to moan. His coins had run out. Julia hung up at once in case he called back, and gazed at the wall above the stairs, where a

145

meaningless scrap of sunlight was climbing. 'Was he drunk?' Laura said.

'Just upset, I think. Never mind, he's on his way home,' Julia told her, and walked slowly back to the kitchen. She was pouring Laura another drink when someone knocked hard at the front door.

If it was Jack, he had either driven so fast she didn't like to think about it or had phoned from so close to home it would have been a joke. When she stepped into the hall she saw two figures silhouetted on the frosted pane of the front door. Perhaps they were house-hunters, but their arrival hard on Jack's call seemed inexplicably ominous. She sent herself along the hall and took hold of the latch. The door swung inwards, catching on a corner of the doormat, and she had to turn the mat over, raising dust like a residue of ash, before she could open the door wide. She had already seen that her visitors were Jody Venable and her father Pete.

He put a finger to his lips. 'Is this a good time?'

'For what, Pete?'

He undoubtedly meant well, but his behaviour didn't do much for her nerves. When Jody covered her mouth Julia saw that she was carrying an envelope. 'If that's a card for Laura, Jody, she's awake. Come in and see her if you like.'

'Hi, Jody,' Laura called.

Jody winced at the sight of her, but said 'You look like a pirate with an eye-patch. We all bought you a card, our class did.'

'Let's see,' Laura said and limped into the front room, Jody following. Julia stepped back further, tramping on the corner of the doormat. 'Come with me while I get Jody a drink.'

As soon as Pete was in the kitchen his demeanour changed. 'I still can't believe what happened. Have the police been in touch yet? Have they got hold of whoever it was?'

'We know where they live, and we've told the police.'

'How many of the swine were there?'

'Three, Laura says.'

'Bloody Christ. Beg pardon,' he said as though he'd belched. 'The teacher told the class that Laura had been

146

mugged, but I didn't think it could be this bad. If it was Jody I'm afraid I'd need locking up or I'd be going round to give them worse than they gave her. It's a good job Jack doesn't have a temper. Is he home?'

'Not just now.'

'Any idea when?'

'Soon, I hope.'

'I wouldn't mind waiting for him.'

'Stay as long as you like.'

'The trouble is I can't. We're one girl down at the Experience. Shall we give him fifteen minutes?' Pete said, and took Jody her drink.

He waited longer. When Julia carried mugs of coffee for him and herself into the front room he was glancing at his watch. His muffled impatience aggravated her anxiety about Jack. Surely he was coming home, but how far did Jack have to drive? Pete gulped the last of his coffee and thumped the carpet with the mug, and peeled back his cuff again to consult his watch. 'What do you think, Jody? Shall we?'

'Aren't we waiting for Laura's dad?'

'We could wait for ever at this rate.' He gave Julia an apologetic smile. 'Julia can tell him.'

'Whatever you say,' Julia said, willing him to come to the point.

'You remember last time you were at the Experience.'

'It was lovely.'

'Are you listening, Laura?' Jody said.

Laura looked up from her Get Well Soon card, which depicted a clown with his leg in traction. 'I am now.'

'You remember getting a bill we didn't want you to pay,' Pete said.

'We would have,' Julia assured him.

Pete shook his head. 'Do you remember something else, Laura?'

'What about?'

'That night.'

'You telling my dad about the job at our school.'

'You're right, that was then too. I don't suppose there's any

147

such thing as a perfect day,' Pete said to Julia, and seemed about to apologise for reminding her when Laura cried 'The competition you said our bill was going in.'

'Yes,' Jody responded at the same pitch.

'You mean we've—'

'You're the lucky winners,' Pete said. 'Your bill was the one that came out of the hat. You've won yourselves a holiday in Greece.'

'Crete,' Laura said as though she were dreaming.

'We thought that might be where you'd want to go.'

Julia felt light-headed, almost drunk. 'That's wonderful, Pete. Just what we needed. How many people is it for?'

'All three of you, of course.'

'It was always for three people?'

'It might have been up to four, depending how many there were on the bill. So you've saved us some money,' he said with an exaggerated wink.

'I don't know how we can thank you, Pete.'

'You just did,' he said, nodding at Laura, and stood up. 'I really have to go. I'm only sorry I couldn't see Jack's face. I'll be giving you a voucher for the travel agent. Look after yourselves in the meantime.'

Jody lingered until he reminded her she had school homework. As she headed uphill while Pete made for the seafront the Orchards stayed at the gate as if doing so might conjure up Jack. When a wind started the For Sale sign creaking Julia said 'Let's go inside. Better keep warm.'

She couldn't help wishing she had heard from Pete before Jack had called; then she would have been able to tell him she knew a secret which he had to come home to learn. She didn't need to tempt him home, there was nowhere else for him. She collected the mugs, and was running hot water into them from the kitchen tap when Laura shouted 'Here's Dad.'

Julia heard the engine die as she turned off the tap. Laura's footsteps hobbled to the front door. By the time Julia reached the threshold Laura was at the van and pulling at Jack's door with both hands. 'Dad, you've got to be happy or we won't tell you our news.'

148

He stared at her as though he wasn't quite sure what he was seeing. He jumped down so suddenly that she almost lost her balance. 'Is this happy?' he said, going pop-eyed and sticking his fingers in the corners of his mouth to produce a toothy grin. 'How about this?' he said and started prancing around the van, lifting his knees high and slapping them each time they came up. 'Am I happy yet? Am I a happy?' he cried, sticking his tongue through his fixed grin and lolling his head from shoulder to shoulder.

Laura giggled and glanced about in case the neighbours saw him. 'Dad . . .'

Julia caught up with him on the far side of the van from Laura. 'Jack, don't spoil it for her.'

He halted, breathing hard, and leaned against the vehicle. When his eyes returned to normal and his tongue retreated between his lips his face appeared to be collapsing. 'Why, is there something to spoil?'

'Let Laura tell you.' As he mopped his forehead Julia said 'You'll be all right, won't you? Can I help?'

'No, no,' he said, so fast it sounded like stammering, and capered around the van to Laura. 'Ready as I'll ever be.'

'Dad, what do you think? We're going to Crete.'

'What, now? That's an idea.'

'Not now, silly. In the summer holidays. We've won the competition at the restaurant.'

'All three of us, Jack,' Julia said, putting both arms around his waist and resting her chin on his shoulder.

'But we didn't pay. I don't see how . . .' He seemed stunned and confused. He lurched against her, then abruptly straightened up. 'When did you hear?'

'Pete and Jody have only this minute gone.'

'Did he say when they made the draw?'

'Sometime today, I imagine. I shouldn't think they waited long to come and tell us. Does it matter?'

Jack squeezed his eyes shut. 'I'm trying to work out when our luck changed,' he said, and swayed against her. 'My God, is that what it takes?'

'I know what you mean.'

149

'What are you doing inside my head?'

He'd straightened again and was staring at her. 'All it took was for the Venables to pick us. Try and calm down, Jack,' she said, glimpsing Laura's disappointed expression as the girl went into the house, and wrinkled her nose. 'Do you want to get changed? You smell of where you've been.'

He recoiled, flapping his hands at himself, his face twisting into a disgusted grin. 'How's that?'

'Don't worry, Jack, I can't smell any fancy woman's perfume. Just petrol and smoke. Was something on fire?'

He grasped the handle on the driver's side as if he meant to climb into the van. 'My bridges,' he said wildly.

'Jack, if there's anything you need to tell me you can, whatever it is.'

'I'd never do anything to hurt either of you.'

'That's one thing you don't need to tell me,' Julia said, and wondered if he had meant it as some kind of answer, his ensuing silence was so protracted. At last he mumbled 'But I'd do anything I thought I had to for you.'

'I really don't think you need to do any more just now except be with us.'

He hadn't let go of the van. He was staring across the mounds of the Crazy Golf course at smoke bulging from the funnel of a tanker on the bay. Suddenly, dismayingly, she wondered if she knew why he wasn't looking at her. 'Jack, you didn't go after the Evans boys, did you?'

'No.'

'I wasn't suggesting you should have. Let the law take care of them and we'll take care of one another.' She shouldn't have asked, she thought; reminding him of the Evanses seemed to have made him feel helpless. 'If by burning your bridges you meant giving up the shop and going back into libraries, you ought to know I couldn't be happier. I'm sure it's best for all of us.'

She let him gaze at the creeping smoke for a few seconds, then she said 'Are you going to let Laura see how pleased you are for her?'

He seized on that as if the idea had only just reached him.

'I should,' he said, and blundered up the path, dragging his sweater over his head.

He seemed revived. It wasn't long before he came downstairs bearing the clothes he'd changed out of and the contents of the washing basket, and he would have stuffed all this indiscriminately into the machine if Julia hadn't stopped him. 'They aren't that urgent,' she said.

'You know me, Square Eyes Orchard. I'd watch an hour of water if the telly wasn't working,' he said, gazing expectantly at the machine until she had to laugh and load his smelly clothes in. 'That's great,' he said to Laura. 'Really great, going to Crete. Really Crete. Really Greek. I'm chuffed that you'll be going after all.'

'You'll be coming too.'

'Will I? There's always a drawback.' He grinned at her with one side of his face. 'Don't mind me. Just a clown with too much patter. You know clowns aren't supposed to talk. Tell you what, why don't we go and say thank you and see what nationality the Venables are now.'

'I've already made dinner, Jack,' Julia protested. 'We can go and celebrate at the weekend. It'll wait.'

'Hope so. Where's your tape?' he asked Laura.

When he calmed down sufficiently to make it clear that he meant Jody's, she fetched it and her player from her bedroom. As the bouzouki music filled the front room he sat and gazed from the window as if he could see Greece. Only his head moved, turning to watch the occasional car that passed along the darkening street. A car slowed as it approached the house, and Jack rose into a stiff crouch above the chair, but the car was giving way to another vehicle. Their brake lights glared red, and then they were past. 'Not for us,' he said, sinking into the chair.

'It's a bit late for house-hunters,' Julia said.

'Later than you think,' he said, and added quickly 'Not than Laura thinks. She thinks it's time for dinner.'

At first he picked at his food, then he began to eat as though he were miming hunger. Between mouthfuls he announced what was visible in the window of the machine –

'Trousers now showing ... And now the eight o'clock socks ... The sweater wins the marathon ... Will the sock find its long-lost twin? Tune in next week' – until he saw that Laura still found laughing painful. Once the machine had churned to a halt he started the Greek tape again, and they sat in the front room, Laura exploring the Cretan guidebook in search of places to visit. Just before nine o'clock he stood up. 'There's an old comedy show I want to hear,' he said. 'I'll listen in the van.'

'It's all right, Dad, I'll turn the music off.'

He was already in the hall. 'We don't want you laughing and hurting yourself,' he called back.

Julia could only assume that he found the broadcast disappointing, because less than ten minutes later she heard the slide and slam of the van door. 'I don't think Dad believes it yet,' Laura said.

True enough, as he came up the path Jack looked bemused, as if he didn't quite dare to trust their luck. 'He'll get used to it,' Julia assured her. 'Don't turn the tape over, love. I think we'll all be early to bed.'

Laura headed for the bathroom as Jack closed the front door. 'Wasn't it much fun?' Julia asked him.

'What?' he said, so sharply that it sounded like an exclamation.

'The comedy.'

'I don't think I know what's funny any more.'

He sounded as if he didn't know how he felt at all, and so she went to him. 'It's real, that's what matters,' she said. 'What happened is real.'

'I'll stake my life on that,' he said. 'God, what a joke.'

If she was unable to grasp what he was saying, that mightn't be his fault; the last two days were catching up with her. 'Do you feel like going to bed yet?'

'You go ahead. I'll be here,' he said, sliding past her into the front room.

She took her time over preparing for bed, hoping he might follow, but when she slipped between the chilly sheets he was still downstairs. Sleep began to jumble the jigsaw of her senses

152

and her thoughts and widen the gaps between them. Once she almost wakened, hearing the radio downstairs playing the jingle which heralded the local news, and some time later she felt Jack beside her, sitting up as though to listen for some sound outside the house. Nobody could have been outside, since Julia went back to sleep.

Jack's snoring wakened her. She might go to the office when he'd slept enough. She eased herself out of bed and had a shower that confirmed she felt refreshed. She was turning it off when the doorbell rang. 'Can you see who it is, Laura?' she said from the top of the stairs.

Laura was hesitating between the stairs and the front door. 'It's a policeman,' she said.

NINETEEN

For Laura the worst moments had been at the hospital: worse than being dragged off her bicycle by her hair, worse than the punches which had felt like being hit with bricks, worse even than the shame and dismay she'd experienced at the thought that her parents would see the state she was in as she'd lain on the bench. Being accused by the mother of her attackers had been horrible enough, but then Laura had thought that one or both of her own parents had been about to attack the woman, and that would have been worst of all. If they weren't in control of themselves, if they could turn into people she didn't know and mightn't want to know, then nothing was to be trusted; anything could happen to her life.

It seemed strange that her own rage didn't disturb her half so much. When she'd lashed out at the boys on the promenade her fury had been indistinguishable from panic until one of her kicks had connected, and then her emotions had instantly changed from being uncontrollable into a possible means of taking control. The way the eldest boy had doubled up as her kick had landed between his legs had encouraged her to grab the leader by his crotch, and twist, and keep twisting until he'd let go of her hair. If she hadn't attempted to climb on her bicycle and ride it away, if she had flung it at them to slow them down, she might have escaped. All the same, the memory of how the boy had screamed as the contents of his scrotum ground together in her fist had gone some way towards compensating her for all the aches and unpredictable sharp pains that had kept her awake in bed.

Now she had the prospect of the holiday in Crete as

compensation too, and it was more than enough. Surely it would make up for what had happened to her as far as her parents were concerned, once her father got over the shock of their good luck. Grown-ups weren't supposed to be at the mercy of their feelings; surely learning not to be was part of growing up. Sometimes she felt at the mercy of hers, but that was meant to be just a phase of her life. Last night she had slept soundly, enveloped in a sense that their win had surrounded her and her parents with good luck, and this morning she was first out of bed.

Her ankle, on which the eldest boy had trampled as a parting shot when she was lying on the tarmac, still hurt if she put her weight on it, but not as much. Her face felt slightly less like a stiff lumpy unfamiliar mask. She limped to the bathroom and saw that the livid colours of her bruises had begun to fade. At least she could open her empurpled eye. She filled the bath and lowered herself carefully into the water, her ribs and arms and legs twingeing, and lay for a while dreaming she was in the Sea of Crete, kicking her uninjured leg gently to create waves. When a chill crept into the water she dried herself and got dressed.

Her parents were asleep. She thought of waking them with a mug of coffee each, but decided to wait until she heard them beginning to stir. She sat in the front room and leafed through Jody's guidebook. Even the names seemed magical – Knossos, Aghios Nikolaos, Heraklion, Minos Tava – and she could almost believe that their magic had altered the family's luck. She heard someone go into the bathroom, and the sound of the shower reminded her of the hoses at her father's shop. As the sound dwindled, she glimpsed a policeman passing the house. The latch of the gate clicked, and then the doorbell rang.

Laura was limping into the hall when her mother came out of the bathroom, clutching a towel around herself. 'Can you see who it is, Laura?'

Laura could distinguish his cap, patterned like a licorice allsort, through the frosted glass. 'It's a policeman.'

'See what he wants, love, would you? I'll be down as soon

155

as I wriggle into something,' her mother said, and tiptoed into the bedroom.

Laura felt reluctant, though she couldn't have said why: policeman were supposed to be your friends. She used her limp as an excuse to go slowly to the door, and when she inched it open she saw Jackie Pether's father. For a moment she wanted to laugh. He always affected her that way, his face so resembled a little kid's drawing, the pale prim mouth a fraction too low on it, the mousy brown eyes an inch too close to the hairline that was hidden by the cap, the small nose stranded between the other features; she couldn't imagine him arresting anyone. Perhaps he sensed that, because he looked uncomfortable and all the more determined to perform his duty. 'Is your father in, Laura?' he said.

'I think he's asleep.'

His expression set firmer. 'Your mother?'

'She's just getting up. Getting dressed, I mean. She says you're to come in,' Laura decided, and stepped back as far as the front room.

He glanced along the hall and up the stairs as he trod into the house. Perhaps policemen were trained to scrutinise everywhere they went, but he was suggesting to Laura that there was something she ought to have noticed in the house. 'In here?' he said, taking off his cap and pointing into the front room with it as his brownish hair wavered erect like trampled grass.

He picked up the guidebook from the nearest armchair and sat down, dropping the book beside the chair and folding his hands over the cap on his lap. 'Shall I get you a drink?' Laura said.

'No thank you.'

She waited for him to add 'Not while I'm on duty', which would make her feel even more as though they were acting out a scene from some old film, but he only stared at his cap and drummed his fingers on its flat crown. It occurred to Laura that he must be especially uncomfortable about the reason for his visit, otherwise surely he would have asked how she was feeling. She stooped to retrieve the guidebook and sucked in a hiss as a pain revived in her side, and was sinking into the other armchair when Mr Pether said 'Jackie was wondering when you'll be back at school.'

No doubt Jackie meant that more slyly than he made it sound. 'Jody brought me some homework,' Laura said.

'And a card from all your friends, I hear.'

He was beginning to annoy Laura, too much so for her to bother being tactful. 'And Jackie,' she said.

He either didn't understand or was pretending not to have heard. He turned his cap over and peered inside it like a magician who'd forgotten a trick, and Laura had had enough of him. She turned the pages of the guidebook, unable to concentrate, until she heard footsteps coming downstairs.

When he saw her mother Mr Pether's expression rearranged itself in a way Laura couldn't grasp. 'Oh, it's you, Mr Pether. Laura didn't say,' her mother said. 'What can I do for you?'

'Is your husband available?'

'He's sleeping the sleep of the just. Will I do?'

'So long as you're present while I take a statement from Laura.'

'Is that all? You sounded as if it was something – I don't know.'

For a second Laura was certain that there was more to his visit. 'Would you like a hot cup?' her mother asked him.

'I've already refused one, thank you,' he said, and taking out his notebook, turned to Laura. 'Your full name is.'

If he was going to do his policeman act she thought he should put on his cap. 'Laura Orchard,' she said.

He gave her a look as though he knew better, and she saw that he'd caught her out. 'Laura Julia,' she said, feeling obscurely disloyal. 'Mummy used to say she'd lent me her name in case I wanted it when I was older.'

He started writing then, using a ballpoint bandaged with adhesive tape. 'Do you know your date of birth?'

'Of course I do. Doesn't Jackie know hers? The second of February nineteen-seventy-eight.'

'Just after midnight or just before,' her mother added,

'depending on whose watch you believed.'

He frowned at his pen before writing Laura's date, but that was the whole of his response to her mother. He raised his head then and pointed the pen at Laura's face as if she might need to be reminded of its appearance. 'Tell me in your own words what happened.'

Whose words did he think she was going to use? Presumably he was warning her mother not to interrupt. Laura couldn't help resenting his insistence that her mother had to be there – it made her feel much younger than she was, and besides, what she had to say was bound to upset her mother. At least telling it seemed more like a story which had happened to someone else, and she tried to convey that feeling to her mother. When Laura had finished, Mr Pether read her what he'd written, not her words but a summary of them. 'Is that what you say happened?'

'That is what happened,' her mother said.

He gazed at Laura with ostentatious patience. 'Yes,' Laura said.

'It isn't only what you say, love. There's a witness.'

'He didn't see how the incident started,' Mr Pether said.

'Laura's just told you how it did. You're not suggesting anything different, are you? How else do you imagine she could have ended up like this?'

'It isn't my job to suggest anything, Mrs Orchard. However, you ought to be aware that there are conflicting stories which can't be resolved by independent testimony.'

'No, Mr Pether, there's a story and there's the truth, and I should think you know Laura well enough to judge which is which.'

'What I think doesn't matter, Mrs Orchard. Because of the lack of evidence the police are unlikely to prosecute.'

'Lack of . . .' Laura's mother gestured fiercely at her, then turned on him. 'What have those little sods been saying about her?'

He pursed his lips, then apparently thought better of rebuking her language. 'They contend that she ran over the youngest boy and trapped his fingers in the wheel. He was taken to the hospital for that, you know.'

'I do know,' Laura's mother said as if her mouth had stiffened.

'They aren't claiming she did it deliberately, you understand, only that she panicked. They say that when they tried to get her off the bicycle to free him she must have thought they meant to steal it. They had to defend themselves and their younger brother, and they admit that the situation may have got out of hand.'

'And do you believe them? Don't you dare tell me it doesn't matter what you think.'

The point of Mr Pether's pen retreated into the barrel with a click, and he slipped the pen into his pocket. 'Well, Mrs Orchard, you must recognise that girls of Laura's age can be subject to fits of hysteria. I've known Jackie lose control.'

Laura's mother was visibly shaking. 'So are you telling me those bastards, *bastards*, will go unpunished for what they did to Laura?'

Mr Pether emitted a sound very like the click of the ballpoint. 'Unless you prosecute yourself I'm afraid that may be the case, yes,' he said, and raised his eyes heavenwards. He'd heard the thud of bare feet above him. Perhaps roused by her mother's voice as it grew louder, Laura's father had got out of bed.

Mr Pether stood up, a look of blank impenetrable determination settling over his face. 'If I could have a quiet word with your husband.'

'Be as quiet as you like,' Laura's mother retorted.

He frowned while keeping the rest of his face blank. 'If I could speak to him alone.'

She called out so loudly that Mr Pether's hands jerked towards his ears. 'Company, Jack.'

Presumably she didn't trust herself to say more, but Laura thought she should at least have said it was the police. She listened to her father's footsteps hesitating overhead – he must be putting on a dressing-gown. Then the bedroom door creaked squeakily open and he padded down the stairs.

Laura pushed herself out of her chair and limped to the

159

door just as her father reached the hall. With his unbrushed hair and bare feet he looked vulnerable, and less than awake. 'Dad,' she said, 'it's—'

He was gazing past her, and at once he was fully awake. 'I can see who it is.'

She had the disconcerting impression that he was doing his best to imitate the policeman's blank look. 'May I have a word with you?' Mr Pether said.

'I understand. Do you want me to come with you?'

Laura wondered if finding a policeman in the house had thrown him so badly he meant to go out before he was dressed, though Mr Pether seemed to think her father was having a joke at his expense. 'That won't be necessary,' he said grimly, 'if we can be left alone.'

Laura's mother threw him a furious glance. 'Come along, Laura. It sounds as though our place is in the kitchen.'

Laura trudged after her as her father stepped into the front room. She wanted to hear what they said, especially since she assumed it would be about her. She closed the door behind her, but not quite, and pretended to shut the kitchen door. The sound of it started the policeman talking. 'Well, Mr Orchard, you seem to know why I'm here. Have you anything to say to me?'

'What would you like me to say?'

From where she stood just inside the kitchen Laura could hear every word. Her mother had sat down with her back to her and was breathing slow and hard. After a couple of breaths she looked over her shoulder, dabbing at her eyes. 'Laura,' she said as though she was addressing someone half Laura's age, 'sit down.'

She was turning her anger on Laura, which was unfair. 'Perhaps you should tell me about the fire,' Laura heard the policeman say. 'I want to hear,' she whispered, blinking back tears.

Her mother seemed to focus on her. 'All right, we'll listen,' she murmured, and cocked her head towards the door.

'The fire,' the policeman was saying, 'and more to the point, your victim.'

'How is he?' Laura's father said.

'As well as can be expected. No better for your behaviour afterwards.'

'My—'

'It could be described as harassment, Mr Orchard.'

There was a silence that seemed to express Laura's bewilderment and her mother's. 'Is that bad?' her father said.

'When someone of that age is the victim it most certainly is. Making a fool of him in public is no joke.'

'I'm not laughing.'

'I should hope not. I understand he was led to believe you would buy him a new pair of shoes.'

Laura's mother goggled at her with a mixture of incredulity and comprehension. 'You may well look taken aback, Mr Orchard,' the policeman said. 'Perhaps you were hoping that had been forgotten, but my father isn't as confused as you may have assumed.'

'I'm glad to hear it.'

'You surprise me. Well?'

'What do you have in mind?'

Mr Pether paused before responding. 'I believe a thorough apology would be in order, and you might think a pair of shoes would be as well. Of course you must be guided by your conscience.'

'If that's what it takes.'

There was another protracted silence, then Laura heard the policeman tramp into the hall. 'Mr Pether's father lost a shoe during the fire at the shop,' Laura's mother mouthed at her.

She was obviously angered by what she saw as the policeman's unjust attitude, but the news came as a relief to Laura. It must have been Jackie Pether's grandfather who had been hopping about with one shoe on, not her own father at all. She heard the front door open, and her mother shoved the bench away from the table and went swiftly into the hall. 'Excuse me, Mr Pether, but I couldn't help overhearing. You ought to realise it was partly your father who caused the fire at the shop.'

161

Laura's father gave her a smile so radiant he might have been trying to suppress it until the policeman was out of the way. 'Let it go, Julia. I don't mind sorting things out with the old man. The more people I can bring good fortune to the happier I'll be.'

Mr Pether closed the gate and looked back. 'I'll look forward to hearing that you've done what's necessary.'

Laura's mother glared after him. 'You shouldn't have let him go, Jack. I don't know how he dared accuse you after he'd just told us that the police won't touch the boys who hurt Laura.'

'Won't they? Well, I don't suppose we can do much about that. Maybe bad luck will catch up with the Evanses, or maybe they behave that way because they aren't as lucky as us.'

Laura's mother looked stubborn, unwilling to be placated. 'If that's the best the law can do ...'

'Forget the law. We don't need it,' he said, so like a criminal that Laura giggled. For a moment he looked bemused, then he laughed, nudging Julia, widening his eyes and mouth until he resembled a clown. 'That's it, Laura,' he said. 'We won't go far wrong if we can laugh.'

TWENTY

When the doorbell rang on Monday morning Jack was alone in the house. It was Laura's first day back at school, and Julia was at work. As he shaved he gazed at himself in the bathroom mirror. This was the face of a man about to start a new job, and he thought it looked pretty impressive: alert, ready for anything. He was pleased to discover he'd forgotten none of the classification numbers which he would find on the spines of books. He played with them while the cool wet metal slid over his throat, and was surprised to realise that he couldn't think of even one that added up to either eleven or thirteen. Then the doorbell rang, and he dabbed shaving cream off the unshaven half of his face and went to see who was there.

It couldn't be the police – they had already visited the house, in the shape of Pether – but the man on the front path had the look of some kind of official. He was gripping a clipboard under one arm and tapping his small even teeth with the blunt end of a pencil as he peered at the bedroom window. 'Double glazing,' Jack guessed aloud.

The man took his time over lowering his gaze and then said 'Mr Orchard.'

'I was last time I looked,' Jack said, and assumed he knew why the man seemed bothered by his face. 'The chin? Just call me Two-Face. Safety in numbers, I always say.'

The man knocked on the clipboard with the pencil as though calling a meeting to order. 'You put in an insurance claim.'

'For a bicycle, you mean. You wouldn't have found it up there.'

163

'I'm the adjuster,' the man said, brandishing the clipboard.

'Just a what?' Jack heard his old self say, but he was in control. 'Come in. What shall I show you besides a leg? You'll excuse my informality. I'd have dressed if I'd known you were coming,' he said.

The loss adjuster halted as soon as he was over the threshold, and having scrutinised the hall-stand as though he was looking for evidence of an intruder in his own house, made a note on the topmost sheet on the clipboard. 'I should like to start upstairs,' he said, so curtly that Jack could only think he was concealing shyness.

'Whatever turns you on.'

When the adjuster reached the upper floor he darted into the bathroom as if he needed to use it rather than examine it. He lifted a bath-towel and peered at the radiator, he slid back the mirrors to take stock of the cupboard, he noted the electric ventilator in the wall beside the window, he even craned over the bath. If he lifted the lid of the toilet, Jack thought, he was in for a surprise, since for the last few days Jack's morning productions called for several flushings to carry them away. Instead the adjuster stooped to the label of a perfume bottle which Laura had left by the sink, then he walked at Jack and opened the next door. 'That's my daughter's room,' Jack said.

Though he hadn't meant that as a prohibition, the adjuster's manner suggested that he was ignoring one. When he shook his head at the state of the bedroom – clothes planning a mass escape from the chest of drawers, bottles and jewellery and souvenir ornaments and seashells strewn across the dressing-table as though left behind by a tide, books bunched in every conceivable position on the shelves – Jack felt unexpectedly affectionate towards the chaos. He watched as the adjuster prowled, sounding a terse hum in his throat whenever he found something else to note on the clipboard. When the adjuster began to count Laura's tapes, waving his pencil above them, Jack said 'Some of those belong to her friends.'

'And she's lent some of her own, no doubt.'

'Have you any children?'

Jack was trying to be friendly, but the adjuster seemed to feel criticised. 'I've thirteen years' experience in my job.'

'I should have known,' Jack said as the adjuster opened the wardrobe and pushed hangers back and forth. If the man were to pull any drawers open, Jack looked forward to his struggles to replace all their contents. Perhaps the adjuster couldn't face the prospect, because he strode abruptly towards Jack as if to catch him out somehow. As soon as they were in the front bedroom Jack said 'While you're occupied I may as well get dressed.'

The man twitched his shoulders twice and hastened to the wardrobe. Jack hung his dressing-gown on the door and lifting his penis in one hand, aimed it at the back of the adjuster's head, mouthing 'Don't give us any trouble. This is loaded.'

If he had still been his old self he would undoubtedly have done that just in time for the man to see him in the dressing-table mirror. But the man seemed determined not even to glimpse him, performing such a dance around the room in order to keep his back to him that Jack felt like a puppet-master. He pulled on socks and underpants and trousers and a sweater before taking pity on him. 'Just my feet are in their underwear now if you can bear to look.'

The adjuster glanced in the mirror as he rifled Julia's jewellery box, but all he said was 'Your wife would be well advised not to leave this where it can be seen.'

'I expect she was thinking of you.'

The adjuster made a note on his clipped sheet and swung towards the door. 'I don't know what you feel you'll gain from making my job harder.'

'I wasn't aware that I was.'

As Jack reached the stairs the shoe whose lace he hadn't yet tied flew off and delivered a kick to the man's scalp. At least, Jack saw that happening to his old self as he tied his shoelaces before hurrying down to the adjuster, who was tapping his pencil on the clipboard in a variety of rhythms. 'Use the phone if you like,' Jack said. 'No need to resort to Morse.'

'What do you mean?'

'Just that you've no reason to be nervous of me that I know of.'

In the kitchen the adjuster opened all the cupboards and drawers, squinted into the oven, crouched to look into the freezer. 'How old is this?' he asked, contemplating a clump of Lawson's sausages.

Jack wasn't to be caught so easily. 'Nearly six years old, the freezer.'

'Not that that's relevant,' the adjuster said with what could have been suppressed triumph. 'You're meant to be insured for the cost of a replacement.'

'Then we must be.'

'I rather fear I may have to report you aren't fully covered.'

Jack leaned against the kitchen door and rested one hand on a gas tap. 'Why would you want to do that?'

'It isn't a question of what I want, Mr Orchard,' the adjuster said brusquely, squatting to look under the sink.

'Can't take the responsibility, eh? It isn't there, it's in the van,' Jack said, only just aloud.

The adjuster rose to his feet and glanced sharply at him. 'I wouldn't play with that.'

'Nor would I,' Jack said, holding onto the gas tap for several seconds before letting go.

The adjuster ducked into the cupboard under the stairs and greeted the contents with a muffled sneeze. When he emerged, eyes watering, he looked more irritable than ever. He darted into the front room and continued to make notes, sniffing as if in disapproval of the computer, the armchairs, the table. He halted in front of the carton by the television. 'How much are these worth?'

'Not a lot. They're old black and whites. Keystone Kops, that sort of thing.'

In fact there were no Keystone films among the cassettes, but Jack saw the uniformed figures dashing back and forth, squirting one another and tripping over hoses as the victim they were supposed to extinguish performed a frantic dance. 'I understand that the older the film,' the adjuster said, 'the

166

harder it is to replace.'

'That depends. Anyway, you needn't let it bother you. Those aren't my cassettes. A friend lent them to me overnight to see if I wanted to buy any of them.'

They weren't insured. Jack hadn't increased the amount of the house insurance since he had taken over Fine Films, and previously Gavin had kept them at his own house overnight. Whatever happened now, the adjuster wasn't going to leave until he accepted Jack's assurance about the cassettes. Jack thought that so clearly he wouldn't have been amazed to learn it had been overheard, and in a moment the adjuster raised his head from examining the carton and stared at him. 'I'm afraid, Mr Orchard—'

Don't say it, don't be afraid, Jack thought, afraid for him. 'Here's the owner now,' he said.

Andy Nation had just passed the house. Jack rapped on the window with the knuckles of both hands, but Andy was already on the far side of the road. Jack ran out onto the path, leaving doors open behind him. 'Were you coming to see me, Andy?' he called.

'Hello there, old pip. Should I be? Nothing wrong besides what those lunatics did to Laura, is there?'

'Nothing at all. As a matter of fact, I've a man from the insurance company in the house now checking everything's insured before they stump up for a new bike. I was just wondering if you were here to pick up the videos you lent me.'

'I'm on my way to fetch a drill from where I left it and then I'm off back to a job. There won't be any problem, will there? Let me have a word with him.'

He opened the gate and strode into the house before Jack had a chance to say more. As Jack followed him into the front room Andy was already saying 'How do, Mr Policy. Treating his kid to a new bike, are you? She deserves one after all she's been through, kids bigger than her beating her up and turning her Christmas present into scrap.'

'Andy—'

'Sorry, old pip. Got carried away for a moment. There they

167

are. Those are my videos.'

The adjuster stared hard at him. 'You lent them to Mr Orchard yesterday, I understand.'

'That's what I did.'

'Rather a lot of films for anyone to watch in one evening.'

Jack opened his mouth, but Andy was too quick for him. 'He was just seeing if there were any he could use to cheer his kid up. That's what she needs, I can tell you. Any of them take her fancy, Jack?'

'One or two.'

'Don't be shy. It's not as if they're worth much. Nobody wants black and white these days,' Andy said to the adjuster. 'You wouldn't buy a colour licence if you were colour-blind.'

'You deal in videocassettes, do you, Mr . . .'

'I'm into everything. I've a job waiting now if you'll excuse me. See you, Jack. Pleasure meeting you, Mr Policy, if I've been some help.'

He left as swiftly as he'd entered. The sound of himself and the adjuster being shut in by the front door made Jack feel purposeful and strong. 'Have you reached your conclusion?' he said.

The adjuster was leafing through the pages on the clipboard. He let them drop and slid the pencil between the board and the clip. 'It may be possible for me to recommend payment of your claim.'

'When should I expect to hear? It isn't me who's impatient, it's my daughter. You are when you're twelve.'

The adjuster sounded a last brief hum in his throat. 'I shall be making my report within the next few days.'

Jack opened the door and released him. The scene with Andy couldn't have gone better if it had been rehearsed. He felt surrounded by good luck. He wasn't waking much in the nights any more, and when he did it was only astonishment that was waiting for him in the dark, astonishment at himself and what he'd done to ensure the family's good fortune. He finished shaving and put on a coat and made sure the house was secure, and climbed into the van.

He would be early for work. As he drove along the

168

promenade, the marine horizon put him in mind of the start of an endless voyage. Turning onto the motorway felt like following that promise. He sped for twenty minutes beside fields planted with a few token animals, then he drove down the Ellesmere Port ramp.

It brought him to fire and water. A ship canal began to imitate the river and then refused to follow its meanderings; metal chimneys tipped with fires that looked Olympic towered above the meeting of the waters. 'That's what the world needs,' Jack said, and after a moment thought what he meant: 'Balance.' He drove over a bridge which carried lamps across water, through several sets of flashing amber lights, and into the library car park.

The library appeared to be intended to recall the thirties, though the inlet of a drainpipe was dated 1961. It was a squarish two-storey brick building, fronted by a bay one storey too tall for the revolving door it housed, and attached at the back by a stubby passage to an octagonal extension of concrete and glass. As he passed through the barrel of doors he felt that he was returning to somewhere he had never really left. If you ventured as far as you could, he thought, you would end up where you started from.

He had to grin. The place was staffed by people alongside whom he might have worked during his library career – two humorous young women, a bespectacled man of thirty or so with a permanent wry expression, a branch librarian twenty-ish years older and well on the way to baldness, which made his chubby solemn face seem to be reverting to babyhood. When he shook hands his grip felt like a handful of dough. 'Let me show you where your coat goes,' he said, 'and then please feel free until one.'

'I'll be getting to know the lie of the land.'

The revolving doors had ushered Jack into a video library, beyond which the passage that connected the two sections of the building led to books, as though the whole represented his recent career. The library had eleven sides if you counted those linked by the passage as one, and he would be starting work at the hour of thirteen. 'It fits,' he said under his breath.

From a staircase carpeted in rubber he saw narrow terraced streets beyond a bus station where the shelters appeared to be roofed with blue Lego and the buses were so various that the terminus resembled a transport museum. The upper floor of the octagon contained the reference library beneath a ceiling panelled like a sauna's. He smelled the dry heat from the screen of the microfilm reader just inside the entrance as he headed for the newspapers, which were scattered over several tables barely wide enough to accommodate two people. Each table was divided by a wooden bar about two inches high – not, Jack thought, unlike tables in a prison visiting-room. As he sat down, having collected all the papers that weren't being read, he felt as though someone should be sitting on the far side of the table to balance him: perhaps Jack Awkward, his old self. He tapped the pack of giant floppy playing-cards that were newspapers into line against the table top and began to leaf through them.

He found nothing that concerned him in any of the national newspapers. Even the Merseyside papers weren't making as much of the story as they had last week. According to the *Liverpool Daily Post* the hunt for the killer was continuing, and police were working on the assumption that it must have been someone with a grudge against the victim, which seemed fair enough to Jack. If the papers closest to home were also closest to the truth about the investigation, however, he had to laugh. Between them the Wirral newspapers depicted Jeremy Alston as a pillar of the community, mourned by his many friends who were appalled by his death and by the manner of it, loved by his pupils and his employees at the riding school. If the papers and presumably the police could be so wrong about the victim, Jack felt confident that the police would have no luck in their search.

HESWALL STILL REELING AFTER STABLES MURDER ... POLICE HUNT BLOWTORCH KILLER ... Entire village in state of shock ... Village locks its doors as soon as night begins to fall ... 'Nobody walks on the murder road alone,' Jack murmured. 'After dark nothing is heard there but the whinny of a lonely horse.' There seemed no point in being dishonest

170

about the way the parade of clichés and inaccuracies affected him. As for the metamorphosis of Alston, perhaps you couldn't have a monster without first representing the victim as sympathetic. Perhaps, Jack thought, he'd at last given the public what they wanted without his realising he had. As for himself, he felt as if his new poised personality was settling into him.

You could adjust to anything. His encounter with Jeremy Alston and its aftermath seemed as unreal now as the newspaper reports. He remembered everything as though he'd watched it on a screen – even his panic as he'd driven away down the deserted coast road, his mind feeling seared and trapped between an urge to drive until the engine ran dry and a yearning to speak to Julia. Underlying both and growing had been a wild astonishment. There was more to him than anyone had suspected, including himself.

He'd done what he had to for the family. It had taken him days to accept that it had worked, days where the minutes had sometimes felt like hours of lying awake in darkness, but now that he was convinced, he thought it would be wholly unreasonable for the family's good luck to be ruined by his being tracked down by the police. He stood up and distributed the newspapers among the tables and went downstairs to start his new career. What he owed the world now was a good day's work.

TWENTY-ONE

On the night of the presentation at the International Experience Laura spent twenty minutes making up her face and then washed off the make-up. The more she put on, the more it looked as though her face was something to hide. The bruises had mostly faded except for marks which could almost have been traces of face-paint around her eye. She brushed her hair, which didn't take long since she'd had nearly all of it cut off so that nobody else could use it against her. She adjusted the straps of her party dress and craned over her bare shoulders to see in the mirror that no bruises were visible on them; then she disentangled a denim jacket from the pile of clothes at the end of the bed and slinging it over her shoulder with a finger hooked through the tag, went to find her parents.

They were in the front room, her father turning the pages of a library book by someone called Thorne Smith, her mother pretending to read the local paper. Both of them smiled at Laura, though her mother's smile seemed to conceal a momentary distress of the kind she'd attempted to hide when Laura had come home with her hair cropped. 'Do you think you'll be all right like that?' her mother said.

'Nobody's going to be surprised how I look, Mummy, since it was in the paper.'

It was there on the page her mother had folded open: VICTIM OF PROMENADE ASSAULT WINS HOLIDAY. 'I didn't mean that,' her mother said, perhaps too readily. 'Are you sure you'll be warm enough later?'

'In this heat? I should think so,' her father said. 'And if it's cold on the way home we can run and skip and dance.'

'That would be a revelation,' Laura's mother said, 'you dancing.'

'Give me a banana skin and I'll glide all over the dance floor.'

Laura's mother stuck out her tongue at him. 'If you're sure you're ready,' she said to Laura.

Perhaps she didn't mean ready to be put on show, but Laura thought she did. 'I don't mind if it helps Jody's parents.'

Laura's mother took her hand once they were past the gate, her father claimed the other as they reached the seafront, and Laura felt as though she was weighing hands, her mother's cool and slim and determinedly firm, her father's hot and rough. She let them guide her while she gazed across the bay, where the sun had reached the water. Long bars of cloud stretched parallel to the horizon, their gold fading and blurred as if painted with an almost dry brush, while above them the sky was a mass of folds of copper. The sun flared between the bars, and for a moment a swathe of the bay blazed like oil. Then a line of streetlamps lit up, drawing her attention to the promenade, where cars crowned with the names of driving schools were venturing around the round-abouts, kindling their brake lights. She remembered watching the learners on the last day she'd had her bicycle, and gripped her parents' hands before she knew she meant to do so. 'Never mind,' her father said, 'it won't be long before you're on your wheels again.'

She felt her mother's fingers flex uneasily. 'I'll be all right, Mummy, really I will. I know where not to go by myself.'

'There shouldn't be any such places. There weren't when I was your age.'

'The world has always been more violent than we like to think,' Laura's father said mildly.

'Maybe, but she oughtn't to have found that out at her age.'

'Mummy, at least now I know I can defend myself. Jody and some of my other friends were saying we should join a class and learn how to do it properly.'

Her mother kissed her forehead, hard enough to hurt. 'I'm

proud of you, you know that. I just haven't caught up with you yet, that's all.'

'The world isn't so bad. There are plenty of good people. The man from the insurance turned out to be one, didn't he? And here are some more waiting for us,' her father said as they crossed the restaurant car park.

Jody ran to open the door for them, and several people came to meet them: not only Jody's parents but a red-faced young man wearing a suit whose lapels were each almost as wide as his head, and a dumpy photographer bearing his stomach and the snout of his camera several inches before him. 'Is this the lucky girl?' the photographer boomed in a Father Christmas voice.

'Let them take their coats off at least,' Jody's mother said, and having handed the garments to Jody to hang up, ushered the Orchards to a table by the window. 'We didn't realise the paper was going to pick up the story about Laura,' she murmured. 'If you'd rather we gave the prize to you or Jack, Julia, you know we'll understand.'

'Can't I be given it?' Laura pleaded.

'Whatever the three of you want, love. Only the reporter would like to talk to whoever it is.'

'I don't mind. I like talking.'

The grown-ups exchanged smiles like a code you learned when you were older, but Laura didn't mind that either. She ordered Montezuma's Secret from the menu which Jody's father brought her, then she gazed out at the huge electric fire on the horizon, bars of cloud fading from red to grey before merging with the night. She would have watched longer if the photographer and the reporter with the chestful of lapels hadn't come to the table. 'Forget I'm here, doll. I'll just be shooting candids,' the photographer said.

Laura glanced at her father in case he was about to make a joke, but his expression said so eloquently that he was suppressing one that she had to cover her mouth while the reporter asked his first question, or rather several of them. 'How did you feel when you heard you'd won? Were you excited? Couldn't you wait to tell your friends?'

All his questions came in bunches, and pretty soon she had the knack of interrupting before he told her what he expected her to say. Ten minutes later he left her, saying 'Thanks, sorry, enjoy' as the waitress brought the first course, and for the rest of the meal Laura might simply have been dining out, except for the way diners at neighbouring tables kept smiling at her or raising glasses of wine in her honour. By the time the waitress brought the Orchards coffee Laura felt full and rather sleepy. She had to rouse herself when Jody's father loitered near the table. 'Anything you'd like to put you in the mood?' he asked her. 'An after-dinner mint? Another drink?'

'Just the toilet.'

'I don't think Pete can bring you that,' her father said and ducked as if she might throw something at him.

When Laura emerged from the toilet cubicle she lingered in front of the mirror, feeling like an actress in a dressing-room, before she advanced into the restaurant. Now the diners were an audience. Jody's father was standing by the cashier's chest-high booth, and Jody's mother had come to meet Laura. 'Just hang on here while Pete does his spiel.'

'Ladies and gentlemen, if I can have your attention,' he called.

The blurred murmur which filled the restaurant subsided as though the sound was being turned down. A few stubborn conversations persisted at reduced volume, in the smoking area half a dozen flames sprang up to be applied to cigarettes, and then everyone seemed to be ready. 'I'll be brief,' Jody's father said.

Laura wanted to giggle, because that was all he said. A party of latecomers had entered the restaurant. He seemed to be prepared to wait while they were seated, until Jody's mother gestured impatiently at him on Laura's behalf and he nodded at a waitress to detain the party of four inside the entrance for the duration of his speech. 'I know some of you here tonight were here when we made the draw for the first of our holiday competitions to celebrate the cuisine we were currently offering,' he said, and took a hasty breath, 'but because of circumstances the winners weren't able to be with us that evening. I'd now like to present the prize which we hope will be the first of many we'll be presenting to our customers. If I can ask you to give this young lady your biggest hand.'

Laura found herself smirking in an effort to keep her face straight, both because of the image his turn of phrase and her father's expression conjured up and because she felt more nervous than she had expected. She stepped between the tables as the diners clapped, and reached Jody's father as the applause drizzled into silence. 'Ladies and gentlemen,' he announced, 'the lucky—'

His mouth stayed open. The leader of the party by the door was shouting 'She doesn't deserve it. These do if anyone does.'

The woman pushed past the waitress, her sons following. In the subdued light she appeared to be wearing an overcoat checked like a chessboard, but no doubt it was the coat she had worn at the hospital. She stopped well short of Laura, hands on hips, and butted her head at her, almost shaking a comb loose. 'That's her who told lies to the paper. She's no victim, she's a maniac. Just look what she did to my three who were walking along minding their own business.'

The youngest boy cringed behind her while his brothers lurched forwards with a kind of crippled swagger, and Laura's stomach writhed. She wanted to run, but at once she vowed she wouldn't let them see how she felt, not them or anyone like them, not now or ever. Jody's father and two waitresses moved to block their path as Laura's parents hurried to her. 'I'm sorry,' Jody's father said to Mrs Evans, 'I'll have to ask you to—'

Her voice overwhelmed his. 'Another of her little gang, are you? Look at all the people she needs to protect her, the poor defenceless mite, I don't think. Only the police don't think she is, do they? At least *they've* a bit of fairness to them, they don't pick on a woman just because she's a widow trying to bring up three growing lads on her own. If they'd believed half of what that little liar told them they'd have thrown us all in jail.'

The diners had begun to murmur. Some of them had obviously identified her sons from the newspaper report and were passing the message to their companions. Before Mrs Evans had finished, quite a few diners were jeering at her. Laura heard shouts of 'Chuck them out' and 'Call the police.' A matronly woman in a low-cut black dress who had patted Laura's arm as she'd gone to claim her prize shied the remains of a potato at Mrs Evans' head. When her sons swung menacingly towards the woman at least four men rose to their feet, clenching their fists; one knocked a bottle off his table with a thud and stared at it as though considering it for a weapon. Either the lights had begun to flare and fuse or there was a storm overhead, but it was the flash of the photographer's camera. 'Ladies and gentlemen,' Jody's father pleaded, 'if I can just ask you—'

Laura's parents were trying to steer her back to their table. 'Look, she wants to go for me now,' Mrs Evans screeched. 'Just you keep her on her leash or I'll have the law on you. Don't think I can't afford it, either. I went to see the citizens' advice and they said there's a lawyer who'll take my case if I want to prosecute you for what you did to my boys who are all I've got to look after me in this life.'

By now several tablefuls of diners were stamping their feet or booing through their cupped hands so as to drown her voice, but that only made her raise it. Some people picked up scraps of food as if they might fling them at her, and one customer clad in a bulging waistcoat seemed to be considering going up to her and emptying over her the jug of water he was holding. The camera flashed like a storm which had yet to release its violence, illuminating the grimaces of diners, and Laura wanted to weep at the change which had overtaken her evening. Instead she struggled free of her parents and stayed where she was, folding her shaky arms.

Mrs Evans surveyed the diners with pigheaded dignity until the uproar died down somewhat. 'I've said my say,' she declared, and as the boos and stamping recommenced, dragged her elder sons towards the exit as the youngest darted out of it, letting the door swing back at her. She shoved the two boys out and glared at the Orchards. 'Enjoy your prize if your consciences will let you,' she said, and stalked out.

'Well, ladies and gentlemen,' Jody's father said with a weak smile, 'how can I follow that? The lucky winners, Laura Orchard and her parents.'

The cheers and applause were deafening. Everyone had changed again, thought Laura. The photographer took several quick shots of her and her parents flanked by Jody's while Laura held the envelope aloft, then he and the reporter ran after the Evanses, who were just leaving the car park as two waitresses made sure they did. As the murmur of the restaurant took over from the applause, Laura and her parents returned to their table. 'It's all right, Mummy,' Laura said.

Her mother was kneading her forehead and staring out of the window. She found Laura's hand and squeezed it and then looked at her. 'It *will* be all right. We'll make sure it is. We'll never forget this holiday,' she promised.

'You bet your life,' Laura's father said, and Laura had heard what she wanted to hear. The behaviour of the diners had upset her even more than the intrusion; it had felt as though violence and madness could flare up in anyone before you realised it was there. Not quite anyone, she reassured herself: not her friends, and especially not her parents – she had as good as heard them say so. At least they would never change. Their future was safe.

TWENTY-TWO

THREATS SWAPPED AT PRIZE-GIVING

Patrons of New Brighton's International Experience restaurant on Friday night saw more of a show than they bargained for.

As 12-year-old New Brighton girl Laura Orchard stood up to receive her prize of a holiday in a competition run by Pete and Cath Venable, owners of the restaurant, she was accused by Hilda Evans of Liscard of attacking her three sons, Clint, Lee and Eli.

Laura alleges that the three boys (16, 15 and 11) attacked her, but the police will not prosecute because of lack of witnesses.

As patrons of the restaurant's Mexican promotion watched in astonishment, Mrs Evans threatened to bring a counter-prosecution if Laura's parents try and prosecute any of her sons. Later she told this reporter that she was considering suing the Orchards for distress she claims she suffered after the original incident.

Laura and her parents would not comment on Mrs Evans' statement. 'It would take more than her to spoil our evening,' Mrs Orchard said. 'We're just glad we can afford this holiday.'

'What a world you're growing up in, Tommy,' Janys said to her son, 'where the paper thinks any of that's worth reporting.' She dropped the open newspaper on the breakfast table, and the majority of pages carried the rest over the edge to sprawl on the carpet tiles. 'What a pair of messy slobs we are,' she said as Tommy waved his spoon and chortled while

179

she gathered up the paper. She unstuck the sucker of his yellow bowl from the table of his high chair and dropped the bowl in the kitchen sink, she retrieved the spoon which was at least as thick with mush as he was, she mopped his small broad blue-eyed face quickly with a wet sponge before he could decide to cry, and then she turned on the tap. As the drumming of water on metal deepened, Tommy's face lit up. 'There's the sound you like. What do we call it?' Janys said.

'Waa.'

'Not war, no. That kills people. We don't like war. It's waaa—'

'Wawa.'

'Good boy, Tommy. I'm proud of you. Wa-*ter*. Try saying wa-*ter*.'

'Wawa.'

'Nearly. Water.' Janys turned off the tap and unclipped the plastic table from his chair, and had just dunked it in the sink when the phone rang in the hall, making Tommy wave his hands as if he was conducting the notes. She left the kitchen door open and extended the aerial as she picked up the receiver. 'Portrait Studio,' she said.

'Is that the portrait studio?'

'Certainly is.'

The voice, which was so roughened by age that Janys couldn't sex it, sharpened. 'The portrait studio?'

'Yes,' Janys said patiently, 'it is.'

'Do you take children?'

'Happy to.'

'Children.'

'All ages welcome.'

'Bridesmaids.'

'By all means.'

Janys was already preparing to repeat her enthusiasm, but instead of demanding it the voice said 'Must we bring them to the studio?'

'Not necessarily.'

'Their grandfather and I will bring them.'

'Whatever's best for you.'

'Will a week hence suit?'

'I'm sure it will,' Janys said, carrying the cordless phone into the studio, opening her diary one-handed and then resting her elbow on it while she grabbed a used envelope on which to scribble details. 'What time would you like?'

'About now.'

'Half past nine? And may I take your name?'

The caller gave it, and Janys thought: oh dear. 'How's that spelled, sorry? Haugh, is it?'

'Haw. Haw,' the woman said in a rising tone, and at last spelled it as though to a very young child: 'Hore.'

It could have been worse, Janys thought as she wrote down the address and phone number. 'I'll look forward to meeting the mob,' she said. 'How many bridesmaids are there, by the way?'

'Two.'

Janys rested the phone on her slippered instep while she copied the details neatly into the diary. The back of the envelope hadn't much space left on it, but the whole of the back of the page which insisted she could turn ill luck into good was blank. She already had, thank you very much, by getting a divorce. At least the letter was good for something – just about everything was. She tidied the diary and the pile of scrap paper into the drawer of her desk and reinserted the receiver in its plastic stand on her way to fetch Tommy, repeating 'Two' in the tone Mrs Hore had used, as though the number couldn't have been more obvious. When that made Tommy giggle she picked him up, burying her nose for a moment in his hair which smelled as blond as it looked, and said 'How old are you, Tommy?'

'Toooo.'

'That's right, my big two-year-old. Soon be three.'

He gazed expectantly at her, but she said no more until she had carried him along the hall, past the framed portraits which he often greeted but which he wasn't interested in just now, and planted him in the playpen in the corner of the studio, where the lights were well out of his reach. 'Two,' she said then in Mrs Hore's tone, and tried to keep a straight face as Tommy's giggling exposed all thirteen of his teeth. It was no use; his giggling infected her so much she almost didn't hear the doorbell.

'Someone's early,' she told him, and shouted 'Hold on' as she dashed into the hall. On her way upstairs she kicked off her slippers and grabbed them as she caught up with them. She sat on the bed, dropped them, slipped her feet into her nearest pair of flat shoes, took the stairs two at a time and unchaining the front door, pulled it open. There was nobody on the doorstep or on the garden path – no sign of anyone except a faint smell of fuel.

She'd been as quick as she could be. She hadn't wanted to appear any sloppier than she was, that was all. Artists might wear slippers when they met their subjects, but she was a professional. She hurried down the path and unlatching the gate, stepped onto the pavement to survey the road. Sunlight glared from the windscreen of a neighbour's Jaguar parked opposite the house, and even when she shaded her eyes she could see only a pale blotch, expanding like smoke. She was trying to blink her vision clear when she heard footsteps behind her, and the squeal of the hinges of the gate.

She almost panicked. Being unable to see had revived her old fear that one day Tommy's father would take him, although she was sure he wouldn't except to spite her; Tommy had been the reason why he'd gone off with that bitch. Janys closed her eyes and groped onto her path, and as the obscured patch of her vision began to shrink, she bumped into someone standing just beyond the gate.

'I beg your pardon,' he said at once. 'Are you all right? Can you see where you are?'

Now she could, however overexposed her house and garden looked, and she saw a young couple, the woman cradling what was obviously her first baby, the man waving away the trace of fumes in the air. 'We need to get that exhaust fixed,' he said. 'I rang your bell and then I thought I'd better park around the corner in case I blocked your road. You're not expecting us till ten o'clock.'

'Nothing my little one and I like better than surprises,' Janys said, ushering them into the house.

TWENTY-THREE

Three days after the presentation at the restaurant Julia was still experiencing surges of rage. She walked to the ferry on her way to work, hoping the walk would calm her, but the sight of the stretch of promenade where Laura had been attacked made her dig her nails into her palms. It didn't help that Laura kept trying to persuade her to forget the Evanses or that Jack had managed to retain his equanimity. If she was the only unreasonable member of the family, she didn't care: she wanted the Evanses to suffer as badly as Laura had. Now that both she and Jack were earning, they could afford to prosecute.

They wouldn't, not when that would need Laura to relive the attack and to be subjected to cross-examination by whatever lawyers Mrs Evans found to take her case. Once they had paid off the debt the thieves had charged to their credit card they ought to consult Luke about investments. Surely if there was any justice the Evanses' own lives would catch up with them.

On the ferry businessmen were strolling round and round the upper deck, hands behind their backs, some stooping forwards as if challenging a wind to oppose them. Julia stood at the rail and watched the Liverpool bank of the river swing towards her like an immense ship laden with warehouses. A party of schoolchildren wearing smiles on their round symmetrical faces met the ferry at the landing-stage. At the top of the exit ramp, people who looked inert enough to have been there all night were smoking cigarettes in the all-night café. A stray dog raised an explosion of pigeons from a scattered sandwich as Julia crossed the flagstones of the Pier

183

Head. Beyond the dock road she climbed a wide old street between office buildings pierced by arcades and turned along the side street to Luke's office.

Though the parking meters outside were hooded, a Ford saloon was parked under the window. A traffic warden peered at the windscreen and turned away without writing in her book. Luke must have an important client, Julia thought as she let herself into the building. Then she hesitated with her hand on the knob of the office door. Someone was crying.

Julia inched the door open until she could see into the outer office. Only three of Luke's staff were in the room. Lynne was at her desk and sobbing into a handkerchief. More disconcertingly, neither of her colleagues was comforting her; Susie was on one phone, Luke's appointment diary in front of her, and Val was using the other phone to put off a client of Luke's. Julia went forwards and touched Lynne's shoulder. 'Lynne, what's wr—'

Lynne jumped up, blowing her nose while pushing Julia towards the door with her free hand. She'd cut off her tears like a tap. 'Don't come in,' she whispered indistinctly. 'Call you later.'

'I should at least speak to Luke.'

'He's busy. Can't see anyone,' Lynne whispered, pushing harder. 'Don't hang around. Go home and I'll call you, I promise.'

'Come outside and tell me.'

Lynne nodded, but it was too late. The rest of Luke's staff had come downstairs from the Ladies and were blocking the hall. As Julia sidled around Lynne to make way for them the door of the inner office swept open, and a man emerged. Though he looked somehow proprietorial, he wasn't Luke. Given the sombreness which had settled over the office, Julia wondered if he was in mourning: so much about him was black – shoes, socks, suit, tie, even his glossy receding hair – though his shirt was uncomfortably white beneath the fluorescent lighting. 'Do you work here?' he said.

Julia didn't care for his tone, nor for his assumption of the right to ask. 'I'm responsible for the computers.'

'In that case I should like a word with you.'

Lynne sat down quickly and covered her face with her hands, and Julia was aware of having made a bad mistake. 'Not until I've had a word with Mr Rankin.'

'I regret that won't be possible.'

'Then I want him to tell me so.'

Lynne interrupted, her voice muffled by her hands. 'Julia, he's from the Fraud Squad.'

So the dark blotch on the frosted glass of Luke's office door was another man in black standing over Luke at his desk. The first man crossed the office to Julia, who held his gaze, trying to feel brave rather than trapped. 'Why are you here?' she said.

'We can talk privately in the car.'

'Why, are we going somewhere?'

'That isn't necessary,' he said as if he meant it as a rebuke. As she followed him she glanced back at Lynne, who refused to meet her eyes, and it occurred to her that Lynne might have been trying to protect her by hustling her out of the office.

The Ford saloon smelled of upholstery and after-shave and very faintly of petrol. The policeman closed the passenger door behind Julia and walked around the front of the car to slide into the driver's seat. Julia was reminded of her first and only driving lesson, not least by her present nervousness. As he locked his door she heard hers lock too. 'May I ask your name?' he said.

'Julia Orchard. May I ask yours?'

'Inspector Dicker,' he admitted, lounging in his seat so as to watch her face. 'Tell me in what way you're responsible for the computers.'

'I train the staff in using them.'

'Including Mr Rankin?'

'Very much so. He still needs some training. I wonder if there's been a misunderstanding.'

'By whom?'

'I don't think Luke is capable of any tricks with the computer.'

He met her eyes with no expression at all. 'How long have you worked for Mr Rankin?'

'Nearly a year.'

'And before that?'

'I taught beginners at a night school for three years.'

'So it would be fair to say that your knowledge of computers is . . .'

It felt like an English test where you had to fill in the blanks. 'Reasonably extensive, unlike Luke's.'

'Which might imply that you would have to be familiar with the information stored in his computer.'

It wasn't a test, it was several kinds of trap. 'Luke's always kept as much to himself as he can,' she said carefully. 'I mean, he locks the kettle and the milk in his office overnight. There's nothing sinister about it. It's just him.'

'Surely you must have access to the information on the computer if you taught him how to store it.'

'Not if he renamed the files,' Julia said without thinking, and remembered the Sunday when Luke had been anxious to learn – remembered the name he had given a file. She'd thought HIDEYHO had expressed his growing confidence, but suppose he had been thinking 'hideyhole'? 'He'd have to restrict the access as well,' she added quickly, 'if he really didn't want me seeing what was there.'

'Did you teach him how to do so?'

'No, he never asked.'

'Which suggests that he didn't want it to be realised that he knew.'

'You're assuming he does know.'

'Hardly assuming, Mrs – it is Mrs – Orchard.'

The hint of sympathy in his voice only made her feel more vulnerable. 'What's he supposed to have done?' she asked.

He considered her for an uncomfortably prolonged few seconds, then he said 'It would appear that your employer has been trying to conceal his use of monies entrusted to him by his clients.'

'What kind of use?'

'We have reason to believe that he intended to make it

186

impossible to trace a considerable amount of money until he had used it for his own purposes.'

'But why? That doesn't sound at all like him.'

'Financial difficulties of his own that have supposedly been building up for years.'

That did. Julia could imagine Luke panicking, growing secretive and desperate, and so she tried to deny the possibility. 'Can you be sure he's done anything wrong?'

'Sure enough to arrest him.'

The policeman was gazing at her, and for a moment she thought he was going to arrest her too. 'I've told you everything I know,' she said.

'You may have to tell it in court, Mrs Orchard.'

The heat of the car and the smell of petrol, which wasn't as faint as it had initially seemed, were conspiring to make her feel sick. 'If you've finished with me,' she said, 'I could do with some fresh air.'

His hand moved, but not to the lock. He reached inside his jacket for a pen and notebook. 'Let me have an address and phone number.'

He might almost have been inviting her to provide false information. Of course she told him the truth, but he didn't release the lock until he had finished writing. As she stepped onto the pavement she found that her legs were unsteady, and there was more of a smell of petrol outside than inside the car. 'I may as well hang about for a while,' she said.

'I wouldn't advise that, Mrs Orchard. There won't be anything for you to do. We'll let you know if we need you. Thank you for your help.'

Being thanked made her feel as though she had betrayed Luke, though if what she had been told was true, hadn't Luke betrayed her and the rest of his staff, not to mention his clients? She turned her back on the office and walked to the station as steadily as she could.

A descending lift, the train, New Brighton station. Those consumed forty minutes of her life during which she felt walled in by her thoughts. She pushed past the ticket barrier and ran downhill, crossing the road to avoid Cath Venable;

she wanted to talk only to Jack. His van was still outside the house. She dug her key into the lock of the front door and slammed the door behind her. 'Jack, are you here? Jack?'

He appeared from the kitchen, lowering a milk bottle and wiping his lips. 'Here I am, love. What's up?' he said, and amplified that as he saw her. 'What's upset you?'

'The police.'

His frown was so swift she hardly saw it. 'Not about Laura again?'

'Not Laura this time.'

He turned away in order to replace the bottle in the refrigerator. 'Who, then?' he said, his voice hollowed by the box.

'Luke. He's been arrested by the Fraud Squad. They're closing down the business.'

Jack came to her at once, shoving aside the kitchen door so that he walked out of a sudden blaze of sunlight. She knew that he was on his way to comfort her, yet she found his immediate reaction disconcerting. 'Not again,' he said aloud to himself with a sigh like an escape of gas.

TWENTY-FOUR

It might take nothing more than a meeting face to face, Jack told himself. That morning he held his own gaze as he shaved and saw no sign of weakness. 'That's all it takes to get what you want,' he heard Andy Nation saying, 'looking fierce and sounding as if you mean to get it.' He donned his best suit, then he took it off again; it wouldn't do to seem too prosperous. He put on one not quite so good and waited for Julia to emerge from the bathroom. 'What do you think?' he said. 'Am I irresistible?'

'You'll do.'

'If we're lucky, you mean?'

'Can't hurt, can it?'

'Never has.'

'Only, Jack, whatever happens, let's not care. We're lucky so long as we have Laura and each other.'

In a way she was right, but it was no longer enough; it hadn't been since the fire at the shop. 'You're sure you want to come,' he said.

'Any reason why I shouldn't?'

'Every reason why you should.' He must be careful not to let himself assume he had to act alone when there was no need. He might have to do things which he couldn't mention to the family because they couldn't be expected to understand, but he mustn't let that attitude spill into their everyday life. 'Maybe going to see him last time without you was my mistake,' he said as they made for the bank.

As he rang the bell beside the enquiry window he found himself willing someone unfamiliar to answer his summons, but it brought him the same young woman. 'We can't go on meeting like this,' he said, and when she blinked her bluish eyelids at him, 'Jack and Julia Orchard for eleven o'clock.'

'You want Mr Hardy.'

He ought to take care not to sound like his old self. Rather than 'You're darn tootin'' he said 'That's the man.'

She seemed to be examining his words for hidden meanings as she turned away to fetch the manager. Third time lucky, he told himself, especially since Julia was with him. He squeezed her hand while he watched the minute hand of the clock creep towards the vertical. Just as it pointed at the zenith Mr Hardy came to the door beside the enquiry window. 'Exactly right,' Jack said.

Mr Hardy gave Julia a polite smile and pursed his lips. 'I didn't catch that, Mr Orchard.'

'You know my wife.'

'Of course,' the manager said as though Jack had meant it as a sly rebuke, and opened the door of the interview room. 'Won't you step through?'

When Jack and Julia both hesitated he edged towards the doorway. 'Please,' Jack said with a magnanimous gesture which might have been indicating Mr Hardy's paunch. 'I'll be the back legs,' he said. 'I'll bring up the rear.'

Lord only knew what Jack Awkward might have felt compelled to add, but his new self knew when he'd said enough. He wafted Julia and Mr Hardy into the interview room and closed the three of them in while the manager, having waited for Julia to seat herself, sat as far forwards as the desk and his paunch would allow. 'I hear you're to be congratulated,' Mr Hardy said to her.

'About the competition? Thanks.'

'I trust your daughter is improving.'

'On the mend,' Julia admitted. 'You're looking well.'

'Fed,' Jack Awkward would probably have added, hoping it would be inaudible, but Jack only took his place on the remaining chair. 'Anyway, Mr Hardy, you wanted to see us,' Julia said.

'That is the case.' Mr Hardy raised a fist in order further to conceal a discreet cough. 'Have there been any developments with regard to the employment situation?'

'I'm still out of a job.'

'How permanent is that likely to be?'

'As far as that job goes, very, I'm afraid, which is why I'm looking for another.'

'With any success?'

'So far people don't seem keen on hiring someone who may have to take time off work to be in court, and I'm restricted by the distance I can travel to work.'

'If the work won't come to us, Mrs Orchard, we must go to the work.'

'I appreciate that.'

She sounded anything but appreciative. 'Are you suggesting we should move further than we meant to?' Jack said.

'That might seem a solution,' Mr Hardy said, and collected another cough in his fist. 'Unfortunately, it may present a problem.'

'More like several.'

'In the immediate context, your mortgage in particular.'

'What about our mortgage?' Julia said.

'In view of the fact that there is no longer duality of income, I fear we may have to adjust our offer accordingly.'

'What are you saying?' Jack demanded, telling himself there was no need to be rude: knowing what he was capable of should give him the strength to be direct and clear. 'You must realise we can't buy anywhere worthwhile for less than you're offering.'

'Were offering, Mr Orchard. I'm afraid we must think in the past tense.'

'A good trick if you can do it, but no use to us.'

Mr Hardy concentrated on Julia. 'I'd hoped to have better news for you, but given what you've just told me I fear I have no choice.'

'Everyone has a choice,' Jack said.

'And the bank's has been made, Mr Orchard.'

'Banks don't make choices, people do,' Julia protested. 'The house is too small for the three of us now. What are we supposed to do?'

'I trust you will be able to make the best of it until your situation improves.'

'That isn't good enough,' Jack said, holding his voice steady despite the blaze of images which filled his head, Mr Hardy dancing wildly as the firemen fell over their hoses. 'Maybe we should think of moving banks before we move house.'

'I doubt that any other bank would welcome your account in its current state.'

'So you think you can do what you like with us.'

'I don't think there's any need to go that far,' Mr Hardy said, bumping the desk with his paunch.

'I'll go as far as I have to,' Jack said, feeling as though at any moment he might begin to hear music to accompany the ritual fire dance in his skull. 'Suppose I take up your attitude with your head office?'

'That's your privilege, Mr Orchard, but I'm afraid—'

'Privilege my sphincter. The bank's been happy enough to have our custom over the years. Your predecessor certainly was.'

'My happiness isn't at issue, Mr Orchard.'

Jack heard him say 'atishoo', but it wasn't worth a joke. 'That's right. Ours and our daughter's is. And keeping your customers happy is part of your job.'

'Not at the bank's expense.'

'The bank can stand the strain better than we can.'

Julia reached for Jack as if she wasn't seeing too well and gripped his hand. 'We'd better go.'

'Let's be clear first,' Jack said, and slipping his hand out of hers, stood up and leaned on Mr Hardy's desk. 'We've done everything we can and despite that you're refusing to help us.'

'Please take your hands off my desk, Mr Orchard.'

'Where do you think I should put them?' Jack was looking at Mr Hardy's fat throat, which seemed to squirm like a grub. 'I don't like to see my family kicked while they're down.'

'If you think such language will achieve something, Mr Orchard—'

'I was hoping language would.' Jack lifted his hands from

the desk. Mr Hardy rocked backwards so as to get up, and Jack saw the manager shrinking from him, saw how a push would send the man sprawling. It would only upset Julia. 'I expect to hear from you soon,' he said.

Mr Hardy pressed his lips together so hard they turned white, and held the door open. 'I'm sorry not to have been able to offer more in the way of encouragement,' he said as Julia came abreast of him.

She said nothing until she was out on the street, blinking rapidly as if she had sand in her eyes. 'We did our best.'

She was asking for at least that reassurance, but Jack knew he hadn't even begun. How much more did he intend to let her and Laura suffer before he did what was necessary? Did he always need a dose of bad luck to spur him into action? Prevention was better than cure, and the family had been through enough. 'Don't tell Laura anything until we've been to the top,' he said.

He could see that Julia wanted to believe that would work. Of course it wouldn't by itself, but he could hardly say so to her. He left early for work and drove towards Seacombe, along the street full of charity shops and second-hand stores, and bought an old pram which he hid in the back of the van.

TWENTY-FIVE

On Monday Jack phoned home after work. 'Who is it?' Laura said.

'Don't speak so loud, I'm in the library.'

'Have you got to be quiet?'

'As an egg.'

'What are you doing?'

'Watching people turn tomes into notes.' When she didn't respond he said 'See if you can do that in eleven moves.'

'Oh, Dad, not another puzzle.'

'We're living one, aren't we? By the way, if you ever need me to look up anything for your homework while I'm here, just ring. I'll take notes and tote the tome notes home.'

His amusement, which felt like utter freedom and which had been gathering for hours, was threatening to overwhelm him. A man whose broad red face was half-concealed by a moustache and sideboards glanced at him over a rampart of law books that occupied most of one side of a table. 'How's your day been?' Jack said. 'How was cycling to school?'

'Lovely. My new bike is. I take off the back wheel and chain it on the front so nobody can steal it when I leave it.'

She was learning about the world. That made him feel nostalgic for her innocence, but also safer. 'Mummy wants to talk to you,' she said.

'She has my ear.' When Laura giggled he said 'Tell her to return it when she's finished with it.'

After a brief muffled dialogue, Julia took her place. 'Had a decent day?' he said.

'Sorting out what's been lurking around the house. I've thrown some old clothes of yours on the bed for you to say goodbye to before they go to anyone who'll have them.'

'I'll take them in the van. There's nothing urgent waiting, is there?'

'Only ...' She let out a breath as though she hadn't the energy to turn it into words. 'Not waiting, no.'

'What were you going to say?'

'Just that the old couple whose house we looked at by the river wanted to know if we'd sold ours.'

'The Woolidges? Did you tell them we were still trying?'

'It wouldn't have been fair, Jack. Someone else has made them a definite offer.'

Jack grinned so furiously that the hirsute student looked down at his notes. 'Does Laura know?'

'I thought I'd better tell her.'

'How's she taking it?'

'She understands.'

Jack clenched his teeth. He ought to go home to the family, but mustn't he already have allowed their luck to worsen by delaying what he had to do? 'Why were you ringing?' Julia said.

He couldn't think of any explanation other than the one he had already concocted. 'I was going to say I'll be home late, but now ...'

'We don't mind waiting if there's a good reason.'

'Only that I've met someone I used to work with and we were planning to go out for a couple of pints.'

'What, now?'

'That was the idea.'

'How long will you be?'

'Say a couple of hours. Less if you prefer.'

'It isn't up to me, Jack.'

'We'll say two hours, then.'

'If you're not back we'll start dinner without you,' Julia said in a tone which suggested she didn't care either way. He would have to bear her low opinion of him, and surely she would forget the incident once their luck improved. 'You and me and Laura will go out one evening as soon as we've something to celebrate,' he said, hoping she would catch his

195

optimism. 'I won't be any longer than I have to be,' he told the empty receiver, and saying goodbye to his colleagues, made for the van.

His grin was hidden under his face now, where it felt more fixed than ever. He resented having been forced to give Julia the impression that he was uncaring, a resentment which was likely to intensify until he found who was responsible. It seemed to harden the five o'clock sunlight and hold his surroundings still so that he could see everything clearly – a vandalised branch hanging from a sapling on the edge of the car park, a low-lying fog left behind by an elongated motorcycle as it roared towards the main road, the remains of a cigarette smouldering as a breeze sent it rolling across the tarmac. 'That could be dangerous,' Jack said, waiting by a line of parked cars until the butt ventured close enough to tread on. The sensation of the object yielding and dying beneath his heel invigorated him. He scraped it in an arc, leaving a trail of fibres of tobacco and cork like a sketch of a comet with an ashen head, then he climbed into the van and swung the vehicle out of the parked rank.

The lights which were doling traffic onto the main road delayed him for five minutes, and the procession of cars crossing the bridge towards the motorway might have been heading for a funeral. Speeding at last up the ramp onto the motorway felt like an awakening of purpose. Slender chimneys rose to meet him, bearing flames or pennants of white smoke so keenly outlined they looked unreal, and beyond them the Mersey curved towards distant hills. The stilted road followed the curve of flames and water to the Manchester motorway, where a bunch of lorries joined the race. Jack outdistanced them, though the van suffered a fit of the shakes. He heard the pram thumping the partition at his back as though it was impatient to get going. 'Nearly there,' he said, and left the motorway at the next junction.

He'd already traced his route on a road map in the library. 'Third time lucky,' he murmured to the clown's head dangling from the ignition as he drove around the roundabout at the top of the ramp. Surely a repairer of musical instruments had

196

to be sensitive and would listen to Jack more sympathetically than Jeremy Alston had or Veronica Alan would have. Jack tuned the dashboard receiver to Radio 3, and a Chopin sonata began an ungainly dance as he sped along the Helsby road.

He had just reached the edge of the village, where each side of the road bore a 30 on a pole, when a sports car red as a traffic light caught up with him. The driver, a flat-capped man with a puffy face, appeared to be mouthing at Jack. Was he drunk or mad? The car veered around the van as Jack slowed to the limit, and he realised from a snatch of music which the sports car left behind that the driver had been singing along with a car radio. It was too easy to call people mad; most folk – maybe everyone – must seem that way sometimes, especially when nobody was there to see them.

At the end of half a mile of semi-detached houses interrupted by a petrol station Jack turned right where the road forked. A humpbacked bridge led him to a steep road called The Rock, on which garden paths were carved out of the hillside which a row of houses climbed. Two blond children stood at a garden gate and watched a horse cantering up and down a field across the road. At the top Jack steered left at a crossroads and drove between scattered cottages until he reached a signpost indicating a walk over the brow of the hill. He urged the van up the steepest road yet and parked by a stile at the edge of a wood.

Two crows flapped croaking out of a tree as he walked around the van, and a transistor radio so muffled he could hear only the percussion of a rock song was playing in one of the houses on the slope he'd just conquered, but those were the sole signs of life. His timing seemed perfect. The locals were all in their houses, and in any case nobody would remark on a vehicle which had been left at the start of a walk. He unlocked the rear doors of the van and wheeled the pram out, then he headed back towards the crossroads.

He had to dig his heels into the road all the way down the slope. The pram or its contents seemed more eager than ever to arrive at their destination. Pushing them uphill again

197

might give him some trouble, except that now he felt ready for anything. But he wasn't ready to be hailed as he pushed the pram alongside the cottages at the foot of the slope. 'Has the little man been up on the hill?' a woman was calling to him.

Jack turned, jerking the pram to a stop. She was in her seventies, wearing tweeds and muddy boots and leaning on an eccentric stick with which she thumped the tarmac as she bore down on him. 'Sorry, who?' Jack stammered.

'The wee fellow. Been out for some air, has he?'

Jack was struggling to cope with his growing hilarity, wondering whether she was referring to some legend of fairies on the hill or accusing him of having exposed himself, when she halted in the middle of the road. 'You men,' she said, shaking her head. 'You wouldn't know which end to put the nappy on if we didn't tell you which.'

'Oh, you mean the baby,' Jack said, rocking the pram as he used to rock Laura's to put her to sleep. 'It's a girl, that's why I didn't know who you meant. I'd better keep moving in case she wakes.'

He took one step, and the woman came thumping three-legged after him. 'Don't cover up the poor mite like that. Here, let me show you how she ought to be.'

'She's fine. That's how my wife has her in the pram. That's how she likes it herself,' Jack said, walking and pushing, cursing the woman's rude rustic health that was letting her catch up with him. 'And the doctor approves.'

'I've never had to call a doctor in my life, and that's because I was always out in the fresh air. It's cruel to deny light and air to a child on a day like this.'

She was still gaining on him. He imagined trying to outrun her, dashing away with the pram while she sprinted after him, waving her stick. That's me, Mr Unobtrusive, he thought wildly as she said 'Can't I at least see her little face?'

'Believe me, you don't want to come face to face with this baby.' He wasn't sure which of him might have said that, his old self or his new, but at once he knew what to say aloud. 'She doesn't like being wakened by strangers. If you waken her she'll scream all the way home.'

'Good heavens, I've had longer than you to learn how not to waken babies. I've put a good few to sleep in my time. I'm a nurse.'

She was about to grab the pram, Jack thought. She would lift the cover, and then ... At that moment he heard a car approaching swiftly up a side road just ahead of him. If the driver didn't see the old woman in the roadway ... But she retreated to the corner of the junction and leaned on her stick, ready to take up the chase again as soon as the car passed.

Jack wheeled the pram past the junction while she was trapped by the car. 'If it's all the same to you I won't take the risk,' he called across the wake of fumes. 'I'd have to answer to her mother when I got home.'

If that didn't satisfy the woman it at least confirmed her opinion of him. 'You men,' she said, digging her stick into the triangle of verge at the junction as though she was thinking of launching herself after him, then contented herself with a parting shot. 'What's her name?'

Jack took a long breath and released it through his nostrils. 'Bernie,' he said.

She didn't think much of that, and shook her head as she plodded down the side road. Jack watched her out of sight before he set off for the crossroads. He could already see his destination, a house standing by itself several hundred yards beyond the shimmering cross of tarmac. 'Let's hope we won't need to wake you up, Bernie,' he said.

The house was a steep-roofed block of red brick, almost featureless except for a satellite dish protruding from beneath the gutter like a toadstool from a tree. The large square garden was surrounded by a six-foot privet hedge. At first Jack thought the metallic gleam within the hedge was an illusion caused by the quivering of the air above the tarmac. He was almost at the gate before he realised that the inside of the hedge was reinforced with barbed wire. The plaque on the gate, which he'd assumed showed the name of the house, proved on closer acquaintance to say NO TRESPASSING. He pushed the pram across the gateway and stopped with one hand on the latch.

A wiry man dressed in slacks and sandals was lying on a striped recliner beside the cobbled path to the front door. One arm lay across his eyes, the other held a tumbler half full of what Jack deduced was gin and tonic balanced on his bushy chest. As Jack unlatched the gate the man raised his head and shaded his eyes to squint unwelcomingly at him. 'Mr Arrod?' Jack said.

'Nobody else here, so I must be.'

'Stephen Arrod?'

'I've said so.' He peered past Jack and saw the pram. 'Ah. No thank you,' he said at once.

'Excuse me, what do you think you're saying no to?'

'Whatever. Newspapers, household goods, free samples. I want none of it, whatever it is.'

'It's nothing like any of those.'

'You aren't telling me you've got something for me to repair in there.'

'In a way I suppose I have,' Jack said, and pushed the pram through the gateway.

'You're a beggar, aren't you.'

Jack assumed Arrod meant that to express some kind of grudging admiration; at least, he did until he turned from closing the gate and saw Arrod staring at the pram. 'No trespassing means no beggars,' Arrod said. 'And if you think your brat can soften my heart you're out of luck.'

'I'm not here to beg, Mr Arrod.'

'I don't want you here at all. You're interrupting my cocktail hour. And I especially don't allow brats on my property. I've taken enough pains to keep them out.'

He was referring to the barbed wire, Jack thought, shivering. The shiver was at least partly of fear on Arrod's behalf. He pushed the pram towards Arrod, and felt the contents stir as the wheels trundled over the cobbles. 'You'd be doing yourself a favour by listening to me,' he said.

'I don't do favours for anyone. Incidentally, before you leave, how the devil do you know my name?'

'It was on the letter I sent you.'

'What letter?'

'One like this,' Jack said, reaching beneath the cover of the pram.

'Don't bother. Whatever it is, I don't want to know. The only thing I want to see is you out of the gate.'

'Please, Mr Arrod. For your own sake,' Jack said, unfolding the letter.

'What the devil's my sake got to do with you?' Arrod swung his legs off the recliner and dumped the tumbler on the lawn, where it toppled over, spilling gin and ice-cubes. 'It's yourself you should be worrying about,' he snarled. 'Worry about what'll happen to you if you aren't gone before I call the police.'

As Arrod shoved himself off the recliner Jack ran the pram along the path and used it to block the front door. 'No need for that, Mr Arrod. I haven't harmed you.'

Arrod's face darkened so instantly it put Jack in mind of a special effect in a film. He lurched at Jack and trod on an ice-cube. His sandalled foot slipped from beneath him, and Jack watched him sprawl backwards on the recliner, which gave way, depositing him on the ground with all his limbs flung out. Swallowing his mirth, Jack went towards him, the letter fluttering in his hand as a wind trembled the hedge. 'Here, let me—'

Arrod screamed with rage and tried to heave himself to his feet, only to sprawl again. 'Don't you come near me or it won't be the police who fetch you, it'll be an ambulance,' he shouted. He managed to get his knees under him, and as he staggered upright he saw the letter Jack was holding. For a moment Jack thought the writhing of his face was a distortion caused by heat in the air. 'It was you who sent me that, was it?' Arrod said.

'One like it.'

'And what do you think happened to it?'

'I'm hoping you'll tell me.'

'Shall I give you a hint? Shall I tell you what to do with the one you've got there? If you're so hard up, use it to wipe your brat's arse.'

As he finished speaking he rushed at the pram and ripped back the cover. Jack imagined him doing that to a pram with a sleeping baby in it, and felt a grin tighten over his teeth. Arrod stared into the pram and turned to Jack, still staring. 'What the blazes is this for?'

'I wish you hadn't done that, Mr Arrod.'

Arrod swung back to the pram and reached in. 'Who are these, my fellow victims?'

He had picked up the letters and was reading the names and addresses on the envelopes. Up to that moment Jack had intended to give him a choice, but now— 'Put them down,' he said through his teeth, and strode forwards. 'They're none of your business.'

Arrod dropped a handful of envelopes into the pram. Still peering at them, he seized the blowlamp from beside them and heaved it up with one hand. Apparently he meant to use it as a shield or a weapon, but its weight took him unawares. He let go of the handle with an outraged cry as it bruised his fingers, and then he gave a howl which hurt Jack's ears. He'd dropped the blowlamp on one sandalled foot.

As the blowlamp rolled onto the grass Arrod hopped backwards wildly as if he could somehow outdistance the pain. He appeared to have no idea where he meant to go, except perhaps away from Jack. He didn't stop hopping until he had backed into a corner of the hedge, where he began to struggle and jerk.

The wire fence must be electrified, Jack thought. Arrod's eyes bulged as he flung himself back and forth; even the hair on his head was quivering. Jack lifted the blowlamp with both hands and advanced on him. By now his jerking had grown so violent that in the midst of his uncontrollable hilarity Jack pitied him. He raised the blowlamp as high as his arms would reach and brought the tank down with all his strength on Arrod's skull.

He was afraid that a single blow wouldn't suffice, especially when Arrod stared at him with a mixture of disbelief and reproach as the dull knell of the impact continued to resound in the tank. Perhaps that lasted only a second or two, but it

202

seemed much longer. Then Arrod's eyes rolled up to show the whites, an effect Jack had thought was purely a cliché manufactured by films, and his head and torso slumped into the hedge.

His hair continued to quiver, and so did the top of the hedge, in a wind. The fence wasn't electrified after all. The belt of Arrod's slacks had caught on the barbed wire; his jerking had been a desperate attempt to free himself. Jack had never seen such panic. At least he would be putting the man out of his misery, he thought, now that Arrod had read the envelopes and left him no choice. He put down the blowlamp and made sure that nobody was in sight; he jumped several times to see over the hedge. Then he stood upwind of Arrod and lit the gas with his lighter, and covered his nose and mouth with his free hand, and closed his eyes until he could see only the flame.

TWENTY-SIX

Laura was writing a long decimal in her homework book when she heard her mother finish talking to Laura's father on the phone and come upstairs. It sounded to Laura as if they'd had the beginning of an argument. Usually she enjoyed mathematics, the more complicated the better – she supposed she took after her parents – but now the numbers seemed just to lie there in the textbook and where she'd written them, and she felt as though her head was cluttered with numbers left in the wake of those she'd written in her book. She tidied her schoolbooks off her bed into her satchel and went to find her mother.

She was lying on top of the quilt of the double bed, staring up. Her eyes were as blank as the ceiling. 'Are you all right, Mummy?' Laura said.

Her mother turned her head to her with not much more expression in her eyes. 'Just trying to relax for a few minutes.'

'Oh, okay,' Laura said quickly. 'I'll—' She was about to say she would go out cycling for half an hour, but that wouldn't help her mother relax. Her not being able to go for a ride made the house feel smaller, and so did knowing they weren't going to move to the house by the river. 'I'll be downstairs,' she said.

Her mother managed to smile. 'I wasn't sending you away, love. Have you finished your homework? Then keep me company if you like.'

Laura kicked off her shoes and lay down, resting her head on her mother's shoulder. Her mother patted her tummy and stroked it, and Laura felt that relaxing both of them. When she felt it was safe to do so she said 'What did Daddy want?'

Her mother laughed with so little feeling that the sound barely rose out of her mouth. 'Oh, just what all men need sometimes, apparently.'

'What?' Laura said, not sure that she wanted to know.

'An evening out with the boys. One boy, at any rate, by the sound of it. I assume it's a boy, I mean a man.' She rolled her head from side to side on the pillow and gave an even feebler laugh. 'If I'm not careful I'll be starting to sound like a wife in a Laurel and Hardy. I know he needs to unwind like the rest of us. I just never realised how much harder that is when you're out of work.'

Laura didn't know what to say to that. After a while she said 'Mummy?'

'Yessy?'

'Could we sell our holiday?'

Her mother propped her chin on her hand so as to look down at Laura. 'Why would we want to do that?'

'I thought we could put the money towards a house.'

'The bank would gobble up the money, love, and go on refusing us a mortgage. Would you really want to sell that holiday?'

'No,' Laura admitted.

'Then don't even think about it. We'll see to it that Crete makes up for everything, won't we?'

When she was convinced that Laura agreed she lay back. At least being fierce seemed to have cheered her up. Laura snuggled against her, feeling comfortable and safe, and said 'When's Dad coming home?'

'About seven, I'm told. I'll get up soon.'

Laura remembered being as young as lying in her mother's arms was making her feel. She'd built a town of upturned bucketfuls of sand on the beach and had tried not to cry when she'd seen the river coming to wash away her houses. The memory seemed deliciously sad; she found herself feeling sorry for the little girl she'd been. She could almost hear the waves and smell salt water and hot sand, but now they were in Crete, and the music bright as sunlight was so loud that she didn't need to get up and switch on the tape. The rhythms of the slow waves and of her breathing merged, and the bed floated away on a calm blue sea. Lying in her mother's arms had turned into sunlight and warmth. It seemed to Laura that if she lay quite still this might go on for ever, and she thought it almost had when she heard the van draw up outside the house.

Her mother was asleep. Laura eased herself off the bed and closed the bedroom door quietly behind her. As she reached the top of the stairs she heard the key fitting into the lock. The front door opened and her father came in.

She saw him before he saw her. He looked dazed, though perhaps that meant he was so deep in himself as hardly to know where he was; after all, Laura had just been in that state. 'Did you have a good time?' Laura whispered, and clutched her mouth to trap a giggle; either he was putting on a show for her or he really didn't know where her voice was coming from. He spun round and stared at the letter-box, he made a visor of his hand and peered along the hall, and only then did he raise his eyes to her. She thought he was going to perform a double-take, but instead he said 'Hmmm?'

'Did you have a good time?'

'I thought that's what you said. I've had worse.'

'Are you drunk?'

'I suppose you could say that,' he told her as though the possibility had only just occurred to him.

'Who did you go out with?'

He responded with most of a smile. 'You'll be a good wife,' he said. 'Just someone I thought might be able to help.'

'Did they?'

'We'll have to wait and see, won't we?' he said, pushing open the door of the front room. 'Where's Julia?'

'Asleep.'

'She needs it. Let's leave her that way. I'll make dinner if you'll trust me not to set the place on fire.'

'I'll help.'

'What, to set fire to it?' This time his smile was even more lopsided. 'I'm getting tasteless. I'll have to watch myself.'

'We tell worse jokes than that at school.'

'I'll bet you do. Well, that's one thing jokes are for, to let us own up to our secret selves. Come on and we'll find something to keep me out of mischief.'

He seemed disappointed that the casserole was already filled and simmering. He lifted the earthenware lid and poked the ingredients with a fork to see what they were. 'No leeks,' he said. 'What this needs is leeks. We'd better take a leek.'

Laura couldn't tell how much of this was an act which he was performing to amuse her. His jokes seemed to be coming in waves. She watched him take a bunch of leeks out of the vegetable rack and wash them and chop them up. When he started to drop them in the casserole she said 'Don't you think you should cook them a bit first?'

'Is that right? It's a good job you're here to keep an eye on me.' He filled a saucepan with water and let the leeks plop into it, then he took out his lighter and turned on the gas. 'Dad,' Laura shouted.

'Sorry. That was a stupid joke,' he said, but she wasn't sure he'd meant it as a joke; he'd appeared to be entranced by the hiss of gas. He snapped his lighter and lit the jet, and moved the saucepan onto it quickly, hiding the flames. 'Don't ever—' he said, and fell silent, hearing Laura's mother in the hall.

He looked suddenly awkward, uncertain of himself. Laura's scalp began to tingle unpleasantly. If they were going to have an argument she hoped they would hurry up. Though her mother would have heard the voices in the kitchen, she wasn't approaching. After a while Laura's father opened the kitchen door. 'I'm sorry if we woke you,' he said.

'You didn't. This did.'

She was holding an envelope which must have been slipped through the front door while Laura and her father were talking, and she seemed not quite able to believe what it contained. 'I think we'd better take it to the police,' she said.

TWENTY-SEVEN

SECOND MERSEYSIDE BLAZE HORROR

Police are so far refusing to confirm any similarities between the murder of 49-year-old Helsby man Stephen Arrod and the burning to death several weeks ago of Jeremy Alston in Heswall.

Mr Arrod, a violin-maker, was found burned to death in the front garden of his Helsby home on Monday. He had apparently been beaten unconscious and then set on fire.

. An extensive murder hunt has been launched by Cheshire police. Door-to-door enquiries are currently being pursued in the Helsby area. Chief Inspector Puce, who is leading the hunt, described the murder as 'the most brutal, sadistic and sickening I have ever seen in twenty-two years on the force'.

Mr Arrod was a well-respected local figure. None of his many friends in the community have been able to suggest any motive for the killing. Police are appealing for witnesses. Anyone with any information should call

'Chuck that away when you're finished with it,' Andy Nation said. 'I've better things to do than read that sort of stuff.'

'Don't you think it might be doing some good?'

'I think they print it to sell papers, that's what I think.'

'You don't believe there's anyone who saw either of these men coming to an end who's just been waiting for the paper to remind them to get in touch with the police?'

'About as much as I believe that someone might have seen this character walking around with a blowlamp like the one you've got there and not bothered telling anyone. You don't have to give it back to me, old pip. You'll have me thinking you're trying to get rid of the evidence.'

'You know we haven't much room, Andy, and there's no point in our keeping hold of it when there's no sign of our moving house.'

'I was only joking, you know. I'm just not as good at jokes as you.' Andy unlocked the tailgate of his car and picked up the blowlamp from the pavement. 'Not as heavy as I remember. You must have got some use out of it at least.'

'I did, at the shop.'

'Dear God, of course you did. Kick me hard,' Andy said, and took care not to turn away from Jack as he slammed the tailgate. 'Coming in for a cuppa or a mugga?'

'I'd better not, thanks, or I'll never get anything done.'

'Just be sure it's worth doing, old pip, and next time try and have some good news.'

'I've got some now.'

'Spill.'

For a moment Jack thought of a wand with a flame on the end, and then he heard what Andy was requesting. He reached into his jacket and producing the envelope, unfolded the contents. 'Someone put his through our door.'

Andy glanced at it and turned it over. 'Now that's really interesting, a bit of newspaper.'

'You see what it's about.'

When Andy turned the torn square of paper the right way up he noticed the item in which part of a sentence was underlined by wavery lines of blue ink. 'Threats swapped at prizegiving,' he read aloud. 'It's about you winning that holiday.'

'See what's been underlined.'

'"She was considering suing the Orchards for distress she claimed she suffered." Don't tell me she has, the woman who brought up those thugs.'

'Not yet.'

'Not ever if there's any justice. So who sent you this?'

'Anon. There wasn't even any writing on the envelope.'

Andy shoved the cutting at him with a kind of undirected

209

anger. 'Do you think it was that old bitch who lets her sons run wild trying to put the wind up you?'

'Raising the wind was involved, but not that sort. I did say it was good news, remember. This wasn't all that was in the envelope.'

Andy peered into it as Jack reinserted the cutting, and looked as if he suspected Jack of playing a joke on him. 'So what was?'

'Almost a thousand pounds in used notes.'

Andy leaned on the roof of his car so hard it emitted an audible creak. 'You're joking.'

'We thought someone was, I can tell you. We took the notes to the police, and they aren't forged or stolen. As far as the law is concerned the money's ours to do what we want with.'

'Who do they think . . .' Andy said as though he couldn't catch his breath. 'Don't they have any idea . . .'

'They figured as I do, a well-wisher. Maybe someone who knows the Evanses. Julia's worried it might be a pensioner who's sent us their life savings. She'd give it back if she could, but the trouble is if we advertise it the Evanses are bound to get wind of it, not to mention the bank manager.'

'Sounds like it's almost more trouble than it's worth.'

'Well, it's worth quite a lot. At least we won't be hard up for spending money in Greece.'

'There's that. And it shows there are some good folk left in the world.'

'I never thought otherwise, Andy.'

'Never said you did,' Andy said, and pointed at the murder report which Jack was holding. 'You'd wonder how something like that gets started, that's all.'

'Easier to imagine how it could carry on.'

'You reckon?'

'I think you can get used to anything if you're convinced it's necessary.'

Andy shook his head, grimacing. 'Who can?'

'Anyone. People like you and me. If ordinary people couldn't get used to killing there wouldn't be any wars.'

210

'Listen, old pip, this is the sort of discussion to have over a drink.'

'You're right, we've both got work to do. Let's keep that drink in mind,' Jack said, and set off to walk home. If they went out drinking he would be sure not to revive the discussion; the topic obviously upset Andy, and it wasn't worth losing friends over. Andy couldn't be expected to understand, any more than Julia ought to be.

She was out shopping. Jack reached home just after twelve o'clock. He still had time before he was due at the library. He drove to the nearest Oxfam shop and donated the pram, feeling as though his gesture might have earned him some luck.

But not enough. Life could turn on him and the family. Mrs Evans might decide to take them to court. Someone might learn of their windfall – Mr Hardy, or a burglar. The Fraud Squad might conclude that Julia was less innocent of abetting Luke than in fact she was. If Jack was beginning to feel wellnigh invulnerable, that was all the more reason for him to make certain the family was safe from harm. He'd had enough of waiting for bad luck to force him to react. Prevention was better than cure. On his way to work he called in at a builder's merchants and bought a blowlamp small enough to fit into a briefcase or a rucksack.

TWENTY-EIGHT

As the van sped out of the tunnel into a blaze of sunlight Julia said 'What are you going to do when you've got rid of me?'

'I'll find something to keep me busy. If you like we could meet for lunch.'

'We won't have time before you have to go to work.'

He'd known she would make that point, and now she would think he was going off on his own at her suggestion. He felt ashamed of manipulating her and yet pleased with his skill. 'I expect I'll drive round for a bit and maybe find somewhere to walk.'

'I wish I could come with you.'

'We'll all go walking soon. We can go up above Helsby.'

'Isn't that quite a way if the van's not too happy?'

'Not too far, and worth the journey. So I've been told by someone at work.'

He drove into the centre of Liverpool, where mid-morning deliveries all but blocked the streets, and dropped Julia at the doors of the Adelphi Hotel, opposite the stone penis of the statue on the front of Lewis's department store. 'All the luck in the world,' he said to Julia, dragging at the handbrake.

'Let's not get carried away, Jack. This computer firm is holding interviews up and down the country. They're bound to be pretty competitive.'

'So are you.' He leaned over to give her a kiss for luck, and when her tongue met his, tasting faintly minty, he kissed her hard. Three black cabs drew up behind him on the road which separated the hotel steps from the front entrance, and he glimpsed them drawing together like a concertina in the driving mirror, but he didn't let go of Julia until the foremost cab honked. 'Don't expect too much,' she told Jack, sliding her door open.

'Of you? I never could.'

As the van reached the end of the steps he turned to wave, but she had already passed beyond the revolving doors. A rectangle of sunlight shone like the entrance to a furnace, then the glass door pivoted away. Jack blinked and drove uphill, slowing as students crowded across the road outside the University. He wasn't sure what time Julia would be called in for interview, but he wanted to have done by then if he could.

The road grew more like an obstacle course as he approached the industrial park. Cars darted out of side streets, lorries attended shops, flashing their hazard lights repetitively as flints which were failing to ignite wicks. Jack overtook one that was parked on the scribble of white paint trailing from a set of traffic lights. The lights climbed down from red to amber, and as the amber began to pulsate a man stepped onto the deserted crossing, straight into the path of the van. It was Gavin Edge.

He didn't recognise Jack. He gave the van a disparaging glance and walked a little slower, balancing a polystyrene cup of coffee on top of a wad of sandwiches inside a plastic wedge. If the brakes didn't work, Jack thought, neither would Gavin; he would be over his edge. He trod hard on the brake pedal and sounded the horn.

Perhaps Gavin had been ignoring the van so thoroughly he'd forgotten it was there. He flung out his hands to ward it off and staggered away from it, not towards the pavement but along the road. His cup and sandwiches described elegant arcs in the air. The cup struck the lights, and Jack thought he heard coffee sizzling on the sign of the walking man, who'd turned bright red. The van screeched to a halt, though not before driving over Gavin's sandwiches. Jack heard and felt their shell crunch.

Gavin staggered onto the pavement and clung to a concrete lamp-standard with one hand while he thumped it several times with the side of the other. Jack stopped the van

213

a few yards beyond him. As he rounded it he found Gavin storming towards him, gritting his teeth and thrusting out his large square jaw and looking almost blind with fury. 'What the bloody devil ...'

'It's me, Gavin. I just meant to say hello.'

Gavin seemed momentarily incapable of hearing him, but then stopped short of him, more or less opening his fists. 'Oh,' he said, and with an effort at generosity, 'Oh, it's you, Jack.'

'I'm sorry, I didn't mean to—' Jack glanced past him at the dripping signal in an attempt to distract himself from his growing mirth. 'I was trying to make you look at me.'

'Head somewhere else.' Gavin waggled several fingers at his cranium. 'Mine was, I mean. Mad's off home early, sick. She's holding the fort while I went to bring back my lunch.'

'Let me restore it for you.'

'Thanks anyway. I need to lose some weight. Maybe you did me a favour. I take it you're doing well for yourself if you were offering to buy me lunch.'

'I think I've identified my problems. And you're prospering, I hope?'

'Doing my damnedest to keep the accountant happy. He has to see there's always a risk of overestimating a new market. You and I did.' Gavin was glancing at passers-by as if he disliked thinking they had seen his comic turn. 'Regards to the family, anyway,' he blurted and dashed back to the crossing as the green man started to bleep.

Gavin hadn't struck Jack as needing to diet. He looked thinner and more haggard than the last time they had met. Jack watched him sprint across the road, then he moved the briefcase from the back of the van onto the passenger seat before driving off.

Five minutes later he was at the motorway. Beyond the starting line marked by traffic lights hitch-hikers held up placards naming towns. Jack stayed in the outer lane until he'd outdistanced the rest of the traffic. Whatever had been wrong with the van seemed to have righted itself, and he didn't slow down until he reached the first exit to Warrington.

The gentle slope of the road curved gradually between fields and solitary houses selling vegetables and eggs. At Great Sankey the houses started to cluster, and the road became a dual carriageway shaded by trees and divided by a wide strip like an elongated football field. Soon Jack had to brake for the centre of Warrington, a maze populated by shoppers and walled in by store-fronts. It didn't faze him. Even when the road sprouted concrete roundabouts and split into lanes painted with destination numbers, he knew where he was bound: through the centre and out again towards the other motorway. Road signs shone green as traffic lights as they caught the sunlight, and in five minutes he was driving leisurely along the road he had located on the map.

Long blocks of thin-faced houses, packed with bay windows and interrupted only by narrow side streets, enclosed the road, which felt to Jack as much like a prolonged village as part of a town. A few minutes later it crossed a canal staked out by fishermen. He parked the van in a side street near a building society and a bank, and walked the last few blocks.

He had every reason to expect Enid Bellows' shop to be in the side street to which he had addressed the letter, and a van marked BELLOWS FLORISTS was. The street, however, consisted of two terraces like reflections of each other; there was no sign of a shop. He turned back to the main road, and a scent of flowers reached him through the air that was heavy with heat and exhaust fumes. The shop was on the opposite corner of the junction, which seemed to be just about the busiest part of the road.

He made sure the briefcase was securely fastened as he crossed to the florist's. Beyond a window banked with flowers he saw a man and a woman behind a counter at the back of the shop. The man was leafing through slips of paper, the woman was arranging a wreath. With all the flowers in the window Jack found it gratifyingly difficult to see into the shop.

Presumably the woman was Enid Bellows, but he needed her to be alone. He walked to the end of the block, past a

215

greengrocer's and a post office, and strolled back. Could he call the man out of the shop on some pretext? He supposed he could regard this visit as spying out the situation, except that doing so little felt like putting Julia at risk.

He pretended to examine the display outside the greengrocer's while he tried to plan, and when nothing useful occurred to him he went in to buy a pound of Granny Smiths in case anyone had noticed him dawdling. Before leaving the shop he put the bag of apples in the briefcase, where they nestled against the blowlamp, except for one apple into which he bit. The green sharpness seemed to blaze through his teeth into his skull as he stepped onto the pavement and saw the man who had been behind the florist's counter emerging from the shop.

Jack walked to the post office next door to the florist's and faced the advertising postcards in the window while he spied sidelong on the man. Whenever he remembered not to look conspicuous he bit into the fruit and glanced at the postcards, at least three of which advertised the value of his name: a house numbered 11, the digits of a postcode, two consecutive digits of a phone number. He had just located the third appearance of eleven when the florist's van turned out of the side street and chugged towards the centre of Warrington, trailing smoke.

Jack took a last bite of the apple, crunching a seed between his teeth, and dropped the core on top of a newspaper in a waste-bin, obscuring whatever the headline said. Either the man was delivering flowers or he'd taken the van to be overhauled; in either case he ought to be gone for a while. Swinging his briefcase jauntily, Jack was at the florist's in two strides.

Nobody was in the shop, not even the florist. There must be a back room, out of sight from the street. A bell pinged like a timer as Jack closed the door behind him. None of the passers-by so much as glanced at him as he pushed down the catch on the Yale lock and turned the placard outwards so that it said CLOSED to the world. 'I'll be with you now,' the woman called from the back room.

Jack had just counted eleven when she came to the counter. She was larger than she had appeared through the wreath, but otherwise nondescript: brownish hair which looked less natural than uncombable, a rotund face whose plumpness blurred its features. 'How can I help?' she said.

'Help what?' Jack Awkward might have said or thought of saying, but he had to be quick and decisive; there was no telling how soon she might notice that the door was locked. He snapped the briefcase open. 'I wrote to you.'

'Did you? That's nice. I look forward to the postman's knock.' She leaned her hands on the counter with two wooden thuds, the second of which sounded like an echo. 'Don't I know you?' she said.

Jack gazed into the depths of the briefcase. The nozzle of the blowlamp made him think of the snout of some creature holding itself still in its lair. 'I do know you,' the florist said. 'Give us a clue, come on.'

Jack gazed at her and reached into the briefcase. 'I know that grin,' she said, and slapped her cheek lightly with her left hand, two fingers of which had knuckles wrapped in plaster. 'It was at her wedding up the road. Weren't those your little ones everyone remarked on?'

'Depends what they were saying about them.'

'They were a delight, that's what everyone said.' She peered at him with a comical grimace that discovered dozens of wrinkles around her eyes, then her face relaxed. 'Tom, that's your name.'

'And you're Enid.'

'That's me all over,' she said, gesturing as though she was sketching a larger and more shapeless body for herself, and cocked her head on one side, rucking the flesh of her neck. 'But I don't remember you writing to me.'

'It was about luck.'

'Well, we can all use more of that,' she said, and glanced past him. 'Let him in, will you?'

Jack turned his head without moving his body, and realised that by standing midway between the counter and the door he was blocking her view of the placard. A boy in his mid-teens with a luminous green headband was shading his eyes and squinting through the glass. Sunlight on it seemed to be the problem, and Jack thought it unlikely that the boy could distinguish his face. He drew a breath which tasted of flowers and more faintly of gas, and as he did so the boy stepped back and ran across the road to flag down a bus. 'Impatient customer,' Jack said, and found that Enid Bellows was gazing at him. 'I've remembered,' she told him.

As his grip on the briefcase shifted, the blowlamp touched the back of his other hand. Perhaps because of the unexpectedness, the metal felt suddenly hot. 'Remembered,' he said.

'What you must have sent me. The letter that's supposed to bring good luck.'

'And did it?'

'I hope it will.'

Jack's hand hesitated between the wad of letters and the blowlamp. 'What have you done with it?'

She raised her eyebrows as if she had already answered him. 'Sent copies to the next thirteen customers who came in after I got it. You never know what may help, I always say, though the old man shouts at me if I so much as cross the road instead of walking under a ladder.'

'You never know where help may come from.'

Jack felt both relieved and robbed of impetus, and stood with his hand in the briefcase until she spoke again. 'Was that all you wanted?'

Jack snapped the briefcase shut. 'No, I'd like a bouquet for my wife.'

'They start at six pounds, or seven delivered.'

'Six will be fine,' Jack said, moving to the door. 'I'll just be popping in the post office while you make it up.'

As she turned towards the back room he reversed the placard and pushed up the catch on the lock, muffling the click with the heel of his hand. Having walked slowly to the end of the block, he returned to the florist's. His surroundings seemed to have brightened and clarified, as though the sunlight was penetrating everything it touched. Enid Bellows looked up from wrapping the bouquet in cellophane, and he saw that her features were by no means unclear now that he was familiar with them. He experienced a surge of affection and well-being as she said 'What's her name?'

'Who?'

'Your lady love,' she said, tutting at his forgetfulness.

'Julia.'

'Really? I thought—' She looked embarrassed; perhaps she thought she'd caused him to betray himself. 'Take a card,' she said.

'Why, are you going to show me a trick?'

She emitted a sound as much like a groan as a laugh. 'You're too quick for me. I should have remembered from the wedding.'

Jack selected a card from the revolving stand, and she clipped it to the cellophane. 'Remember me to your wife,' she said as he reached the door, 'and, oh—'

Jack halted with one hand on the latch. 'You've remembered something else?'

'Remind her she was going to drop me in a recipe the next time she was passing.'

'Are you certain that was Julia? It doesn't sound like her.'

'I keep thinking that wasn't her name.' The florist lifted a flap of the counter and stumped over to open the door for him. 'Maybe the old brains are addled. Maybe it was three other people.'

'Aren't we all,' Jack said, and headed for the van, where he stood the bouquet on the passenger seat and held it upright with the briefcase. Soon the streets fell behind, and the road swooped between fields to the motorway. He wasn't at all surprised to find he was joining it at junction 11, nor that the first junction after 12 was 14. Of course it was silly to imagine that the landscape had somehow been arranged as a sign to him, but he felt that the family's bad luck might have disappeared as though, like junction 13, it had never been. 'Thank you, Enid Bellows,' he murmured as the scent of flowers filled the front of the van.

TWENTY-NINE

On Sunday afternoon he was back on that stretch of motorway. As he drove up the ramp at junction 14, towards a sky like an inverted sea inhabited by a single glinting fish, Laura said 'Do you think we'll ever get a car?'

'Why, are you tired of Old Faithful?'

'I just feel a bit sick sometimes. Maybe it's riding in the front, or the petrolly smell.'

'Perhaps we could fix up a seat in the back,' Julia said.

'It wouldn't be safe,' Jack told her. 'Don't we all quite like riding in the front like this? We won't be together for ever.'

'You don't have to say that,' Laura protested. 'You'll bring us bad luck.'

'I'll do my best not to,' Jack said, driving around the ample roundabout at the top of the ramp and taking the Helsby road. 'And I'll see what I can do about the petroleous smell.'

'You made that word up.'

'How much do you bet?'

'Everything we've got.'

'Then we'll have nothing, because you'll find the word in the dictionary if you look it up.' When Laura glanced at him, hoping he was joking, he said 'It's a good job I didn't take your bet.'

Traffic lights halted the van at the edge of Helsby, and Jack patted her hand. He wanted her and Julia to share his optimism. Though he hadn't yet been able to contrive himself the chance to visit any of his addressees since meeting Enid Bellows, his encounters with her and with Gavin had left him with a lasting sense of rightness. Returning to Helsby wasn't just a celebration, it was a way of proving to himself that he and the family had nothing to fear.

When the traffic lights released him he drove into the village, over the bridge where the road forked, up The Rock. Today the verge was loaded with cars, and guests were arriving at a barbecue in one of the elevated gardens as the blond children who he'd seen watching the horse ran to greet them. Jack almost waved, but of course the children hadn't noticed him the first time. He felt invisible, and all the better for it, as he drove to the top of the road.

He was turning left when he caught sight of Stephen Arrod's house. It looked disused, and somehow darker than the rest of the sunlit landscape. All the curtains were drawn, and the chimney seemed bereft of smoke – not that Jack would have welcomed the sight of smoke above the house. He saw the Kops tripping over their hoses as a blazing puppet pranced frantically, and hummed a snatch of the Ritual Fire Dance to dispel the images before they came any closer. Even once they'd vanished he didn't feel relieved until he had parked the van where he'd left it last time and was making for the stile rather than for the downward slope.

Beyond the stile a path led through a small wood that sounded like a generator. The hum of bees faded as the path emerged into the open and wound upwards over limestone slabs bristling with gorse. A scrap of blue paper pinned to a large fern unfolded its wings and kept fluttering ahead of Jack. The path smelled of grass parched the same colour as the dusty earth. The undergrowth buzzed as if it was primed with miniature alarms, set off and then silenced by his approach. 'Try and count the grasshoppers,' he said mischievously to Laura.

When the path climbed to a plateau Jack walked to the edge and let the distance come to meet him. Beyond the insects racing on the motorway, flames hovered like earthbound souls of the industrial landscape. Further out were models of the Liverpool cathedrals, two bridges which he could have placed across the Mersey at Runcorn with a finger and thumb, the brown mass of Warrington fretted with roofs. 'Welcome to the Count's domain,' Jack murmured.

'Whose?'

221

He hadn't expected either of the family to hear him, but Laura had. 'The Count of Eleven,' he said.

She sat on the jagged flat edge, Julia grabbing her shoulder to steady her, and dangled her legs. 'Who's he when he's at home?'

'I suppose you could say I am. That's what my name adds up to.'

'How do you reckon that?'

'J is the tenth letter of the alphabet, A is the first. Add them all up and see what you get.'

She was silent for a time. Julia sat beside her and plaited stalks of grass while Jack scrutinised the horizon, which looked sunbleached. Quite soon Laura said 'Not eleven.'

For a moment Jack felt dizzy and too close to the edge, as though a support on which he was relying had been snatched away. He stepped back quickly. 'Of course it does.'

Laura shook her cropped head. 'Ninety-two.'

'And what do nine and two add up to?'

'*Dad.*'

He wasn't sure whether she was admitting defeat or thought he was cheating. 'Laura and Julia add up to it too,' he said.

She seemed to ponder that, then said 'We're really thirteen.'

'I certainly hope not,' Jack said, feeling it was safest to sit down. 'Where do you get that from?'

'It's what Orchard adds up to.'

She was right, of course. Though he was seated he felt more precarious than before, as if all his calculations had been erroneous. 'None of our full names does,' he said, 'and Orchards doesn't either.'

Julia lay back and sighed. 'Does it matter? I'd quite like to get away from numbers for a bit.'

'You can,' Jack said, and lay back too, but not for long. When sunlight kept swelling behind his eyelids like an impatient fire he said 'Anyone coming for a walk?'

Julia murmured a sleepy refusal, and Laura said 'I like it here.'

He was happy to walk by himself; he wanted to walk off his doubts. He picked his way along the stone edge, gazing down at houses which looked as if he could trample on them. Laura's discovery needn't trouble him, he thought; if anything, it proved he was on the right track, since he had instinctively prevented her from adding up to thirteen. 'Trust the count of eleven,' he said to himself.

His walk brought him to a burned patch of the hill. It ran alongside the path for about twenty feet, an irregular plot of blackened earth strewn with ash. Several beer cans crumpled by the fire lay in the midst of it, near a bunch of charred stubs protruding from the earth, the remains of a bush. He stood and stared at the vandalised patch. When people felt themselves to be meaningless, he thought, they were capable of anything. He imagined how the bush had looked, flaming orange in full daylight with the unassailable conviction of a dream, or blazing in the twilight as if it marked a region between waking and dream, or illuminating the hillside at night, rousing the bushes around it to dance. He gazed until the smell of ash scratched his throat and the stubs began to resemble burned fingers, and then he turned quickly and hurried back.

He was almost in sight of Julia and Laura when someone hailed him. 'Where's the rest of the family today?'

If he should recognise her, he didn't know from where. She was wearing a purple track suit, a straw hat and sunglasses, and carrying a straight black stick. Her vague familiarity seemed like an omen, but of what? 'Over there, I hope,' Jack said, pointing ahead.

She came tramping down through the ferns as Julia and Laura waved to him. When she reached the main path she leaned on her stick and raised her sunglasses like a visor. 'Where's the baby?'

She'd seen him on his way to visit Stephen Arrod. He felt as if she and his family had trapped him between them, isolating him in the relentless sunlight. He had to answer her – he mustn't let any of them suspect that he had reason to hesitate – but Julia was quicker. 'Here she is,' she said, hugging Laura.

223

The woman cut down a swathe of ferns with her stick and stared hard at Jack. 'Not her. The baby in the pram.'

'We haven't had one of those for years,' Julia said.

'He knows what I mean,' the woman said, still facing Jack, and demanded of him 'Weren't you up here the other day with a baby in a pram?'

'Would you try and wheel a pram over this terrain?'

'Someone did,' she insisted. 'And if it wasn't you—'

'If it wasn't me it must have been someone else.'

'Someone with less sense,' Julia added.

The woman poked the scythed ferns with her stick and eventually turned to her. 'I could have sworn I'd seen your husband with a pram quite recently.'

'Not unless he's got a second family hidden somewhere.'

'Or a little niece or nephew.'

'Not even one of those,' Julia said. 'We've just got us.'

The woman bowed over her stick and gazed at Jack as though she was determined not to move until she recalled where she had previously encountered him. She opened her mouth, looking almost sure of what she was about to say – perhaps that Jack had been taking a neighbour's baby for a walk. She pursed her lips instead and jammed the sunglasses over her eyes before trudging towards the woods, slashing at the undergrowth. 'Sorry to have bothered you,' she called as an afterthought.

'What was up with her?' Laura said.

'People get stranger as they get older.'

'As you can tell by looking at me,' Jack said.

Julia threw a handful of grass at him. 'Maybe she saw you somewhere when Laura was still in the pram.'

Jack sat on the edge for a few minutes to ensure that they didn't meet the woman on their way to the van. He felt he'd learned something today on the hill. The feeling persisted as he drove home, and lingered as he lay in bed. It seemed entirely benign, no reason for him to lie awake.

In the morning Julia learned that she hadn't been short-listed for the job regarding which she had been interviewed at the hotel. She had resigned herself to the possibility in advance, and Laura was doing her best to seem resigned too. 'Only thirty-three days to Crete now,' she said.

Jack realised she was being cheerful, but he felt as though she was telling him to be quick. Belatedly he realised why the woman on the hill had seemed an omen. He'd learned from their encounter that even if people looked straight at him they didn't see a criminal; he was invisible because nobody could know what he meant to do. Thirty-three days, he thought: what could be clearer? It wasn't just time enough, it was like hearing the Count undertaking to finish his labours before he and the family left for Crete.

THIRTY

Jack came downstairs looking for his briefcase. He couldn't go to work without that, he thought; he couldn't do the job. Of course he knew not to ask Julia where it was, and in a few moments he remembered that it was still in the back of the van; where else would it be? He was opening the front door, intending to wait on the path until she was ready to go, when she called 'What do you think about this in the paper?'

'What?'

'Come and see.'

He closed the front door with his heel and used the impetus to send him towards the front room. Julia was sitting on the couch, holding the local newspaper, which she folded inside out and then in half horizontally before passing it to him, one finger indicating a paragraph. 'What do you think?' she said again before he'd had time to look.

It was among the job vacancies. COMPUTER TUTOR, the heading would have said, except that the typesetter had spelled the last word 'tuter'. The job required applicants with a knowledge of financial management and word processing, and it was at a college in Withens Lane, no more than fifteen minutes' walk away. 'Should I give it a try?' Julia said.

'Definitely. I'm amazed you're even asking.'

'But they say they'd prefer someone with a teaching degree.'

'You earned one of those at Rankin's.'

'That isn't what they mean.'

'Then it should be. Anyway, you won't know unless you try, will you?'

'Do you think I should write to them now?'

226

'I do. And while you are I'll go for a stamp.'

'For a tramp, you mean.'

'Vagrants have enough to put up with without me going for them.'

Julia groaned and waved him away, and he walked to the newsagent's which sold postage stamps. 'We've thirteens and sevens in now if you want some,' the newsagent said.

'I'll take one of each.'

She seemed to feel rebuffed, as if she had put herself out on his behalf, and so he bought half a dozen of each; the encouragement she'd given him was worth at least that much. Like the woman on Helsby Hill, she'd shown him that he needn't be afraid of anyone who remembered having seen him. By the time he strolled home Julia had written her letter and sealed the envelope. 'What did you put?' he said.

'Myself on a piece of paper.'

'I'd like to see anyone try and reduce you to that.' As he gave her the stamps he said 'Maybe you shouldn't tell Laura you've applied for another job unless she asks.'

'Why?'

'Just in case, and I *mean* just in case, she might be disappointed.'

'There's that,' Julia admitted, and looked askance at him, the thirteenpenny stamp resting on her tongue. She picked the stamp out of her mouth and smoothed it onto the envelope. 'If she has to be we'll let her show it, won't we? She's at one of the times of her life when she needs to let her feelings out, and there's nothing wrong with that. You aren't afraid of yours, are you?'

'No, not at all.'

'No need to be,' she said as if she thought he wasn't being entirely honest with her. 'Well, let's send me off to try my luck.'

On their way to Birkenhead she posted the letter in King Street, where Jack had bought and subsequently donated the pram. Less than fifteen minutes later they were at Charing Cross, a five-armed star of shopping streets. 'Shall I buy you some trunks?' she said. 'I should think even you might learn to swim in Greece.'

227

'Fish and chips do, but it isn't worth more than a couple of quid to find out.'

'You just have to learn not to be scared of water,' she said, jumping down as the traffic lights changed.

Jack followed the most direct route to the motorway and was there in eleven minutes, feeling as though nothing could stop him. When the motorway rose towards Ellesmere Port he had a sense of not being there to be seen. Today was his day off from the library, and he meant to make at least two visits. Past the merging of the motorways he raced along the stretch where a thirteenth junction would have been, and left it at junction 11. Though the next exit would have been closer to his first destination, this one seemed too good an omen to waste.

Where the road through the fields forked he turned right beneath a gathering of foliage. The route would take him through the outskirts of Warrington, where two of his subjects lived. Depending on how well his visits went, he might have time to make a third before heading home.

Soon the road led him through villages – Stockton Heath, Grappenhall – half-submerged in suburbs. Grappenhall was where, to quote the directory precisely, Edw Byrne Cobbler worked and perhaps lived. Beyond a new estate a humpbacked bridge led the van onto a cobbled road, where Jack heard the briefcase jumping about behind him. The cobblestones gave out, and the road bridged a canal to a main road. He knew that the address wasn't beside a canal, but it was more by instinct than by consciously recalling the map that he crossed into a side street which brought him to a major road. Among the blocks of long thin houses were occasional clusters of shops, and the cobbler's was in the second clump he passed.

Jack drove to the next shops and parked outside a bookmaker's, then took the briefcase out of the van and walked back half a mile. Around him everything was luminously defined: the milky drip about to fall from the pointed base of an ice-cream cone which a small boy beside the opaque window of the bookmaker's was licking, the molten spillage of

228

sunlight which slid over the window of each car that passed Jack, the tiny bright round eyes of a sparrow bathing in the dust of a yellowing front lawn. Everything was as clear as he himself was unnoticeable, even if there had been anyone on the pavement to see him.

The cobbler's was beyond a restaurant that was closed until the evening and the frosted windows of a bank. There was no name above the cobbler's, but surely there couldn't be two such businesses on this road. Jack opened the door without glancing around him and stepped into the shop. It was a small room that smelled of leather, and a small leathery man was at work behind the counter piled with hanks of shoelaces and circular tins of polish. He was fitting a boot onto a last in the gloom among a copse of shoetrees and whistling through his teeth as though he would know the tune and rhythm once he heard them. 'Give us a minute,' he grumbled, apparently speaking for the boot as well as for himself.

If the blinds on the door and the window were down, nobody would be able to see into the shop. Jack shifted the briefcase into his left hand and reaching his free hand over his left shoulder, coughed to cover the sound of the catch on the lock. The cobbler must have thought he was expressing impatience, because he hunched over the last to show he wasn't to be hurried. Watching him, Jack thought his skull resembled a kind of last onto which his face had been tugged until the bald scalp fitted snugly, while the rest of the face grew looser and more wrinkled the closer it approached the chin. Eventually the cobbler gave the boot a grudging nod and stared over the sole as if Jack had prevented him from doing his best. 'Got your paper?'

'It depends what—'

'No goods without a receipt,' the cobbler said with relish.

'I knew that was what you meant. I'm not collecting.'

Jack barely hesitated, but the cobbler nodded hard at his briefcase. 'Well, open it up if you're opening and give us whatever you've got.'

Jack didn't need reminding that he should be quick, but

hasty was another matter. 'You're Edward Byrne?'

'I'm Byrne. Who wants to know?'

'Edward Byrne,' Jack repeated, suddenly wondering if the contraction in the directory could have denoted Edwin.

'Edward Byrne wants to know if Edward Byrne is Edward Byrne?' The cobbler had begun to slap his open palm with a metal shoehorn. 'Shape up, son. Some of us have better things to do than talk tripe.'

'I was just making sure it was you I wrote to. Now I am—'

Byrne struck the counter with the shoehorn. 'Don't want any. These are the laces I stock and that's the polish. They're what my customers want, and if they don't they can bugger off.'

'I'm not a salesman, Mr Byrne.'

'Are you anything at all besides a bloody nuisance?'

The clang of the shoehorn was still reverberating in Jack's brain. It reminded him of the sound the tank of the blowlamp had made on coming into contact with Stephen Arrod's head. 'I'm just a man like you,' he said, taking hold of the lock of the briefcase.

'We've all got our jobs to do, right enough, those of us who don't sit around all day whining about how no bugger will give us one.' The cobbler gave Jack what for Byrne might be a relatively sympathetic look. 'I'll wish you better luck wherever you're off next, but that's the best I can do.'

He turned away from the counter and threw out his arms to shoot back the cuffs of his shirt and jacket. As Jack quietly opened the briefcase he thought Byrne resembled a crucifixion viewed from behind. He was reaching into the briefcase when the cobbler swung round. 'What did you write to me? When?'

'A few weeks ago, to give you the chance to turn ill luck into good.'

Byrne exposed his teeth in something like a grin and tapped them several times with the shoehorn. 'How was that?'

'Don't you remember the letter?'

'I won't forget it as long as I live, son. What I'm asking is why I was lucky.'

Jack felt a sigh of relief building up inside him. 'I suppose because the letter must have worked for you if you did as it said.'

Byrne came to the counter and leaning on it, thrust his face at Jack. 'What I'm asking you is why you singled me out when I've never seen you before in my life.'

'Will it make a difference?'

Byrne raised his left hand and made a gesture of crushing an object between finger and thumb. 'That much.'

Though Jack wasn't conscious of tilting the briefcase, the blowlamp seemed to fit itself into his hand. 'So I don't need to ask what you did with the letter.'

'You're quick, you are. If I blink I reckon I won't see you going.'

Jack's fist closed around the blowlamp. He wanted to be fair, despite the exhilaration which had begun to make him feel elevated, viewing himself from above. 'What did you do with it, Mr Byrne?'

The cobbler shoved himself away from the counter so violently that the shoehorn fell off the edge with a resounding clang. 'Wrote to thirteen other lucky buggers, what do you think?' he shouted. 'Now if you're satisfied, some of us have to work for a living.'

Jack let go of the blowlamp. He felt abruptly deflated and in danger of being confronted by himself. If he went out now he would feel as though he'd left some task unfinished – and then a thought struck him. 'I don't suppose you sell shoes as well as mend them.'

'There's a few people never called back for,' Byrne allowed with some reluctance.

'That's what I should be here for. I promised weeks ago to buy a chap a pair.'

'What size?'

'Mine would fit him. Nine.'

Byrne scowled and trudging to the back of the shop, began to rummage in the gloom. He was making so much noise that Jack didn't bother to muffle the sound of releasing the lock. He had just released it when Byrne stalked forwards and dumped two stout black boots on the counter. 'That's the only pair of nines I've got.'

Jack was reminded of playing cards with the family. 'You win,' Jack Awkward might have said now, or even 'Beats my ace of spades.' Instead he asked 'How much?'

'Call it a tenner,' Byrne said as if he would have accepted less to see Jack out of the shop.

'Sounds too good to be true.' One ten to buy nine twice — two sets of figures that each made eleven. Jack closed the briefcase and dug in his pocket for a ten-pound note, which Byrne received with little grace. 'I've no bags,' Byrne said, morosely enjoying that triumph.

'You've given me all I need.' Tucking the boots under his arm, Jack went to the door. He grasped the latch and said 'You really did mean—'

But Byrne was at his last again, whistling louder and more haphazardly. Of course he'd spoken the truth about the letters, Jack assured himself, pulling the door open. He stepped out backwards, watching in case Byrne glanced up and let Jack see his eyes, but the cobbler seemed intent on his work. Jack shut the door and bumped into a policeman.

The policeman appeared not to notice him. He was talking into a receiver which emitted a hiss like an imperfectly doused fire before each response. As Jack walked around him, murmuring an apology, he headed for the bank, whether answering a call or on his own behalf wasn't clear.

Jack walked to the van, hearing cars dusting the road, feeling satisfied with a job well done and ready for another. 'I'm invisible when I have to be,' he told the clown on the key-ring as he started the engine. 'Invisible and invincible, they're the Count's Is.'

He closed his eyes so as to visualise the map before moving off. The road would bring him to a bridge, beyond which he should turn left and follow a road alongside the canal. He did so, and drove steadily beside the water, keeping an eye out for a sign for Walter Foster, Waterways Bookseller. When the next road bridge brought an end to the houses, however, he had seen no shops at all.

Two vans which he presumed belonged to fishermen were parked in a layby near the bridge. He left the van behind them and walked back. He was at the start of the house numbers, and number 155 would be several minutes' walk away, which was all to the good. A hedge obscured his view of the canal from the pavement in front of the pairs of houses. He could hear water coursing gently, and birds fluttering in the hedge. Now and then a fishing-rod would rear up beyond it, or dip towards the canal as a hook plopped into the water.

By the time Jack came in sight of the address on the letter, the canal opposite seemed to be clear of fishermen, and nobody was to be seen in any of the front rooms. He went swiftly up the drive beyond a wooden gate which someone had left open, and rang the doorbell.

A garage concealed him from the ground floor of the next pair of houses, even when he stepped back a few feet to scrutinise the house. Both of its front windows, upstairs and down, had their curtains drawn. He pressed the brass button again, longer this time, but the ringing was the only sound within.

His sense of being let down had returned, stronger than it had been in the cobbler's. Could he have mistaken the address? He squatted by the briefcase on the doorstep and leafed through the envelopes. Assuming that he hadn't copied it wrongly, the number was correct. He clutched the briefcase shut and rose to his feet, and was staring at the house as though that might conjure up its owner when a voice said 'Who are you after?'

Taken off guard, Jack had to resist the impulse to hide his face with the briefcase. 'If you're after books,' the voice said from the canal path, 'you're out of luck.'

'Is Mr Foster away?'

'He's here.'

It wasn't the same voice. Whereas the previous speaker's accent had been plummy and cultured, this man sounded proud to hail from Lancashire. Jack could do nothing if the bookseller wasn't alone, but a retreat at this point would look suspicious. He crossed the road and craned over the hedge that bordered the canal.

There was only one person on the towpath, a shirt-sleeved man sitting on a canvas stool. He'd turned to peer through the hedge, a flat tin in one hand, the hook at the end of his line in the other. He wore half-moon spectacles low on his nose, making his already lofty forehead seem even higher. 'Walter Foster?' Jack said.

'You've found me out.'

'I thought you were with someone.'

'Just my little wriggling friends.' Foster held up the tin of bait. 'This is how I answer the phone,' he said in the cultured voice, then let the accent drop. 'Buying or selling?' he said as though either would be a trial.

'Not precisely either.'

Foster squinted at the label on the tin. 'Are we waiting for you to be precise?'

'Let me come down and talk to you,' Jack said, and strode two hundred yards or so along the hedge to the nearest gap. All the way sunlight showed him empty front rooms, and once he stepped through the hedge he was out of sight from the road and the houses. As he walked along the dusty unkempt path, Foster shuffled round on the stool to meet him. 'Fancy some lunch?'

'That's very kind,' Jack said, then saw that Foster was offering him the tin, in which fat white grubs were squirming. 'I'm saving myself, thanks,' Jack said.

'Strong stomach, eh? There's a few I've shown the wrigglers who've lost their bread and dripping in the canal. One way of keeping the fish fed. They'll gobble anything, just like some folk.' Foster jerked his head to fling back a dangling lock of grey hair. 'Much time for books?' he said as if the relevance was obvious.

'I'm a librarian.'

'Then I imagine you'd say we're in the same business.' Foster pinched a grub between finger and thumb and raised it to his face, opening his mouth in a loose grin, and Jack thought he intended to hold the bait between his teeth while he closed the tin. Instead he placed the open tin on his lap and holding the grub above it, took what seemed to Jack an

234

unnecessarily long time to pierce its body with the fish-hook. 'I like them to know what's in store for them,' he explained, closing the tin and dropping it into the hamper beside him, and shied the hook into the middle of the canal. 'So are you in uniform today?' he said.

'I'm not here as a librarian.'

'I don't need to put my voice on, then.' Foster pushed his hair back with one hand like an actor. 'You weren't thinking you could have a free read of my stock.'

'I'm sure nobody could.'

'I didn't get where I am by not knowing what things are worth,' Foster said, and having propped his fishing-rod on its stand, raised his face to Jack. 'So what's the secret? Have I had a clue yet?'

He was asking why Jack was there. 'I wrote to you a few weeks ago,' Jack said, feeling as though he was playing the same scene with yet another actor.

'Sending me money?'

'Not directly.'

'An order?'

'More of a request.'

'Go on. You've got me drooling. I'm agog.'

A car swept by beyond the hedge, and Jack reminded himself that he couldn't be seen. 'I sent you a copy of a letter that worked for me. It said—'

'It wished me luck.'

'Well, yes. That's it exactly.'

'It said if I made thirteen copies it would make it worth my while.'

'Precisely.'

'You think all it takes to get on in the world is sending thirteen copies of a letter.'

'Not all it takes, no, but it helps. And not sending them—'

'Nothing is for nothing in this world, my friend. Maybe you think it is because you're paid out of the rates. You should be glad you came. You'll be going away wiser.'

'I can guess what you did with my letter, then,' Jack said, grasping the lock of the briefcase.

'It went where all the junk mail goes. Some days I believe half a rain-forest lands on my doormat.'

'And if I happened to have brought you another copy in case the first one never reached you—'

'Then I'd take it off you.'

Jack pulled the briefcase wide. The blowlamp caught the sunlight as though it was impatient to flame, and beneath it Foster gazed up at him, eyebrows high on his creased forehead. 'And do what?' Jack said.

'What I'm told. Anything for a quiet life.'

'You'd send copies to your friends or someone?'

'What do I have to do to convince you, pull out my hair?'

Jack shoved a hand into the briefcase and covered the blowlamp to blot out the illusion of flame. 'I ought to be honest – I'm not being completely unselfish. When you didn't follow the instructions in the letter the bad luck somehow boomeranged on me and my family. So you'd be well advised to be sure of the people you send your copies to.'

'Well, I never would have known that if you hadn't told me. Is that mine?' Foster held out his hand as Jack found the appropriate envelope. 'Now have you finished scaring the fish?'

'Of course. Excuse me,' Jack said, and handing him the letter, made for the gap in the hedge. The light he had seen in the briefcase seemed to have entered his surroundings, the glossy green leaves of the hedge, the pebbles gleaming through the dust underfoot, the earthy beads of water which fringed splashes at the edge of the path, the patterns swaying and expanding on the surface of the canal. An underwater movement caught his eye, and he stopped to watch a large dappled fish swimming towards Foster. It looked as though a portion of the canal-bed composed of earth and stones had been brought to life by the sunlight and rippling water. 'Here comes some of your luck,' he called to the bookseller.

The last word was sucked back into his mouth by a gasp. As he turned he caught Foster in the act of tearing up the letter and depositing the fragments in the hamper. The sunlight seemed to flare up and focus on the seated man. 'You shouldn't have done that,' Jack said regretfully.

Foster didn't hear him. He didn't look up until Jack had halved the distance between them, and then he glanced towards Jack to see what was causing the unfamiliar sound. The flame of this blowlamp wasn't nearly as loud as the blowlamp Jack had returned to Andy Nation, but it still produced a satisfying roar. 'What are you—' Foster demanded, and more shrilly: 'Good God, what—'

Jack let the blowlamp do his talking for him. He need only walk, because the sight of him was twisting the bookseller's face into a caricature of disbelief struggling with panic. Jack was at least ten strides away from him when the bookseller lurched to his feet and tried to run. Foster's haste sent the stool skittering into his path. He dodged it wildly, slipped on a patch of moss and sprawled into the canal.

The splash was spectacular. If Jack hadn't retreated, his trousers would have been soaked. The fish flicked its tail as if in disapproval and swam out of reach with grace that looked positively aloof. As thick ripples collided with the far bank and began to multiply, Foster floundered to the surface about six feet from the edge of the path, spewing water and clawing at his face to clear away locks of hair plastered across his spectacles. 'Help,' he screamed, 'I can't sw—'

'Neither can I,' Jack said, but Foster couldn't have heard him. He must have lost his footing, because his face tilted back in the water, which filled his ears and mouth, drowning his last word. He was going to float, Jack thought, remembering Julia assuring him how easy that was. The sensation obviously terrified Foster, who started to flail his limbs as though he was desperate to touch solid ground with some part of himself. His face canted upright again, streaming and spluttering, and then it sank.

Jack set down the briefcase and the blowlamp on the path. His surge of hilarity at the sight of the Hardyesque pratfall had given way to a sense that he ought to intervene, but how? He couldn't jump into the canal, and he couldn't very well run for help; Foster was bound to accuse him of causing his fall. On the other hand, if Foster came close enough for

Jack to haul him out, mightn't he be sufficiently grateful to return the favour by sending the letters? Jack turned off the blowlamp and waited to see where the distorted agitated lump, which seemed for the moment unable to do more than ruffle the surface of the canal, would bob up.

Apparently Foster couldn't see where he was going. He was yawing towards the middle of the canal, but to gain the far bank he would have to flounder a good few yards further than to return to the path. What looked like a lungful of bubbles swarmed helplessly to the surface, and Jack wondered if that was the end, though weren't the drowning supposed to rise three times first? Then, as if the expulsion of breath had lightened him or the agony in his lungs had lent him extra strength, Foster's head and shoulders wallowed up from the canal, and he made a wild grab for the tip of the fishing-rod.

He missed, but not entirely. Though his other hand was only clutching at the air, it snagged the line. This bent the rod towards him, and he dragged it down until he was able to seize it with both hands. 'Help,' he gargled, spitting and retching. 'Help!'

He was trying to haul himself along the rod to the bank. The support on the path was wobbling dangerously, but it had caught on an exposed brick at the edge. Jack came to a decision. 'Hold on,' he called, 'I'll—'

As soon as Jack turned towards the rod, Foster began to scream 'Murder! Keep him off! Help! Murder!'

'I only want—' Jack said, and halted. Foster ceased screaming, presumably in order to concentrate on inching hand over hand along the rod, but it was clear that he would recommence his accusations if Jack moved. He would if he ever got out of the canal – he would tell people about the blowlamp – and so there was nothing Jack could do but wait for the rod to topple into the water.

He watched as the metal support creaked and scraped against the brick. Suddenly it keeled over, and the rod whipped the surface of the canal and immediately sank. Foster plunged forwards, a movement Julia had frequently tried to teach Jack, and managed to plant his fingertips on the margin of the canal.

The effort seemed to have exhausted him. He hung against the bank, his head and shoulders a bedraggled bust exhibited by the canal. Jack imagined his waterlogged body pressing against the slimy bank, but even those sensations must come as a relief, for an expression not entirely unlike triumph flickered in Foster's eyes. It lasted until Jack began to speak. 'I can't . . .' Jack mused aloud.

Foster tried and failed to heave himself out of the water. A patch of moss came away in his hand, exuding moisture. His arms were shaking, and his body must be as his feet scrabbled underwater at the slippery bank. Jack continued to pity him until Foster commenced screaming, louder than ever. 'Someone help! He's killing me! Murder!'

'Just as you say,' Jack said, and grabbed the blowlamp. Impatience had got the better of him. The hiss of gas sounded like a whisper, wordlessly urging him. The flame spouted from the nozzle, growing invisible almost as soon as it emerged into the open air. He kicked the hamper into the weeds beside the path and stooped towards Foster, whose face had taken on exactly the look of mingled incredulity and panic with which it had originally greeted the sight of the blowlamp. If he didn't believe in it, Jack thought angrily, why had he made so much noise about it? He might have been able to save himself.

Jack was hoping that the nearness of the blowlamp would cause Foster to retreat out of reach of the bank, but the bookseller began to drag himself along the margin, his fingers leaving snail-tracks on the moss. In two strides Jack was above him and aiming the flame at his fingers. Even that didn't dislodge him from the bank. Instead his fingers started wriggling wildly — not unlike the grub on the hook, Jack thought — as they hauled him along the edge. It wasn't clear to Jack what fraction of the wriggling was an illusion produced by the heat of the blowlamp, but the spectacle struck him as distressingly pointless; Foster was simply prolonging his own agony. 'Have to be cruel to be kind sometimes,' Jack told him, and played the flame directly on his fingers. 'Do yourself a favour, for heaven's sake. No point in hanging on.'

Foster had ceased crying for help as he tried to flee, but had kept emitting a groan like someone struggling to waken from a nightmare. It rose to a shriek as his fingers turned red. They continued to writhe and to try and dig into the soil at the edge of this stretch of the path – just like worms, Jack thought, that were searching for holes in which to take refuge – until the skin on the back of Foster's right hand started to smoulder. Then they recoiled, and a convulsion of his whole body sent Foster jack-knifing backwards several feet. 'Murder,' he shrieked, 'murgle, murglub,' and sank.

'Stay down,' Jack murmured. 'Third time lucky.' He was experiencing a sadness which might have felt like guilt if he hadn't been certain that he had pursued the only course of action open to him. He began to count aloud. He hadn't reached eleven when Foster erupted from the canal, at least a foot closer to the bank than when he'd sunk, waving his blistered hand as if he could shake off the pain. His impetus carried him towards Jack, both hands clutching for the edge.

'This is silly,' Jack protested, his voice starting to crack. 'You know perfectly well—' Talking was useless, especially since Foster had lost his spectacles underwater and presumably couldn't see him. He trained the jet of flame on the largest target within reach, the top of Foster's head. In a very few seconds the man's hair hissed and withered, and he was both bald and piebald. During these seconds he emitted an almost inarticulate crescendo of sound – 'Mmmur' – and Jack had the dismaying impression that he was crying out for his mother. His hands were convulsively slapping the water and keeping him afloat, so that he was unable to move out of range of the flame. His scalp was peeling by the time shock or helplessness or a yearning for the cool water caused him to sink.

Jack took hold of the control of the blowlamp but made himself wait before turning it off. To his distress, some kind of struggle was continuing in the depths of the canal. A cluster of large bubbles spent themselves on the surface, then another bunch rose from between Foster's legs. Surely that was all, Jack thought, just as Foster's scalp bobbed above the water. It resembled an old weathered rock rather than anything human. It protruded for several seconds, ripples streaming around it like a replacement for its hair, and finally sank.

Jack turned off the flame and stood listening to the liquid harmony of the canal. Though it sounded like a promise of eternal peace it couldn't quite assuage his dismay. He dropped the blowlamp into the briefcase and snapped the lock, and shuddered from head to foot, which left him feeling somewhat better. 'Horrible. Horrible,' he kept muttering to himself as he strode to the gap in the hedge.

There was nobody in sight on the road or alongside it, though he could hear mowers working on more than one back lawn. He kept his eye on the fishermen through the hedge as he walked to the van, but they all had their backs to him. 'Horrible,' he told the clown as he inserted the key in the ignition, and thought of a word which summed up Foster's demise more accurately. He started the van and drove towards the motorway. 'Unnecessary,' he repeated, feeling each time that it had more to tell him. By trying to explain too much to Foster he had only succeeded in confusing the issue. In future he would come straight to the point. It was only fair, and he wanted to be fair.

THIRTY-ONE

Janys' first client of the day was determined to be good with children. When she met him at the front door with Tommy in her arms he immediately said 'What's his name?'

'Tommy.'

He stuck out a hand for Tommy to shake, a hand so large and hairy that she could imagine his pupils at school deriving as many nicknames from it as from his name. 'I'm Mr McGrotty,' he said, challenging his audience to keep a straight face. 'Is your name Tommy, Tommy?'

Tommy's response was to bury his face between his mother's breasts. 'Come on, Tommy Tommy,' she said, 'you can be the birdie to watch.'

The teacher followed her along the hall and lingered, hands behind his back, to appraise the photographs on the walls. 'Are these your work?'

'All mine.'

'Good. They're good.'

'Thank you, kind sir.' She took the repetition as a double compliment, but perhaps he had another intention for it. Once Tommy was deposited in his play-pen Mr McGrotty said 'Shall I show Tommy what I've brought him?'

'What would that be?'

He was addressing Tommy rather than her, which reminded Janys of how Tommy's father had behaved before the divorce, playing with Tommy in ways that seemed designed to blot out the child's awareness of her even when she was in the room. 'I've brought Tommy a book,' the teacher said. 'Books are good, Tommy. Would Tommy like to look?'

At least he wasn't offering sweets spiked with additives, which had been her ex-husband's favourite way of simultaneously antagonising her and making her appear unreasonable to Tommy. He snapped open his battered briefcase and produced a book not much larger than his hand. 'This is a good book, Tommy. Would Tommy like to look at the book?'

Tommy held onto the side of the play-pen and peered at the book with a pained expression that seemed to retort he was already doing so. When that didn't work he stood on tiptoe and reached for it. 'Ook.'

'Correct, book. If Tommy says book he shall look at the book.'

'Oo.'

'Who? Tommy shall. Tommy is a good boy who can say book.'

'I think you might have to make another appointment for that,' Janys intervened. 'The nurse says we're doing pretty well for two years old.'

'Is Tommy two? Two is a good age to be. Can Tommy say two?'

Tommy could, but was bored with having the book waved at him. He sat down with an abruptness that left him undecided whether to cry or laugh, then began to throw his alphabet bricks about instead. 'Is Tommy going to spell a word for me?' Mr McGrotty said.

'I wouldn't count on it.'

'Look, Tommy,' the teacher persisted, virtually ignoring Janys. 'There is a word. Tommy has made a word. That word is am. A,' he pronounced as though Janys had dug him in the ribs, a tempting notion. 'Mmmm,' he said like a diner expressing pleasure, just as Tommy kicked the bricks away.

'Thank you for the lesson, Mr McGrotty. Now I wonder if we should—'

'Shall I put the book here for Tommy to look at?' Mr McGrotty said, balancing it on the corner of the play-pen. The instant he moved away, Tommy staggered to his feet and grabbed the book. 'That's a good boy. Books are good for you,' the teacher said.

'You were saying you wanted me to shoot you with a prop.'

Janys wouldn't normally have put it that way, but she was distracted by the prospect of his continuing to talk in the accents and vocabulary of a reading scheme even when he was addressing her. 'Did I say so?' he said.

'You said you were bringing something you wanted in the picture.'

'So I did.' He dug in his bag again. 'Here it is. This is it,' he said.

'That's right, your diploma, you said. Ah, it's under glass.'

'Will that make for difficulty?'

She was so relieved to hear him use a word of more than two syllables that she might have promised almost anything. 'I just need to light it right,' she said, feeling as if she was performing the reading scheme now. 'Don't worry, I can cope.'

She sat him in the sitters' chair and waited while he posed with the framed educational diploma on his lap, then she adjusted the lights so that they weren't reflected by the glass. To make her sitters smile she often asked them to look at Tommy, which nearly always worked, but she didn't think she could bear to have Mr McGrotty notice that Tommy was holding the book, which contained pictures of a circus and a few words in large print, upside down. She directed the teacher to look at the lens, and when he'd composed his face into the expression he apparently favoured, one that suggested that he felt he had received no more than he deserved, Janys took half a dozen quick shots with the Pentax, the last of which he spoiled by waving at her. 'No, no. I don't want that many,' he protested.

'I'm giving you a range to choose from. How many would you like?'

'Just the one. Wasn't that understood?'

'I'm sure you made yourself clear. Let me just try a couple more angles.' She photographed him slightly in profile from both sides, then placed the camera next to the pile of scrap paper on her desk. 'All done,' she said.

'When may I view them?'

'I'll put them in the post to you tomorrow. Is whichever you choose for your wall?'

'My mother lives down south,' he said briskly, lowering the diploma into his bag. 'Shall I leave Tommy the book?'

'That's very kind of you.'

He wasn't talking to her. 'Is the book good, Tommy? Is it a good book?' he said, and made to turn it the right way up. As soon as his outsize hand reached for it, Tommy began to howl. 'Don't cry, Tommy,' the teacher said, recoiling. 'No need to cry. Boys don't cry.'

'Oh, I think they should,' Janys said, giving Tommy a wink that stopped him. 'What do we say to Mr McGrotty for the book? What do we say?'

'Ta.'

'Tar's something sticky on the road. You mean thank you, don't you,' she said and ushered the teacher, who was continuing to look uncomfortable, to the front door. 'Where have you taught?' she couldn't resist asking.

'Nowhere as yet.'

'Good luck,' she said, and having watched him to the gate, went back to Tommy, who was grinning at a picture of a clown. She released the laughter she had been suppressing until Mr McGrotty couldn't hear, and Tommy joined in. He didn't know what she was laughing at, but she looked forward to telling him when he was older.

She copied the details of an appointment she'd scribbled on the back of a letter just before the teacher had arrived, then she made to drop the page into the bin, since it offered no more space. Instead she turned it over to remind herself of what it said. 'Turn ill luck into good, Tommy, that's today's free offer, except it means sending thirteen letters, so it isn't so free after all.'

She was rambling. Surely there was only one place for the letter; she didn't understand why she was hesitating. She didn't really believe in luck, except the kind she'd earned for Tommy and herself, but deep down she must be superstitious after all, or she wouldn't still be holding the letter. She supposed she ought to thank it for showing her herself. She

245

held it up for Tommy to see. 'What do you say we should do with it? Try our luck, or is it for the bin?'

Tommy dropped the book and trotting to the bars, held out his hands for the letter. Behind him the clown in the open book grinned at him. 'Is it a joke, do you think?' Janys said, handing Tommy the letter.

He blinked at it, turned it over and gazed at her hasty scrawl, turned it over again. Holding it by the two top corners, he gave Janys a look which asked so eloquently whether he was allowed to commit wickedness that she laughed. 'Trust your instincts.'

He frowned at her, then began gravely to tear the letter into ragged strips which fell to the carpet outside the bars. When he'd finished he smiled at the pieces. 'Bin,' he said.

'I won't argue.' Janys collected the strips and threw them in. 'Bin indeed. That's the safest thing to do with rubbish.'

THIRTY-TWO

Jack shook hands with a laughing man who immediately burst into flame. The heat fused their hands together, and Jack's arm was on fire. The lack of any sensation frightened him, so that he did his best to cry out, though it felt as if he was attempting to use someone else's voice. The feeble groans sounded familiar, and he thought he would rather not remember where he'd heard them. He sucked in a breath which sent a sharp pain through his teeth, and darkness extinguished the flames.

Julia gave a sleepy murmur of protest and turned away from him. He gazed at the ceiling until the dark wiped out the memory of the dream, except for a trace which felt as though a charred mote had lodged in his brain. It had only been a nightmare, and he was safe at home. All the same, he seemed to spend a considerable time alone in the dark before he fell asleep.

He didn't dream again, but neither did he sleep well. At some point he was vaguely aware of movements in the house. The next he knew, Julia was standing by the bed. 'Jack, are you there?'

'Of course I am,' he said, blinking his cindery eyes at the sunlight. 'What do you mean? What's wrong?'

'Only that soon it'll be time for you to go to work.'

When he peered at the bedside clock he saw it was nearly eleven. 'Why did you let me sleep?'

'I thought you might appreciate it. You've been seeming—'

'What?'

Her expression made her face look heavier. 'Less unfriendly than you're being now, at any rate.'

By the time he regained some control of his words she was

247

on her way downstairs. Stumbling into the bathroom with the mug of coffee she had brought him, he clambered into the bath. He stayed under the shower until the water had cleansed him of at least some of the grubby feeling left behind by his restless night, though the inside of his head still felt charred, then he dressed and went down to Julia.

She was reading a computer journal in the front room. 'I can't be expected to know what you're doing if you don't tell me,' she said without looking up.

'There's nothing to tell, Julia.'

'Or if you'd rather not be in the house while I am.'

'What on earth makes you say that? You know perfectly well—'

'I'm not sure what I know, Jack, the way you've been behaving recently.'

'You were going to tell me what way that was.'

She dropped the journal, open at a page of calculations which were incomprehensible to him, and met his eyes. 'For weeks you've kept seeming as if you'd rather be away from us than here, as if you're getting ready to leave.'

'Oh, now, Julia—'

She held up a hand to ward him off. 'Don't try and smother me. Just stay where you are and talk.'

'I don't know what to say. I can't understand where you got the idea. If you've been worrying like that I wish you'd told me sooner.'

'It's my fault, you mean.'

'I don't mean anything of the kind. Look, what exactly have you been imagining? Do you think there's someone else?'

'Is there?'

'Who else would have me?'

She gave him a hint of a smile. 'That's supposed to be my line, not yours.'

'About me, I hope you mean.'

'But of course.' She raised her hand again to forestall him. 'I still keep feeling you'd rather be off on some adventure when you're with us.'

'You're not still thinking of that night I went out for a drink with someone I used to work with.'

'Suppose I am?'

'I told you at the time I thought they might have been able to help you find a job. Anyway, if your interview at the college went as well as you say, it doesn't matter. So that was one of my adventures. Tell me another.'

'I told you it was just a feeling.'

'Shall I tell you what I think?' When she didn't answer he said 'I think you'll stop feeling like that about me when you get another job.'

'It isn't about you, it's ...' She grimaced at herself. 'Oh, I don't know. Maybe you're right and it is my fault.'

'It isn't at all.' He knelt down beside her and took her hand. 'Let me show you there's nobody else.'

She kissed him briefly and stood up. 'Later, when Laura's asleep.'

He would have hated himself for lying so glibly to Julia if it hadn't been for her sake. He was glad she didn't want to make love now; he would have time to get rid of at least one task. Maybe then he wouldn't feel so nervously eager to be out of the house. Oversleeping had thrown him, as had their talk, so that when she said 'Were you meaning to go somewhere?' he said the first thing that occurred to him. 'I was going to see if we had anything in the library for Laura's history project.'

It didn't sound very convincing to him, but perhaps Julia wanted to believe him. 'Don't let me stop you,' she said.

He made himself eat a bowl of cereal in order not to seem too eager. He counted one hundred and twenty-one while brushing his teeth. 'Just make sure you come home,' Julia told him at the front door.

'What could stop me?' he said, thinking where to go on his way to work.

The noonday sun blazed into his face as he unlocked the van. The interior was even hotter than the street, and he rolled both windows down before driving off. The journey uphill smelled of heat and petrol fumes. He parked just out of sight of the Evanses' house and mopped his forehead with his handkerchief before opening the back of the van.

His burden felt unexpectedly heavy. It must be the heat, he thought as he waited to cross the road. When a learner driver slowed the traffic down, Jack ran across and up the steps of the police station.

The counter was unstaffed. A trill of the enquiry bell brought a policewoman out of the inner room. 'Is Constable Pether in?' Jack said, feeling as though he was asking if Pether could come out to play.

'Who shall I say?'

'The Count of Eleven,' Jack heard himself announce, though he wasn't sure which of his selves would do so. 'Jack Orchard,' he said.

She went back into the room and closed the door, and shortly Pether appeared beyond its glass panel. He glanced at Jack and said something to the policewoman, who gave Jack a glance of guarded appraisal. Jack was about to raise his hands above the counter and deposit his burden when Pether emerged from the room. 'Headline news, I see,' he said.

'Who is?'

Pether came to the counter and extended a hand. Jack thought he meant to grab him, but Pether was pointing at him. 'News to me,' Jack said, unable to think past the joke.

'Wait there a moment.'

When Pether moved, Jack was sure he was about to come round the counter, but the policeman stepped back into the room. Disconcertingly, Jack didn't know how the prospect of being detained had made him feel, and his unsureness kept him standing there until Pether reappeared, holding that week's local newspaper, which he folded open about halfway through before dropping it on the counter. 'Not you so much as your family,' he said.

TEA COSY TERROR STRIKES AGAIN ... BUDGIES LEFT TO STARVE TO DEATH ... CRASH MAN SPAT ... BINMEN ESCAPE IN CHAINSAW ATTACK TERROR ... DOG'S LEGS TIED UP AND THEN THROWN OUT ... BLACK MARKET TRADE IN PARROTS SPELLS MISERY FOR PET SHOP... CAR CRASH DRIVER

250

TRAPPED BY LEGS ... At last Jack found the item, a paragraph at the bottom of the page, beneath the headline NEW BRIGHTON GIRL'S COURAGE REWARDED BY MYSTERY BENEFACTOR. 'How did this get out?' he demanded.

'I believe Laura told her classmates.'

'Doesn't the paper have to ask permission to print her name?'

'I hardly think so, particularly if the story's true. Besides, most children of her age like to be the centre of attention.'

'That's not the point,' Jack said, growing less sure what was, though he knew he didn't like the sense that part of the family's life had got out of control. He lifted the boots and stamped them on the counter. 'Anyway, there's another promise kept.'

Pether stared at them. 'You're giving me these for my father?'

'If you think that's a fair exchange,' Jack managed not to say, nor 'Unless you're standing in your bare feet.' 'I'll take them to him if you like,' he said. 'I just wanted you to know I don't forget.'

'He isn't much of a boot man.' Nevertheless Pether picked up the boots. 'He hasn't been too well this week. I'll deliver them and see what he says. Was that all?'

'Tender my apologies.'

Pether looked suspicious of Jack's phrasing. 'Thank you,' he said as if that might be only a temporary response.

Jack lingered by the pay telephone next to the counter. He hadn't time to make the calls he intended to make, and indeed he hadn't yet ascertained the numbers he should call, but the notion of phoning from the police station appealed to him now that confronting Pether had restored his faith in himself. He sprinted to the van and drove to the motorway, feeling that whatever happened until he made his next contact would be leading him to his goal. Even so, he didn't expect the library to be such a help. Almost as soon as Jack arrived at work the librarian asked him to go on a quest for some expensive overdue books.

251

THIRTY-THREE

Jack was left in charge of the reference library while the librarian went for lunch. Once he was alone with the readers, all of whom seemed intent on their work, Jack carried the Merseyside telephone directory to the table behind the counter. His briefcase was in the van, but he knew all the names and addresses on the remaining envelopes by heart. He found the number of the name whose address he would be closest to that afternoon, then he moved the phone from the counter to the table and sat down out of sight of the public. When the other phone had rung eleven times – five and a half pairs – he broke the connection and tried again. 'Nine, ten,' he chanted softly, 'eleve—' and the bell was silenced. 'Dail's Signs,' a man said.

Until he'd heard it spoken Jack wondered if the name in the directory might be a misprint for 'Dial'. 'Mr Dail?' he said.

'He's the only one you'll find here this late on early closing day.'

'Forgive me. Can you spare a few minutes?'

'Depends what for.'

'I sent you a letter a few weeks ago.'

'Folk do.'

'It was a copy of one I'd received, asking me to send out thirteen copies. I was wondering—'

'Is that all you called me back from going home for?'

'Just to follow it up, to see if you've done as it asked.'

'I don't take kindly to being sent letters that aren't even signed.'

'So you're saying that if I were to tell you my name—'

'I'd be interested in that, believe me, and where I can get hold of you.'

'And you'd send out copies of the letter?'

'It's as good as done. You can trust me as much as you can trust your letter.'

He didn't sound entirely convincing, perhaps because he assumed Jack was too stupid to notice. 'So you've kept it,' Jack said.

'Need you ask? The place wouldn't be the same without it,' Dail said, beginning to tire of the game. 'Hang on, it looks as if one of the girls has chucked it out. The things staff do if they aren't watched.'

'Suppose I were to send you another one, signed?'

'Why don't you bring it yourself and then you can see what I do with it.'

'Which would be—'

'Stuff it in your gob to shut you up.'

'Am I to take that as a refusal, Mr Dail?'

'Do you know,' Dail said in a mincing parody of Jack's tone, 'I really think you should.'

'You've an adequate ear and a certain raw talent for mimicry,' Jack said as a clatter at the other end cut him off. He imagined Dail marching out of the shop, convinced he'd got the better of Jack. Jack felt almost sorry for him, though he was mostly experiencing relief, which renewed his sense of power; at least he knew where he was with Dail. He looked up the first of the names he hadn't yet contacted and dialled the number.

'. . . Ten, eleven,' he counted. 'One, two—' and the phone emitted a shriek of tortured metal. 'Yeh, wha?' a young male voice enquired.

'Is that Colloran's Car Repairs?'

'It's the garridge.'

'Could I speak to Mr Colloran?'

'Danny,' the voice shouted. After a while the shriek of metal ceased and a different voice said 'Colloran.'

'You don't know me, Mr Colloran. I sent you a letter a few weeks ago inviting you to improve your luck.'

253

'He sent me that fucking letter about luck,' Colloran shouted, and Jack really needed no further response. 'So what's your problem?' Colloran demanded.

'I was wondering if you'd had a chance to do as it asked.'

'Plenty of chances, pal. Just no inclination.'

'Have you still got the letter?'

'It's hanging on the shithouse wall, isn't it, Mark? Don't worry, pal, we've put it to good use.'

Jack had started to grin. 'Do you think I should give you another chance to change your luck?'

'The cunt's asking if I want another chance. The only fucking chance I want, pal, is the chance to kick your fucking head in for sending me that crap.'

'That seems unambiguous enough,' Jack said, and pressed the receiver rest delicately until it terminated the sound of jeering. He found the number for the name which most appealed to him, but Fazackerly of Fazakerley must be out on a plumbing job. Maybe a woman would give him a more sympathetic hearing than he'd had so far today, he thought, and phoned the first name that suggested itself. The phone rang eleven times, then eleven again, and Jack was about to abandon it when it was picked up. 'Janys Day?' he said.

'That's me.'

'You don't know me. I sent you a letter a few weeks ago inviting you to improve your luck.'

'I know.'

She meant she remembered, Jack told himself. 'I was wondering if you'd had a chance to do as it asked.'

'I'm afraid not.'

'It's important, Miss Day. I can assure you from my own experience—'

'It's Mrs Day, not that it's more than a name any more. I'm sorry, I've no time for your kind of thing.'

'I hadn't either until I found it worked for me. Have you still got the letter?'

'I'm afraid it's been torn up.'

'I could provide you with another copy if you'd care to reconsider. It really would be in your best—'

'You'd be wasting your money as much as you're wasting your breath now, and my time. Who are you, by the way? Am I supposed to know you?'

'Just a mystery benefactor.'

'I don't like mysteries, and I don't like receiving any kind of call from someone who won't identify himself.'

'I never knew who sent me the letter. It's the luck that counts, not who the sender is. If you'll give me just a few minutes I'm sure I can—'

'That's men for you, always sure of themselves,' Janys Day said, and cut him off.

'You do know me, or you will,' Jack murmured. 'I'm your bad luck.' He was leafing through the directory when someone coughed behind him. 'Sorry, have you been waiting long?' Jack said.

'Only a few moments. I only wanted to know where I could find local history.'

'You're talking to a piece of it. You were seeing it in the making.' Jack escorted the small nervous woman, who cleared her throat several times in the thirty or so seconds it took him, to the secluded alcove where books about Merseyside were shelved, and then he spoke. 'I was just phoning in search of some overdue books.'

'I thought that was what it might be.'

Another reader asked Jack to help her discover the law on trading from her house, which took an armful of massive books and over half an hour. Jack had never realised the law was so convoluted; he was glad it didn't touch him. By the time the reader was satisfied, the librarian was back from lunch. 'Ready for the road?' he asked Jack.

'Whenever you give me the licence.'

'You'll be dealing with an odd customer.'

'I'm used to handling people.'

'Lives by Bromborough Library. They know him there, so he came here.' As Jack set off the librarian added 'The scenic route is via Eastham.'

That sounded to Jack like an invitation to take his time, though he didn't intend to take any more than he needed. He drove out of Ellesmere Port, between brick blocks of 'thirties flats and then clumps of increasingly newer and similar houses, and onto a road which paralleled the motorway and which made him feel rather as though he was excused from participating in a race. Sunlight fluttered through a rank of poplars before the road climbed over the motorway and wound through fields. A long rodent darted out of a hedge and into the hedge opposite. An oil refinery blocked off the fields to Jack's right, then the road was claimed by Eastham, a village of white cottages built around a churchyard. A dual carriageway divided it from Bromborough, the next village. This radiated from an old stone cross, but most of the buildings around the cross had been occupied by modern shopfronts, one of which said Dail's Signs. Several hundred yards around the corner, closer than Jack had anticipated, was the library, and he found himself a space in its car park.

The borrower of the overdue books lived in a small house squeezed between two larger ones overlooking a green in front of the library. As Jack crossed the thirsty grass, he glimpsed a net curtain falling into place at a window not much larger than a car windscreen above the front door. He reached gingerly for the bellpush, which was dangling from a single screw and exposing its wires, and pressed the grubby plastic button. When even leaning on it provoked no response, he managed to raise the brass knocker and slam it against the tarnished plate on the knurled black door. The knock was answered by a screech of rage, and the door was flung open. 'Mr Samson?' Jack said.

The door had been opened by a tall thin stoop-shouldered man with very red prominent ears. His trousers were bright blue except for the faded knees; his old tweed jacket, like his skin, seemed at least a size too large for him. 'Eh?' he shouted, glowering and shoving one ear forwards with a cupped hand.

'Mr David Samson?'

'What do you want?' he demanded, adding 'Eh?' before Jack could open his mouth.

'Those books on the stairs, Mr Samson. I'm from the library.'

Behind Samson, at the end of a short dim hall whose carpet was dusty with fallen plaster, Jack could see a pile of large books halfway up the stairs, which also bore some tins of food and an indeterminate crumpled item of clothing. Among the titles on the spines were the names of all the artists who were the subjects of the books Jack had been sent to reclaim. That much he saw before Samson moved to block his view, shouting 'You're not from the library' and pointing across the road.

'Not this one. Ellesmere Port.'

'Ellesmere Port? Half the time you can't get a bus to it. They say one's coming and it never does. If you ask me they want to keep us in our houses so we won't be able to use our bus passes,' Samson yelled, and glared accusingly at Jack.

'I'm not from the bus company,' Jack said, aware that an interested audience was gathering outside the library. 'I just want the books.'

'Eh?' Samson shouted, pushing both ears forward.

'The books, Mr Samson,' Jack said, lowering his voice.

'You want to take away the only pleasure I've got left, do you? Those books belong to everyone. We pay for them out of our poll tax, them and your wages.'

'It's because they belong to everyone that the library would like them back.'

'Eh?'

'I don't think you're as deaf as that, Mr Samson,' Jack said in an ordinary voice.

'You don't, eh?' Samson shouted, and his face crumpled with fury. He rose to his full height, towering unsteadily over Jack, and shook a finger at him while haranguing the dozen or so people outside the library. 'Look, here's the latest thing. Here's how we can expect to be treated in future. Better not borrow any books, because if you're too ill to return them the authorities will send a thug to break into your house.'

'I haven't touched you or your house,' Jack said for only him to hear. 'But I won't leave without the books.'

'Come and look at him. He's enjoying himself.' When nobody made a move Samson peered at Jack's face and shuddered. 'You're mad. You're dangerous.'

'Only when I have to be.'

Samson ducked into the cottage. 'Don't you take one step closer,' he said, no longer shouting. 'Here, have your books if they'll get rid of you. God help the world if there are many like you in it.' He stalked rapidly along the hall, his feet crunching fallen plaster, and grabbed the top book from the pile. 'El Greaso, he's yours, isn't he? He sounds like he paints,' he said, and shied the book along the carpet. 'Who else are you after? Piss Arrow? Pick Arso?'

'If you throw the books I'll have to come in to stop you,' Jack said.

Samson clutched the entire pile of books to his chest and staggered towards Jack. 'Nobody comes in, not even to read these,' he shouted, nodding sideways at the gas and electric meters just inside the cottage. 'When they come to carry me out in a box, then it'll be open house. Here, take the lot if it'll make you happy, if it'll wipe the grin off your face,' he said, his voice beginning to falter, and dumping the books at Jack's feet, slammed the door so hard that the dangling bellpush danced against the wall.

They were all library books. Jack loaded them against his chest and made for the car park. Most of the audience had gone inside the library, but an old couple with a wheeled basket and a Yorkshire terrier walked along with him. 'You did better than the gas man,' the woman said.

'We could use a few like you to chase our tenants,' her husband told Jack. 'And we never even saw you lay a finger on him.'

'I didn't.'

'Of course not. All it requires is not taking no for an answer.'

'More power to you,' the woman said. 'You're an asset to the community.'

By the time Jack unlocked the van they were out of sight. He piled the books on the passenger seat and strolled towards the shops. Those which faced Dail's Signs were closed for the afternoon, and the view of the shop from near the stone cross was obscured by a bus shelter. As Jack left the car park a small queue of people with their backs to him climbed on a bus for Ellesmere Port. The bus swung round the crossroads, and then the street was deserted.

Both Dail's shop window and the glass panel of the door were opaque with signs: KEEP OUT, BEWARE OF THE DOG, NO TRESPASSING, NO CREDIT, NO SMOKING ... Jack squatted in front of the door, his briefcase nudging his calves, and prised open the letter-slot, which was only a couple of feet from the ground. The floorboards in the gloom were bare, and directly in front of him a gap between two of them, as wide as a gap drawn with a felt-tipped pen, led to a counter encrusted with plastic signs. 'The line of fire,' he murmured, and applying his lighter to the nozzle of the blowlamp, poked the flame through the metal slot.

He remembered the gong-note of the old blowlamp as it had struck Arrod's skull: bonggg-gg-g ... g ... But the new tool was far more efficient. It was virtually inaudible from outside the shop, yet in a few seconds flames began to feel their way along the gap between the floorboards. When he saw the lowest signs on the front of the counter start to curl up and sputter, he turned off the blowlamp and returned it to the briefcase before rising to his feet. 'I hope you're insured,' he told the shop. 'A little expenditure can save a lot of heart-ache.'

He walked invisibly to the van and drove back to the cross. A woman surrounded by several carrier bags was standing by the bus shelter now, and beginning to sniff the air. Any moment she would notice the smoke oozing from beneath the door behind her. If she ran to the nearest phone, the fire brigade should be in time to save the adjoining shops. Jack winked at the clown. 'Never thought we'd be glad of early closing day, did you?' he said.

THIRTY-FOUR

The librarian was delighted with Jack's haul, which included books borrowed years ago under names other than Samson from libraries in Birkenhead and Chester. 'We may send you out again soon,' he said, and Jack mentally crossed another name off his list, though he didn't yet know which.

When he arrived home Laura was asleep in bed. Though he didn't like to leave the situation unresolved – it felt like a flaw in their life – he couldn't very well wake her up. In the morning he was waiting for her at the breakfast table. She ran downstairs late as usual, ready to linger over toast and Marmite and run to brush her teeth before hurrying to school. He had the newspaper open at the paragraph about her. 'Laura, do you know anything about this?'

'Can't it wait until she comes home?' Julia said.

'Won't we all feel better once it's out of the way?' When neither of them spoke he said 'So what do you know about it, Laura?'

'One of my friends' mums is a reporter.'

'And?'

'She asked me about the money while me and Stephanie were walking home.'

'She interviewed you, you mean.'

'I didn't know she was until she'd finished and she said it might be in the paper.'

'I'll be having a few words with her.'

'Dad, please don't. Stephanie's my friend. Her mum didn't write anything bad about us.'

Jack gave in, though he wasn't entirely happy. 'I suppose we'll just have to get used to being news for a while.'

It seemed to him that there was more to it, but he wasn't sure what until the post came, consisting of a letter from the bank. 'Please contact me at your earliest convenience to arrange an appointment,' he read aloud to Julia. 'Sounds as if Hardy's after our money.'

'Unless he wants to give us some.'

'I wonder if I could make that happen,' Jack mused, and phoned the bank.

Mr Hardy wasted no time once Jack was put through to him. 'When would be convenient for you to come in to discuss your financial situation?'

'How about now?'

'My diary is full until lunchtime. This afternoon, perhaps?'

'I'll be at work.'

'And your wife?'

Ignoring that, Jack said 'Tomorrow as soon as you open? That's if it won't take long.'

'I don't foresee much discussion.'

'I'll look forward to it,' Jack said, baring his teeth at the phone. 'I get the impression he's read the paper,' he told Julia.

'Does he want us both again?'

'It doesn't matter what he wants, only what you want.'

'Then I'll come.'

Jack might have been able to take a harder line on his own, but Julia's presence needn't enfeeble him. He was trying to think of an excuse to leave early for work and finish making his phone calls when she commandeered him to help tidy the house. With just the two of them in it, it didn't seem so cramped; it wasn't for lack of space that they kept touching each other. They hadn't finished cleaning their bedroom when they started to undress each other, and they weren't even half naked when Julia pulled him down on the bed and clasped his waist with her legs. He felt huge and hot inside her. As she cried out and dug her nails into his shoulders he thought it was the loudest cry he'd ever heard.

They lay embraced until it was time for him to leave for work. Perhaps he would have a chance to use the phone this afternoon, he thought as he drove to the library. He arrived a few minutes early, and manned the reference desk while his colleagues headed for the staffroom. He was making for the phone directory when he caught sight of the headline on the front page of one of the newspapers. CANAL MURDER 'MAY BE WORK OF MERSEY BURNER', it said.

Jack went quickly to the table, reminding himself that there was no need for stealth. The newspaper report said that the police believed Walter Foster had jumped into the canal to avoid being burned alive. They had also found similarities between his death and those of Jeremy Alston and Stephen Arrod. It wasn't clear to Jack whether the police had invented the nickname in the headline. He was scrutinising the report, having scanned it, when the librarian approached him. 'Jack?'

'Just glancing at the paper,' Jack said, and turned his back on it. 'I'll be at the desk.'

Something about the librarian's expression halted him. 'Or do you want me somewhere else?'

'I don't, no.' The librarian was trying to make it into a joke, stretching his mouth in a clown's grimace. 'Your fan club is downstairs. The police.'

THIRTY-FIVE

Jack's first thought was that he had been too slow. Instead of making the phone calls and perhaps even visiting one of his list he had dallied with Julia and allowed bad luck to catch up with them. It wasn't just bad luck, it was the worst, because it entailed his abandoning her and Laura to it. He felt unworthy of them. He'd had the chance to assure them a good life and failed. He turned away from the librarian, embarrassed by the prospect of being seen to be found out, and made for the stairs.

The rubbery treads seemed to adhere to the soles of his shoes. The sensation was unpleasantly reminiscent of a dream, but in dreams one was never aware of the future, whereas now he was imagining Julia and Laura learning what he'd done on their behalf. Shouldn't he at least phone Julia and tell her before she learned from someone else? He couldn't think how to begin: he couldn't think of a single joke.

Reaching the foot of the stairs put an end to his thoughts. He was hesitating between the two sections of the library when Stella came out of the video section. 'What have you been up to, Jack?'

She was treating it as a joke too. Of course, he thought, the police hadn't told his colleagues why they wanted him. 'Where are they?' he said.

She jerked her head back, jingling the bells which dangled from her ears. 'Waiting for you.'

Over her shoulder he saw a police car parked outside the revolving doors. A uniformed policeman was standing beside the car, his back to the library. He must know that was the only exit Jack could use which wouldn't set off the alarm, unless someone else was posted beyond the other door. It occurred to Jack that he would be able to phone Julia from the police station; he was entitled to one phone call. He trudged towards the doors, his inability to think what he could say to her slowing him down until it seemed as though he might never reach them.

He was pressing his hand against the metal plate on the foremost door, the coolness of the plate fading as he did so, when the policeman with his back to him raised both hands to his face. Jack heard a match scrape, and smoke began to puff out of the policeman's face. If Jack could lure him to the van and reach the blowlamp— It wouldn't be fair; the man was only doing his job. Jack squared his shoulders and marched through the barrel of doors into the sunlight and a sweetish aroma of pipe-smoke. 'I believe you're looking for me,' he said.

The policeman emitted a couple of puffs before turning to him. Perhaps the pipe was meant to counteract the school-boyishness of his face. He appraised Jack for several seconds before admitting 'That's right.'

'Well, you've got me.'

The policeman gave him a stern look which impressed Jack as restrained under the circumstances. 'Remind me what I should call you, if you will.'

'Call me—' Not the Mersey Burner, but the Count of Eleven would require too much explaining. 'How about sir?'

'As you wish, sir.'

There was no point in antagonising him. 'The name's Jack Orchard.'

'Mr Orchard. This shouldn't take long,' the policeman said, relighting his pipe. The match flared before his face, and Jack felt as if the man was playing with him, trying to taunt him into a confession. A couple of readers with whom he had discussed books stared at him and the policeman before entering the library. 'Can we do this in the car?' Jack said.

The policeman took the stem out of his mouth and used it to point at his colleague in the driver's seat, who was studying a street map. 'He doesn't appreciate the pipe.'

'Then put it away, and your matches before I show you what to do with them.' Whichever of Jack's selves would have said that, it was headed off by a fear that the librarian might be calling Julia. 'What did you say to my boss?' Jack demanded.

The policeman gave him an expertly blank look. 'What should I have told him?'

'Why you wanted to see me.'

'Just that, of course.'

The policeman seemed about to go on, but Jack interrupted him. 'Do you mind if I make my phone call now?'

'We're quite busy, Mr Orchard. Is it anything that can't wait a few minutes?'

Surely that couldn't be another taunt; perhaps the man didn't realise— 'I'm married,' Jack told him.

'Congratulations,' the policeman said with what sounded like irony. 'Still getting used to the idea?'

Perhaps after all he knew what he was doing to Jack. He opened the matchbox, and Jack felt his fingers stiffen. 'Been married long?' the policeman said, watching him over the flame.

'Nearly thirteen years.'

'Lucky for some. Children?'

'A daughter.'

'One can be enough, I keep telling my wife.' The policeman waved smoke away from Jack's face. 'Is your daughter the problem?'

'This conversation is.'

'I see, sir.' The policeman's face could hardly have turned redder if Jack had trained a flame on it. With a briskness which all but convicted Jack of having wasted police time he said 'We'd better establish the facts of the case.'

'Here?'

'As good as anywhere. Between two-thirty and three o'clock yesterday you were—'

'In Bromborough.'

'For what purpose?'

If he insisted on playing games he would have to play by the Count's rules. 'Collecting overdue books,' Jack said.

'So we gather from the gentleman you collected them from. He had a good deal to say about your methods.'

'There were witnesses.'

'Oh, quite. I didn't know if you realised there were.'

If he was only to be accused of arson, Jack thought, shouldn't he confess? Could the police connect the fire at Dail's Signs with anything but arson? After a pause the policeman continued 'What time would you say you returned to your vehicle?'

'The first time or the second?' Jack wasn't about to ask that, and he mentally challenged the policeman to do so. 'It must have been a few minutes before three.'

'Do you recall driving past a signmaker's shop?'

Jack was losing patience. 'I may have.'

'Please try to concentrate. Perhaps the name will jog your memory. Dial's Signs.'

'Not Dial's, Dail's,' Jack refrained from saying, and managed not to smile at the obviousness of the trap. 'I don't remember any such name,' he said.

'Between the library car park and the cross.'

'Then I must have passed it. Why do you ask?'

'Because we're questioning everyone we can trace who was in the area about that time, Mr Orchard. We need to find out if they noticed anything suspicious, anything at all.'

Pipe-smoke drifted towards Jack and gave him an excuse to cough into his hand while he controlled himself. 'Was there a break-in?' he said when he was sure he could appear concerned.

'Arson. Someone set fire to the shop for no reason we've been able to discover so far.'

'Dear me. I certainly saw no-one who looked capable of such a thing. Is the shop near a bus shelter?'

'Just by one.'

'I seem to recall a lady with a load of shopping at the bus stop, but I'm sure she couldn't have been who you're looking for.'

'She sounds like the person who called the fire brigade. What vehicle do you drive, if I may ask?'

'A blue van. There it is.'

'Then we can eliminate that. She said she saw it passing.' The policeman gazed at Jack as if reluctant to let him go. 'Please let us know if anything further occurs to you, however unimportant it may seem. Now you'll be wanting to make your phone call.'

'I don't suppose it was that urgent. I expect as a father you'll know how it feels.'

'Nothing too serious, then.'

'Our daughter was in the news. She was beaten up by three boys, and now someone's sent us quite a sum in case we have to go to court.'

'I heard about it.' The policeman gave his pipe a final suck before opening the passenger door. 'If those scum ever end up in custody overnight I shouldn't be surprised if they put one another in hospital.'

The police car pulled away, and Jack stood in the sunlight, trying to grasp what the encounter had meant. He wanted somehow to recapture the sense of relief which had seemed to underlie his feelings when he'd thought the police had caught up with him. He walked into the car park and around the van, and then he saw that his luck was still taking care of him. Being questioned by the police had shown him not to visit any of his list while he was out on behalf of the library, since that way his whereabouts could easily be traced. If this hadn't been the first time the police might well have been suspicious, but instead the Count had triumphed again; he hadn't even needed to explain what phone call he had wanted to make. He strode back into the library, feeling absolutely on course. 'I see from your face that it wasn't too serious,' Stella said.

Jack put a finger and thumb to the corners of his mouth, for his expression felt capable of splitting his cheeks. 'Quite the reverse.'

THIRTY-SIX

The next morning Julia had a headache. Once she had made Laura's breakfast she went back upstairs and lay on the bed. When Jack had showered and dressed he sat by her and stroked her forehead. 'We should be thinking of going to the bank soon.'

She pressed his hand to her forehead and relinquished it. 'Would you mind very much if I weren't to go after all?'

'Of course not. I can handle him. Will you be all right, though?'

'I'll give myself and the computer journals a rest. It's them and too many late nights in front of the screen.'

It was also, Jack suspected, the strain of waiting to hear about the college job. 'Shall I ring when I get to work and tell you what happened?'

'I'll ring you when I'm up and about.'

Jack wondered if one source of her headache might be the thought of yet another confrontation with the bank manager. 'I'll have good news.'

She frowned and immediately winced. 'Don't say anything you might regret.'

'I'll go as easy on him as I can,' Jack said, kissing her forehead smooth. He refilled her tumbler from the bathroom tap, water slipping between his fingers, and took a sip from the tumbler before setting it down by the bed. When he touched her forehead with his fingers chilled by water she responded with a subdued smile. 'Dream of Crete,' he said, and left the house.

Sunlight was pivoting into the street, pushing shadows back under the houses. Jack rolled his window down to ease the heat and the faint sharp smell as he drove to the bank. He was ten minutes early, and his nerves were urging him to deal with the manager on Julia's behalf. He swung the van into the side road whose corner was occupied by the bank, and stopped behind a Capri which was being parked. The black car's reversing lights shone white, then its brake lights reddened, and the driver hauled himself onto the road. It was Mr Hardy. 'Caught you,' Jack said.

The manager glowered at the van and marched to Jack's door. 'Excuse me, perhaps you could—' he exhorted, and recognised Jack.

'Good morning. I won't be any longer than you keep me, and I don't suppose you'll be going anywhere until you're done.'

Seen from above, Mr Hardy appeared more than ever to consist of his most prominent features: balding dome, thick lips, pinstriped paunch. He expressed a breath that made his lips quiver and tramped to his car for his briefcase. When he made for the entrance to the bank Jack was already there, and took a step as the manager unlocked the door. 'If you'd like to wait outside,' Mr Hardy said.

'I've told my boss I may be a few minutes late for work, since you made this sound so urgent. You won't be long, will you? You wouldn't want me to lose my job.'

'I shall be as quick as practicable,' the manager said heavily, stepping aside to admit someone else. Jack thought they were jumping the queue which consisted of himself and the Count of Eleven and the Mersey Burner, until he saw that they were the staff of the bank. He moved back, but not far, and had the satisfaction of seeing Mr Hardy bump his own paunch with the door as he shut Jack out. Jack stared at the door as if his gaze could burn a hole in it, and considered fetching his briefcase in order to appear more businesslike. He hadn't done so when Mr Hardy unlocked the door.

'Please,' he said, inviting Jack in with a curt nod which seemed designed to show that Jack should do as he was told. 'One of us might well be frightened of the other,' Jack murmured as he followed Mr Hardy into the interview room.

The manager sat down, gazing at Jack and pulling in his paunch so as not to bump the desk with it. 'I understand you have been in contact with my head office.'

'I said I would be.'

'I don't know what you imagined you would gain by it, but I have to tell you that they fully support my decision.'

'Don't they have to? Tell me, I mean.'

'No doubt a communication will be in the post.' The manager sat forwards gingerly, resting his folded arms on the blotter. 'That wasn't why I wrote to you. I believe there has been a change in your circumstances.'

'They're on the mend.'

'I should like to remind you that you still have an overdraft with us.'

'Then I should think you'd be pleased we don't need to borrow any cash to spend in Crete.'

'I should have thought you would be well advised to consider delaying any holiday.'

'You win the battle of the tenses. I can't get any more remote than that,' Jack said, and didn't wait for a response. 'Tell me why.'

'I shouldn't think your employers would look too favourably on your taking time off so soon after starting work for them.'

'They've been more than reasonable,' Jack said, and was mentally adding to his score when he saw from Mr Hardy's face that he was saving the worst. 'What else?' Jack challenged him.

'I should have thought it ill-advised to plan a holiday that might have to be cancelled at short notice.'

He sat back smugly, and Jack resisted the temptation to shove the desk at his paunch. 'Why on earth should we have to do that?'

'In the circumstances that your wife is needed by the court or the police.'

'I don't think even the law is that unreasonable,' Jack said, feeling as if the manager was wishing Julia bad luck. 'Excuse me while I fetch my briefcase. I've got something to show you that may change your attitude.' He didn't say that, but he imagined Mr Hardy's eyes bulging as he was trapped behind the desk, and knowing he could make that happen gave him strength. 'Are you going away, Mr Hardy?'

'My wife and I always go to Devon,' the manager said with a hint of chauvinism.

'I shouldn't like to think your holiday might be spoiled by thoughts of how ours was.'

Was there the faintest trace of unease in Mr Hardy's eyes? The impression was sufficient to encourage Jack. 'Imagine how much better you should feel lying on the beach and knowing you'd authorised our mortgage.'

'I can't imagine what would make me do so, Mr Orchard.'

'Knowing my wife had a good new job.'

'Has she?'

The question wasn't quite dispassionate enough; to Jack it sounded like another hex on Julia. 'All the signs point to it,' he said.

'Ah, signs. I'm afraid in business we need something more definite.'

'So if she definitely gets the job you'll authorise the mortgage.'

Mr Hardy almost pouted. 'I should be prepared to look at it again.'

'And I'm sure your head office would.'

The manager's eyes flickered before he could conceal his uncertainty. 'May I ask how you can be so dogmatic that your wife will be selected?'

'I think it's best if I keep that to myself,' Jack said, and rising to his feet, looked down on the manager. 'Was there anything else you wanted me to deal with?'

Mr Hardy tilted his face up, and Jack thought he was finally going to bowl over backwards. 'I should like you to pass on my advice to your wife. I would have expected her to be here.'

'The pressure's given her a headache. May I give her your best wishes for her future?'

'Please do, and if you would like to keep my other comments in mind . . .'

'Rest assured I'll do everything in my power to make things come out as we all want them to,' Jack said, and reached across the desk to shake Mr Hardy's hand and help him up. He was pleased to find that the manager's palm was sweating. 'Until we meet again,' Jack said.

He'd done all he could at the bank, but it wasn't enough. Mr Hardy had planted a doubt in his mind, and any delay might put Julia at risk. The cab of the van had grown hot and oppressive, and remained so even with the windows open. As the van sped along the motorway he felt he was racing to discharge the breathless heat somewhere. 'Successful start to the day?' the librarian greeted him.

There were books to be shelved, readers to be guided to the books they wanted, information to be located, a panting mongrel to be chased out, a woman of about Jack's age to be read a letter from the Department of Social Security – not because she was blind, Jack realised belatedly, but because she was illiterate. He was wondering if any of the recipients of his lucky letters might have been unable to read, and if so how he should deal with that, when Stella called him to the phone. 'I think it's your wife.'

Was he already too late? In his haste to speak he almost lost his grip on the receiver. 'Jack?' Julia said.

She sounded as though she might well have bad news. 'I'm here,' he said.

'How did the interview go?'

'At the bank? We came to something like an understanding. What's wrong?'

'Just the headache. I was going to ask if you'd get me some paracetamol on the way home.'

'Sooner if you want. I can bring them at lunchtime.'

'I'll be fine so long as I have some in case I need them in the night. And maybe you could bring a pizza home for you and Laura.'

'Not for you?'

'I may have a nibble.'

'You deserve more than that,' he said, experiencing a blaze of yearning for her that was inextricably bound up with his sense of relief. The future had renewed some of its promise, and he meant to assure it before the day was over.

His appointment at the bank had made him a few minutes late for work, but he still had most of his lunch hour to play with. As soon as he was free he hurried to the nearest chemist's for a jar of paracetamol. 'I can't sell you those at the moment,' the girl behind the counter told him.

'You're joking.'

'I'm not allowed to sell any drugs unless the pharmacist is here. It's the law.'

'Then the law is—' Jack began, and saw that he was being offered an excuse. 'Makes sense to me.'

He sprinted to the van and drove to the all-night chemist's in Birkenhead. He was back at the library with a few seconds to spare, feeling efficient and nervously eager. The Birkenhead address on the wrapping would explain his lateness to Julia, so long as he wasn't home too late.

More books, readers, enquiries. The afternoon seemed to be passing at a distance from him even as he lived it. When he left the library he found himself tingling as though the sunlight had reached his nerves. He drove along the motorway, breathing heat and fumes, and came off onto the New Chester Road. The houses grew thinner and more closely packed as he approached Rock Ferry, and by the time he swung the van off the dual carriageway into the dockland suburb they were squashed into gardenless terraces. He stopped at a telephone box in sight of an urban freeway, across which he saw cranes rearing up from the Mersey. Counting out change, he let himself into the booth, which smelled of petrol from the freeway and of the previous user's cigarette.

Jack didn't abandon the call after five and a half pairs of trills. The bell had repeated itself thirteen times when it was interrupted by a clatter. 'What?' a voice demanded.

'Could I speak to Danny Colloran?'

'Who do you think this is, pal?'

Jack could hear no background noise, but wanted to be sure. 'Sorry if I stopped you working. Is there someone else there I could speak to?'

'D'yer think I'd be answering the phone if there was?'

'Sorry to have troubled you. Maybe I'll call again tomorrow. And maybe I won't,' Jack added to the reflection of his face entangled in the numbers displayed in a frame on the wall. A louder clatter cut off Colloran as he muttered 'Silly fu—' By the time the door of the booth wobbled shut, dragged by its crippled metal arm, Jack was already driving away.

In a few hundred yards the road bent sharp left to avoid the urban freeway, and Colloran's Car Repairs was just around the corner. It was a windowless brick shed two storeys high and as broad as a pair of houses, and it was alone on this stretch of the road, which doubled back almost immediately. Jack parked the van outside and climbed down, holding the briefcase.

On the freeway each vehicle sped by with a whoosh whose pitch barely had time to fall before the next whoosh came. Twin doors, each bearing half of the name of the business, occupied almost the whole of the front of the garage. The I of the last word was painted on a wicket. Jack glanced around, noting that the registration number of the van would be visible only to someone on this stretch of the road, and let himself through the wicket.

The garage was full of cars and parts of cars. A fluorescent tube, one end of which was at least a foot lower than the other, dangled from the ceiling. The entire contents of the garage looked oily, even the telephone and its directory, even a kettle and a huddle of tin mugs. At the back, beyond a Volvo on a hoist, a man was using a blowtorch on the far side of a Range Rover. He hadn't yet noticed that he had company, and when Jack kicked a Datsun wing that was lying on the floor, the roar of the torch drowned the clatter. Jack had almost reached the Range Rover when the man raised his head and saw him through the windows of the car.

His face was a blank metal barrel with glassed-in eyes. Of course he had to wear the mask while using the torch. He switched off the roaring and lifted the mask, revealing an oily grimy squeezed-together face. 'I'm closed, pal.'

274

'Alas, I think you are.'

The mechanic's eyes seemed even smaller than they had under glass, and shrank as his expression grew yet more suspicious. 'Got something in your ears? I said I'm shut.'

'I wouldn't be too happy about that if I were you.'

Colloran glanced with distaste at Jack's briefcase. 'If you're from the tax, the ould woman deals with all the paperwork.'

'That's not my game, Mr Colloran.'

'Don't tell me the bitch was wrong about me not having to pay VAT.'

'That isn't my line either.'

Colloran smeared his forehead with the back of one grimy hand. 'Are you going to stand there until I fucking guess?'

'As long as you've cast me as your guilty conscience, you might want to satisfy me.'

Colloran reached into the breast pocket of his overalls for a grubby plastic lighter. 'I don't know what you're fucking on about, pal. Take your big words out of here before I lose my rag.'

'You're risking losing more than that.'

Colloran flicked the lighter, which emitted a puff of smoke. 'Says who?'

'Says the letter I sent you. I wrote to you, I phoned you, and now I'm here in person to offer you a last chance.'

Colloran's finger froze on the lighter. 'You mean that shit about good luck.'

'I invited you to better your luck, yes.'

'You had to come and see what I thought of it and you, did you, pal? Take a good look,' Colloran said, and raised two fingers of the hand which held the lighter.

A finger doubled plus nine digits gave eleven, Jack thought, and said 'You're saying that to your luck.'

'No, I'm fucking saying it to you, pal,' Colloran shouted, grinding the flint with the wheel of the lighter. 'Get out while you've got some luck of your own left.'

'I'm afraid my luck is why I'm here, Mr Colloran.'

Colloran pressed the wheel viciously, and a flame sputtered up from the lighter. 'That's it. I warned you,' he said, and

275

pulling his mask down, lit the torch and turned its nozzle towards Jack.

Though Jack was about ten feet away he felt the heat on his chest as if a ray of sunlight had been focused on him. He imagined producing his own blowlamp, imagined the Count of Eleven joining combat with the helmeted Black Knight, grinned at the thought of how surprised the eyes behind the glassed-in slit would look – except that producing the blowlamp would take time, and Colloran could hardly be expected to wait for Jack to light it. As the mechanic gestured menacingly with the blowtorch, Jack dropped his briefcase next to one door of the dismantled Datsun.

Colloran took a step towards him as Jack grasped the inner handle of the door. 'The Count needs no weapon but a shield,' Jack said, and lifting it in front of him, strode at the mechanic, almost running.

For at least a couple of seconds Colloran watched him in disbelief, and then he jabbed the roaring torch at him. Jack met it with his shield. The door clanged against the nozzle, knocking the blowtorch around in Colloran's hand. At once the chest of his overalls began to smoke, and he gave a muffled hollow sound of pain and rage as he stumbled backwards. The next moment he trod on a spanner and crashed onto his back on the concrete floor with such force that the mask jerked up, exposing his chin.

He must be stunned, because he didn't move, even though the jet of the blowtorch was pointing straight at his face. His hold on the blowtorch slackened, and it would have rolled off his chest if Jack hadn't placed one foot on it. The damage had been done, and it was best to finish what had started. Jack pulled out his handkerchief and wiped the handle while resting the door against his chest and his other arm, then he let the shield fall and wadded the handkerchief over his nose and mouth so that he could stop holding his breath. He felt the beginnings of a struggle underfoot, but the movements ceased before he would have had to look. As soon as he sensed that it was safe to take his weight off his foot he did so and picked up the briefcase, let himself into the deserted street, wiped the handle of the wicket as he closed the door, climbed into the van and released a long sigh.

He rolled the window down and drove into Birkenhead. By the time he reached the pizza parlour the breeze had blown away the hint of queasiness he'd begun to experience. He kept the window shut on the way home, and the aroma of pizza made his mouth water. As he carried the boxed pizza up the garden path, Julia opened the front door. 'How are you feeling?' he said.

'Much better. Starving. I didn't need to send you after all.'

'Don't be so sure,' Jack told her, and smiled so that she wouldn't wonder what he meant. 'Let's get it while it's hot,' he said.

THIRTY-SEVEN

The first person Jack tried to phone at lunchtime, a dress-maker by the name of Amy Conning, was represented by an answering machine. 'No, no,' Jack murmured, wagging his finger at the receiver, and tried Fazackerly of Fazakerly. The phone began to beep like a toy car running wild. A woman with a toddler in a buggy was doing her best to catch Jack's eye in the mirror on the wall of the phone box, but he avoided looking at her until she moved away. He wanted to finish his calls, and he was hoping that at least one of the people he contacted would prove to have responded to his letter.

A tanker thundered towards the motorway, shaking the booth and shrouding it in fumes, as Jack placed the next call. This one seemed promising, even though he didn't believe in what the woman stood for. 'Hello,' she said almost at once.

'Ursula Gemini, the clairvoyant?'

'It's Ursa, dear. What would you like?'

Jack hadn't predicted her briskness. 'I wrote to you a few weeks ago,' he began.

'I don't do postal readings, dear. I believe in the personal touch. Would you like to arrange a time?'

'Perhaps I can just talk to you now. It won't take long.'

'I only do it face to face, dear. Were you planning to make an appointment? I've a lady here now waiting for her future.'

Though Jack felt he had been outmanoeuvred he was more amused than irate. 'How long is a session?'

'That depends on how clear you are, dear. A trial is usually about half an hour.'

'Monday morning?'

'I could fit you in at eleven.'

'Perfect. I'll see you then,' Jack said, and was lowering the receiver when she said 'I need a name.'

Names raced through Jack's mind like the symbols in a fruit machine, two of which came to rest. 'Bernard Onze,' he said.

'Can you spell that for me, dear?'

Jack did so and rang off. She didn't sound much of a clair-voyant – she hadn't seen through his false name – but if anyone should believe in the power of the letters, she should. He tried the plumber's number again, and this time he got through. 'Fazackerley of Fazakerley,' a woman said.

'Could I speak to Mr Fazackerley?'

'I'm sorry, he's not here at the moment. Can I take a message?'

'It's rather difficult to explain. Have you a number where I could reach him?'

'How urgent is it?'

'Very.'

'You could, I suppose, but I don't know what good it'd do. He's out on a big job, and he does them all by himself.' She rustled papers like a pet building a nest, then said 'Here's the number, anyway. Bill doesn't like to let anyone down.'

'That's kind of him.'

'In case you don't manage to get him, who shall I say? This is his wife.'

'Don't worry, I'll get him,' Jack said, depressing the receiver rest gently. As he dialled he found himself willing her husband to have responded to the letter, or failing that, to be open to persuasion. He didn't like to think of causing her pain.

The phone rang eleven times, then eleven. Jack imagined the plumber busy with a blowtorch, and willed him to turn it off. Five more pairs of rings, and perhaps one more had just begun when the phone was lifted. 'Aye, who's this?' said a slow male voice.

'Bill Fazackerley?'

'Aye.'

He must be alone in the building, Jack reflected, and tried

not to begin thinking prematurely along those lines. 'Your wife told me where to find you.'

'Aye.'

'I'm sorry to trouble you at work,' Jack said, making a wish as he took a breath. 'It's about a letter.'

'Oh, aye.' Fazackerley's tone had become guarded. 'What kind of letter would that be?'

'About good luck.'

'Oh.'

Jack closed his eyes, feeling heat waver through him as though he was turning into it. Fazackerley's syllable – a weary groan – seemed to have told him all that he needed to know. 'Mr Fazackerley,' he said into the blaze behind his eyelids, 'if I could just—'

'God love us,' the plumber said with such ponderous force that each word sounded like a knell. 'Don't tell me you're another.'

'Another what?'

'Another she sent one of them letters.'

Jack steadied himself by pressing one hand against the hot glass of a window. 'Who?'

'The wife.'

'Forgive me, but are we talking about the same letter?'

'The one about thirteen bringing you good luck.'

'The very one,' Jack said, opening his eyes to a world renewed by sunlight. 'I just wanted to let you know it works.'

'Oh, aye.'

'Believe me,' Jack said, for Fazackerley sounded less than convinced. 'I didn't tell your wife, but I hope you will, and thank her for me. Good luck to you both.'

'Aye,' the plumber said, retreating with what might have been embarrassment into his initial brusqueness, and Jack hung up at once. He felt enormously relieved for the Fazackerleys, and grateful to them for confirming his impression that anyone sympathetic must respond to his appeal for good fortune. 'Let's keep this simple,' he said to the mirror as he placed the next call.

'Doctor Globe's surgery.'

'Could I speak to the dentist?'

'What concerning, please?'

'It's easiest if I explain to him.' Then a child started crying in the background, growing louder, and the receptionist said 'I think he's finished. Who shall I say?'

'He won't know me.'

'I see,' the receptionist said dubiously, and Jack heard her hand cover the mouthpiece. After a few seconds the seashell hollowness went away, and a male voice said 'Edwin Globe. Is there some problem?'

'Sounds like it,' Jack admitted as the crying was done away with by the slam of a door. 'I'm following up some correspondence.'

'What firm are you?'

'There's no firm, just you and me. I wrote to you a few weeks ago inviting you to improve your luck, and I was wondering—'

'That's the reason for your call.' The dentist gave a sound too curt to be called a laugh. 'Professionalism gets everywhere these days.'

'Apparently,' Jack agreed through his teeth. 'I wonder if you've had a chance—'

'If you're asking after your letter, it went in the bin with the rest of the day's waste.'

'I thought it might have. I don't suppose you'd reconsider if I sent you another.'

'You suppose correctly. Now unless you—'

'Thank you for helping make my mind up,' Jack said, putting a full stop with the receiver rest halfway through the sentence. He'd taken a dislike to the dentist as soon as he'd heard the crying. A glance at his watch showed him that he was due back at the library in a few minutes. He redialled the dressmaker's number.

'Amy Conning. I'm not able to come to the phone just now. If you'd like to leave your name and number—'

'I wouldn't,' Jack said, and cut her off.

She could be there in the flesh, listening in order to decide

281

whether to pick up the phone, but if she wasn't he would have had to record a message more explicit than he cared to leave. She would wait, he told himself, and crossed the road to the library, feeling invisible and safe. All the same, his failure to establish whether she had helped his family nagged at his thoughts, and so he resolved to phone her again from the safest place he could think of. He was almost home at the end of the afternoon when he parked the van and went into the police station.

There was no risk. Nobody would overhear him. The counter was deserted, and in any case he was invisible. He fed the phone some coins and watched the display tot them up to thirty-three. 'Amy Conning,' the voice said after three pairs of rings, as usual. Jack was awaiting the rest of the message when she repeated 'Amy Conning.'

'Sorry, I thought you were— You sounded like—' Jack watched the display of his credit linger over twenty-three, and began again. 'I believe you received a letter about good luck.'

'Have you a problem with that?'

'I haven't, no,' Jack said, rather thrown. 'Have you?'

'I hope not. Why not start by saying who you are.'

'I don't think that's necessary.'

'Then I won't discuss it over the phone.'

'You should have,' Jack said regretfully, dropping the phone on the hook and collecting his unused change from the chute. She would find him altogether surer of himself when they met face to face. He thought of phoning again as Bernard Onze, if a name was all she wanted, but it seemed clear from her tone that she hadn't responded to the letter. He pocketed his change, the clown's head nudging his fingertips, and turned to the door. Three policemen and four other people were coming towards him, blocking the width of the steps, and one of them was pointing at him.

Those who weren't policemen were the Evanses, Clint and Lee and Eli and their mother. 'There he is,' she protested at the top of her shrill voice. 'He's the one you should be locking up.'

Each of the policemen was leading one of her sons by the

arm, and the one who had hold of Eli was Pether. He shouldered the door aside and met Jack's eyes as the policeman leading Clint said 'Mrs Evans, I should advise you—'

'Don't you try to shut me up. You wouldn't if I had the sort of money your friend has. Nobody listens to a mother on her own who has to skimp and scrape. It was him and his daughter who he lets run wild who gave my sons a bad name, so whose fault is it if they get into trouble? You'd be taking *her* away if there was any justice in the world instead of letting them keep the fortune them and the paper tricked someone into sending them at me and my boys' expense.'

During her diatribe the policemen had herded the boys onto chairs in a waiting area off the lobby. As Pether stood on guard, Jack went to him. 'You won't need me, will you?'

Pether shook his head. 'We caught them in the commission of a burglary,' he murmured, sounding almost apologetic. 'I think you can safely spend any money you've been saving for court costs.' As Jack moved towards the door, ignoring Mrs Evans, Pether added 'My father said to thank you for the boots.'

'You're in league, the lot of you,' Mrs Evans screamed, and continued along those lines as Jack descended the steps. Screams could be music, he thought with a grin, and hastened home to tell the family as much of his good news as he could.

THIRTY-EIGHT

The early hours of Monday were so hot that Jack dreamed he was in Greece, where the colours burned and the sea felt more like sand than water. He awoke feeling parched and had several glasses of water for breakfast. 'I hope you won't have to queue long in this heat,' Julia said.

'It'll be worth it to make sure our passports are on the way through the system.'

'I could go if you like.'

'Don't say that, or you'll have me feeling I'm no use.'

'We'll still keep you as an ornament,' Julia said.

He returned her grin, though he felt embarrassed by his subterfuge. There wouldn't be many more scenes like this, he promised her. Of course their passports, like everything else in their lives, would take care of themselves so long as he did what was necessary. 'I'd better be off before it gets too hot,' he said, and made for the van.

The hard-edged sun in the desert sky looked shrunken by its own heat. The tunnel under the river offered the only available shade. The route to the clairvoyant's led through the suburbs of Liverpool into Skelmersdale, a newish town which appeared to have been built in anticipation of a future yet to be filled in around it. Enormous circular slices of lawn interrupted roads split down the middle by fields, and the roadsides were scattered with isolated clumps and rows of identical houses like the first growth of some new boxy vegetable encased in corrugated chocolate bark. Crumpled sheets of greasy paper lay on the verges as if maps had been forsaken by walkers who'd given up trying to find their way or any pavements. When Jack began to suspect that he'd driven around the same roundabout twice he stopped the van and opened the road map.

He was leafing through the book when four children, three boys and a girl, came into sight wheeling a supermarket trolley alongside a row of maisonettes identical except for the patterns of their net curtains. All the children looked about eleven years old. They saw Jack and went into a muttering huddle, then they approached the road with four inventively varied kinds of swagger which were presumably meant to imply that they had every right to be off school or that it was none of Jack's business. The girl glanced at the van and nudged the nearest boy, and the two of them came to the passenger window while the others dawdled past with the trolley. 'Do you sell dishes, mister?' the girl demanded.

'Dishes of what?'

She grimaced as though at a childish joke. 'You know. *Dishes.*'

For a moment Jack continued to assume that she'd mistaken the van for a mobile café – both she and her companion were undernourished, their thin pale faces raggedly framed by lank hair – and then he remembered the trademark which was still faintly visible on the rear doors. 'Satellite dishes, you mean.'

'Yeah,' the boy said with spectacular aggressiveness. 'Give us one.'

'I haven't any to give away or even to sell. Can you tell me how to get to—'

'What've you got if you haven't got dishes?' the girl said in open disbelief.

'Nothing much. Nothing you'd like.'

'Give us ten pee, then.'

'Each,' the girl added.

'I might if you tell me—' Jack said, and imagined being observed in the act of handing money to them as if to lure them into the van. It wasn't that thought which made him break off, however; it was a muffled sound at the rear of the vehicle. 'What's happening back there?' he shouted, and sliding his door open, jumped down onto the tarmac.

The rear doors were wide open. As Jack sprinted to them, one of the boys leapt out of the van and flung the briefcase into the trolley. The girl and her crony had already run along the passenger side of the van. They grabbed the handle of the trolley without faltering and raced away along the road.

For a moment Jack didn't know who he was. People might have robbed Jack Awkward, but surely not the Count. He slammed the rear doors and glared after the children. 'You don't want to steal that,' he said in a voice which cut through the air like a jet of flame.

Perhaps they faltered, but they didn't halt. His power mustn't work at that distance. 'I warned you,' he said, and bolted after the children, who squealed in chorus. Two of the boys darted across the road, either abandoning their friends or trying to decoy Jack. He was gaining on the trolley when the girl and her companion reached the junction and dashed towards the roundabout, into the path of a car.

The car veered aside with a screech of brakes and a short dirty yell from the driver. The children ran the trolley onto the central island, which wasn't as broad as the distance Jack had yet to run to it, unless the perspective was confusing him. He put on speed, his breath blazing in his aching lungs. He had just reached the edge of the roundabout when the children arrived at the far side of the island.

They couldn't cross. Cars were streaming two abreast onto the roundabout, the gaps between them too small for even these children to brave. Jack sprinted onto the dry grass of the island and managed to suck in enough breath for a shout as the children saw him. 'Leave it. I don't want you, I only want my bag.'

The boy swung round and snatched the briefcase out of the trolley. Cars were still cutting off his escape. He held up the briefcase, and Jack's innards twinged as he realised that the boy meant to fling it into the traffic. 'Do that and I'll kill you,' he warned, stumbling to a halt in the middle of the island.

His intention was to give the boy a chance to drop the briefcase without feeling threatened, but the girl grabbed the trolley and pushed it towards Jack with all her strength. It stopped yards short of him, slowed down by the grass. He had already sidestepped, and now he ran at the boy. 'Bastard,' the boy yelled, hurling the briefcase across the island, and fled onto the road.

The briefcase landed at the very edge of the grass and sprang open. The blowlamp rolled out onto the island. The children dashed across the road, dodging cars, and began to shout at Jack upon reaching the verge. Their insults grew fiercer as they put more distance between him and themselves, but Jack was scarcely aware of them. So long as he ignored them, he felt, they couldn't draw attention to him. He replaced the blowlamp quickly in the briefcase and stood up. Once the traffic permitted he strode off the island and onto the parched verge. He was halfway to the van when he saw that someone was waiting for him.

The man was leaning on a baseball bat, a pose which, like his bright red singlet, seemed designed to show off the muscles of his hairy arms. Jack bore down on him without breaking his stride. He was the Count now that he had his case back.

The man straightened up as much as he could without lifting the bat from the tarmac and thrust his flattened mottled face, whose most prominent feature was its dislocated nose, at him. 'What were you doing with them kids?'

'The absolute minimum, considering.'

The man made a face that squashed his top lip under his nose. 'Less of the fancy language, bud. What were you after?'

Jack held it up. 'My case.'

The man considered it and the answer at length, then allowed his lips to sag. 'You'll be wanting to report it, then.'

'No point. I didn't see their faces.'

Perhaps he should have asked the way to the police station, because the man looked laboriously suspicious. 'What were you doing stopped round here?'

'Trying to find my way, and I wouldn't object to some help.'

'You wouldn't, wouldn't you?'

'If I can find something called the Concourse,' Jack said as though his patience was almost exhausted, 'I'll know where I am.'

The man started to knock on the roadway with the tip of the baseball bat, until Jack wondered if he could be signalling to another vigilante. The gesture was apparently an aid to thought, however. Eventually the man lifted the bat and pointed with it towards the roundabout from which Jack had retrieved the briefcase. 'Across there and the next one. And the one after it, and you'll see the caterpillar.'

The last Jack saw of the man was a glimpse in the rear-view mirror of him poking the grass verge with the bat as though he regretted having put it to so little use during the encounter. Then the roundabout swung him out of the mirror and there was only tarmac and grass. The road sloped upwards for no particular reason and down again to the next roundabout, where a sign directed Jack to the town centre. A one-way system wandered around the Concourse, a large windowless box containing all the shops. On its roof there did indeed stand a giant bespectacled caterpillar. Jack left the van in the car park over which the caterpillar kept watch and made straight for his destination, across the one-way road.

All the street names were grouped in alphabetical order as if they might have been invented and then placed by a computer. On one side of the road were Flamstead, Flaxton, Flimby and Flordon, on the other were Harsnips and Hartshead and Hawksclough. Fomble should be just around the bend, and there it was, opposite Hazingly. The clairvoyant's was the end house, which had sprouted a lanky stained-glass porch to distinguish it from the rest of the chocolate terrace. Before Jack could ring the bell a woman stepped into the porch, colours spilling down her ankle-length white dress as if she had just upset half a dozen pots of paint over herself. 'I sensed you were near,' she said. 'Mr Onze.'

'Who else.'

Her wide face looked tautened by earnestness and by the rainbow hairband from which her red hair flowed over her shoulders. 'Come in, dear, so we can keep the heat out,' she said.

The narrow hall smelled of incense and a fried breakfast. Framed photographs of figures outlined by flaring colours hung on the staircase wall. Ursa Gemini ushered Jack into the first room, which was darkened by curtains embroidered with silver crescent moons and pentagram stars. One corner of the small room was occupied by shelves of books in shabby jackets – Nostradamus, Strieber, von Daniken, Vogh – and much of the rest of the wall space was concealed by greenery in pots. 'Sit at the table, dear,' the clairvoyant said like an aunt having a child to tea.

The top of the round table which occupied the centre of the room was covered in green baize. This, and the Tarot pack that lay on it, suggested to Jack that they were about to play a game which the Count would win. The large white globe dangling above it imparted a glow to the baize while keeping the rest of the room dim. Jack took his place on one of the twin straight chairs as Ursa Gemini faced him across the table. 'You've an unusual name, dear. Where are you from?'

As Jack met her green-eyed gaze she held up one hand glittering with rings. 'Don't tell me. Have you something to do with water?'

'Not directly.'

'I see you near water, and the letter – could it be N or M?'

'I'm sure it could be.'

'Could I be seeing a river, dear?'

'If you say so.'

'I see you by the river. Would that have an M in it?'

'Among many other things.'

The clairvoyant waved her ringed fingers at him. 'Try and help me a little, dear, so that we can establish a rapport. You live near the river, don't you? The Mersey, I believe.'

'True so far.'

'And the name of the place, dear, would that be the N?'

'Good heavens.'

'I nearly see it, but it won't come clear. Is it quite a long word?'

'Even longer.'

'Yes, of course, two words. It's by the Mersey, isn't it? New Brighton, am I right, dear?'

'Amazing. However do you do it?'

'We all of us have the gift, dear. It's a question of putting your faith in it and making it work for you.' She sat forwards, brushing the Tarot pack aside, and took his hands. Hers were soft with plumpness, but their skin was rough. 'Now, dear, tell me how I can help you,' she said.

'I wanted to tell you that over the phone, if you remember. You don't think you could say now without my having to.'

'I'll do my best if that's what you want, dear,' she said like the aunt indulging the child. 'I never ask anyone to pay unless they believe in me.'

She grasped his hands more firmly and closed her eyes. After a while she said 'I get the impression you're concerned about someone besides yourself.'

'I think you could safely say that.'

'I feel it may have to do with how you make a living.'

'That may be the case in a manner of speaking.'

Her hands had grown absolutely still, and Jack sensed her trying to read any movements of his, but he let them go limp. 'I see danger,' she said. 'Do you make your living by taking risks, Mr Onze?'

'Doesn't everyone?'

She appeared to be listening intently, but Jack thought that was only to him. 'I still get danger,' she insisted. 'Has it to do with protecting other people, what you do?'

'Yes indeed.'

'Are you worried about someone at the moment, dear?'

'Come to think,' Jack said with surprise, 'I suppose I am.'

'Someone close to you?'

'Couldn't possibly be closer.'

'I feel it's a woman.'

'Right in one.'

'It must be your wife.'

'Even closer than my wife just now.'

Her hands shifted uneasily, then she opened her eyes. 'You

could try to help me a little, dear. I'm beginning to wonder if you're really here for a reading.'

'Why else do you think I would be?'

'I'm not sure I care to know.' She gazed at him and flexed her fingers. 'Do you want to hear the truth?'

'I'm counting on it.'

'I don't believe Bernard Onze is your real name.'

'I can't quite see a birth certificate saying Ursa Gemini.'

She let go of Jack's hands and pushed them away. 'If you came to try and discredit me, dear, I'm afraid I must ask you to leave. I've no time for anyone who wants to destroy other people's beliefs because he's no faith of his own.'

Before she could stand up, Jack closed his hands around her wrists. 'Let go of me, dear,' she said, loudly enough to be preparing to cry for help.

'I want you to feel that I'm telling the truth. Don't make me let go until we've reached an understanding.' He tightened his grip, gently but firmly enough that she would bruise herself if she tried to break free. 'I don't know why you should feel discredited. You were closer to the truth than you seem to think.'

Her hands were flattening themselves under his as though they were doing their best to be inconspicuous. 'You said everyone can see the future if they work at it,' he said. 'Let me tell you what I see for you.'

He felt the pulsing of her veins, her tendons growing tense. 'If you keep up your correspondence,' he said, 'all will be well.'

He thought she might be impressed by his being specific so quickly, but she looked resentful. 'Who with?' she demanded. 'What about?'

'With thirteen people, and you didn't need to compose a single letter.'

She stared at him, and her hairband shifted as a ripple passed through her forehead. 'I don't hold with such things, dear. They're superstition. If that's all—'

'If you believe in what you do you must believe in them. They work.'

291

Something froze her: his gaze, or his hands on her wrists, or the tone of his voice. 'You must be able to sense if I'm telling the truth,' he said. 'Am I trying to deceive you in any way?'

She seemed to have some difficulty in moving her lips. She belched suddenly, and her right hand twitched as if she wanted to cover her mouth. Eventually she whispered 'No.'

'Have you kept the letter you received?'

'No,' she said in a small high pleading voice.

'If you were to get another, would you do as it says?'

Her voice was shrinking as though it was trying to hide. 'Yes.'

'If you don't I can't see any future for you at all, just a blank. You're certain?'

'I've said.'

Her tone was edging closer to resentment. Jack let go of her wrists but kept his eyes fixed on hers while he reached for the briefcase on the floor. He didn't need to glance away in order to find her letter on top of the remaining wad. He slid the letter across the table and waited for her to look.

Her face tightened as she saw the envelope. When she raised her eyes he could see that she was disappointed and perhaps rebellious. She must feel tricked. 'I told you I was worried for you, and I am,' the Count said. 'Whatever you do, don't go back on your word. I've seen the consequences, and you wouldn't like them.'

He was willing her to believe him. She had almost used up her chance. He watched as she took hold of the envelope with both hands. 'Don't tear it,' he heard someone murmur under his tingling scalp.

When she stood up, pushing the envelope into the hip pocket of her dress, he covered his mouth to quieten a breath of relief. 'Does this count as a reading?' he said, reaching past the clown's head in his pocket for a sheaf of banknotes.

'You don't owe me anything,' she said loudly and clearly, reasserting herself. She hurried to the curtains and shoved them open, brightening the jungle of the room. She waited until Jack preceded her into the hall and opened the door to the porch, where slivers of glass flared up like jagged flames to meet him. As soon as he stepped out of the porch she closed the door behind him. 'I did see water,' she said.

He glanced back as she retreated into the house, slamming the inner door with one hand and crossing herself repeatedly with the other. He'd made such an impression on her, he thought, that she was unlikely to break her promise. He strode back to the car park, swinging his briefcase and feeling the blowlamp roll. A uniformed attendant with a book of parking tickets was making his morose way along the rank of vehicles which included Jack's. 'Enjoy your day,' Jack called to him, wreathing him in fumes as the van pulled out of the rank.

Once he was past the outbreak of roundabouts the road brought him to yet another motorway. His route led past Warrington and Helsby, and the landscape seemed increasingly like a record of the Count's adventures. Soon they would come to an end. He wasn't sure how he felt about that, but until the end came he wouldn't need to know.

He was almost forty minutes early for work. He parked by the library and strolled to a pub where he quenched his thirst with a pint of Wobbly Bob, then contented himself with another half and a ham roll. He ambled to the library, feeling amiably vague, and arrived at twelve minutes to one. As he emerged from the staffroom Stella caught sight of him. 'I didn't know you were here,' she said.

'Why, was someone wanting me?'

'Yes,' she said, shifting a sweet which rattled against her back teeth. 'Your wife wants you to call her. Something about where she used to work.'

THIRTY-NINE

The Count took most of Saturday afternoon to make a call he should already have made. The first time he heard the answering machine he replaced the receiver at once, and had to remind himself that the dressmaker might be waiting to hear a voice before she accepted the call. He dialled again, and said 'Hello' when the recording invited him to speak. 'Hello? Hello?' There was no response, and a student was waiting at the reference library counter.

He fetched the last two weeks' issues of three newspapers and carried them to a table as the student followed him, her metal crutches clicking. Once she was seated he phoned again. 'Amy Conning. I'm not able to come to the phone just now. If you'd like to leave your name and number after this short tone I'll get back to you,' she promised, and emitted a shrill beep.

'Hellou?' the Count said in a deep cultured unctuous voice. 'Is there anyone there, hellou?' This met no more success than Jack's voice had. After thirty seconds or so the tape beeped again and gave way to the dialling tone as a rotund man plodded over to Jack for help in discovering the origins of his surname, Sarney. By the time Jack had settled him with a pile of genealogical tomes the student wanted last month's newspapers. As Jack sorted those she'd finished with, several headlines caught his attention – HAS MERSEY BURNER KILLED AGAIN?; HORRIFIC GARAGE MURDER; ROCK FERRY MURDER 'MAY BE COPY CAT' SAY POLICE – and seemed to be urging him not to waste time.

'—after this short tone I'll get back to you. Beeeep.'

''Allo, annyboddee? 'Allo?' Bernard Onze's trace of a

294

French accent earned no response either. Soon Stella came upstairs to staff the desk while Jack had his tea break, and when he returned there were queries waiting to be answered. Picking up the receiver when eventually he was left alone was so automatic he didn't need to think of the number.

'—back to you. Beeep.'

'Miss Conning? Mrs Conning? I don't suppose you're there, by any chance?'

'It's Ms Conning. Did you call before?'

She sounded ready to lecture him on the proper use of the answering machine. 'Why, does my voice seem familiar?' he said.

'I really couldn't say. Should it?' Without pausing she said 'Did you want to make an appointment?'

'Please.'

'Who's it for? I don't dress men.'

'My daughter.'

'How old?'

'Twelve.'

'What do you want for her?'

'A fortune,' Jack might have said, but the Count used Jack's voice to say 'An outfit for the heat.'

'Bring her so I can look her over. When do you want?'

'How late do you see people?'

'My evenings are my own. I can measure her when she gets off school on Monday if that's any use to you.'

'Would that be your last appointment?'

'Five o'clock would be.'

'That sounds ideal. We'll look forward to dealing with you.'

'I don't have your name and address.'

'Bernard Onze, 11 Counting Way.'

'Whereabouts is that?'

'On the new estate.'

'Five Monday, then. Please don't be any later. Now you'll have to excuse me while I boot my two-year-old out of the kitchen before she burns herself.'

'I wouldn't want that to happen to her,' Jack said with a grin like the one he was fingering on the clown's head, and held onto the phone until it replaced the dressmaker with emptiness. He hadn't asked about the letter because he felt he didn't need to ask: her whole attitude told him that she would have torn it up. 'Looking forward, looking forward,' he murmured, and let go of the receiver and the clown's head as a bell rang to announce that the library would close in ten minutes. The last reader left the building eleven minutes later, and Jack drove home.

When he unlocked the front door the house was silent. 'Anyone?' he called.

Julia came out of the bathroom with a towel around her hair. 'Where's Laura?' Jack asked.

'Out on her bike. Probably on her way back from the library by now.'

'She'll be fine.'

'I know.'

No doubt Julia was thinking of the self-defence class Laura had helped get started at the school, but she seemed preoccupied. 'Pensive,' Jack said.

'Don't laugh, but I'm feeling sorry for Luke.'

'Well, sympathy comes cheap. And birds go it,' he added when she looked hurt. 'I expect Rankin's clients could use a bit of sympathy, not to mention the people like you he left out of a job.'

'I see all that. Now you'll laugh, but I feel almost guilty after what he just did.'

'Guilty of what, for heaven's sake?'

'I suppose about wishing the worst for him. I didn't know he was going to take all the blame on himself.'

'He didn't take it, it was already his.'

'Unless you think I should have noticed what he was playing at sooner.'

'I don't think any such thing. I'll tell you what I do think – he's hoping the law will go easier on him for not dragging you into court.'

'Maybe,' she said as if Jack had disillusioned her.

'Don't you dare blame yourself any more,' he said, hugging her until the towel down her back started to drip on the hall carpet. He hadn't released her when Laura let herself into the house and greeted the sight of them with a wolf whistle. 'Maybe I'm admitting to myself I was afraid we'd be stopped from going to Crete,' Julia murmured.

'What's going to stop us?' Laura said, so anxiously that Jack began to wonder if anything could. He had weeks to finish what he had to do before they left – long enough to wait for times when Julia wouldn't question where he was. 'Nothing,' he and Julia told Laura in chorus, making her laugh.

In the morning Julia suggested a picnic. 'Shall we go to that place where we went on a train when I was little,' Laura said, 'where the squirrel ran off with my sweet?'

'Freshfield.'

'Sounds good to me,' Julia said.

It sounded better than that to Jack, because it was only a couple of miles from Amy Conning's house. He could leave the family sunning themselves while he drove past the dressmaker's or perhaps even took care of her, but he rejected the notion at once: it brought the Count and his tasks too close to the family. 'It'd be teeming with people on a day like this,' he said. 'Let's just drive until we find somewhere we like.'

They ended up at the edge of a copse on a hillside in Cheshire. Fields were laid out like samples of green on the slopes below. While the Orchards ate cheese and Julia's home-made bread and shared a bottle of Bulgarian Cabernet Sauvignon, two magpies flew out of a hedge, spreading their ebony tails, and strutted about to pick at the hillside. A hawk which looked high as the sun hovered overhead against a flawlessly blue sky. Jack watched it until it sailed beyond the trees, then he turned his attention to the grass on which he was lying and which contained treasures the magpies had overlooked, beetles so small that their glinting colours were invisible from more than a few inches away. He was watching them clamber about the maze of grass when Julia touched his shoulder to draw his gaze where Laura was looking.

A fox was observing the Orchards from the copse. Its gleaming eyes were darker than the deepest shadow under the trees. Jack could see its whiskers twitching, its sides breathing beneath the glossy auburn pelt. It stood with its left front paw upraised, regarding the family as if challenging them to make the first move. They managed to remain absolutely still until it turned and darted away through the copse with a wave of its bristling tail.

'I'll always remember today,' Laura whispered.

'So will I,' Julia said.

'We all will,' said Jack.

Certainly the Count did so on Monday afternoon as he drove out of Liverpool to the dressmaker's. If he hadn't decided against taking this route yesterday, they wouldn't have seen the fox on the hill. The docklands of Seaforth gave way to the villas of Crosby, beyond which a pair of stone lions on the gateposts of Ince Blundell guarded the start of the Southport road. Jack stayed in the fast lane of the dual carriageway until he came in sight of the Formby turn-off.

As he signalled before moving into the left-hand lane a Citroën cut in front of him without signalling. BACK OFF – BABY ON BOARD, said a sticker on the rear window, and there was indeed a toddler in the back seat with a dummy in her mouth. The driver stuck one hand out of the window as if she was turning right and swung left at the roundabout, releasing the stub of a cigarette which showered red-hot sparks across Jack's windscreen. 'No thanks, I don't smoke,' he said.

He felt as though he was tailing the Citroën. The toddler hoisted herself up on the back of the seat and pressed as much of her face as the dummy would permit against the rear window, above a sticker which said GOD MADE MEN BECAUSE VIBRATORS DON'T MOW THE LAWN. If the car had to stop dead, Jack thought, the toddler would fly between the front seats and through the windscreen. He couldn't help feeling relieved at the sight of the left turn ahead, which would lead him away from the spectacle of the Citroën and its passenger. But the car turned left there before he did.

On both sides of the straight road narrow gardens separated by hedges led to paired houses. Amy Conning's house would be about halfway along. Jack kept an eye on the numbers and tried not to watch the toddler, who was attempting to prise open a can of Coca-Cola with a screwdriver. Then the Citroën's brake lights flickered, the car began to slow, and Jack found himself willing the driver to be Amy Conning.

A climbing frame and a swing were visible above a hedge just ahead. They must be either in the dressmaker's front garden or in her neighbour's. The Citroën veered towards the middle of the road and slowed abruptly, and the point of the screwdriver slid off the can. Can and screwdriver banged against the rear window as the car swung into Amy Conning's drive, and Jack coasted by, grinning a grin which felt like a cut as wide as his face.

He turned left into the next road, which would lead him back to the dual carriageway, and parked the van. Two-seater planes from a nearby airfield buzzed overhead like huge slow flies, and he could hear distant shots from a rifle range. As he walked back to the dressmaker's he saw the toddler swing into the air above the hedge. 'Say goodbye,' he murmured.

The driver was unloading groceries from the boot of the Citroën. She wore a white T-shirt and baggy denim shorts, and presumably shoes when she was driving. She had pouchy cheeks and artificially silvered close-cropped hair, and her face was pale except for her prominent lips, whose aggressively red lipstick gave them a pouting appearance. She lifted the last carrier bag out of the boot and pushed the swing higher, and saw Jack at the gate. 'Yes?'

'Ms Conning?'

'That's who I am. Who are you?'

'Onze. We spoke.'

'Come in,' she said with a gesture as though she were flicking an invisible cigarette at the gate, and turned back to him when she reached the house. 'Weren't you supposed to be bringing your daughter?'

'She couldn't make it, I'm afraid. I'll tell you all you need to know.'

'I like to see who I'm togging,' the dressmaker said, and stepped into the house. 'Well, as long as you're here, come in.'

Jack frowned at the toddler while smiling at the same time, and was answered by a loud suck on the dummy. 'Are you leaving her out here?'

'She'll be all right so long as you've closed the gate properly,' Amy Conning said with more than a hint of accusation. 'She can't reach the latch.'

Jack went up the gravel drive, noticing that nobody except the toddler and her mother had seen him, and hesitated on the doorstep. 'Isn't there anyone else to look after her?'

'My parents live up the road. They'll be round in an hour or so.'

They might need to come sooner than that, the Count reflected. There was a phone in the hall, next to a staircase with open treads, and another Conning who lived locally ought to be easy to find in the directory beside the phone; he wouldn't have to say much. He followed the dressmaker past the front room and another which smelled of cloth and which was crowded with torsos in various stages of undress, raised trophy-like on poles. His fingers were straying to the lock of the briefcase when Amy Conning dumped the bag of groceries on the kitchen table and turned on him. 'No need to follow me like a hound. We'll go in the front room.'

It was furnished with a suite whose upholstery displayed frames of timber. Rugs were scattered across the polished floorboards, mirrors hung on the walls. A box of toys was shoved in the corner nearest to the television. The dressmaker sat with her back to the window and gave herself a cigarette which made her mouth look more petulant than ever. 'Smoke?'

'I leave that to others,' Jack said with a broad grin, and produced his lighter.

'We could do with more people like you who live and let live,' the dressmaker told him, cupping her hand around his as he lit her cigarette. The redundant gesture amused him, though her momentary closeness affected him with a pang of dismay; he wouldn't let her come that close again. 'So tell me what I can do for your daughter,' she said.

Through the window Jack could see the toddler struggling

to stand up on the swing. 'I think your child's about to fall. Perhaps you should—'

'You sound like her grandmother. She's got to learn. I can't be looking after her every moment of the day,' Amy Conning said with the briefest glance out of the window, and any dismay Jack had experienced on her behalf was gone for good. 'You were going to tell me what you need,' she said.

Jack placed the briefcase between his feet and sprang the lock open. The toddler spat out the dummy and began to howl. 'She's just trying to get my attention,' the dressmaker said without looking.

Jack reached into the briefcase and rested his fingertips on the blowlamp, which felt cool as a welcome drink. 'You've brought her measurements, have you?' Amy Conning said. 'Let me see or you'll have me wondering what you're hiding between your legs.'

Jack stroked the barrel of the blowlamp. 'I don't suppose you recall our being in touch earlier than Saturday.'

'Oh, do shut up,' she said, and banged on the window behind her. 'What about?'

'Luck.'

Without warning she jumped up and ran out of the house. Jack didn't move except to close his hand around the blowlamp; the Count wouldn't let her escape. He watched as she grabbed the dummy from the lawn and stuck it in the toddler's mouth before shoving her down on the seat of the swing and giving it a hard push. 'Now just try and amuse yourself for a few minutes. Nan and Grandad will be here soon,' she said, and took several drags on the cigarette as she returned to the house. When she came into the room she looked so peevish that Jack had to suppress a snort of mirth. 'I don't see how you could have got that letter,' she said.

The only way Jack could deal with the unexpectedness of this was by glancing past her at the window. 'Never mind her,' the dressmaker said, plumping herself onto the chair. 'You've got some explaining to do.'

'Certainly one of us has.'

She turned defensive at once. 'I only sent them to my

customers, and you aren't one.'

'You're talking about the letters.'

'That's right,' she said defiantly, 'I am.'

'You sent letters to how many of your customers?'

'Thirteen, like it said. Why not? It was only a joke.'

'A joke.'

'What's wrong with that? We can all do with a laugh now and then.'

'Oh, quite,' Jack said, letting go of the blowlamp and regaining his hold on it. 'So how did you make it clear to your customers that they weren't meant to take these letters seriously?'

'I didn't think they needed to be told.'

With a growing sense of disappointment which felt disconcertingly like helplessness, Jack realised she was on the defensive for precisely the opposite reason than he'd expected. 'Are you saying you didn't write anything at all on the letters?'

'Just my summer prices on the back. All right, so it wasn't only a joke, it was a promotional gimmick. I still don't see what it has to do with you.'

Jack touched the blowlamp once more for luck and reluctantly let go of it. 'Because I know someone who didn't know how to take the letter to begin with.'

The Count willed her not to ask for a name, and she only said 'Is that why you're really here?'

'It was at first. Now—' He rummaged in the case and snapped it shut. 'I'm afraid I seem to have wasted your time. I haven't brought the measurements after all.'

'I'd rather see her anyway.'

'I wonder if her mother may have fixed her up. If she hasn't I'll let you know,' Jack said, and stood up. 'Sorry to have troubled you. It could have been worse.'

'I won't ask how.'

If she suspected him of anything, it was of being capable of making life more difficult for her over the letters. Of course, he thought, she'd concluded that he was concerned with trading standards and practices – perhaps that someone had complained to him. 'You didn't do anything illegal,' he told her as he stepped onto the path, then he pointed at the toddler. 'Except that I should take more care of her if I were you. Seat-belts and so forth. Sometimes we don't know our own good luck until it's taken away.'

On his way to the van he couldn't shake off a lingering sense of frustration. If he had found out that she hadn't sent the letters it would have solved so much. Still, the Count's career wasn't over yet, and he set about planning his next visit as he drove home.

When he closed the front door Julia looked out of the kitchen. 'Where were you?'

'Held up on the road. These days they call highwaymen drivers,' he said, not wanting to entangle himself in further explanation. 'You don't look too happy. Anything wrong?'

'I just wanted you to be home to hear the news.'

'Why, what was it saying?'

She sighed and pointed at an envelope on the stairs. It was addressed to her. Jack reached for it, but she'd had enough of waiting. 'It's from the college,' she said. 'I got the job.'

FORTY

In the morning the passports arrived. Jack's photograph raised the biggest laugh, and speculation as to what he had been trying to remember. 'Where you were,' Laura suggested.

'Who you were,' Julia said.

'Where I was bound for.'

'We know that,' Laura protested. 'Crete.'

He couldn't argue. The other photographs appeared to be looking to the future, Julia producing a dreamy smile, Laura more concerned with the face she would be presenting to the world. 'I'll go to the bank before work,' he said.

He had more than one reason to do so, and going out early would give him time to make another call. Delighted as he was with Julia's success at the college, so much good luck in such a short time struck him as precarious, in need of reinforcement. There were few tasks left for the Count to perform, but it seemed best to deal with them as soon as practicable, to give nothing a chance to go wrong.

By half past ten he was at the bank, ordering Greek money and traveller's cheques. 'Shall I debit your account?' said the counter clerk, a young man whose sketchy moustache was glistening with sweat.

'I'll pay cash.'

As if that was a cue, Mr Hardy emerged from his office behind the clerk. 'If the manager's free,' Jack said, 'could I have a word?'

'It was Mr Orchard, wasn't it?'

'It still is.'

The clerk emitted a nervous cough and went to mutter at the manager. Mr Hardy frowned at the clock, but poked his paunch at the enquiry window as Jack finished signing the order forms. 'Some fresh problem, Mr Orchard?'

'Not even a stale one, I hope. I thought we might have another chat about buying a house.'

'I'm afraid my position on that hasn't changed.'

'But ours has. My wife's has, anyway. She's been hired to teach a computer course.'

'Please pass on my congratulations.'

'And an invitation to talk about a mortgage?'

'Not at the moment, Mr Orchard, no.'

The heat of the day seemed to gather behind Jack's eyes. 'You promised that if our circumstances changed—'

'Perhaps you should have informed me sooner. For a variety of reasons the branch's loan allocation for the quarter has been used up.'

'We only heard about the job yesterday,' Jack said, wondering whether, if the letter to Julia had been sent first class, or she'd phoned him at work with the news rather than waiting until he came home, or he hadn't been late home because of Amy Conning, whom he hadn't needed to visit so urgently after all— 'You mean we'll be on your list for the next quarter,' he said.

'I can't commit myself at this stage any more than I did previously. I suggest you contact the bank to schedule an appointment after you return from holiday, assuming that you haven't taken my advice concerning cancellation or postponement.'

'We won't disappoint our daughter. My wife isn't going to be needed in court. Her old boss has said she's innocent.'

'Then I should count your blessings, Mr Orchard, and then put your mind to husbanding your good fortune.'

'Rather than wiving and daughtering it, you mean?'

Mr Hardy leaned forwards over his paunch and lowered his voice. 'I think you might try taking life a little more seriously, Mr Orchard.'

'Believe me, I wish I could introduce you to some of the people who've reason to know that I do.'

It was the Count speaking. He'd leaned forwards too, so

305

that his face was only inches from the manager's. For a moment he felt that the glass was about to melt away and let him take hold of the man. 'I wish you all the luck you've wished us,' he said, 'and I look forward to seeing you when I return.'

Perhaps Mr Hardy had overbalanced, top-heavy as he was, or the buckle of his belt had caught under the ledge beneath the window, but it seemed to Jack that the Count's gaze was holding Mr Hardy in danger of toppling against the glass. 'I wouldn't want us to be enemies. I haven't many of them,' Jack said, and pushing himself away from the ledge on his side of the window, watched the manager bob up like a distorted reflection of himself.

Outside the bank Jack drew a long hot breath. He felt both enraged and wildly hilarious. At least he knew what to do with these feelings before they turned into anything like frustration. He went to the nearest phone box and fed in change and dialled one of the numbers left in his head. 'Doctor Globe's surgery,' the receptionist said.

'When's the latest the dentist sees patients?'

'How late do you need him?'

'Later than you think,' Jack refrained from saying. 'I can't take time off work,' he said.

'Last appointment is normally five-thirty.'

'Is he there later for emergencies?'

'He's here, but the surgery would be shut. In an emergency your best bet's the dental hospital.'

'Thank you for the clarification,' Jack said, and rang off.

He couldn't deal with the dentist that night, since he himself was working late. He went home to tell Julia how Mr Hardy had let them down. 'Oh,' she said, and trying to sound less angry and sad, 'Oh well, nothing is for ever.'

Her disappointment stayed with him throughout the day like a reminder of the Count's next task. Her and Laura's attempts to seem as if they had accustomed themselves to the setback only intensified his sense of purpose. In the morning he told Julia that he would be home late. 'I'm going to see what can be done about a mortgage.'

306

'Don't get involved with anyone who might make matters worse.'

It was almost the last time he would need to deceive her. The deception was ultimately Edwin Globe's fault, and one more reason for the Count to deal with him. 'You know I wouldn't commit us to anything without discussing it with you,' Jack said.

His workday passed like a slow parade in which he was participating at a distance. When at last he returned to the van he felt as though he'd been held up all day by the passing of a funeral. He drove along the motorway past Helsby, to the junction which would have been the thirteenth if there had been such a number, and made for Runcorn.

There wasn't a house to be seen for miles. Only signs stood by the road, pointing an arrow to places he had never heard of and another for 'all other Runcorn traffic'. Presumably by following the latter he would reach The Heath by a process of elimination. Helter-skelter slip roads led him under the carriageway, homebound cars staying close on his tail as he braked at the tight steep curves, and he wouldn't have minded seeing a police car keeping the traffic in check. But the Count never saw police cars; that must be part of his luck.

After ten minutes' worth of curves and underpasses he came to a straight road which led him to The Heath, a series of unfenced playing-fields overlooked by pairs of large houses and more distantly by fat chimneys producing fatter industrial smoke. Several amateur football games were attended by scatterings of supporters. Jack parked at the further end of the line of their vehicles and strolled across the baked field to the dentist's house.

It was larger than its twin by virtue of an aluminium conservatory protruding from the front. As Jack skirted a line of spectators at the edge of a marked pitch a woman emerged from the house and ran for a bus. The time was almost six o'clock. A few seconds later a man in a white smock stalked along the drive and closed the gates which the woman had left ajar, and Jack was sure that the dentist was alone in the house.

The front door slammed as Jack stepped off the grass, noting that there were no cars in the driveways of either of the dentist's neighbours. The brass plaque on the gatepost blazed like a mirror which a child was using to catch sunlight as Jack lifted the latch of the gate. Shouts of advice from spectators followed him up the drive in which a black Jaguar was parked, and pressing the bellpush seemed to produce cheers and applause. Though he didn't hear a bell, it brought the dentist to the door, yanking it open and then raising his hands behind his head like someone at gunpoint. 'Yes?'

'Doctor Globe?'

'Obviously.'

His manner wasn't nearly as submissive as his gesture had seemed, and in any case he had only been untying his smock. His plump dull face, which was adorned by a beard made for a narrower chin, was pink with a threat of losing his temper. 'What can I do for you?' he said in a tone which suggested he hoped it was nothing at all.

'I was wondering if you could give me something for my daughter.'

'My receptionist makes the appointments. She'll be here in the morning at nine.'

'I meant something to ease the pain.'

The dentist sighed. 'How extensive is it?'

'More than one tooth.'

'Then clearly she should take better care of them. I recommend you consult a pharmacist and speak to my receptionist tomorrow.'

Having finished peeling off his smock, he reached out to close the door. 'The chemist's shut,' Jack said.

'I can't do anything about that, I'm afraid.'

'Can't you help? Haven't you got something she could take?'

'Good God, man, this isn't a dispensary. If I start handing out analgesics, before I know I'll have all the walking wounded from the ball games trooping up my drive. Didn't you read my hours on the gate?' He stared at Jack's dismay, which wasn't entirely feigned, and gave a louder sigh. 'Oh, come in for a minute while I see what I can find. I really shouldn't be expected to do this, you know.'

Jack followed him swiftly and closed the door, cutting off the roar of spectators. The hall was wide and very empty apart from a sharp smell of disinfectant which made Jack's teeth twinge. Globe halted at the foot of the stairs and pointed at the nearest door. 'Please wait in there. I'm really not in the business of pain relief.'

Jack heard a child crying behind Globe's voice, and the smell of disinfectant seemed to fill his head like fuel. 'I gathered as much,' he said.

The dentist's mouth worked disapprovingly, wagging his beard. 'We have to believe God made pain. If, of course, you believe in God.'

'Sometimes I have problems believing in myself.'

It wasn't an especially good joke, the Count thought as he stepped into the waiting-room, where half a dozen hard chairs faced a counter and a low table spread with dog-eared magazines that looked dusty with sunlight through the net curtains. He was impatient with both the joke and the deception. When he heard Globe hurrying downstairs he opened the briefcase on the counter. 'These are the best I can do for you,' the dentist said from the hall.

'Don't be so sure.'

The Count's voice seemed to come from within the brief-case into which he was gazing. No doubt it was hardly audible outside the room, because Globe said 'Pardon me?'

'I don't know if that's possible.'

The dentist tramped into the room, shaking the floor. He apparently resented the inconvenience rather than anything he'd heard. 'Here you are,' he snapped.

He was proffering the remains of a blister pack of aspirins which he had presumably found in his bathroom, since the tinfoil was pale with talcum powder. 'Who left those?' the Count said. 'I assume they can't be yours.'

'I don't think that's any of your affair,' Globe said and slid the pack along the counter, the ragged tinfoil of popped blisters scraping the formica. 'Now I must ask you to excuse me. Here's my number if you wish to call tomorrow.'

The Count ignored the tablets and the dentist's card. 'I wish I could. There's something else you should have done for me.'

'Please.'

It was a dismissal, not an enquiry, but the Count gave him a last chance. 'You didn't know me then,' he said, unfolding the letter and laying it on the counter.

The dentist gaped at him as though unable to believe he was still there, then cocked his head to glance at the letter. The next moment the ridged back of his neck turned red, and he thumped the letter with the side of his fist. 'It was you? You sent me this?'

'As you see.'

'You dare to admit it after what I told you?'

'Remind me.'

Globe shoved himself away from the counter, the page fluttering in his wake. 'Didn't I make it clear that I put my trust in God?'

The Count wasn't sure that this was an entirely convincing rebuttal, but that was hardly his problem. 'Then you should look forward to meeting him,' he said as he lifted the blowlamp out of the briefcase and moved between Globe and the door.

As he took out the lighter the dentist's jaw dropped, and he made a sound as though he was about to be sick. 'My God, you're—'

'Don't say it. I don't like that name,' the Count told him, and turning the blowlamp on, flicked the lighter. He flicked it again, hard, then harder. Nothing emerged from it except a thread of smoke.

The sight of the blowlamp appeared to have paralysed the dentist, but the failure of the lighter released him. He lurched to the window and tore at the net curtains. When they slid only a couple of inches along the wire on which they were strung he banged on the window with the palms of his hands, screaming 'Help! The Burner!'

'Help him indeed,' the Count said, shoving the blowlamp

into Globe's face. He didn't want the dentist making a spectacle of himself at the window, and the curtains might catch fire. The dentist's face jerked away from the jet of gas, and he floundered towards the door. The low table tripped him. His head thumped the door, slamming it, and he slid down it until his shoulders were resting beneath the doorknob.

He wasn't quite unconscious, but he seemed not to know where he was; he was trying to shove himself backwards, his heels digging at the carpet, as though he could break through the door. The Count snapped the lighter again without success, then held the nozzle of the blowlamp against the fleshy groove beneath the dentist's nose. Globe began to flail the air with his hands and heave feebly up and down, his shoulders rubbing audibly against the door. His mouth fell open and gurgled a monotonous tune as his head twisted back and forth, unable to escape the gas. After rather too long in the Count's opinion, his eyes bulged and glazed over, and his head slumped against the doorknob.

He was still breathing. A bubble swelled from his left nostril, deflated and swelled again, and the Count had to resist the instinct to pick up the letter and use it to wipe Globe's nose. Instead he flicked the lighter in case the wick had had time to gather fuel, but it emitted only a click. 'Matches, where do you keep your matches?' he demanded, and answered for the dentist: 'In the kitchen, of course.' 'Thank you,' he said and pulled out his handkerchief, not to wipe the dentist's nose but in order to take hold of the doorknob.

Even a two-handed heave at the knob didn't shift Globe an inch. The Count had to grasp him by an arm and an equally leaden leg and drag him, his buttocks bumping along the carpet, until he was propped beside the doorframe – not far at all, but far enough to make the Count feel sprinkled with hot ash. He blew gas up the dentist's nose for a few seconds to ensure that Globe would remain unconscious, then he sidled out of the room.

Sunshine through the pane above the front door felt like a cloak on his shoulders as he ventured along the hall, hands down by his sides so as not to risk touching anything he didn't need to touch – the walls that were so palely papered that he could imagine them dazzling Jack, the blond pine banisters whose newness he would have been able to smell if it hadn't been for the disinfectant in the air. Under the stairs was only a shadow crouching like a large beast, and overhead must be a deserted floor. 'Just you and me, Doctor Globe,' he murmured, turning the kitchen doorknob with the handkerchief.

The kitchen was exactly as he'd expected: cold, metallic, as nearly antiseptic as it was possible for a kitchen to be. There wasn't a speck of dust on the windowsill, nor were there any matches. He scanned the gleaming metal surfaces and the scrubbed pine table for something he could use to carry a flame from the electric stove, then he thought of the letter and strode along the hall, narrowing his eyes at the sunlight. The door to the waiting-room was open just an inch, though he hadn't pulled it to behind him. When he shoved it with his wrapped hand it didn't budge.

'Don't play games with me,' he said. He retreated two paces and drove his shoulder against the door. It shook, and he heard a mumble of vague protest from the other side. 'The sooner you let me in, the sooner you won't feel a thing,' he promised, and launching himself from the far wall, ran at the door. This time his impact dislodged the obstruction, though only long enough for him to stagger into the room before Globe's head and torso lolled against the door again, the dentist making a blurred sound as if he didn't want to be roused. 'Stay asleep as you are,' the Count said and seizing Globe's shoulders, hauled him away from the door and rolled him onto his face. He threw the tableful of magazines on top of him and gave them a taste of gas from the blowlamp, and was stooping to pick up the letter when, in the room from which the conservatory extended, a woman spoke.

The Count froze, but only for a moment. 'You didn't tell me there was someone else,' he whispered at the dentist. 'That wasn't fair to them.' Then the woman fell silent, and he realised she had been a television announcer, because now he could hear music: *dum-de-dum, dum-de-dum, diddleydum, diddleydum* – the Laurel and Hardy theme. Someone must have switched on the television, however. The Count dodged out of the waiting-room and tiptoed across the hall to close his handkerchief around the doorknob.

He turned it minutely, though not quite minutely enough to prevent it from squeaking, and flung the door open, belatedly realising that he still had nothing with which to light the blowlamp. Was sufficient gas left in it to overcome someone else? Whoever was in the room must have heard him approaching and hidden behind one of the obese leather chairs, or the television and its mahogany stand, or in the corner obscured by bookshelves displaying as many saintly figurines as books, or in the conservatory full of vines beyond the French windows. 'Here's another nice mess you've gotten me into,' Oliver Hardy growled, and the Count saw that the television was simply monitoring what the videorecorder had switched itself on to record.

'You almost did,' he called, marching across the hall to the Laurel and Hardy tune, and grabbed the letter from the carpet while he mopped his forehead with the handkerchief. 'I don't know about you,' he told Globe, 'but I'm going to need a holiday after this.' He dropped the blowlamp into the briefcase, which he left at the foot of the stairs, then he screwed the letter into a long spill as he hurried back to the kitchen. He should have switched on the stove, he thought, and then he wouldn't have needed to wait. He switched on the nearest ring and watched it start to grow dull red, and heard a groan from the waiting-room. 'Just wait,' he muttered. 'I hope you've seen this one before. I wouldn't want to deny anybody a laugh.'

As soon as the ring appeared to be hot enough he pressed the end of the spill against it, but all this achieved was to turn an inch of paper brown. 'Why don't you do something to *help* me?' Oliver Hardy pleaded. He counted to eleven slowly, then poked the spill at the ring again, and this time the paper caught fire. 'Well, I couldn't help it,' Stan Laurel wailed, and the Count heard another groan. 'Coming now,' he said.

313

He stuffed his handkerchief into his pocket and walked back along the hall, shielding the flame with his free hand. Globe was sprawled under the magazines in the same position as he had been left, and the Count was relieved to think that the dentist wasn't conscious after all. He pointed the spill downwards to set more of it alight, then shared its flame with the magazines on Globe's body before dropping the blazing spill against his nose. 'Whoomph,' he agreed with the sound it made then. Averting his eyes and covering his mouth and nose with the handkerchief, he stepped quickly into the hall and picked up the briefcase as he headed for the front door.

A burst of applause and cheering greeted him. 'Thank you,' he said. He returned the handkerchief to his pocket, having shut the door and the gate, and lingered at the edge of a football match for a few minutes. He was watching the dentist's house, but there was no sign of movement beyond the net curtains. 'Nearly done,' he murmured as he strolled back to the van.

FORTY-ONE

He was almost home when he started to feel nervous. It made the familiar streets seem aloof from him as he drove through the slanting sunlight, which kept touching him like a memory of fire. For the moment the best he could do with his nervousness was transform it into a show of righteous anger. 'You were right to be suspicious,' he told Julia.

'Was it a waste of time?'

'Anyone who sounds as if they're offering something for nothing has got to be hiding a lot. We'd have ended up trying to borrow money from the bank to pay shysters like those back.'

'What's a shyster?' Laura wanted to know.

'Someone who's shyer than shyest.'

'The bank will have to give us a loan soon,' Julia said, mostly to Laura. 'We don't want to risk getting into difficulties.'

'People like that can get on my nerves, people who prey on the gullible. We can see through them, but they make their living off people who haven't our sense.' Jack ranted along those lines for a while, not least because he was wondering if Julia had helped identify the basis of his nervousness. As far as he could see, all that could go wrong now were their dealings with the bank, and he wouldn't know about those until the family returned from Crete. Would it be best for the Count to make his final visit as soon as possible, or should he wait until nearer the time?

His inability to decide hovered behind him all through dinner. Afterwards they watched a comedy, but Jack was unable to concentrate; while Cary Grant and Katharine

315

Hepburn chased a leopard he felt as if the Count was waiting silently at his shoulder. Even when he made love to Julia after Laura was asleep, he sensed indecision or the Count looming at his back.

He would deal with the problem next week, he thought as he lay in the dark. He couldn't do anything until then, since Saturday was Laura's sports day. On the following Saturday the family would leave for Crete, but he ought to do what was necessary by Thursday, when her school year ended. One evening next week, then, once he had concocted an excuse.

On Saturday the sun made him think of the glass porthole of a furnace. By the time Laura and Jody and two others from the self-defence class gave a demonstration of their skills the playing-field was all but shadowless. The sight of Laura, feinting and throwing her opponents and being thrown, rolling to her feet again bright-eyed and hardly panting, both exhilarated and saddened him; she seemed to be receding from him into a future he couldn't envisage. 'She'll be all right,' he murmured, and Julia squeezed his arm.

The Orchards spent Sunday evening at the bowling alley on the promenade. Laura won, and Julia wasn't far behind. Jack listened to the hollow boom of bowls and the echoing rattle of skittles being set up again and again as though a primitive computer was working out a sum in front of his eyes. He still hadn't thought of an excuse. He wouldn't need one tomorrow, since he was on the late shift, too late for the Count to go visiting afterwards – but the delay was allowing him to wonder if, because this would be the final visit, he was secretly afraid that it might somehow go wrong.

Or was he nervous of telling Julia one lie too many? Simplest was best, he told himself, when it came to excuses. He would see the light in time. Tuesday or Wednesday evening, he thought as he lay in bed. Neither day added up to eleven, but 'Count of' made thirteen, and the 'eleven' after it turned ill luck into good. After a while his anxious counting put him to sleep, and he dreamed of making excuses, none of which he could remember in the morning, so that he had to reassure himself that none of them could have been worth remembering. 'Too hot in the night,' he told Julia when she remarked on his harassed look.

He needed to be on his own. He set out for work with half an hour to spare. Perhaps the drive would give an excuse the chance to take shape, or a walk at the end of the drive would. After ten minutes' driving and not a word from the Count he switched on a local radio station to have a background against which his thoughts might roam.

'Mother Doreen of Clock Face there,' a presenter was saying, 'bringing awareness to us all about the – *situation*, if you like, concerning disabled playgroups. We all hope you find a place for your little one soon, Doreen, yes indeed.'

For a moment Jack had thought she was a nun with an odd name, not a mother. It seemed the programme might be more distracting than he'd anticipated, but perhaps he could use the amusement. 'Your calls are part and parcel of this show each and every day if you wish to add your voice,' the presenter said. 'Calls from here, there and everywhere on every subject under the sun. Let me just give you that item of traffic news again. An oil spillage has blocked the M53 near the Vauxhall terminal, so expect delays if you are travelling eastbound in any way, shape or form. We'd all be better drivers if we adhered to the signs.'

'Thank you,' Jack said, and left the motorway at the next exit. His route would take him through Bromborough onto the Chester road. He opened his window and listened to the song of the hot wind. He was aware only of snatches of dialogue, the presenter interjecting 'some thought in that' or 'a suggestion not to be decried or denied by any manner or means'. The van had almost reached the edge of Bromborough when a telephone voice seemed to grow sharp and close as though he had pressed a receiver against his ear, and he wound the window shut in order to listen. The caller had just said 'the Mersey Burner.'

'Not the sort of person we like to think is roaming our local streets, Margaret. I'm sure every one of our listeners, be they pensioners or – *able-bodied*, so to speak,' the presenter said with a deprecatory giggle, 'must agree with that fact. Not that

'I'm suggesting pensioners aren't able or vice versa, perish the thought, very much so. Is there a hubby, Margaret, to make you feel a bit safer?'

'My husband's dead at the moment. Shut up. Get down. It's the dog,' she explained over an outburst of barking.

'He sounds a good big one, is he, Margaret? I expect you feel more secure with him at your beck and call.'

'She's a she. Basket,' the caller shouted, presumably not at him. 'What I'm saying is I blame your media for making folk of my age terrified to stir out of the house.'

'You've given me a bit of a hot potato there, Margaret, no doubt of that at all. It was mooted to me the other day that the police never called him the Mersey Burner, it was one of the nationals that did, as if Merseyside hasn't enough bad press to compete and combat, as it were. Fair dos, though, the local media has been reporting as much of the police investigation as we've been kept abreast of, I'm led to believe.'

'You oughtn't just— Sit. Sit. Sit. I say you oughtn't just to be reporting. I thought your job was to investigate.'

'Well now, Margaret, our newsroom's pretty sharp. You'd cut your fingers on some of our reporters, I can say without fear of contradiction,' the presenter giggled, and adopted a serious tone. 'Do you have an avenue, in so many words, that you think they should unravel?'

'Basket. Basket. What I'm saying is there's one thing your media never mentions. Whoever this maniac is, he's got to have a family, and you aren't telling me they don't know who he is. You should be trying to make them aware of their responsibilities before he does it to someone else.'

'Margaret there from Higher Tranmere, turning the spotlight on a local angle that should concern each and every last one of us. What say you? Is there a family out there offering – succour and sanctuary, shall we say, to a criminal when they should be going to the police? Your thoughts on this and any other subject are invited, whatever you wish to indulge me in conversation about . . .'

'I hear you,' Jack said through his teeth, which were clamped together so hard that they ached. He swung the van around the cross in the centre of Bromborough and parked it by the library, and dashed back to the phone box opposite the bus shelter. The number which the presenter had kept repeating echoed in his head. He shoved a handful of change into the slot and dialled, and was answered almost at once. 'Phone-in,' a woman said briskly. 'What's your point, please?'

'I want to talk about the so-called Mersey Burner.'

'What's your view on that?'

'That it's grossly unfair to blame the family. Damn near libellous.'

'Have you some special knowledge of this kind of thing?'

'I'd prefer to answer any questions on the air.'

'And what's your name and number, please?'

'Bernard. Bernard from Bromborough,' he said, and read her the number on the dial.

'If you'll put your phone down we'll call you back in a few minutes.'

Most of his change spilled out of the coin-box, and he felt lucky at once, as though he'd beaten a fruit machine. The Count was back. He gazed across the road at the boarded-up front of Dail's Signs, noting with satisfaction that now it looked very much like Fine Films. When the phone rang, everyone waiting at the bus-stop looked at him, but he ignored them and picked up the receiver 'Bernard?' the woman said.

'As you say.'

'We're putting you on air now. Don't speak until you're spoken to. Have you a radio on near you?'

'Hardly.'

Almost at once he heard the presenter. '. . . Vi there from Allerton sharing her eyes and ears with us. Reminding us that we have due regard, as it were, to be proud of Merseyside. Now in a very second or two we'll be talking to Bernard from Bromborough. Do your friends call you Bernie, Bernard?'

'I wouldn't know,' the Count said.

'We'll stick to Bernard then, shall we?'

'Whatever you think my name should be.'

'You'll have heard Vi saying as such that the media detracts

319

employers from coming to Merseyside, and she made reference regarding books and films that seem to want to denounce and denigrate its name. Were you calling to bring some awareness to that subject, Bernard?'

'No, I wanted to defend the family you were attacking before.'

'When we were making mention of the Mersey Burner, that's to say.'

'If that's what you choose to call him.'

'Or her, should we add? We don't know what the police know.'

'Not much if they can't trace a motive.'

'They do moot that,' the presenter admitted, and the Count grinned: it was good to have confirmation of what he had simply assumed. 'So it's the family you're concerned with when all's said and done, is it, Bernard?'

'I should hope so. If anyone's name is being blackened, it's theirs.'

'Some would say the Burner can't help giving him or herself away to them.'

'The police would, but that's propaganda. They also say that every criminal makes a mistake sooner or later, but that's just meant to worry those who don't. If it was true, why did they never catch Jack the Ripper?'

'Well, Bernard, I've heard tell they did and it was hushed up.'

'Unless you take that to mean they don't like to admit they were stumped.'

'The Ripper's a bit of a legend anyway, isn't he or she?'

'Like Robin Hood, shall we say?'

The presenter giggled, more with audible surprise than mirth. 'I was reminding you that the Burner isn't historical by any stretch of the imagination. His victims die after receiving a catalogue of injuries, and he's doing what he's doing here and now.'

'At this moment, do you mean?' the Count said, grinning at the shocked expression he was certain the presenter's face had just acquired. 'We're straying off the subject. You let one of your callers accuse the family of being accomplices and pretty well agreed with her. Maybe you should wonder what would happen if your local luminary gave himself up to the police and proved his family never suspected for a moment who he really was. I'd say they could sue you and your station for a fortune.'

'Well, Bernard, I'm going to put my neck, so to speak, on the block and say I hope they try.'

'I'll think of you in that position,' the Count said, knuckling the receiver rest to terminate the conversation. He walked back to the van, not too fast, even though he wanted to hear the discussion that followed his call. As soon as he was in the driver's seat he switched on the radio. A caller was putting in a plea for playgroups for the blind, and Jack heard no reference to the Count or his broadcast, though he took his time about driving to work.

He strode into the library with a sense of a job well done and more of the same ahead of him. 'Thank heaven it's cooler in here,' he remarked to Stella. He was stamping books when an old lady placed her dry pale hand on his. 'I heard you,' she said.

His throat was suddenly parched, and he had to swallow before he could speak. 'You ... heard ...'

'I heard you saying how hot it is out. I think I'll just sit in here and read my book until there's not so much sun.'

'With my blessing,' Jack said, smiling gratefully at her. She'd thrown him only to remind him that the Count was still invisible, and in that moment of clarity he saw what the phone-in programme had told him. He had only to make sure that Laura and Julia didn't suspect who he was, and the closer to leaving for Crete he made his final visit, the less of an excuse he would need for absenting himself on some last-minute task. He felt at peace with himself and generous towards the world. He might even give the one remaining addressee a last chance.

FORTY-TWO

Halfway through Thursday morning Janys managed to persuade Tommy that he would like a nap. He'd begun the day by demonstrating that a poached egg was no longer his favourite breakfast except for throwing at the kitchen wall, where it had hung for a moment like a picture he might have made of the sun in a cloud. When she'd put him in the playpen he had only wanted to fling his alphabet bricks over the bars and had started to whinge because she wouldn't keep returning them to him, and as soon as she had picked him up he'd commenced howling and bending himself backwards as he often had as a baby when she was giving him the breast and calling him her little suckling pig. She'd tried leaving him in front of the television, a course she only ever followed as a last resort, but he'd kept playing with the controls until she'd had to trap him in his high chair while she attempted to sort out ingredients for his birthday cake. 'You'll be lucky if you live to see another birthday at this rate,' she'd said after a few minutes of his tantrum in the chair, and had carried him upstairs to his cot despite his protests. Once he was behind bars again he'd tried at once to climb over, and so she'd stroked his hair and sung him a lullaby she used to like her mother to sing to her even when Janys had supposedly been too old for it:

> 'Lavender's blue, dilly dilly,
> Lavender's green;
> When you are king, dilly dilly,
> I shall be queen. . . .'

It hadn't seemed to work on Tommy. After performing half an encore she'd left him jumping up and down and screaming furiously while she went back to measuring ingredients. She was listening anxiously for a thud which would mean he'd managed to clamber out of the cot, but instead his protests trailed off, and before long she couldn't hear the faint vibrations which meant he was bouncing with rage. When she thought it was safe she crept upstairs and peeked into his room.

Perhaps the lullaby had worked after all, though she thought he had tired himself out. He was lying with one foot thrust into the pillow, his head resting on one small fist that dug into his cheek. His blond hair looked as though he'd been fighting a gale, his face was mottled and crumpled and sulky, a toned-down version of how it must have appeared when he was absolutely refusing to lie down. Janys was gazing at him, in the state of amazement she experienced whenever she realised how much she loved him, when the phone rang.

'Don't you dare wake,' she murmured, and closing the door quietly, ran downstairs on tiptoe. 'Janys Day,' she said as she snatched up the receiver.

'Sorry, are you busy?'

'Just a mite. Didn't mean to snap at you. Can I help?'

'Are you free just now?'

'The studio's closed today, if that's what you mean.'

'All day?'

'I'm afraid so.' She could have told him it was Tommy's birthday, but that wasn't his business; besides, she was trying to recall where she'd heard his voice before. 'Anything I can do for you?' she said.

There was a pause, and then: 'Do you happen to remember speaking to me a few weeks back?'

'I'm trying. Give me a clue.'

'About — well, about luck.'

She remembered, and her face grew hot. 'You sent me a letter.'

'That was me, yes. I was wondering if you'd let me explain. If you hear me out you might—'

'If there's one thing I can't stand it's men who won't take no for an answer,' Janys said. 'If I hear from you again I'll be in touch with the police.'

She slammed the receiver onto the cradle and stood breathing hard, eyes shut, until the anger faded from her cheeks. She'd thought door-to-door evangelists were difficult enough to repulse, but this clown was worse. Perhaps he was so persistent because what he was trying to sell made even less sense.

Thinking about him wouldn't get the cakes made. Janys listened to make sure the phone hadn't wakened Tommy — she would have been considerably less polite to the caller if she'd thought it had — then she hurried into the kitchen. Eggs, margarine, sugar, flour ... 'Oh, you wretched man,' she cried, instinctively blaming the caller, though of course it wasn't his fault that she had only enough flour for the birthday cake and none left over to make little ones to go with sandwiches and sausage rolls. Without them there wouldn't be sufficient for Tommy and his friends from the playgroup.

She tiptoed upstairs and eased his door open. He was sound asleep, his hand flattened by his cheek now. If she wakened him he would be overtired for his party, and experience had taught her that she couldn't transfer him into the buggy without wakening him. She could be back from the corner shop in five minutes. She blew him a kiss and grabbed her handbag from the post at the end of the banisters, then let herself out of the house.

Apart from a woman wheeling a pramful of free newspapers, the street was deserted. Sunlight massed on Janys's scalp as she turned the sharp curve a hundred yards or so to the left of her house. Now she could see traffic on the conveyor belt of the main road, less than two minutes' walk beyond the junction where a street like hers crossed hers. As she ran past the junction, someone was parking a blue van in the cross street, but she barely noticed it; she was busy counting Tommy's guests again. The roar of traffic overwhelmed the scent of flowers in the front gardens as though

324

one sense was being substituted for another, and then she was at the main road.

Frith's was on the corner. The window was crowded with sunglasses and toys and baby foods and washing-up bowls and rubber bones and felt-tipped pens and sandals, and there was even more variety inside the shop. Miss Frith, a large-boned woman in a voluminous floral dress, was serving as much conversation as goods to a customer, and her new assistant, a teenager with a round face and a frown that announced she was anxious to please, was finishing serving another. Janys saw packets of flour over the assistant's shoulder and went to her as the previous customer turned away, examining his change. 'Just a packet of flour. No, make that two,' Janys said.

The round-faced girl lifted two packets from the shelf and lowered them carefully onto the counter. 'Thank you. Anything else?'

'Not today,' Janys said, digging in her purse for something smaller than a ten-pound note. She had found only a few pence worth of copper when Miss Frith told her customer the amount of the bill and leaned across the counter. 'Mrs Day, could I have a word in just a moment while you're here?'

'Well, it's a little—' Janys began, rummaging in her purse, but Miss Frith had already returned to her customer. The assistant would just have to accept a tenner, Janys thought, and was disentangling it from keys and an emergency tampon when the customer the girl had last served approached the counter. 'Excuse me, I don't think you gave me the right change.'

'Could I just—' Janys said, but the girl was directing her concerned frown at him. 'You gave me a pound for kitchen roll and I gave you eleven pee change,' she said.

'Right, but on the price tag it says eighty-seven pee.'

The girl took the twin pack of kitchen roll and cocked it to one side while cocking her head to the other. 'I'll have to ask,' she said. 'Miss Frith.'

'Just a moment now.' Miss Frith recommended counting change onto her customer's palm, even more slowly than it took her to pronounce each amount. 'Keep your hat on,' she said, which sounded to Janys like a rebuke but which was apparently advice to the customer. 'Now, Glenda, what?'

'This gentleman gave me a pound for kitchen roll and I gave him eleven pee change because that's what the rolls cost that I sold yesterday, but he says the tag says eighty-seven pee.'

'Let's see now,' Miss Frith said, groping for her spectacles among packets of tobacco and cough sweets on a shelf. 'Ah, that's an old tag.'

'Could you take for the flour?' Janys said to the girl.

'I will do,' the assistant said, then trained her frown on the ten-pound note. 'We'll have to wait for Miss Frith. I have to tell her when I give change of a note.'

'Miss Frith,' Janys said, 'I really do need—'

'I won't be a moment. As soon as I've dealt with this.' She lowered her face to the kitchen roll as if to blot out all distractions. 'This is last month's tag. It should have been altered,' she informed the customer. 'It was our fault. Strictly speaking we're within our rights to charge you the current price, but I'll pay you back the two pee for your trouble.'

'Don't bother. I just wanted to get things clear.'

'If you're sure. I don't want to lose your goodwill.'

Make your minds up for God's sake, Janys thought. Her scalp felt hotter than when she'd been under the sun. The customer picked up the kitchen rolls and dawdled towards the door as if he was considering accepting the two pence after all, and it wasn't until he was out of the shop that the assistant said 'Ten pounds, Miss Frith.'

'Ten pounds,' Miss Frith agreed, and turned unhurriedly to Janys. 'Now, Mrs Day, I wonder if I could have a word.'

'If it takes no longer than it takes her to give me my change. I've left Tommy asleep.'

'Ah, the little angel. How is he?'

'Angelic at the moment, I hope. What did you want?'

'I was wondering when you could fit in a portrait of my little nieces. They'll be staying with me for a week now it's the holidays. It'll be a surprise for their parents, the portrait will, you understand.'

326

'When would you like?'

'Whenever's most convenient for you.'

Too late Janys saw that she shouldn't have restricted their conversation to the time it took the assistant to make change, because the girl would wait until Miss Frith had finished talking. Her head was a jumble of panicky thoughts – the number of guests at the party, how much longer she had left him alone than she'd meant to, the fear that his father would take him away, a fear which lingered precisely because it was so irrational. 'My diary's at home,' she said. 'Give me a ring in a few minutes.'

'I haven't a phone, unfortunately.'

'Well then, can't you—' Janys said, and interrupted herself for the sake of swiftness. 'Shall we say sometime next week?'

'I don't suppose the week after might be possible?'

'Even better. Monday?'

'Or Tuesday, perhaps?'

'What time?'

'Whenever would suit you.'

'About now? Eleven?'

'Eleven.'

'I'll just write that down so we don't forget,' Miss Frith said, retrieving her spectacles from the shelf. She found a fractured Biro next to the cash register and crouched behind the counter in search of a notebook. 'If I can have my change,' Janys said to the girl.

'I'll do that now.' But the assistant had to wait until Miss Frith stood up before she had room to sidle to the cash register. She seemed prepared to continue taking her pace from Miss Frith, until Janys stared hard at her own watch. As soon as the girl had handed her the change Janys said 'Thanks' to Miss Frith, who tore out a page bearing the date and time of the portrait session and gave it to Janys, together with a faintly offended look. By now Janys didn't care. She stuffed the page into her handbag and clasped the packets of flour to her breasts and ran out of the shop.

She wanted to let out a gasp of relief, but the sunlight and the noise and fumes of traffic oppressed her. She ran across the minor crossroads, near which no vehicles were parked now. She was calculating in her head how long it would take her to mix the ingredients, how long to cook the birthday cake, how long Tommy might continue to sleep. All this kept her surroundings at a distance, and so when the roar of traffic didn't give way to the silence of the empty front gardens but to the murmur of what sounded like a crowd, it didn't immediately strike her as strange. She was so preoccupied with Tommy's party that when she turned the corner and saw half a dozen neighbours outside her gate she wondered if they were there because of his birthday. In that first moment she thought she was somehow seeing the light of his birthday candles flickering in the house.

FORTY-THREE

On Friday evening there was nothing left for Jack to do. He was hoping to occupy himself with packing the luggage, but Laura and Julia had already finished that. Last night he had been able to go to bed shortly after dinner, since he had been on the late shift, and he didn't think he could bear sitting idly at home tonight while he was so on edge. 'Do you know what I'd like to do?' he said to Julia.

'What?'

'I don't know. I was hoping you did.'

'*Dad*,' Laura said.

'Maybe I do. Why don't we go out for dinner.'

'I thought we were just having fish and chips for a change,' Julia said.

'Dining out will be more like starting our holiday, and it'll be a way of thanking Pete and Cath. Let me phone and see if they can fit us in.'

It felt odd not to have to make any more surreptitious calls, but that wasn't why he was nervous. Why did he feel as though he had forgotten or overlooked something? As soon as Pete Venable offered them a table for seven o'clock Jack wished he could go out for a walk by himself instead. Perhaps whatever he was unable to recall would come to him while he and the family were away. As they walked to the International Experience, towards a sun which the sea wouldn't douse for hours, he felt as though part of his brain was cut off from him.

He failed to see how any aspect of the Count's last visit could be troubling him. He'd parked the van in a side road near Janys Day's house in Old Swan, having phoned her from a call-box on the main road. Her letter-box had been protruding a free newspaper like a rude tongue, but it had looked more like a fuse to him. After ringing her doorbell twice he'd steeped the paper in fuel with the blowlamp and set fire to the paper with his refuelled lighter, then he'd pushed the blazing paper into the house and had watched through the letter-box, which he'd held open with his handkerchief, until he had seen the hall carpet catch fire. He remembered experiencing mostly relief that nobody had answered the bell. Driving away, he'd felt that the simplicity of this visit had been a reward for completing his task.

The International Experience had turned Spanish. 'Iced soup if you can't stand the heat,' Cath Venable said as she gave the Orchards menus. Throughout the meal she kept returning to their table, patting her forehead with a handkerchief, for reassurance that the food wasn't too spicy, until Jack grew hot and bothered: he could do with fewer references to heat while he was unable to sort out his thoughts. His impatience made him feel ungrateful to Pete and Cath, and so he ensured that he caught them together. 'We'll bring you back a surprise from Crete,' he said. 'Thanks for giving us the chance.'

'It was the least we could do,' Pete said.

Jack paid the bill and looked out of the window. Julia and Laura were waiting in the car park. The low sun and its trail on the water were reddening, fire turning into blood. The sight of his family with their backs to him and gazing out to sea gave him a sudden sense of vulnerability, but he couldn't tell if that related to them or himself. Was he uneasy because now that the Count had finished he had no way of guaranteeing their good luck? Surely it was guaranteed precisely because the Count had finished and there was nothing to go wrong. Julia and Laura continued to gaze at the sun as he came out of the restaurant. 'The fire's dying,' he said.

They strolled home through the cooling light, not saying much. Cars with their headlamps lit or blank passed along the promenade; a few seagulls, autumnally tinted by the sunset, wheeled above the bay. The dwarf windmill and castle and cottage extended their longest shadows across the Crazy Golf course as though grotesque holes had opened in the earth. On Victoria Road the Bingo parlours were silent, but one arcade was still lively, reels of symbols spinning in the fruit machines, phosphorescent figures scampering about the video screens, a pinball jangling. As the family crossed in front of an empty bus parked outside the Floral Pavilion and stepped into their street, Jack hesitated, all at once sharply convinced that he was close to remembering. He watched Julia and Laura walking towards the van, and then he knew. The blowlamp was in the briefcase, which was still in the back of the van.

The Count would never have overlooked that, but Jack Awkward had. He followed Julia and Laura in case they wondered why he was faltering, then he halted outside the gate. 'Forgotten something?' Julia asked.

'Just trying to think. I'll be in in a minute.'

Saying so used up all the words in his head. He couldn't leave the blowlamp here while they were away, or he would be unable to relax. As Julia and Laura went up the path he wandered alongside the van, dabbing at it with his fingertips and leaving prints in the grime as though a pretence of incriminating himself might quicken his thoughts. He stared blankly at the rear doors as Julia let herself and Laura into the house. He was writing 'Count' on the left-hand door with his blackened fingertip, having seen that he could do so with eleven strokes if the first letter was drawn like a V turned through ninety degrees, when it occurred to him to wonder how Laura or her mother could be in the front bedroom only seconds after entering the house. He glanced up just in time to see a man dodging across the room towards the door.

In a moment Jack had grasped the clown's head. As he pulled out the keys the one he needed appeared to gleam. He unlocked the rear doors in the same swift movement and ducked in to grab the briefcase, which had slid towards the doors when he was driving home, as though it had made itself ready for him. The Count was still wanted, and it was a mercy he hadn't got rid of his weapon. He shook the front-

door key forwards as he dashed up the path. He would leave
the key in the lock, take out the blowlamp and drop his briefcase, find the lighter in his pocket, and then— If the man had
dared to harm Julia or Laura, he would— But when he flung
the front door open, he was too late.

The stairs were strewn from top to bottom with passports
and traveller's cheques and aeroplane tickets and the balance
of the money sent by the anonymous benefactor. Julia was at
the foot of the stairs, pale-faced and shaken, holding onto the
phone and saying 'Police.' Where the stairs bent near the top,
a man in his late teens was sprawling on his stomach. He was
grey-skinned and scrawny, with painfully prominent veins,
made more prominent by the way Laura was locking his arms
in the small of his back as she knelt on his spine. 'Fucking get
off me, you little whore,' he was snarling. 'I'll fucking kill you.
Fucking let me up.'

Jack dropped the briefcase on the doorstep and squeezed
Julia's waist before charging upstairs. 'It's all right, Dad,'
Laura said, though she was flushed and somewhat breathless.
'I've got him.'

Julia was speaking their address rapidly into the phone.
'Can you be quick? He's here now. I don't know how long we
can hold him.'

'Stay still,' Jack warned in the Count's voice as the man
started to kick the wall at the bend of the stairs. He climbed
over the man's legs and stayed within reach, though Laura
seemed to be in control. A few minutes that felt loaded with
more seconds than he was able to count dragged by. He heard
a police siren, and grew tense as he saw the man stiffen until
Laura redoubled her grip on his wrists. The police arrived
with a screech of brakes and a stampede of boots on the path,
and Julia pushed the door wide. 'Top of the stairs,' she said in
a pinched voice.

Two policemen came thundering upstairs while a third
stayed with Julia. 'Is this yours, madam?' he said.

'No.'

Jack hovered anxiously while the two policemen took over
from Laura. He had difficulty in breathing until they'd got

hold of the burglar and she was out of the man's reach. He saw the other policeman stoop outside the door and pick up the briefcase, saw his finger and thumb closing around the lock to snap it open. 'Yes, that's ours. Mine,' he said.

He hadn't spoken loud enough. The policeman hadn't heard. He was standing on the stage of light from the hall, his heavy face lowering over the briefcase. In a moment he would see within, and then his face would rise and catch sight of Jack. 'Excuse me—' Julia said as if it hardly mattered under the circumstances.

'Just one moment, madam.'

'My husband says that's his. I didn't know.'

'Oh, I beg your pardon,' the policeman said, and handed her the briefcase.

His colleagues were urging the burglar none too gently down the stairs, and there wasn't room for Jack to sidle past them. He saw Julia take the briefcase and stare at it and move her other hand towards it, then she stepped aside to let the policemen usher their captive out of the house. 'I wonder if it might be convenient for me to take your statements now,' their colleague said.

'We're supposed to be going away on holiday tomorrow,' Julia said as though the break-in might have changed her mind, and dropped the briefcase by the stairs with a thud which contained a dull resonance of the blowlamp.

Jack went downstairs, restraining himself from running, and having reassured himself that the briefcase hadn't snapped open with the impact, refrained from picking it up. The back door had been forced, he saw along the hall. 'I'll ring Andy to fix it,' he told Julia.

He hadn't much to tell the police. He was glad that Andy was round in ten minutes; talking to him kept Jack's mind off the briefcase and its secret. By the time Andy had fixed heavy bolts at the top and bottom of the door, the interviews were finished. 'That's all, sir,' the policeman said to Jack. 'Try not to let it spoil your holiday. You must be proud of your daughter.'

'I'd wish the media could get hold of this except we've had

enough of them. People would be better off copying her instead of the Mersey Burner.'

Only Jack Awkward could have said that. He was aware of being heard by the policeman and Andy and Julia and Laura, and he thought he sensed them recoiling from him. Then the policeman grinned wryly. 'You won't hear me arguing.'

Jack saw him down the path and closed the door. Andy was making coffee for everyone while the others sat in the front room. Laura looked exhausted but pleased with herself, Julia as though the shakes might be about to catch up with her. It was almost eleven o'clock, but it felt later. As Jack made to pass the open door of the front room, Julia gestured him to stop. 'Whose is the briefcase?' she said.

FORTY-FOUR

That night none of the Orchards slept much. Whenever Jack's plans came apart in his head as he drifted towards sleep, Julia's restlessness beside him brought him back to himself. She must be suffering from some of the thoughts that were troubling him, though for different reasons: if they went to Crete now ... if they didn't go to Crete ... Being unable to discuss his reasons with her drove him deeper inside himself, where he might have sought the Count's advice. But his instinctive reaction to the burglary had shown him that he'd been nervous for days not because he was afraid the Count might fail on his last adventure but because he was unwilling to relinquish him, which brought the Count too close to the family, close enough to lie beside Julia in the dark.

Shortly after dawn Jack got up. His eyes and brain felt smudged with smoke. He'd heard Laura moving about, and met her coming out of the bathroom. She looked as sleepless as he was, and as though she was trying unsuccessfully to prepare to be disappointed. 'Are we still going?' she said.

It was one plan or the other, though he couldn't foresee either in detail. 'Of course we are,' he said, and at once was convinced this would work; he couldn't bear to think otherwise when he saw her face light up. Julia trudged out of their room just then. 'You two finish in the bathroom while I make us all coffee,' Jack said, leaving them to talk.

By the time they were out there were only a few minutes left for him to use the bathroom. He shaved and brushed his teeth and ducked under the shower, and was dressing when the doorbell rang. 'That'll be Andy. I'll pack my stuff from the bathroom,' he called, and fetched the razor and foam and deodorant. As he heard someone opening the front door he grabbed the briefcase from beside the wardrobe and hid it under the beach towels in the larger suitcase, which he locked. 'I think we're just about ready,' he announced.

While Andy loaded the suitcases into the boot of his car and then waited outside with Laura, Julia toured the house to check that everything which could be locked was locked. When she set out on a second tour Jack thought she might refuse to leave after all, and so he diverted her nervousness towards ensuring that she had the passports and tickets and traveller's cheques and Greek money in her handbag. At last she sighed, and closed and locked the front door and made certain it was locked. They climbed into the car, and as it pulled away he told himself there was no turning back.

The motorway was almost clear. Usually when he was a passenger Jack found himself mentally driving the car, but now he was content to feel he had no control. As he dozed, signboards blue as the sky promised to be sailed past – Bromborough, Helsby, Runcorn, Warrington – like names in a dream, none of which seemed meaningful enough to waken him fully. Then Andy was trying to do so, and the air was laden with roaring. 'Manchester Airport,' Andy said.

The Orchards clambered out of the car, and Laura ran to find a baggage trolley. Julia was blinking at the throng of passengers beyond the automatic doors as if she wasn't sure that the family ought to be here. 'I'll wire up an alarm in your house the moment I get back,' Andy promised. 'Don't worry, Mrs O. With your luck the house would be safe as houses even if it wasn't alarmed. Look how you came home last night just in time to catch the villain.'

Julia nodded a little reluctantly, watching for Laura. 'I'd better be off,' Andy said, but Jack stopped him with the question which he could tell Andy knew he'd provoked. 'What do you know about our luck?' he said for Andy alone to hear.

'I'd really better be going, old pip. They fine you if you park here too long.' Andy gave him a wink and an apologetic

336

grin. 'You've guessed, haven't you? I sent you that weird letter months ago.'

'Sent it to me and who else?'

'Only you. You and the family were the only people I knew whose luck needed a leg up. I hope you didn't take it seriously. I just wanted to cheer you up, seeing as you always enjoy a joke.'

A taxi flashed its headlamps at him, and he waved to the driver and climbed into the car. 'I'll be seeing you,' he shouted to Jack. 'You needn't worry about anything. Just remember to come round for your alarm keys before you let yourself into the house.'

Jack stared after him as the brake lights ignited and the car left a shimmer of fumes in its wake. He felt as though he had yet to awaken. What did it mean that Andy had simply passed on the letter to him? He was still struggling to understand when Laura returned with a trolley. 'They're checking in our flight,' Julia said.

Jack loaded the trolley and pushed it through the automatic doors, which flinched away from him. There were queues at three desks for the flight to Heraklion. Julia appended herself to the shortest queue, and Jack found himself wishing she'd chosen the longest so that he would have more time to finish thinking about Andy and prepare to seem innocent when he reached the desk, or should he take the suitcase to the men's room on some pretext and hide the blowlamp behind a cistern? How long might it stay there without being noticed, and would the police be able to deduce when it had been hidden? 'We're next,' Julia told him.

The entire queue in front of the Orchards had consisted of a single party who were moving away from the desk. No doubt the airport police checked the toilets frequently – perhaps even monitored them with hidden cameras. Leaving the blowlamp in the case was safest, he reassured himself: bombs were smuggled onto planes that way. 'Morning. Hot this morning,' he said to the young woman behind the counter, and wiped his forehead.

She took the tickets and passports and leafed through

them, glancing up at the family. As Jack hauled the larger suitcase onto the weighing platform the handle seemed to grow uncomfortably warm. 'Did you pack your luggage personally?' the uniformed young woman said to him.

Julia laughed. She was going to deny it, thinking it was a joke, and the uniformed woman would sense disagreement between them and insist that he open the suitcase. 'We both did,' he said hastily.

'That's what I like to hear,' the woman said with an approving grin at Julia, and asked Jack the rest of the security questionnaire. He watched the suitcase containing the blow-lamp advance hesitantly towards the conveyor belt, topple onto it, bump into a carton of disassembled furniture and pursue it through an opening half-concealed by trailing strips of plastic. He saw a hand grasp its handle, and then it was gone. 'Can you put your other luggage on for me?' the woman said.

'Sorry. This is all new to me,' Jack said, quickly enough to head off any doubts she might have had, he hoped.

She sent the other suitcase on its way and consulted a screen for details of seats. 'Smoking or not?'

'Not. Very much not, thank you.'

She presented him with the boarding passes and a standard smile. 'Enjoy your flight.'

'I will when it's over,' Jack almost said.

A rubber carpet carried the family up to the next level, a large hall so crowded that they made for the departure hall at once. First came another examination of their passports, followed by a security check. As he watched Julia's and Laura's handbags being conveyed through an X-ray, he imagined the briefcase revealing the silhouette of its contents. The panic he experienced at the thought seemed unnecessary and somehow more distressing because it was. He followed Julia and Laura through an electronic archway which had let them pass unmolested, and set off the alarm.

It didn't matter, he told himself as he stepped forward to meet the security guard who was beckoning to him. The lighter or the keys on the clown's head must have caused the alarm to sound, but he was carrying nothing that could incriminate him. The guard couldn't tell how badly his palms were sweating, though wouldn't he be trained to look for signs of nervousness?

The guard had him raise his arms as though he was about to be crucified, and Jack felt his sodden shirt peel away from his cindery armpits. The guard crouched in front of him, passed his hands along the insides of Jack's thighs as Jack tried not to stiffen them too obviously nor to let them shake, rose until his bland efficient face was level with Jack's. Jack was yearning to swallow to ease his dry throat, afraid to swallow in case the guard noticed. He saw Laura giggling at the spectacle of her father being treated like a criminal, and managed to wink at her, though it felt like the beginning of an uncontrollable twitch, especially when the guard fixed his gaze on it. The alarm sounded again behind Jack. 'Thank you, sir,' the guard said, and stepped aside.

Jack succeeded in walking away without drawing more attention to himself, though his feet were sweating so much he thought the guard must be able to hear them unsticking themselves from his sandals at each step. 'Did they think you were a terrorist, Dad?' Laura said.

'There must have been too much change in my pocket,' Jack said, too loudly. 'Let's go and spend some on a drink.'

'It's a good job you didn't bring that poor man's briefcase by mistake,' Julia said. 'That might have taken some explaining.'

Last night he had simply told her that he'd picked up a reader's briefcase without thinking as he'd left the library but hadn't wanted to say so in front of the police. There was nothing in it, he'd explained, and so returning it could wait until they came home. 'Never mind,' Julia said now as he tried to suppress his anxiety. 'We know you didn't mean to take it. It's more like the Jack we know and love.'

For the moment he preferred not to examine what she meant. He bought drinks at the bar, on which the barmen left saucerfuls of change to encourage customers to do so, and searched for a No Smoking area in which nobody was smoking. The only unoccupied seats had no view of the announcement screens, but at least that gave him an excuse to be restless. As he came back from yet another wander past the screens, the public address system asked someone to return to the check-in desk. 'Do they want us now?' Laura said.

'Is the flight boarding, do you mean? No movement yet,' Jack said, straining his ears so as to be ready if the call to the desk was repeated. The mumble of the crowd seemed to close around him, and he resisted the temptation to use the Count's voice to demand silence. He drained the last trickle of a pint of bitter in an attempt to ease the dryness that was spreading through his mouth, and made for the screens again as soon as he reasonably could. Just as he saw that the gate for the flight to Heraklion had been announced, the public address system repeated its message. It was for someone he'd never heard of, and he hurried back to the family. 'They're calling us.'

Another walkway conveyed the Orchards to the boarding gate. Now that she seemed to be on her way, Julia was growing as excited as Laura already was. 'Lucky for some,' she said as she caught sight of the number over the gate.

'For everyone who uses it, I hope.' Jack avoided looking at the lit 13 and gazed out through the plate glass. The aeroplane was on the tarmac, the staircases were attached to it, so why were the passengers having to wait? Here came someone in uniform towards him along the corridor, surely to check the passengers through the gate, but she strode past without even a glance at him. Of course the Count was invisible, but was Jack? He might soon know, because a guard with a radio at his belt was striding towards him – straight towards him.

If Jack had kept hold of the briefcase he could at least have defended himself once he was out of sight of the family, could perhaps even have made his escape. He should have feigned illness, he thought with sudden agonising clarity: he should have insisted that Julia and Laura take the holiday while he stayed at home. Now the airport security had found the evidence and him.

The passengers crowded towards the gate, delaying the

guard, though not for long enough to let Jack do anything meaningful. Julia and Laura came to him, and he saw the guard dodging them as though they had fended him off, except that he hadn't been coming for Jack after all. 'Hurry up, Dad. Everyone's getting on,' Laura said.

The crowd was forming itself into a queue at the gate. As the Orchards joined it Jack saw the guard returning along the corridor, looking harassed. Jack had a not entirely reassuring sense of watching a mime of his own nervousness. He held his passport ready as the queue shuffled forwards, but the stewardess wanted to see only his boarding pass. He walked down a staircase onto the sunlit tarmac and up a wheeled staircase at whose top uniformed figures were waiting, and felt as if he'd passed the point at which anyone would want to check up on him.

There were five seats in each row. The Orchards sat together, Laura by the window, Jack by the aisle. He closed his eyes to rest them and then opened them. Passengers were stuffing items into the overhead lockers. When he opened his eyes again all the passengers were seated, and it was time for the plane to take off.

Stewardesses took up their positions in the aisles as if they were performing the umpteenth take of a scene and began to mime to a voice which Jack thought was recorded. They stretched out their arms on either side of them as he had for the body check, placed masks over their faces, modelled life-jackets, though drowning was the least of Jack's worries, he found. Surely the plane was about to move. The stewardesses were advancing down the aisle now, glancing at passengers to make sure they were belted into their seats and had no baggage on their laps, no briefcase. The briefcase must be in the hold, the baggage handlers had finished loading; what was there to delay the plane?

'I think we're waiting for someone to get on. This must be them now,' Laura said, gazing out of the window, and a hand took hold of Jack's shoulder. 'Excuse me, sir.'

He didn't start – there was no point – and he managed not to let his sense of inevitability make his shoulders slump, but he felt as though his body had turned to stone as he lifted his face to the stewardess. 'Are you sure it's me you want?' the Count said.

'We were wondering if you would mind changing seats, sir. We've a lady with a babe in arms in smoking, and she'd rather not have it there.'

Jack was so thrown that he turned to Julia for reassurance. 'Up to you,' she told him.

'I'm sorry, I must have mistaken the seat,' the stewardess said. 'I hadn't realised you were together.'

'I don't mind changing,' Jack assured her, and stood up. The number of his seat – 8C – meant nothing in particular, after all. 'Everyone's on board. We'll be taking off just as soon as we get clearance,' he heard her saying to Laura, and realised that his seat number had added up to eleven. 'Which seat are you sending me to?' he said.

'I'll show you, sir.' She led him towards the back of the cabin, to a trio of seats in the middle of which a tousled woman with a baby buttoned into overlarge rompers was sitting. 'This gentleman says he'll change with you.'

'Thanks,' the woman said distractedly to Jack, and waited while the wheezing man who occupied more than the seat next to her hoisted himself to his feet.

'I'll be up and down,' he warned Jack. 'Want the aisle?'

'You need it more than I do.' Jack squeezed past him as the stewardess carried the woman's tote bag up the aisle. He snapped his seat-belt shut and gazed at the number of his seat: 29B. It didn't matter, he told himself as the wheezing man crashed onto the seat beside him. The plane would move now, it would move when he'd counted eleven, it would move when he'd counted eleven three times. That much he managed silently before he felt his lips opening. 'Actually, I wonder—' he mumbled, and pretended he hadn't spoken; what kind of clown would insist on changing his seat because of the number? The plane began to inch forwards, and he felt as though it had been shifted by his refusal to believe.

It coasted for at least five minutes, then it halted. He could just see the top of Julia's head over the seats in front of him.

All at once the sight affected him with a piercing sense of finality. He closed his eyes and clenched his fist around the clown's head, and was holding his breath when the note of the jets rose sharply. A few seconds later the plane raced along the tarmac and into the air.

Suburban streets shrank into a maze, and Jack saw a police car speeding along a motorway, all its lights flashing. 'Too late,' he murmured. The land tilted like a dish, spilling the police car out of his vision and showing him an elaborate pattern of fields and water which the sunlight set ablaze, then the horizon fell out of the sky and there were only clouds. A stewardess was distributing newspapers, but the soundless touch of clouds on the windows seemed to be inviting Jack to drift and dream.

His neighbour kept wakening him. Whenever he came back from the toilet the row shook, and his wheezing sounded like a puncture, as if the air pressure was about to fail. Eventually he said 'I think it's time I introduced myself.'

'Even more of yourself?'

'Inspector Wheezer of Interpol.'

'Pardon?'

'Je pense qu'il est temps que je m'ai introduit. L'inspecteur Ouiser d'Interpol. J'ai été sur vous pour quelque temps, Monsieur le Comte.'

'Oh merde.'

'Voulez-vous venir doucement, Monsier le Comte? While it's hot.'

'What's that?'

'I said, get it while it's hot,' the man wheezed, and Jack discovered that a table had been folded down in front of him to support a plastic tray containing food in its hollows. He ate the bland meal and drank the quarter-bottle of wine Julia had paid for, then he gazed out of the window at an unbroken plateau of cloud until the monotonousness gathered on his eyelids. 'Êtes-vous prêt, Monsieur le Comte?' Wheezer said.

'À vous batailler, oui.'

'Où?'

343

'Dans le compartiment des bagages.'

'Il nous faut parler au capitaine.'

'Je l'appellerai. L'avion peut aller sur pilote automatique,' Jack said, reaching for the button which would summon a stewardess, and woke up. His neighbour was expansively asleep and wheezing. Before they could pursue their adventure, a blaze of sunlight from beneath the plane disoriented Jack so much he had to waken fully. The mirror was the sea, and the plane was beginning its descent to Crete.

Some doubts had wakened with him. He had to keep reminding himself that Greek airport security was reputed to be the worst in Europe. When the plane came to earth with a bump and began to coast along the runway he saw passengers relaxing all around him. Soon he could relax too, he promised himself.

At last the plane dawdled to a halt and the stewardesses opened the doors. Jack followed Wheezer as he plodded down the rear staircase, which shuddered at his every step, onto the tarmac in front of the terminal building, a long three-storey concrete box the colour of a bone dried by the uncontested sun. Crowds stood on open balconies or straggled across the airfield, and it looked to Jack as if nobody would bother anyone unless it was absolutely unavoidable. He met Julia and Laura at the foot of the other staircase. 'Dad, you smell all smoky,' Laura said, wrinkling her nose.

The immigration officer at the barrier inside the terminal flirted gravely with her and glanced at her parents' passports. Beyond the barrier the passengers were gathering around a baggage carousel. The Orchards found a space near the belt which would produce the luggage from behind the scenes. Laura went to the toilet and came back, then Julia did while Jack stared at the plastic curtain which presumably concealed the baggage handlers. Soon people began to sigh loudly and fan themselves and light cigarettes. 'Is this usual?' a woman behind Jack said when the carousel had remained immobile for a quarter of an hour.

'Something's wrong,' said a man in a shirt like an illustration from a child's first botany textbook.

'Maybe,' said his wife, wafting smoke away from her face with a frayed straw hat, 'they've found something in the baggage.'

'Here comes another flight. That should get things moving,' the man said, flapping his shirt-front. A plane-load of passengers from London was converging on the immigration barrier. Their only effect, however, was to increase the hubbub and heat and smoke until it seemed to Jack that these elements had coalesced into a single oppressive medium, perhaps the very medium that was gumming up the works. He began to count eleven slowly, and then counted it again. He felt he'd repeated the count far too often by the time the belt crawled forwards and suitcases began to stumble through the plastic curtain. People stepped forwards to welcome their luggage, and the crowd thinned gradually until all the voices Jack could hear had London accents. Then Laura said 'There's ours.'

It was the smaller suitcase – the one he'd checked in last. Of course their order of precedence could have been reversed between Manchester and Crete, but suppose the larger case had been flown to another airport by mistake? The longer it was in transit, the more liable its contents were to be examined. Julia lifted the smaller case off the carousel as he watched the parade of luggage pushing the curtain out of the way. The yellowing plastic slithered over a metal trunk and drooped, only to be raised by a pram stuffed with knotted newspapers, pursued by a suitcase which could almost have been Jack's except that it didn't bear a label in his handwriting. 'There's the other one,' Julia told him, and he watched listlessly as it tottered along the belt and fell on its side with a muffled metallic rattle from within. Why, it was his suitcase after all, minus the label. 'I'm glad you're here,' he said, almost sprawling on the carousel in his eagerness to retrieve the case.

He was so exhilarated that he carried both suitcases out to leave them by the coach to which the courier directed him. 'Apologies for the delay. The luggage carousel broke down,' she said into a microphone as she took her seat beside the driver. As the coach swung out of the rank with only inches to spare she bade her passengers good afternoon in Greek and tried to coax an echo out of them. She put on a tape of bouzouki music as the coach veered through the narrow shabby baked streets of the capital, and Jack was already in love with Crete. The vehicle climbed out of Heraklion and began to follow the coast road, beyond which the sea stretched to the horizon. Jack gazed at the blue water dotted with swimmers and decorated with ripples of tame fire, and thought he was almost safe.

FORTY-FIVE

Aghios Nikolaos was an hour and a half's drive from Heraklion, and the hotel was five minutes' drive out of the town. The hotel consisted of about a dozen buildings like blocks of sand two storeys high, half-embedded in a terraced hillside which overlooked a small beach. Young bare-breasted women were sunning themselves on recliners at the edge of the lazy waves or insinuating themselves through the transparent water, while further out a man was falling off his water-skis and being left behind by a speedboat. The coach reversed laboriously between the hotel and a taverna and halted with a heartfelt gasp of its air brakes, and the driver climbed down to release the Orchards' luggage from its belly. They were the only remaining passengers on the coach. The courier ushered them into the reception area, a room displaying photographs of a gorge and notices reminding guests not to flush toilet paper and a library of old paperbacks on a shelf beneath the counter, and arranged to meet the Orchards the next day for a chat about tours. The porter gave them keys attached to metal coshes and carried their luggage to the second terrace up, where he unlocked 14 and 15. 'Shall we go for a swim?' Laura said.

'Give me a chance to unpack, love.'

'I'll deal with our case if you two want to go down to the beach,' Jack said. 'I won't be long.'

'Are you thinking of trying to swim, Jack?'

'Shouldn't I be?'

'I think you can do anything you want to if you want to hard enough.'

That was true of the Count, not him, since it seemed he

couldn't even keep the suitcase away from her long enough to open it unobserved. Then she said to Laura 'Well, let's have a look at your room.' As she followed her into 15, Jack grabbed the larger suitcase and ran next door.

There wasn't much in the room: whitewashed walls, a curtained recess of which contained hangers on a rail above a chest of drawers; twin beds with a single sheet on each; two bedside tables, each draped with a cloth on which stood a mosquito repellent; two low chairs, vaguely related to a round table which was the only other furniture. Floor-length windows on the seaward side gave onto a stone balcony. Jack dumped the suitcase on the nearer bed and unzipped it, thinking how lucky he was that it no longer locked. Strewing the towels across the bed, he dragged out the briefcase and was at the windows in two strides and sliding the panes back.

The balcony was bare except for a frail table and two plastic chairs. It offered even less concealment than the room did, though it was hidden from its neighbours by walls as wide as itself and as high as the stone ceiling. A couple were playing Trivial Pursuit on the balcony to his left – 'How many ghosts were there in a film by William Castle?' a girl with a Birmingham accent said – but when he craned out, searching for a hiding-place, the wall concealed the players. Fifteen feet or so beneath him, at the foot of a featureless wall, was the cracked stone path alongside the lowest terrace; above him, about two feet higher than the ceiling, was the roof. He was leaning backwards over the edge of the balcony and gazing up, wishing he could think of a better idea, when Laura poked her head around the dividing wall. 'Dad?'

Her sudden appearance made him dizzy. 'Yes,' he snapped. 'It's lovely, isn't it?'

He'd almost started the holiday by spoiling it for her. 'So it is.'

'What are you looking at?'

'Nothing. There's nothing to see.'

'Mummy says she'll be with you in a minute.'

'No hurry,' Jack said for Julia to hear, and dodged behind

348

the wall to open the briefcase. He'd left it on the table, and Laura hadn't seen it. He crumpled the last letter, the one addressed to Janys Day, and stuffed it into his trousers pocket before seizing the blowlamp. Placing the briefcase on top of the wall at the edge of the balcony, he pushed a plastic chair against the wall, put one foot on the seat, grasped his knee and levered himself up.

He ducked just in time. The ceiling would have knocked him silly. A man from Birmingham said 'Which film comedian brought his friend hard-boiled eggs and nuts in hospital?' and Jack heard Julia murmuring in Laura's room. Reaching up with his left hand, he took hold of the edge of the underside of the roof, which felt cumbersomely large, and placed his left foot on top of the wall, which was as broad as his heel. 'Here goes,' he said in a voice which wasn't quite the Count's. Gripping the overhead edge as firmly as he could, he heaved himself up onto the wall, his right foot wavering in the air.

He had to lean out; he couldn't duck his head any lower. The heat and the path below seemed to sway at him. He pressed the thumb of his left hand under the stone edge to steady himself, then he raised his right hand until the tip of the nozzle of the blowlamp was touching his left thumb. 'Take it,' he muttered in a voice which felt as if it might leap out of control, 'take it now,' but his thumb wouldn't budge – not until he leaned on the blowlamp. His thumb faltered away from the ceiling as the rest of his hand struggled to keep hold, and then his thumb was holding the nozzle against the stone. His right hand slapped the ceiling, wedging him between it and the wall. He closed his left hand around the nozzle and lifted the blowlamp, which rang dully against the stone. He couldn't see the roof above him, and he poked the blowlamp towards it for some seconds before discovering that it was inches out of reach.

He couldn't just throw the blowlamp. He would need to recover it once he decided where to dispose of it for good. He had to plant both feet on the wall and lean out far enough to stretch his arm above the roof. 'You can do it,' he told himself. 'Luck's on your side.'

He inched his palm along the ceiling, which was warm and painfully rough, and leaned out a fraction. A scent of flowers mixed with the stony smell of sunbaked dust surged into his throat. The roof of the building below him shuddered up towards him as though it was being inflated, and he saw what he'd missed seeing: if that roof was visible to him, the blowlamp would be visible from all the higher balconies. 'Clown,' he said through his teeth, and stepped down with his right foot onto the chair.

'Stan Laurel,' the Birmingham girl answered at last, and Jack felt the chair slide from beneath him. He was falling. He couldn't hold onto the edge of the ceiling without letting go of the blowlamp. The world tilted as though some organ of balance had come loose behind his eyes, and his left foot kicked the briefcase off the balcony. His backward plunge lasted long enough for him to think what he could do to save himself, which was nothing. At least his chin was still tucked into his chest, so that only his shoulders thumped the dividing wall, scraping on the rough stone as he sprawled on his back. 'What was that?' said the Birmingham girl.

Jack's skull had started to ache rhythmically, his back felt as though it had been stripped like wallpaper, but he had no time to recuperate. He rolled over, and the balcony rolled with him. He closed his eyes and made himself lie still while he counted eleven, slowing down over the last few numbers, then he swayed to his feet and grasped the sliding frame of the right-hand window before wobbling into the room.

When his knees collided with the end of his bed he bowed forwards almost helplessly and began to ransack the suitcase. As soon as he found his swimming trunks he lowered himself onto the bed, which was further beneath him than he'd thought, and found himself toppling backwards. He kicked off his sandals and dragged off his trousers and underpants – the easy part – then he attempted to thread his legs through the trunks. At the third try he managed to locate both legholes, but the trunks were the wrong way round. He heard Julia saying 'See you in a few minutes' and tottered to his feet.

He hauled the trunks up and grabbing the nearest towel, wrapped the blowlamp in it just as Julia came in.

She halted as she saw him, and he willed her to be letting her eyes adjust to the relative dimness of the room, but she was gazing at him. 'So much for your unpacking,' she said. 'More like a dog after a bone.'

'Woof,' he said, and repeated it so that it didn't sound at all like 'Whoomph.'

'You're worse than Laura ever was.'

'I must take after myself.'

'Never mind, I said I'd do it.' Then she stared harder at him. 'You're back to front.'

'New fashion.'

'Don't go out like that, Jack. You'll have Laura imagining everyone's looking.'

'If she even notices,' he said, but arguing would waste time. He shoved the towel and its contents more firmly beneath his armpit and yanked the trunks down past his scrotum, then he wriggled until they slid to his ankles. His movements were rubbing his shirt over his raw shoulders, and he was afraid there might be blood for Julia to notice. He turned around carefully, his headache beating like a drum machine, once he was free of the trunks, and sat on one of the chairs near the beds, the thin-skinned upholstery pricking his buttocks. He was hooking the trunks to him with one foot when someone rapped on the door. 'Is that Laura?' Julia called.

'Yes.'

'Come in then, and stop putting on that funny voice.'

'Hang on, I don't think—' Jack said, reeling to his feet and clutching at the towel with one hand while attempting to drag his trunks up with the other. They had only reached his knees when the Birmingham girl, who proved to be in her twenties but who had sounded younger, stepped into the room. 'Well, excuse *me*,' she said, backing out fast. 'I was only going to ask if you'd lost this.'

Julia ran after her and did her best to appear solemn. 'Sorry about the misunderstanding. Our daughter's called Laura too.'

'Really,' the other Laura said as if that made the situation even more suspect.

'What did you say you were wanting to ask?'

The length of the question gave Jack time to stumble to the door. 'If you'd dropped this,' the Birmingham Laura said, holding up the briefcase.

'I don't think so,' Julia said. 'I'm sure it can't be ours. Though now you mention it, it does look a bit—'

'It looks like an old briefcase,' Jack interrupted. 'It isn't ours.'

Their neighbour kept her gaze fixed on his chest as though she was determined not to look higher or lower. 'Sorry to have bothered you, I'm sure,' she said, and retreated into the next apartment.

Julia contained her giggles until Jack shut the door. 'I should have let you keep your trunks on after all.'

He wished he could stay and share the joke. 'I'll see you both on the beach.'

'I should think our Laura's just about ready if you want to wait for her. You've got her towel, by the way. Here's yours.'

Jack took it from her and ventured into the sunlight, which collided with his head, reviving the ache. 'Are you ready, Laura Orchard?' he called.

'Almost. Why are you calling me that?'

'I'll leave your towel next to mine on the beach,' he told her, and stumbled down the nearest flight of steps. At the bottom he glanced both ways before shoving the blowlamp down the front of his trunks. They hid it, and he felt comfortable enough with it until he tried to walk; then it began to nudge his penis with a gentleness which he suspected would soon become unbearable. He stuck Laura's towel under his arm and reached into his trunks to adjust his penis as he moved towards the lowest set of steps, and glanced up in case either Julia or Laura was watching him. Neither of them was, but the Birmingham couple were, and looking decidedly dubious. 'Just dealing with my equipment,' he mumbled wildly, and fled down the steps.

Below the road in front of the hotel a concrete slipway led

352

down to the narrow pebbly beach. Most of the bare-breasted young women were lying face down on recliners, except for one who was bouncing a baby in the waves. Several Greek children were skimming stones across the water while their grandmother, a large swarthy woman in a bathing suit and cap and with varicose veins so pronounced they looked like rubber tubes inserted beneath the skin of her legs, plodded through the shallows. Jack spread the towels on the slipway and unbuttoned his shirt, wincing at the prospect of peeling it off his shoulders. When he removed it, however, he found there was no blood on it. He dropped it on his towel and wriggled his feet out of his sandals – the blowlamp wouldn't let him stoop – then, hoping that the bare young women wouldn't take his posture as a response, he waddled down to the sea.

He expected it to be warmer than it proved to be. When he trod in it he had to restrain himself from jumping back. In a couple of seconds it felt more welcoming, and he waded forwards until he was knee-deep. Waves tugged gently at his legs, pebbles appeared to sway back and forth underwater, and he felt in danger of losing his balance. He couldn't loiter in case Julia or Laura saw him. He floundered into the leisurely waves, and the water closed around his trunks.

It felt as though the blowlamp at his groin had extended a cold grasp around his hips. The largest wave he'd met so far broke at his waist, splashing his chest, and he thought the impact had knocked him over. He pulled the blowlamp out of his trunks and held it underwater. Now he could stoop, but there was no hiding-place in sight. Pebbles dug into the soles of his feet, a swarm of tiny fish nipped at his ankles. Though the water seemed capable of floating his legs from under him and carrying him helplessly away, he would have to go deeper if he wanted to be certain that the waves wouldn't return the blowlamp to him.

He shouldn't have come into the sea, he thought; he should have gone up the hill. Perhaps he still could. Then he heard Laura calling 'Look at Dad,' and he wallowed forwards, having glimpsed a large underwater rock that appeared to be

353

almost within his reach. It seemed to raise itself and inch towards him, but that was an illusion produced by the water, as was its closeness to him. The sea was halfway up his chest when he gained the rock and fell to his knees on top of it, water filling his nostrils and stinging his shoulders. He snorted his nostrils clear and shook his throbbing dizzy head and sucked in a lungful of air, then he plunged his face into the sea and reached beneath the rock.

It was lying on sand. Something squirmed away from his fingers and burrowed deeper. He dug as deep a trench in the heavy sodden sand as he could without raising his head out of the water. His vision was blurring, his lungs were beginning to struggle to keep the air down; he felt as though the sea which was thundering dully in his ears was penetrating his skull. When it seemed that all the air in his lungs was about to burst out of him through whatever exit it could make he thrust the blowlamp into the trench, nozzle first. The nozzle dug its own hole, and the body was well under the rock. He shoved himself away from it and reared up out of the water, spitting and blinking and gasping, so desperate for air that his impetus threw him backwards. The sea replaced the sky, and a wave held him under.

It could only happen to Jack Awkward. He'd come all this way solely in order to drown himself. He flailed at the water with his arms and legs, but he could neither regain his footing nor find the surface with his face. Everything around him seemed to be infected by his dizziness. Another wave carried him for some distance, and he realised he was floating, out of control. Then pebbles scraped the knuckles of his right hand and he bruised his toes on a stone, and managed to crouch on all fours and shove his face above the water. For a few seconds he could only splutter and try to blink his salty eyes into focus, then he saw that the wave had carried him in the direction of the beach. Laura was swimming towards him. 'Dad,' she called without breaking her stroke, 'you nearly swam.'

'If that's what it's like I'm glad it was only nearly.'

When he'd recovered, however, he turned on his back and let the water buoy him up. All he needed to do in order to float was relax, and he thought he was entitled to relax at last. He counted the seconds as another wave returned him to the beach: eleven, twelve, thirteen, and pebbles grazed his shoulders. It was lucky that he didn't need to swim, he thought, struggling to his feet and trudging through the waves.

'That was impressive,' Julia said, paddling to meet him; then her smile faltered. 'What have you done to yourself?'

'Didn't you see me fall on the rock?'

'Oh, Jack.' She made to touch his shoulders and grimaced sympathetically instead. 'Have a shower before the salt gets in.'

Despite her sympathy, he thought that she also welcomed his clumsiness. The Count had existed to look after her and Laura, and now she was happy to take care of Jack. As he stood beneath a shower outside the reception office the Birmingham couple strolled by, both of them giving his crotch a disparaging glance. 'I left it for the fish,' Jack said, not caring whether they heard.

Julia interrupted her swim on seeing him returning to the beach. 'Better?' she said.

'As never.'

'You shouldn't have tried so much so soon. We've nearly a fortnight if you want to learn to swim.'

'I think I've seen the end of my adventures. You go ahead, and I'll catch up on my sunshine.'

He lay face down on the towel while she and Laura swam and came back with tales of caves and of fish that pretended they were patches of the sea floor. So long as they didn't tell him they'd found a blowlamp he would be content, and even if they did, it no longer had anything to do with him. The sun felt like balm on his head and shoulders. When Julia and Laura began towelling themselves in the golden light he was able to sit up quite steadily. 'If you're hungry, we are,' Julia said.

The family changed in their rooms and met outside Laura's door. A green lizard skittered down the steps, above which generous red blossoms on vines were closing their petals around bright yellow candles dusted with yellow pollen. Old women dressed from head to foot in black were converging on a graveyard by the sea; beyond the stones and glassed-in marble shrines to the dead Jack saw a ship at anchor. The Orchards meandered for a while, past a restaurant on the ground floor of a building from which the roof had been omitted to save on tax, round the harbour where old men sat sipping ouzo outside cafes and watching the somnolent bobbing of yachts, up a hill where tavernas spilled onto the pavement and young Greeks sped past on motorcycles with girl tourists on their pillions and candles flickered in the gilded gloom of an Orthodox church. At the top of the hill palm trees shaded a square, off which they found a restaurant called Itanos that served wine from barrels into tin carafes and displayed its food behind a glass counter. They chose their meals and ordered a litre of wine and sat near the open end of the large hall, watching a donkey being led through the twilight. 'Well, here we really are,' Jack said.

'Thanks to Pete and Cath,' said Julia.

'Here's to them.'

'Pete and Cath.' The Orchards touched their glasses together, and Julia said 'I wouldn't have dreamed they could be so kind.'

'Putting our bill in the draw when we hadn't paid, you mean.'

'That as well.'

'As well as what?'

'Jack.' She glanced at Laura and decided that Laura had no illusions about it. 'Don't tell me you didn't know they let us win.'

'They couldn't have stopped us, could they? Not that they would have wanted to.'

'*Dad*,' Laura said as though he was carrying a joke too far.

'You're saying they—'

'They fixed it for us to win because of what happened to Laura.'

'Are you telling me they told you so?'

'They didn't have to tell us,' Julia said, and Laura agreed: 'I knew.'

If they hadn't been told, Jack tried to think, it was possible that they were wrong, but he felt as if they were forcing him to own up to having known. Surely it didn't matter if they weren't here because of their luck, and in any case, perhaps they were: perhaps if the Count hadn't worked to preserve it some unforeseen event would have obstructed them. He concentrated on tearing up a piece of bread to dip into taramasalata. 'Anyway,' he said, 'it's good to have friends to count on.'

'That's because you like counting,' Laura said through a mouthful of hoummus.

'What do you mean?'

'What should she mean? It was a joke.'

'I know, love,' he said quickly to Laura. 'I didn't quite hear what you said at first. That's why you shouldn't speak with anything in your mouth.'

Laura looked as if she felt that comment deserved a retort, but she only said 'I just meant you like numbers.'

'Some more than others.'

He thought she was going to ask which were which. Instead she looked pensive. 'Dad?'

'Address me.'

'What's the power of thirteen?'

'Something multiplied by itself thirteen times.'

'Like that letter.'

'Which was that, now?'

'That silly letter you sent thirteen copies of to people.'

'I sent—' The waiter removed their used plates, and Jack had to make himself breathe. As the man moved away Jack tried to sound amused. 'You said I sent—'

'You're as silly as that letter. I meant you were supposed to, not that you did. Have you got a piece of paper?'

'What for?'

'I want to work something out.'

'I may have.' Jack groped in his pocket and touched a crumpled piece of paper. 'This is the letter you're talking about, isn't it?' he would have had to say if he had given it to her. 'I haven't any,' he told her. 'Can't you do it in your head?'

She gazed at the arched ceiling and moved her lips silently as the waiter brought their meals. 'Don't let it get cold,' Julia said to her after a minute or so.

'Right, Dad. How many people are there in the world?'

'I haven't counted lately. A good few.'

'If you sent thirteen people a letter, and each of them had to send it to another thirteen people, and then those hundred and sixty-nine all had to, and those—' She closed her eyes for a couple of seconds. '—those two thousand one hundred and ninety-seven did, and on and on like that, how long would it be before all the people in the world were used up?'

'Beats me.'

'More than thirteen times all that?'

'It would have to be.'

'Bet it wouldn't be much more.'

'I don't know, and I'm not going to try and work it out when we're supposed to be on holiday. Besides,' Jack said with a mixture of relief and triumph, 'not everyone does what the letter tells them.'

'How do you know?'

'Are you saying I did?' the Count said.

'No need to speak to her like that, Jack, just because she's given you a problem.'

'You're right,' he said, and smiled at Laura until she was convinced he meant the smile. 'You win.'

What she'd pointed out was irrelevant now – after the fact, he told himself, and tried to put it out of his mind as he finished his meal. Afterwards they walked down the far side of the hill to a lake surrounded by young tourists dining at tables beneath awnings. A path led the Orchards above the lake, which was full of inverted luminous hotels, and down to a children's playground where they all had a swing in the dark. Another street took them over the hill again, past shops that seemed to have been abandoned half-built among their thriving neighbours, and eventually the Orchards came back to the road to the hotel. In the cemetery flames in jars stood on graves; stars flickered above the hushed almost invisible sea. 'I'm beginning to wish we could never go home,' Julia said.

'Have you had enough of where we're living?' Jack said.

'I don't mean that. I just mean I love it here.' She was silent while they watched a bat like a scrap of the night flutter out of a cypress opposite the graveyard. 'When we do go home,' she said, 'maybe we need to think of making a few sacrifices so that we can move.'

'I've made several,' the Count wanted to respond. 'Let's see what we all can think of,' said Jack.

'I do want to go home,' Julia declared as if he'd implied the reverse. 'Though I don't mind telling you, when the woman by me on the plane asked where I was from I was ashamed to say, seeing she was reading the paper.'

'What difference did that make?'

'Of course, you didn't see it. You were busy catching up on your shuteye. Just a report of what that Mersey maniac did to a mother and her little boy,' she said. 'I didn't want to admit I came from anywhere that could produce such a monster.'

FORTY-SIX

Thank God, it had all been a dream except for their being in Crete. At the end of the holiday Jack would reopen Fine Films while Julia went back to Rankin's. The credit card hadn't been stolen, and Jack had never had to confront the bank manager; but what had he forgotten which was threatening to disturb his sleep? Of course: he needed to insure Fine Films in case there was a fire, or because once it was insured there would be, providing them with cash to help them move house and giving him an excuse to find a better job. Though that didn't quite make sense, surely he needn't ponder it now; if he didn't put it out of his head it was liable to spoil the holiday. But he'd forgotten something else, which felt like an inexorable slow explosion in his brain, and it did worse than mar the holiday – it wakened him.

He was lying alone in thick sweaty darkness, and held down on the bed by a sodden sheet. For a moment he thought he had been incarcerated in a Greek asylum, then he realised he was in the hotel room. He could hear Julia's breathing across the room. There wasn't space for the two of them to sleep together on either of the beds, but he felt as though she was trying to stay away from him. If she found out who he was she would, and he would be the last to blame her. He only wished he could dissociate himself.

He hadn't killed Janys Day's child. That much he'd learned from Julia. A neighbour had reached the child's room with a ladder and smashed the window and brought the child out safe before the fire had penetrated the room. Jack imagined flames swarming up the cot, trapping the toddler in a cage of fire, and tried to writhe away from himself. Even the thought

360

of the neighbour carrying the toddler, no doubt struggling and screaming in her arms, down the ladder above the fire brought him close to fainting. He hadn't killed the child, but he might have. He *had* killed five people, and Julia was right to loathe him.

He couldn't reassure himself that she didn't know who she was loathing; that only made him feel more outcast. He couldn't tell himself that he'd killed in order to protect her and Laura; he was no longer certain that he'd needed to. In any case, he had no right to hold her and Laura responsible. He was.

Acknowledging that didn't help either. It seemed as if all he could do was wait to be found out, and he didn't think he could bear to wait for very long. You could get used to anything, he reflected, and crammed the sheet into his mouth to stifle a cry of disgust at himself. 'Who?' Julia mumbled, then turned over with a sigh, and Jack began to shiver from trying to lie absolutely still until he was certain she was asleep.

Judging by last night, now that he'd awakened he could look forward to hours of wakefulness. The charred darkness felt as if it was as much within him as outside him. When he opened his eyes he saw vague smoky lights, when he closed them his eyes felt almost too raw to suffer the weight of their lids. Whenever exhaustion seemed about to let him doze, one or other of the thoughts he'd already had flared up again in his skull. He could hardly believe that he slept, but at one point he found the room had grown perceptibly less dark without his noticing, and then sunlight was streaming through the windows and Julia had left a kiss on his forehead. 'Wake up or we'll miss the coach for Knossos,' she called from the bathroom.

When he heard the bathroom shower reduced to a drizzle he pushed himself off the bed. He felt as though the night had left a sooty residue on his eyeballs. He was trying to grasp an impression that there was something else he should remember, something crucial. He stood under the shower, hoping that the water might rouse his thoughts, but he'd had no success by the time he felt obliged to go to Julia for fear that she might wonder why he was delaying. He dressed, trying not to avoid meeting her eyes, and collected Laura on the way to breakfast. Appearances had to be maintained, he heard one of his voices remark.

The breakfast room above the bar was already almost full. There were tablefuls of tanned young Germans, a blind Norwegian and her female companion, the couple from Birmingham. Jack loaded his plate with bread rolls and feta cheese and cold meat and bade the Birmingham couple good morning, and received stares and mumbles in response. They had every reason to be dubious of him. Might one or both of them be police? He almost welcomed the idea, except that the prospect of being arrested in front of Julia and Laura, or even of their learning about him, was unbearable. 'Aren't you hungry, Dad?' Laura said, and he made himself pick at the food on his plate.

On the way into town the sun felt like a light in an interrogation room, the sea appeared to be glittering a relentless incomprehensible message at him. The coach would meet the Orchards at a telephone kiosk on the near edge of town. Jack found his attention drawn to the phone, and then he could hardly speak but had to. 'I'm just going round the corner,' he managed to say in his ordinary voice.

'So long as it isn't round the bend,' Julia said.

'Don't be long, Dad. The bus might come.'

Once they were out of sight he began to snarl through his teeth like a ventriloquist 'You clown, you clown, you clown.' A fisherman on his way up from the harbour with a pole full of squid glanced reprovingly at him, but Jack was nearly blinded by dismay. The names of his victims spelled out his name; the police had only to decode the numbers of the pages in the phone directory. 'You clown,' he snarled, he didn't know how loud.

But could the names of the people he hadn't harmed be used to trace him? Since the Count hadn't made his later visits in alphabetical order, could they be seen to spell Jack's name? He closed his eyes and faced the sun while he recalled the order of the names. Burning figures pranced in his head. He was safe after all, he was invisible; the Count had taken care of him. He dodged into a store and grabbed a litre of water from among the bottles of retsina and Metaxa, and almost dashed out without paying when he heard the coach. For a moment he thought it was leaving without him. One panic felt much like another just now, yet the notion of being left behind by Julia and Laura seemed momentarily welcome. But the coach was drawing up beside the telephone kiosk. 'Here's Dad now,' Laura said as if she had been close to panic.

The coach laboured up the slope above the town, past a donkey lying down for a rest, and turned towards Heraklion. Solitary churches gleamed white on the mountains, then the road was threaded through towns which appeared still to be under construction in order to house the throngs of tourists. The veering of the coach had put the burning figures out of Jack's head, but his brain felt stuffed with ash. He was sitting in front of Laura and her mother, and every so often he gave in to a compulsion to turn and reassure himself that they hadn't deserted him.

The coach climbed through Heraklion to the site of the palace of Minos. The guide led the coachload of passengers through the ruins, past parties which were being advised in German and French and Dutch. Here on the hill surrounded by olive groves and cypresses were fragments of great porches supported by red pillars, giant horns carved on ancient pavements, exposed subterranean rooms full of jars larger than a man, a stone throne guarded by mythical animals, even a queen's privy. Finally the guide brought her party to the road along which Minoan royalty would walk between their palaces. Jack gazed along the path of stone slabs outlined by moss and saw where it was crossed by a mirage of a stream, heat transformed into water. 'We didn't see where the Minotaur lived,' Laura said wistfully.

He could show her a labyrinth, he thought. It was himself. He was the monster in it too, and he'd trapped himself at the centre with no way out. 'There's no magic here, only history,' he opened his mouth to say, but a thought silenced him.

Perhaps there was magic after all, because he had grasped what he'd been trying to remember. The world seemed to brighten as if a fire had been lit, and he felt as though an oracle had helped him. He could still protect the family, and he had to. He was all at once certain that one or more of those who'd claimed to have sent the letters, or had promised to do so, had lied to him.

FORTY-SEVEN

On the morning of their last full day in Crete Jack said 'Have we done everything you wanted to do?'

'We have now,' Julia said.

'Everything,' said Laura.

They were at Lató, a ruined city about three miles' walk from the main road. On one side of the hill ancient altars faced a valley below a jagged peak, on the other the white streets led below a second peak towards Aghios Nikolaos, piled in the distance against the pale sea. Apart from a few goats and a shy snake and a chorus of insects, the Orchards had the ruins to themselves. Laura kept wondering aloud whether any of the thick stones which made up the pavements and the remains of the houses and workshops and shops were really three thousand years old, until Julia told her gently not to bother so much about numbers. Jack stood by the altars and gazed at the greenery which overgrew the crags and let the growing heat catch up with him, and eventually Julia called 'Penny for them.'

'They're worth a lot more,' he said, smiling easily at her.

'Shall we head for humanity before it gets too hot?'

'If you've seen all you wanted to see.'

'You too, Jack.'

'Oh, I've got what I wanted out of the trip,' he said, resting his hand for a few seconds on the slab of the altar. Its warmth felt like a secret it was sharing with him. He slithered down the path, dislodging a few pebbles that rattled after him, and took Julia and Laura by the hand as they returned to the dirt road.

An old woman in black was selling her embroidery near a

shrine at the edge of the ruins, and later the Orchards encountered a couple of jeeps bound for Lató, but otherwise the road was deserted. It wandered downhill between groves and fields where the only sign of cultivation was the occasional abandoned farming implement. After half an hour of trudging Jack felt as though he had been walking for ever while the sun rode his back, yet the experience was peaceful because his outlook was. When the Orchards halted for a mouthful each of bottled water, Laura said 'What did you like best?'

'Sailing to Santorini,' Julia said.

'You mean when we first saw it and we thought all the houses on the top of the island were snow?'

'And having to ride up on donkeys because the streets were so steep.'

'And when they let us dive off the ship on the way back and we swam over the drowned city.'

'Was that your favourite, Laura?'

'No, the Bounty beach.'

'Even though it took us half the day to get there and there weren't any Bounty bars at the beach shop and they'd had to hang coconuts on the palm trees when they were filming the advert?'

'Yes, because the sand was so white and we swam out to that little island. What was your favourite, Dad?'

'All of it. Being with you two. You don't realise how much you can fit into thirteen days until you have to.'

'At the top Mum said not to worry so much about numbers.'

'I'm not worried,' he said, feeling their hands in his, Julia's rougher than it had been when they'd first held hands but still essentially soft, Laura's almost as big as Julia's now and both of them slim though, he reflected, anything but frail. 'Come on or we'll miss the next bus,' he said, worried after all. 'We mustn't have you two getting sunstroke on our last day.'

When at last they reached the end of the rubbly path the bus was pulling away from the stop, but sighed to a halt when the driver saw them despairing. The conductor gave Laura the tickets once she'd treated him to her six words of Greek, and then an old woman who was taking a basketful of produce into town engaged her in a conversation which soon turned into smiles and gestures, and gave her a handful of olives which Laura didn't like to refuse. Jack ate most of them and held the stones in his fist, having counted them: 'Florist, plumbress, psychic, dressmaker, rich girl.' Their bitter taste lingered in his mouth all the way to the bus station by the harbour.

The driver inserted the bus into the rank of vehicles with, it seemed, hardly an inch to spare. As the Orchards climbed down from it an Orthodox priest strode by, the hem of his robe flapping. Jack could smell fish, the sea, the fumes of the bus, the spicy meat of a kebab, the faintest hint of Julia's body lotion. They walked away from the roaring of engines and the distorted shout that announced the destinations of the buses, and Jack heard the cries of gulls seesawing above the wake of a fisherman's boat. 'Shall we come here next year?' Laura said.

'Let's make the most of now for now,' Jack told her. He felt ambushed by unhappiness until she said 'I'm going to look in the jewellery shop' and ran ahead.

Julia watched her long tanned legs moving gracefully, her body slim in shorts and a T-shirt, her red hair no longer so cropped. 'She's growing up.'

'We all are.'

'I'm not so sure about you,' Julia said, and became thoughtful. 'I wish you could have seen her when we found the burglar in the house. She ran straight at him as he came out of our room before I could stop her. I don't think he knew what hit him.'

'I can imagine.'

She put one arm around Jack's shoulders and kissed him, gazing into his eyes. 'I'm glad you managed to unwind. I didn't know what was wrong with you the first couple of days we were here.'

'Just getting used to the heat and trying to catch up on my sleep.'

367

'I think it's turned out to be our best holiday ever.'

'I think you're right,' Jack said, walking ahead of her for a few steps so that she couldn't read his face. 'Let's go back to the hotel and have lunch in the shade,' he said, catching her and Laura by the hand.

The family sat under the awning of the taverna beside the hotel. A man wearing a wide-brimmed straw hat was paddling a plastic boat hired from the next beach, and a group of new arrivals were braving the height of the sun on recliners below the hotel. A breeze set the waves glittering and brightened Julia's and Laura's eyes, touched up their freckles, twined and untwined Julia's hair over her shoulders. The waiter brought swordfish and retsina, and Jack wanted the meal to last for ever. All too soon Julia finished her brandy and coffee and said 'I'm going up for a shower.'

'I'll get the keys,' Laura said, and ran to the office while Jack waited for the bill. When he went inside the taverna to pay, the proprietor offered him a shot glass of raki from a plastic bottle that had once contained water. Jack knew about the drink – Greek moonshine – and drained the glass at a gulp. 'Dutch courage,' he told the proprietor, who assumed that was a toast and raised his own glass.

Jack stood beneath the awning for a few moments, feeling the spirit burn down into his stomach and rise into his brain, then he sent himself towards the hotel. There was no point in wishing that the day would never end; he'd saved the holiday only by knowing what he would have to do. Suddenly anxious to be with Julia, he hurried to their room.

She opened the door to him and retreated, towelling herself. Ghosts of her swimsuit emphasised her breasts and the bushy ginger division of her thighs. Her hair, sleek with water that dripped down her back, made him think of a wildcat's pelt. He heeled the door shut and put his arms around her and threw the towel on the bed, and was running his hands down her spine to her naked bottom when Laura knocked on the door. 'Mummy, there's a cockroach in my room.'

'It's a good job it wasn't an insect that burgled our house,'

Julia murmured, and called 'Don't worry, Laura, it's twice as scared of you as you are of it.'

'Can't I come in?'

Julia pressed her cheek against Jack's and her body against him. 'What for?'

'Just for a little rest. I won't be able to sleep for thinking that's in my room.'

Julia hugged Jack, then eased herself away from him. 'You don't mind, do you? We'll be alone later.'

He gave her a last kiss, chasing her tongue with his, then turned away quickly – not so quickly, he hoped, that she would wonder why. It was for the best, he thought as he opened the door; by the time Julia had gone to sleep Laura might well have been awake. 'It was this big,' Laura said.

'If it was that big we should have caught it and had it stuffed.' He stood back to let her in while Julia finished towelling herself. 'Where's Daddy going to sleep?' Julia said.

'You can have my bed, Laura. I'm going to read.' He picked up the guidebook from Julia's bedside table and stepped onto the balcony, leaving the windows ajar.

He took his time over leafing through the guidebook. They hadn't found time to walk down the Samarian Gorge; they'd never seen the rare flowers or the bearded vultures or the goats whose horns bent back. Perhaps one day, he thought, and told himself he mustn't try to plan for them. He examined the map that showed the Sea of Crete. As he'd noted on the way to Santorini, there were very few islands, and the whole of Britain could have been fitted into this sea. He gazed from the balcony at the glittering of the water, a message he understood now, and then he looked into the room.

Julia and Laura were asleep. They didn't stir when he tiptoed in and found a pen in Julia's handbag. On the balcony he smoothed out the envelope addressed to Janys Day and tore off the back before stuffing the rest of it, together with the letter, into his shirt pocket. *Gone to hire a boat from the next beach for a paddle*, he wrote, and glanced at his watch: nearly three o'clock. *Back by 4.30*, he wrote, and bit his lip

369

and rubbed the corners of his eyes hard. He drew eleven kisses and turned to the window again, but had difficulty seeing until he wiped his eyes with one forefinger and thumb. Then the heat dried his eyes and the sight of Julia and Laura gave him strength.

It was only right that they'd crowded him out, he thought; they didn't need him. Eleven was the number of a team – a winning team – and Julia and Laura added up to that without him. His worst mistake had been to think that the Count had won Julia her new job. It showed how much Jack underrated her that he hadn't realised she had achieved that herself.

He slipped the keys with the clown's head out of his pocket and crept into the room. Placing the guidebook on the otherwise bare table near the window, he laid the note on top of the book and weighed it down with the clown's head. As he stood between the beds he felt as if he was already nothing more than his shadow on the wall. He knelt between the beds and kissed Julia's forehead, then Laura's. 'Murn,' Julia said, and Laura greeted him with almost the same sleepy contented sound. Once he was certain they were still asleep he stood up carefully. 'Look after each other,' he whispered, and tiptoeing out of the room, inched the door shut.

He felt unexpectedly exhilarated as he went down the sunlit steps. There was something to be said for being able to see the future so clearly. He tore the letter and the remains of the envelope into small pieces and dropped the fragments in a waste-paper basket beside the reception counter. 'Just going to hire a boat for an hour,' he told the receptionist, and pointed along the coast towards the next beach.

A road closed by bollards led in that direction. Five minutes' walk brought Jack to the public beach. A man and a woman were splashing and ducking each other a few hundred yards out from the edge of the waves, but the beach was deserted apart from a bearded Greek on a canvas chair beneath a wide umbrella next to several canoes. He gestured at the sun with one thick calloused hand and set his face in an advisory grimace when Jack held out the hire fee, then he shrugged and accepted the money. 'One hour,' he said.

The canoes were made of moulded plastic. Near the back of each was a flat ridge for sitting on, flanked by pedals that were no more than U-shaped pieces of metal. Each boat had a number – and yes, Jack saw, one was number 13, the digits and the red plastic dulled by sea and sun. He cradled it in his arms and staggered across the pebbles and sand to drop it in the water, almost falling on top of it. The man and woman splashed inshore towards him, competing to see who could drench the other worst. They were the couple from Birmingham.

When they recognised him they finished their game with one last defiant splash each and then seemed to be trying to pretend that he couldn't have caught them at anything so undignified. As they paddled towards him Jack sat on the boat, which immediately touched bottom and tilted to one side, nearly throwing him off. 'More awkwardness between my legs,' he said.

'I beg yours?' the woman demanded in a shocked shrill voice, and her companion emitted a sound halfway between 'What?' and a protracted splutter. It would be just like Jack Awkward to be foiled at the eleventh hour by a punch-up. The owner of the boats was shouting 'Go out, go out' and flapping his hands at the canoe, and Jack floundered off it in order to push it away from the shore. 'Water,' he mumbled, 'that's what we need.'

'What are you asking for now?' the Birmingham man growled.

Jack straddled the canoe and lifted his feet onto it, and found that it floated. 'Just needed pushing deeper,' he told the Laura, who looked as if she suspected him of innuendo. 'Feets, don't fail me now,' he said.

'*What* did you just ask my wife?'

'I was talking to my feet, not her. Not that I'm suggesting there's any similarity.' Jack shoved at the pedals with the heels of his sandals, which skidded off the metal. 'I was telling them not to let me down, like that tanned gentleman used to.'

'Eh?' the man said, a sound like the Birmingham accent reduced to its essence, and stared at the owner of the boats as

371

if Jack was referring to him.

'The actor. The black. You should know, you're fond of films.' Jack managed not to panic. He exerted a more gradual pressure on the pedals, and the canoe glided between the couple. 'Feets, don't faaaiiil me now,' Jack cried to demonstrate what he'd meant, and sailed out from the beach.

In a few strokes of the pedals he established a rhythm. He passed the caves to which Julia and Laura had swum, where the reflections of ripples lapped the shadowy ceiling, and then the hotel came into view. Suppose Julia were to step onto the balcony? Even at that distance she might recognise him, in which case she would try and call him back out of the sunlight which was beating on his skull. Suddenly he wanted her to appear – wanted it so much that he forced himself to face away from the hotel and keep paddling until he thought it was safe to look back, until he'd thought so for minutes and hadn't looked. When at last he couldn't resist glancing over his shoulder he was hoping that he would see Julia waving at him to return or swimming after him. But there was no sign of her, or the hotel, or the beach: nothing but the sea.

He felt as though he'd been relieved of a burden or an obligation. He was experiencing a sadness so profound it was peaceful. All around him the sea glittered in the rhythm he was pedalling. He trailed his fingers through the water, which was cool, a refuge from the heat if that became unbearable. After a while he rested from pedalling, and found that the boat continued to drift away from the land. He would let it drift so long as nothing appeared anywhere on the enormous disc of water that surrounded him. He seemed to be attaining a state beyond action or thought. The sea whispered to him, the sun began to lower itself towards his baked cranium, and it was purely by chance that his gaze fell on his watch.

The time was almost five o'clock. Julia and Laura would be awake. By now one or both of them would have been down to the beach to see what was keeping him. Perhaps they had already questioned the receptionist, and eventually they would speak to the owner of the boat and no doubt to the Birmingham couple. At some point they would contact the police. He thought Julia would be the first to understand that he wasn't coming back, but in time Laura would have to ask. Beyond that he couldn't think.

The alternative was even less endurable – that they would discover who he was. Even if he escaped the notice of the police, he was sure that Jack Awkward couldn't fool his family for the rest of his life. There might be nothing other than himself to betray him, but that would be enough. The panic he'd experienced when the policeman had handled the brief-case was aching to be revived. During their first days in Crete it had nearly driven him out of hiding, and only knowing that he had to take the course he was taking now had assuaged it. Besides, more than panic was lying dormant in him. Despite his being almost certain that the Count's adventures hadn't affected their luck, if he went home the Count would feel compelled to make sure. The prospect sent a shiver through him, which he translated into a push at the pedals which sped him towards the receding horizon.

After a few minutes he let the canoe drift again. The sun was at his back, which meant he was continuing to leave Crete behind. His skull had begun to feel weightless. Soon he felt close to disembodiment, as though his body and the canoe no longer had anything to do with him. Perhaps he was already a ghost who was remembering the sea as he watched over Julia and Laura, because he could see them. They'd had to go home days later than they'd planned, the tour operator having taken pity on them, and the house was just the right size for the two of them. If they still wanted to move house the life insurance which was linked to the mortgage would have paid off the last of the debt, and if Mr Hardy dared give Julia any trouble, he'd better keep looking behind him; the Count might be watching over the family too. They weren't troubled now, they were reminiscing. 'Remember all the happy times in Crete,' Julia was saying, and Laura said 'I remember that day when we saw the fox with Dad.'

His gaze wavered to his wrist, and he managed to focus. His watch showed a quarter to six. Julia must be struggling not to panic. However vividly he might imagine that, the reality must be far worse. He yearned to go back to her, to ask how she could have thought for even a moment that he could ever leave her, and then he wondered how the police would search for him. Weren't they likely to use a helicopter? The possibility, and his need to place himself beyond giving in to his longing for her, made him disengage his feet from the pedals and, lifting himself from the seat, inch backwards along the canoe until he sensed that it was about to tip up. Before panic at the prospect could get the better of him, he leaned backwards and kicked the boat away from him with all his strength.

The canoe shot away, bouncing out of the water, while he floated in the opposite direction. He was aware of the unseen depths below him, which for the moment were buoying him up. He was floating on his back, as Julia had often tried to teach him and as he'd succeeded in doing after burying the blowlamp, but he didn't think he could sustain the position for long. Soon the depths would reach for him. Foreseeing his last moments had been easy, but living through them mightn't be. He made himself relax as if he was lying in bed, about to fall asleep, and closed his eyes, and began to count aloud slowly as the salt water lapped at his ears. When he reached eleven he would see if he had any luck left. Perhaps the Count could swim.